A FIRE IN THE SKY

Julie had figured out what she'd done wrong in the first attack on an enemy airship. This time she fired far enough ahead that the machine gun's bullets ripped gashes in the envelope and the gas bags beneath. She was using the rounds to mix the gases as well as ignite them.

Then it occurred to her she'd overlooked something.

"Laura, pull—!"

The gas plume ignited—just as the Vasa flew into it. Fortunately, the Vasa had flown fast enough that it suffered no damage beyond scorching parts of the fuselage—but only enough to discolor it, not to set it aflame.

"I guess that's what they call baptism by fire," said Laura.

1637
THE POLISH MAELSTROM

ERIC FLINT

1637: THE POLISH MAELSTROM

A Baen Books Original

Baen Publishing Enterprises
P.O. Box 1403
Riverdale, NY 10471
www.baen.com

ISBN: 978-1-9821-2472-4

Cover art by Tom Kidd
Maps by Michael Knopp

First printing, April 2019
First mass market printing, July 2020

Distributed by Simon & Schuster
1230 Avenue of the Americas
New York, NY 10020

Library of Congress Control Number: 2018061008

Printed in the United States of America

10 9 8 7 6 5 4 3 2 1

To Harry Meserve

Contents

Contents

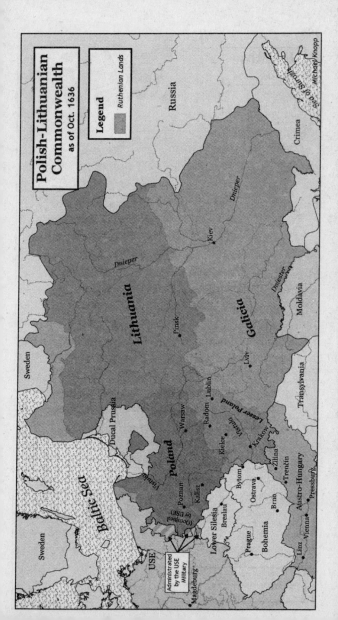

Polish-Lithuanian Commonwealth
as of Oct. 1636

Legend
Ruthenian Lands

Russia

Sweden

Baltic Sea

Sweden

Michael Knopp

Sea of Suprus

Crimea

Dnieper

Kiev

Dnieper

Lithuania

Pinsk

Galicia

Dniester

Lviv

Moldavia

Lublin

Transylvania

Ducal Prussia

Prussia

Warsaw

Radom

Lesser Poland

Vistula

Kielce

Krakow

Žilina

Trenčín

Poland

Poznan

Kalisz

Occupied by USE

Bytom

Ostrava

Austro-Hungary

Pressburg

Lower Silesia

Breslau

Brno

Vienna

U.S.E.

Administered by the USE Military

Magdeburg

Prague

Bohemia

Linz

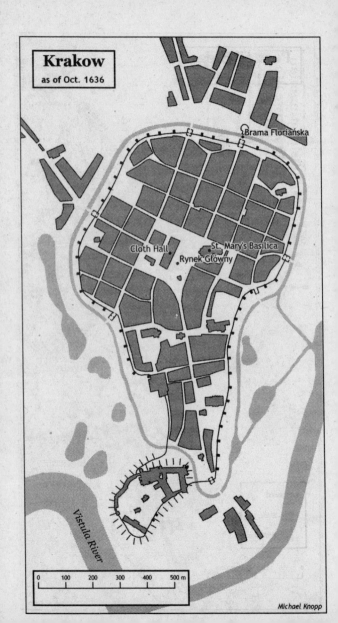

Krakow
as of Oct. 1636

Brama Floriańska

Cloth Hall

St. Mary's Basilica

Rynek Główny

Vistula River

0   100   200   300   400   500 m

Michael Knopp

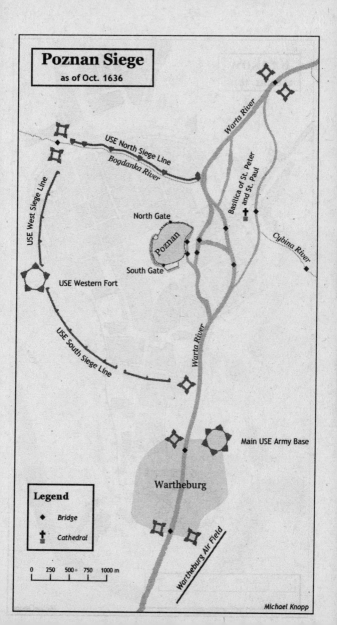

Poznan Siege

as of Oct. 1636

Warta River

USE North Siege Line

Bogdanka River

Basilica of St. Peter and St. Paul

USE West Siege Line

Cybina River

North Gate

Poznan

South Gate

USE Western Fort

Warta River

USE South Siege Line

Main USE Army Base

Wartheburg

Legend

♦ Bridge

✝ Cathedral

0   250   500   750   1000 m

Wartheburg Air Field

Michael Knopp

Prologue:
The Anaconda Project

November 1633

Prague, capital of Bohemia

"This is absurd," said Morris Roth, as forcefully as he could. He had a bad feeling that wasn't very forceful at all, given that he was wearing an absurd costume—he thought it was absurd, anyway, although it was just standard seventeenth-century courtier's clothing. The entire situation was absurd.

A bit desperately, he repeated the statement. "This is absurd." After a couple of seconds, he remembered to add: "Your Majesty."

Fortunately, Wallenstein seemed to be in one of his whimsical moods, where the same possible slight that might have angered him at another time merely seemed to be a source of amusement. General Pappenheim—damn his black soul to whatever hideous afterlife there

1

might be even if Morris didn't actually believe in hell—was grinning outright.

"Ah, Morris. So modest!" Pappenheim's scarred face was distorted still further as the grin widened. "How can you claim such a complete absence of heroic qualities? You! The Don at the Bridge!"

Morris glared at him. "It was just a job that needed doing, that's all. So I did it. But what sort of lunat—ah . . ."

Calling the king of Bohemia a "lunatic" to his face was probably not wise. Morris was nimble-witted enough even under the circumstances to veer in midstream.

" . . . misadvised person would confuse me with a blasted general? Your Majesty, General Pappenheim, I am a *jeweler.*"

"What sort of person?" asked Wallenstein, chuckling softly. "A lunatic, perhaps. The same sort of lunatic who recently proclaimed himself King of Bohemia despite—yes, I will say it myself—a claim to the throne that is so threadbare it would shame a pauper. But who cares? Since I am also the same lunatic who won the second battle of the White Mountain."

They were in the small salon in the palace that Wallenstein favored for intimate meetings. He planted his hands on the armrest of his rather modest chair and levered himself erect.

"Levered" was the correct term, too. Wallenstein's health, always delicate, had been getting worse of late. Morris knew from private remarks by Wallenstein's up-time nurse Edith Wild that she was increasingly worried about it. Some of the new king of Bohemia's frailty was due to the rigors of his past military life. But most of it wasn't. Wallenstein, unfortunately, was superstitious and still placed great faith in the advice of his new astrologers—including their advice on his diet. Morris had once heard Edith mutter that she was *this close*—a thumb and fingertip indicated perhaps an eighth of an inch—to getting her revolver and gunning down the astrologers.

It was not an inconceivable thought. Edith was quite ferocious, as she'd proved when she shot dead the assassination team sent to murder Wallenstein a few months earlier. The reason Wallenstein had new astrologers was because they'd replaced some of the old ones who'd been implicated in the plot.

"A jeweler," Morris repeated. Even to his ears, the words sounded like a whine.

Pappenheim waved his hand airily. "And what of it? Every great general began his life as something else. Even a baker, perhaps."

Morris glared at him again. "'Began his life.' I am in my fifties, for the love of God."

"Don Morris, enough," said Wallenstein firmly. "Your reluctance to assume the post of general in my army simply reinforces my conviction that I have made the right decision."

"Why, Your Majesty?" demanded Morris, just as firmly. One of Wallenstein's saving graces was that the man didn't object to subordinates challenging him, up to a point, provided they were polite about it. "My military experience is limited to that of an enlisted soldier in the American army of another universe. What we called a 'grunt'—with exactly the connotations you'd expect from the term. I wasn't even in a combat unit. I was essentially a quartermaster's clerk, that's all, keeping military supply records."

Smiling, Wallenstein looked at Pappenheim. For his part, Bohemia's top general still had the same wolflike grin on his face.

"Limited to that? Oh, surely not, Don Morris," said Pappenheim cheerily. "You forget the Battle of the Bridge. Which you led—not even you will deny that much—and which has since entered the legends of the Jews all across eastern Europe."

Morris grit his teeth. "I said. It was just a job that needed to be done, and—"

"Enough, Morris," repeated Wallenstein.

Morris fell silent. The fact that the king of Bohemia had dropped the honorific "Don"—which was an informal term, but significant nonetheless—made it clear that he considered the argument at an end. Whether Morris liked it or not, his new post as a general in the Bohemian army was a done deal.

"Follow me," said Wallenstein, heading toward one of the doors in the small chamber. Even though Wallenstein was only fifty years old, he moved like a man twenty years older. It was rather painful to watch.

After following Wallenstein and Pappenheim through the door, Morris found himself in a chamber in the palace he'd never been in before. The chamber, also a small one, was completely dominated by a large table in the center of the room. The table itself was dominated by huge maps that covered its entire surface.

Once Morris was close enough to see the map on the

very top of the pile, he had to restrain himself from hissing.

So. Here it was. He'd heard rumors of the thing, but never seen it.

The map had no legend, but the title of it was plain enough even if invisible. *The Future Empire of Wallenstein the Great* would do quite nicely.

Wallenstein and Pappenheim said nothing, for a while, giving Morris time to study the map.

His first impression never changed. The map could also have been titled *How Little Bohemia Became an Anaconda.*

Indeed, the "Bohemia" that the top map projected into the future did look like a constrictor, albeit a fat one. On the west, serving for the serpent's head, lay Bohemia, Moravia and Upper Silesia. Then came a neck to the east, in the form of a new province that Wallenstein had labeled "Slovakia." Presumably, he'd picked the name from one of the future history books he'd acquired. Which was all fine and dandy, except that in the here and now there was no country called "Slovakia." What there was in its place was the northern part of the region of the Austrian empire known as Royal Hungary, the rump of Hungary that had been left to it by the Ottoman Turks after their victory over the kingdom of Hungary at the Battle of Mohács in 1526.

So. War with Austria. Check.

Of course, that was pretty much a given, with Wallenstein not only a rebel from Austria but allied to the USE. Hostilities between the USE and Austria had died down lately, since Gustav Adolf was preoccupied with his war against the League of Ostend. But nobody much doubted that they would flare up again, unless he lost the war against the alliance of France, Spain, England and Denmark. Assuming he won, everyone with any political knowledge and sense at all knew that Gustav Adolf would turn his attention to Saxony and Brandenburg, and the Austrians were likely to weigh in on the opposite side.

Still, rebelling against Austria and establishing an independent Bohemia was one thing. Continuing on to seize from the Austrians territory that had never been part of Bohemia was something else again.

It got worse. Or better, Morris supposed, depending on how you looked at it. He had to remind himself that, after all, this *was* the ultimate reason he'd come to Prague and decided to throw in with Wallenstein. The worst massacre that would ever fall upon Europe's Jewish population prior to the Holocaust was "due to happen" in fifteen years, in the Chmielnicki Pogrom of 1648, unless something was done to upset the applecart.

Morris had finally decided that the best chance for upsetting that applecart—a very intractable applecart, given the social and economic factors involved—was to ally with Wallenstein and rely on him to be the battering ram.

He still thought that was the best alternative. What he hadn't figured on was that Wallenstein would return him the favor and propose to make *Morris* the battering ram.

But he'd leave that aside, for the moment. He went back to studying the map.

East of "Slovakia," the proposed new Greater Bohemia started getting fatter, like an anaconda that had just swallowed a pig. The big new belly of the new empire would consist of the southern part of the region that was often called Lesser Poland, a huge territory which comprised close to half of the Polish–Lithuanian Commonwealth. In the future history Morris came from, most of that would eventually become part of Ukraine.

War with Poland. Check.

Being honest, Morris knew that was pretty much a given also, if he was to have any hope of forestalling the Chmielnicki Pogrom. The noble magnates who dominated the political life of the Polish–Lithuanian Commonwealth were bound to be hostile to any project which removed the corrosive social tensions in Lesser Poland. Much of their wealth and power came from those tensions.

From there, the map got rather vague. The northern boundary of Wallenstein's proposed empire was not clearly defined, running somewhere south of Lviv and Kiev until it reached the Dnieper River, at which point it expanded southward to the Black Sea, gobbling up Moldova, Bessarabia and the city of Odessa. The exact boundary on the southeast was not distinct, either, being indicated by a shaded area rather than clear borders, although it generally seemed to follow the Dniester River. Morris suspected that Wallenstein wanted, if possible, to avoid any outright clashes with the Ottoman Empire. He'd take what he could, but stop short of challenging the Turks directly.

Marked in faint pencil lines further east was what amounted to a long tail that stretched into the southern regions of what Morris thought of as "Russia," although in the seventeenth century the area—this was true of much of Lesser Poland, as well—was very much a borderland thinly inhabited by a wide mix of peoples.

So. War with Russia and the Cossacks. Check. Tatars too, most likely.

Morris let out a slow breath. Maybe war with the Muscovites and Tatars could be avoided. As for the Cossacks . . .

Mentally, he shrugged his shoulders. Morris had as much sympathy for the Cossacks as any late-twentieth-century Jew with a good knowledge of history.

Zilch.

Fuck 'em and the horses they rode in on. The same bastards who led the Chmielnicki Pogrom—and then served the Tsars as their iron fist in the pogroms at Kiev and Kishinev.

Wallenstein and Pappenheim still weren't saying anything. Morris leaned back a little and started scrutinizing the map again, west to east.

The plan was . . . shrewd. Very shrewd, the more he studied the map.

Morris didn't know exactly where the ethnic and religious lines lay in the here and now. Not everywhere, for sure and certain. But he knew enough to realize that what Wallenstein proposed to do was to gut the soft underbellies of every one of Bohemia's neighbors.

Silesia, in this era, was not yet really part of Poland, as it would become in later centuries in the universe Morris had come from. Its population was an ethnic mix, drawn from many sources—most of whom, at least in the big towns and cities, were Protestants, not Catholics.

Despite the name, "Royal Hungary" in the seventeenth century was mostly a Slavic area, ruled by the Magyars but with no real attachment to Hungary. Morris wouldn't be at all surprised if most of its inhabitants would view a Bohemian conquest as something in the way of a liberation. They certainly weren't likely to rally to the side of their Austrian and Hungarian overlords.

Moving still further east, the same was true again. Parts of "Lesser Poland" had little in the way of a Polish population—and that often consisted mostly of Polish noblemen grinding their Ruthenian serfs under. As for the Ruthenians themselves, the name was not even one that they'd originated, but a Latin label that had been slapped onto them by western European scholars. In a future time, most of them would eventually become Ukrainians. But, in this day and age, they were a mix of mostly Slavic immigrants with a large minority of Jews living here and there among them.

Most of the Jews lived in the larger towns and were engaged in a wide range of mercantile and manufacturing activities. The Polish–Lithuanian Commonwealth did not maintain in practice the same tight restrictions on Jewish activity that most realms in Europe did. Unfortunately, a number of them had also moved out into rural areas.

"Unfortunately," from Morris' viewpoint, because these Jews did not spread into the countryside as farmers. Instead, they spread as rent collectors and overseers of the large landed estates maintained by mostly absentee Polish and Lithuanian magnates. They were universally hated by the Ruthenian peasantry—who, in the nature of things, did not make any fine distinctions between the small class of Jews who exploited them and the great majority of the Jewish populations in the towns who were simply going about their business.

Wallenstein's shrewdness was evident wherever Morris looked on the map. He did not propose to take Kraków, for instance. Looked at from one angle, that was a little silly. At the end of the year 1633, the population of Kraków was also mostly non-Polish. Wallenstein could even advance a threadbare claim to the city, since it had once been under the authority of the kingdom of Bohemia.

But the Poles had an emotional attachment to Kraków, since it had once served as their capital city—and still was, officially, although the real capital was now Warsaw. Kraków's Jagiellonian University was still Poland's most prestigious center of learning. So, Wallenstein would seize everything south of the Vistula but did not propose to cross the river and seize Kraków itself. Thereby, he'd avoid as best he could stirring up Polish nationalism, while establishing a defensible border.

Sum it all up and what you had was what amounted to Wallenstein's preemptive strike at every existing realm in eastern Europe. He would seize all the territories that each of them claimed—but for which none of them had really established any mutual allegiance. The end result, if his plans worked, would be a Bohemian Empire that rivaled in territory and population any of the nations in Europe.

Morris scanned the map again, west to east. With Prague as the capital—it was already one of the great cities of Europe—the rest of Wallenstein's empire would consist of mostly rural territory stitched together by a number of cities. Pressburg, and possibly Lviv, Lublin, Kiev—maybe even Pinsk, way to the north, in what would someday become Belarus.

Morris couldn't help but chuckle. Pinsk, which already had a large Jewish population and would, by the end of the nineteenth century, have a population that was ninety percent Jewish.

There weren't many Jews in Pressburg. But Lviv, Lublin and Kiev were heavily Jewish.

"You propose to use us as your cannon fodder," he said. "Jews, I mean."

"Yes, of course. It's either that or serve the Cossacks as mincemeat fifteen years from now. Make your choice."

Idly, Morris wondered where he'd gotten the term "mincemeat," which Wallenstein had said in English. Probably from Edith Wild.

Make your choice.

Put that way, it was easy enough.

"I'll need the Brethren," Morris said.

"Yes, you will. Not a problem." Wallenstein's long finger came to rest on Lublin. "There is a very large concentration of the Brethren here, you know. And others, scattered throughout the region."

Morris hadn't known the Brethren had a presence in Lublin. The news caused him to relax a little. If the Brethren could *also* serve as what amounted to Wallenstein's social garrisons in the major cities of his proposed empire, that would remove some of the tension on the Jews. They were themselves Christians, after all.

So . . . it might work—assuming Morris had any chance

of translating his pitiful military experience into something worth a damn on the battlefield.

It was Pappenheim who crystallized the thought that Morris was groping toward.

"Stop thinking of being a 'general' in narrow terms," said the man who was perhaps the current world's best exemplar of a general in narrow terms. Pappenheim was a man of the battlefield, with little interest in anything else. "Think of it in broad terms. You simply have to organize the military effort, while you concentrate on political matters. Let others, better suited for the task, lead the troops on the field."

He grinned again in that savage way he had. Then, jabbed a thumb at Wallenstein. "That's what he does, mostly, you know."

Morris stared at Wallenstein. The recently crowned king of Bohemia and proposed usurper of much of eastern Europe stared right back at him.

It was true, actually. Wallenstein hadn't been so much a general as what you might call a military contractor. He put together armies—and then found men like Pappenheim to lead them into battle.

Put that way . . .

It didn't sound quite so bad. Of course, Morris would still have to find his equivalent of Pappenheim, since he had no doubt that Pappenheim himself would be fully occupied in the next few years fighting Bohemia's immediate enemies. That'd be the Austrians, mostly.

Morris looked back at the map, trying to estimate the territory Wallenstein expected him to seize and hold over the next few years. At a rough guess, somewhere around one hundred thousand square miles. About the size of Colorado or Wyoming, he thought. Just what a former army supply clerk-cum-jeweler had always expected he'd wind up doing.

"Piece of cake," he said.

October 1634

Vienna, capital of Austria-Hungary

"So, what do you think?" asked Piccolomini. The Italian general from Florence who was now in Austrian service raised his cup.

The man sitting across from him at the round little table in the small but very crowded tavern frowned down at the cup in front of him. He'd only had a few sips of the dark liquid contained therein. He still didn't know what he thought of the stuff—and he certainly would never have ordered it himself, as expensive as the concoction was.

His name was Franz von Mercy. He came from a noble family in Lorraine, not Italy, as did his table companion. But in other respects, they were quite similar. Like Piccolomini, von Mercy was a general and a professional soldier. They were long-acquainted, if not quite friends.

There was one critical difference between them, however, which explained part of von Mercy's skepticism toward the black substance in his cup. Ottavio Piccolomini was gainfully employed by the Habsburg ruler of Austria and von Mercy was not.

In fact, he was not employed by anyone. Just a short

time earlier, he'd been in the service of Duke Maximilian of Bavaria. But after the traitor Cratz von Scharffenstein surrendered the fortress of Ingolstadt to the Swedes, von Mercy had taken his cavalrymen and fled Bavaria. He'd known full well that, despite his own complete innocence in the affair, the murderous duke of Bavaria would blame him for the disaster and have him executed.

So, he'd come to Vienna, hoping to find employment with the Habsburgs. But he'd been turned down, with only this bizarre new hot drink offered by way of compensation.

He looked up from the cup to the window. He'd wondered, when they came into the restaurant, why the owners had defaced perfectly good windowpanes by painting a sign across them. And he'd also wondered why they chose to call their establishment a café instead of a tavern.

Now he knew the answer to both questions.

"God-damned Americans," he muttered.

Piccolomini winced at the blasphemy, even though he was known to commit the sin himself. Perhaps he felt obliged to put on that public display of disapproval since he was now quite prominent in the Austrian ranks. They were, after all, right in the heart of Vienna—not more than a few minutes' walk from either St. Stephen's Cathedral or the emperor's palace.

"Damned they may well be," said Piccolomini. Again, he lifted his cup. "But I enjoy this new beverage of theirs."

"Coffee," said von Mercy, still muttering more than talking aloud. "We already *had* coffee, Octavio."

His companion shrugged. "True. But it was the

Americans who made it popular. As they have done with so many other things."

He set the cup down. "And stop blaming them for your misfortunes. It's silly and you know it. They had nothing to do with Scharffenstein's treason—they certainly can't be blamed for Maximilian's madness!—and it's not because of them that the emperor decided not to hire you. That, he did for the same sort of reasons of state that have led rulers to make similar decisions for centuries." He paused while he picked up the cup and drained it. "I happen to love coffee, myself."

He gave his fellow officer a look of sympathy and commiseration. "Tough on you, I know. Tougher still on your men. But look at it from Ferdinand's perspective, Franz. He's expecting a resumption of hostilities with the Swede and his Americans by next year. No matter how badly Maximilian has behaved and no matter how much the emperor detests him, do you honestly expect Ferdinand to take the risk of escalating the already-high tensions between Austria and Bavaria by hiring a general who—from Duke Maximilian's peculiar point of view, I agree, but that's the viewpoint at issue here—has so recently infuriated Bavaria?"

He shook his head and placed the cup back on the table. "It's not going to happen, Franz. I'm sorry, I really am. Not simply because you're something of a friend of mine, but—being honest—because you're a good cavalry commander, and I wouldn't be surprised if I have need of one before long."

Glumly, von Mercy nodded. He realized, in retrospect, that he should have foreseen this when he left

Bavaria. He knew enough of the continent's strategic configurations, after all, being by now a man in his mid-forties and a very experienced and highly placed military commander.

He'd have done better to have accompanied his friend von Werth to seek employment with Bernhard of Saxe-Weimar. Bernhard would certainly not have cared about the attitude of the Bavarians, seeing as he was already infuriating Maximilian by threatening to seize some of his territory. Or so, at least, Maximilian was sure to interpret Bernhard's actions—but, as Octavio said, it was the Bavarian duke's viewpoint that mattered here.

Nothing for it, then. He'd have to head for the Rhine, after all, and see if Saxe-Weimar might still be in the market. Von Mercy could feel his jaws tightening at the prospect of leading a large cavalry force across—around—who knew?—a goodly stretch of Europe already inhabited by large and belligerent armies. Most of whom had no reason to welcome his arrival, and some of whom would actively oppose it.

Alternatively, he could head for Bohemia and see if Wallenstein might be interested in hiring him. But . . .

He managed to keep the wince from showing in his face. *That* would be certain to infuriate his Austrian hosts, who'd so far been very pleasant even if they'd declined to employ him and his men. He had even less desire to fight his way out of Austria than he did to fight his way to the Rhine.

He heard Piccolomini chuckle, and glanced up. The Italian general was giving him a look that combined shrewdness with—again—sympathy and commiseration.

"I have another possible offer of work for you, Franz. And one that is rather close at hand."

Von Mercy frowned. "The only possibility I can think of, close at hand, would be Wallenstein. And why would you or anyone in Austrian service be sending me to Wallenstein? Like as not, a year from now, you'd be facing me across a battlefield."

A waiter appeared. Piccolomini must have summoned him, and Franz had been too preoccupied to notice.

"Another coffee for me," the Italian general said. He cocked a quizzical eyebrow at von Mercy. "And you? What's in your cup must already be cold."

Franz couldn't see what particular difference the temperature of the beverage would make. Hot or cold, it would still be extremely bitter. But . . .

Piccolomini was obviously in an expansive mood, and under the circumstances Franz felt it prudent to encourage him. "Yes, certainly. And thank you."

After the waiter was gone, Piccolomini leaned across the table and spoke softly.

"Not Wallenstein directly. In fact, part of the agreement would be that you'd have to be willing to give me your oath that—under no circumstances—would you allow yourself or your soldiers to be used directly against Austria. But . . . yes, in a way you'd be working for Wallenstein. He wouldn't be the one paying you, though, which—"

He gave von Mercy a vulpine grin. "—is always the critical issue for we mercenaries, isn't it? Or 'professional soldiers,' if you prefer the circumlocution."

Franz felt his shoulders stiffen, and forced himself to

relax. He *did* prefer the circumlocution, in point of fact. If that's what it was at all, which he didn't believe for a moment. The difference between a mercenary and a professional soldier might be thin, but it was still real. A mercenary cared only for money. A professional soldier always placed honor first.

As Piccolomini knew perfectly well, damn the crude Italian bastard—or he wouldn't have made this offer in the first place. He'd take Franz von Mercy's oath not to allow himself to be used against Austria as good coin, because it was and he knew it. He'd certainly not do the same for a mere mercenary.

"Who, then?" he asked.

Piccolomini seemed to hesitate. Then, abruptly: "How do you feel about Jews?"

Von Mercy stared at him. His mind was . . .

Blank.

Piccolomini might as well have asked him how he felt about the natives in the antipodes—or, for that matter, the ones that speculation placed on the moon but which Franz had heard the Americans said was impossible.

What did Jews have to do with military affairs? They were the least martial people of Europe. For any number of obvious reasons, starting with the fact that most realms in the continent forbade them from owning firearms. About the only contact professional soldiers ever had with them involved finances, and that was usually only an indirect connection.

Belatedly, Franz remembered that he'd also heard some rumors concerning recent developments among the Jewry of Prague. They'd played a prominent role in repulsing the attack of General Holk on the city, apparently. That had allowed Wallenstein to keep most of his army in the field and defeat the Austrians the previous year at the second battle of the White Mountain.

They were even supposed to have produced a prince of their own, out of the business. An American Jew, if he recalled correctly.

Throughout the long pause, Piccolomini had been watching von Mercy. Now, he added: "Yes, that's right. Your employer would be a Jew. An American Jew, to be precise, who is now highly placed in Wallenstein's service."

Franz rummaged through his memory, trying to find the name. He knew he'd heard it, at least once. But, like most such items of information that didn't seem to have any relevance to him, he'd made no special effort to commit the name to memory.

Piccolomini provided it. "His name is Roth. Morris Roth." He smiled, a bit crookedly. "Or Don Morris, as the Jews like to call him. They fancy their own aristocracy, you know. At least, the Sephardim always have, and it seems the Ashkenazim as well."

Franz noted—to his surprise; but then, he didn't really know the man that well—that Octavio knew that much about the inner workings of Jewry. So did Franz himself, from a now long-past friendship with a Jewish shoemaker. But most Christians didn't, certainly not most soldiers.

He realized, then, the purpose of Piccolomini's probing questions. And, again, was a bit surprised. He wouldn't have thought the outwardly bluff Italian soldier would have cared about such things.

"I have no particular animus against Jews, if that's what

you're wondering." He smiled crookedly himself. "I admit, I've never once contemplated the possibility that one of them might wish to hire me. For what? In the nature of things, Jews don't have much need for professional soldiers."

"Or a need so great that it is too great to be met," said Piccolomini. "But, yes, in times past you'd have been quite correct. But the times we live in today are ones in which the nature of things is changing. Quite rapidly, sometimes."

The waiter returned, bringing two hot cups of coffee. Piccolomini waited until he was gone, and then picked up his cup and leaned back in his chair. Still speaking rather softly, he said: "Well, then. Let's savor our coffees, and then I'll take you to meet someone."

"Roth?"

Piccolomini shook his head. "No, Roth himself is in Prague, so far as I know. The man I'll be taking you to is one of his agents. Uriel Abrabanel, of the famous clan by that name." The Italian blew on his coffee. "Famous among Sephardim, anyway."

Quite famous, in fact. The Jewish shoemaker whom Franz had known in his youth had once told him, very proudly, that he himself was—admittedly, rather distantly—related to the Abrabanels.

"Famous to many people, nowadays," said Franz, "seeing as how the wife of the prime minister of the United States of Europe is an Abrabanel. And has become rather famous herself—or notorious, depending on how you look at it."

Piccolomini nodded, and took an appreciative sip of

his coffee. "She has, indeed. The redoubtable Rebecca Abrabanel. I've been told that Cardinal Richelieu himself remarked upon her shrewdness—which, coming from him, is quite a compliment."

"Yes, it is. Although many people might liken it to one devil complimenting another on her horns and cloven hoofs."

"Oh, surely not," chuckled Piccolomini. "The woman is said to be extraordinarily comely, in fact. So I'm told, anyway."

He chuckled again, more heavily. "What I know for certain, however, is that she's the niece of the man you'll be meeting very soon. So do be alert, Franz. Uriel Abrabanel would be described as 'comely' by no one I can think of, not even his now dead wife. But he's certainly very shrewd."

It was Franz's turn to hesitate. Then, realizing he simply needed to know, he asked: "At the risk of being excessively blunt, Octavio, I must ask why you are doing me this favor?"

Again, the Florentine issued that distinctively heavy chuckle. "Good question. You'd really do better to ask Janos Drugeth. Know him? He's one of the emperor's closest advisers."

Von Mercy shook his head. "The name's familiar, of course. He's reputed to be an accomplished cavalry commander and I try to keep track of such. But I've never met him and don't really know much about him."

"Well, Janos is also one of Ferdinand's closest friends, and has been since they were boys. This was his idea, actually, not mine." Piccolomini made something of a face. "For my taste, the reasoning behind it is a bit too convoluted. Quite a bit, being honest."

Franz cocked an eyebrow. "And the reasoning is . . . Indulge me, if you would."

"I suppose there's no reason you shouldn't know. Drugeth is not in favor of continuing the hostilities between Austria and Bohemia, and thinks we'd be wiser to let things stand as they are. Personally, I disagree—and so does the emperor, for that matter. But Ferdinand listens carefully to whatever Janos says, even when he's not persuaded. And Janos suggested this ploy as a way of encouraging Wallenstein to look elsewhere than Austria for any territorial aggrandizement. We know that he's appointed Morris Roth to expand his realm to the east. But how is Roth supposed to do that without a military force? So, Drugeth thinks we should help provide him with one."

Von Mercy nodded. Up to a point, he could follow the reasoning. War had a grim and inexorable logic of its own. Once the Bohemians began a real effort to expand to the east, in all likelihood they would find themselves getting drawn deeper and deeper into the effort. The more they did so, the less of a threat they would pose to Austria to the south.

There came a point, however, at which the logic began to crumble. Granted, Franz was more familiar with the geography of western Europe than central Europe. Still, one thing was obvious.

"'Expanding his realm to the east' will take him directly into Royal Hungary, Octavio."

Piccolomini grimaced. "So it will, indeed—and don't

think I didn't point that out to the emperor and Janos both. I thought that would end the business, since the Drugeth family's own major estates are in Royal Hungary. But Janos—he's an odd one, if you ask me—didn't seem to feel that was much of a problem. In the end, the emperor decided there was enough there to warrant making the connection between you and the Jew in Prague."

He gave Franz a stern look. "But I stress that we will want your vow not to take the field against us."

"Yes, certainly. But you understand, surely, that if I enter—indirectly or not, it doesn't matter—the service of Wallenstein, that I will simply be freeing up some other general and his forces to come against you."

The Italian shrugged. "True enough. But they're not likely to have your skills, either. I think what finally convinced the emperor was Drugeth's point that if we simply let you roam loose as a free agent, since we didn't want to hire you ourselves, the end result was likely to be worse for us than having you leading Wallenstein"—he waved his hand toward the east—"somewhere out there into the marshes of the Polish and Lithuanian rivers."

Once more, that heavy chuckle. "It was hard to dispute that point, at least."

After they left the tavern—or "café," rather—Piccolomini glanced up at the sky, which had grown leaden.

"Getting cold," he said, reaching up and drawing his cloak around him more tightly.

Von Mercy followed suit. The temperature wasn't too

bad, but there was something of a wind that added considerably to the chill. "Where are we headed? Unterer Werd?"

Piccolomini shook his head. "No. The ghetto would be too far from the center of things for Abrabanel's purposes. And he's got plenty of money." With his chin, he pointed straight ahead down the street. "Just up there a ways. Less than a five-minute walk."

Franz was a bit surprised, but only a bit. Although Jews in Vienna usually lived in the ghetto located on the island formed by the Danube and one of its side branches, the city did not enforce the provision strictly if the Jew involved was wealthy enough.

As they walked, Franz noticed two other taverns sporting the new title of "café."

"I swear, it's a plague," he muttered.

Glancing in the direction of von Mercy's glower, Piccolomini smiled. "If you think it's bad here, you should see what it's like in Italy. My younger brother is the archbishop of Siena and he told me there was almost a public riot there a few months ago, because of a dispute involving the rules in a game of soccer."

"A game of . . . what?"

"Soccer. If you don't know what it is, be thankful all you have to contend with is the occasional tavern with pretensions. And pray to God that you never have to deal with the intricacies of baseball."

"Intricacies of . . . what?"

"Never mind. Stick to the cavalry, Franz."

A few dozen yards further along, Piccolomini pointed with his chin again. This time, at a small shop they were nearing. There was a sign over the door, reading: SUGAR AND THINGS.

"There's the real money," said the Florentine general "That shop's owned by a partnership between two local merchants and one of the American mechanics whom the emperor hired recently to keep his two automobiles running. Sanderlin's his name—although it's really his wife who's involved in the business."

"They are sugar importers?"

"Yes—but mostly they process it into something called 'confectioner's sugar' and sell it to the city's wealthiest residents and most expensive restaurants." He shook his head. "Sugar is already worth its weight in gold. What they do with it . . ."

He shook his head again. "But people are besotted with things American—especially anything they can find involving Vienna in those up-time tourist guides. So, they say Vienna needs its cafés with coffee and pastries—and the best pastries require confectioner's sugar."

"A plague, as I said."

"May as well get used to it, Franz," Piccolomini said heavily. "When Wallenstein's Croats failed in their raid on Grantville, all of Europe was doomed to this lunacy. Even in Paris, I'm told."

He stopped in front of a nondescript doorway. Just one of many along the street, marked in no particular way.

"And here we are."

Uriel Abrabanel proved to be, just as Piccolomini had said, a man whom no one would think to call "comely." He was saved from outright ugliness only by the fact that an animated and jovial spirit imparted a certain flair to his coarse and pox-marked features. It was hard to believe, though, that the man was closely related—uncle, no less— to Rebecca Abrabanel, reputed to be one of the great beauties of Europe.

But von Mercy was skeptical of that reputation, anyway. He didn't doubt the woman was attractive, probably quite attractive. But he was sure that the near-Helenic reputation given to her appearance was mostly the product of the same glamorous aura that surrounded everything American by now, almost four years after the Ring of Fire. An aura that was just as strong—probably stronger, in fact—among the peoples who were the USE's enemies than those who lived under Stearns' rule directly or counted themselves as his allies. Unlike the Swedes or the Germans or the Dutch, who had had many occasions to encounter Americans or their Abrabanel associates directly, for most Austrians or French or Italians (outside of Venice)—to say nothing of Spaniards or Poles—they remained mostly a matter of legend and hearsay.

And if much of the hearsay and many of the legends involved their wicked ways and nefarious schemes, there was no reason those couldn't be combined with other qualities. So, if Mike Stearns was a relentless savage bent upon destroying all that was fine and sensible about Europe's social and political arrangements, he was also surely the most cunning and astute barbarian who had stalked the earth since Attila raged out of the east. So also, if his Jewish spymaster Nasi was evil incarnate he was also intellect incarnate—just as Stearns' Jewish wife combined the appearance of a goddess with a spirit fouled by the demons of the Pit.

For, indeed, the same aura extended to those closely associated with the Americans, even if they were not American themselves. That was especially true of the Jews, especially the Sephardim of the widely flung and prominent Abrabanel clan.

Franz believed none of it. He'd read some of the philosophical and theological speculations concerning the nature and cause of the Ring of Fire. But, in the end, he'd come to the same conclusions that, by all accounts, the Americans had come to themselves. Namely, that they had no idea what had caused the miraculous phenomenon, and they were certainly not miraculous themselves. Just people, that's all. Granted, people from a distant future possessed of incredible mechanical skills and knowledge. But no more exotic, for all that, than visitors from Cathay.

Less exotic, in most ways. They spoke a well-known European language, and most of them were Christians. And all of them except a small number of African and Chinese extraction were of European origin. Solid and sturdy origin, at that: English, German, and Italian, for the most part.

As von Mercy had been ruminating over these matters, Abrabanel had spent his time studying Franz himself. Eventually, he seemed to be satisfied with something he saw, if Franz interpreted his expression correctly.

"Not a bigot, then," Abrabanel said softly. "Octavio told me as much"—here he gave the Florentine general a sly glance—"and I was inclined to believe him, even though he is an Italian and thus of duplicitous stock. So unlike we simple and straightforward Hebrews and even simpler and more straightforward Lorrainers."

Franz couldn't help but laugh. Partly, at the jest itself; partly, at the truth lurking within it. For, in point of simple fact, the seemingly bluff Piccolomini was a consummately political general, as you'd expect of a man from a prominent family in the Florentine aristocracy. He'd spent a good portion of his years as a military officer serving more in the capacity of a diplomat or even—in truth if not in name—as what amounted to a spy.

Duplicitous, as such, he might not be. But Franz didn't doubt for a moment that lies could issue from Octavio Piccolomini's lips as smoothly and evenly as a gentle tide sweeps over a beach.

He recalled himself to the matter at hand. "No, I am not a bigot. I claim no particular fondness for Jews, mind you. But I bear no hostility against you, either. What I don't understand, is what any of that has to do with your purpose in asking me here." He nodded toward Piccolomini. "Nor why you needed to use him as your conduit."

"In answer to the second question, I am not actually using Octavio as my conduit to you. It would be more accurate to say that I am using him as my conduit—say better, my liaison-at-a-comfortable-distance—with Emperor Ferdinand."

The logic was clear enough, once Franz thought about it. "Ah. You feel that if you employed me directly, the Austrians might fret themselves over the purpose of the employment. And then, out of anxiety—"

"Oh, that's far too strong a term, Franz!" protested Piccolomini. "Don't give yourself airs! We would—at most—be motivated by reasonable caution."

He bestowed a fulsome grin upon von Mercy and Abrabanel both.

Franz returned the grin with a thin smile. "Out of reasonable caution, then"—he looked back at Uriel—"they would take steps that you might find annoying."

"Oh, ridiculous!" boomed Piccolomini. "That he might find disastrous to his plans! Utterly destructive to his schemes. Might lay waste his entire project for years to come." The grin returned. "That sort of thing. Much the better way to put it."

"Indeed," said Uriel, smiling also. "This way, at every stage, the Austrians are kept—to use a handy little American expression—'in the loop.' I think that will serve everyone nicely."

Piccolomini brought a fist to his mouth and cleared his throat noisily. "Except . . . well, Wallenstein, perhaps. If he finds out that I'm involved in any way. I assume he's still holding a grudge?"

"Well, yes. Of course he is, Octavio. His name is Albrecht von Wallenstein and you *did*, after all, plot and carry out his murder."

Piccolomini waved a meaty hand. "In another world! In this one, it never happened! And that, only according to a detestable play by a German of very dubious reputation. Why, the man hasn't even been born yet. How can anyone believe a word he says?"

All three men laughed, now. Friedrich Schiller's drama *Wallenstein* was now one of the best-known plays in central Europe and very widely published and performed—despite the fact that it wouldn't have been written until the year 1800 and only one copy of it had existed in Grantville. Partly, because the subject was still alive and now king of Bohemia, a position he'd never achieved in Schiller's universe. And partly—such was the universally held suspicion—because Wallenstein secretly financed the play's publication and many of its performances. Although *Wallenstein* had its criticisms of the man who gave the play its title, the portrait of him was by and large quite favorable.

When the laughter died away, Uriel shook his head. "But I saw no reason—and see none now—for Wallenstein to know anything of your role in this business. All he will know, if all goes well, is that I met a fortunately unemployed cavalry commander of excellent reputation in Vienna and hired him on behalf of Don Morris."

Piccolomini rubbed his jaw for a moment, and then nodded. "Well. You're probably right."

Uriel turned to von Mercy. "My proposition is simple enough, General. As you may or may not know—and I suspect you do, at least the gist of it—the king of Bohemia has entrusted Don Morris Roth to see to Bohemia's interests to the east. Among those interests—this is at the center of Don Morris' own concerns, as well as mine—is included a reasonable and just resolution of the Jewish issues involved."

Franz managed not to wince. He could think of several possible resolutions to what Abrabanel was very delicately calling "the Jewish issues involved" in the politics of the Polish–Lithuanian Commonwealth and the sprawling lands and peoples of Ruthenia. But neither "reasonable" nor "just" was likely to be part of them.

But all he said was, "Not so easily done. And if it can be done, it won't be done by cavalry."

Uriel now grinned. "And an honest man, too! No, General, it can't be done by cavalry. In the end, in fact— such is Don Morris' opinion, and I share it—the matter can't be resolved by any sort of military force. But what cavalry *can* do, as we wrestle with the problem, is keep someone else from imposing their own very unreasonable and unjust solution."

"Possibly. Although it will take more than one regiment of cavalry."

"Quite a bit more, in fact." Abrabanel leaned forward in his chair. "But here's the thing, General. We can train—so we believe, at least—a powerful enough military force out of our own resources."

Franz raised an eyebrow. "From Jews? Meaning no offense, but I find that unlikely."

Abrabanel shrugged. "It was done in another universe. A very powerful military force, in fact. But it won't simply be Jews, in any event. The Brethren are with us also, and—"

"Socinians." That came from Piccolomini, who, for all his cosmopolitanism and sophistication, had more than a little in the way of straightforward Italian Catholic attitudes. The word was practically sneered. "Heretics who make Lutherans and Calvinists look sane. And I thought they were pacifists, which just proves how mad they are."

"No, you have them confused with the Polish Brethren. The Brethren I speak of are the Bohemian

Brethren, the ones descended from the Hussites. They're quite Trinitarian, I assure you." He made a little fluttering motion with both hands. "But whether they are heretics or not—and as a Jew, I would not presume to judge such Christian matters—I can assure you that they are quite capable of fighting, Octavio. They did very well against Holk's forces last year."

He turned back to von Mercy. "But here's the thing— as you well know from your own experience. Without the traditions involved, there is no way we can forge a good cavalry force on our own."

After a moment, Franz nodded. At least, this Don Morris and his Abrabanel agent were not so wildly impractical as to imagine they could conjure up good cavalry from the ranks of ghetto dwellers and rustics.

Infantry . . . yes. Perhaps even artillery, if not too much was demanded of it in the way of maneuvering. But cavalrymen, like archers, almost had to be born to it. At the very least, they had to have spent years learning all the necessary skills.

"So. And for that, you seek to hire me. Yes?"

"Exactly."

"And the terms?"

Abrabanel's description was short, clear and to the point. When he was done, von Mercy studied him for a few seconds.

"And all this is going to come from the purse of one man? Who is not even a duke, much less a king. Pardon me, but I find that hard to believe. I'm not a village peasant, who thinks a 'rich Jew' is some sort of devil-summoned creature with bottomless coffers."

Uriel smiled. "You might be surprised, actually, at how rich some of these up-timers have gotten. The Roth fortune derives largely from cut jewelry, of which at the moment they have an effective monopoly and is a rage sweeping Europe. More than one monarch—and any number of dukes—are opening up their coffers to obtain the new gems. And, at that, Don Morris' wealth is rather small compared to the fortune being amassed by the Stone family with their pharmaceutical and chemical works. Still—"

He waggled fingers in a gesture that simultaneously dismissed the problem and cautioned the need for discretion. "Not all of the funds, of course, will come from Don Morris himself. Probably not even most of them. I said that Wallenstein was not *directly* involved here. I did not say he was not involved at all."

Von Mercy leaned back in his chair, and felt the tension caused by the Austrian emperor's refusal to hire him begin to ease. It seemed he would be able to keep his regiment intact, after all. Some of those men had been with him for years and would have been very difficult to replace quickly if at all.

In fact, he *had* heard tales of the wealth of the man Roth in Prague. The intricately carved new jewelry he and his partners had introduced to Europe was, indeed, all the rage—at least, among those circles who could afford such gems at all. But there were a lot of noblemen in Europe, many of whom were very wealthy themselves—and it seemed as if each and every one of them was bound and determined to acquire one of the dazzling new "Prague jewels," as they were now being called.

And if Wallenstein was also involved, even if only at the level of providing funds through the back door . . .

Yes. Roth *could* afford to employ an experienced general and a regiment of cavalry, even on the munificent terms he was offering.

"Done," he said. "Where do you want me to take my troops? And by what date, and by what route?"

"As to where, Brno. Wallenstein—Roth is in charge of it—has launched an armaments industry there, so it seems a good place to station your regiment. Especially since Brno is in Moravia, not Bohemia, which should reassure Emperor Ferdinand that you are not a threat to Austria."

"It's not far from the Moravian Gate, either," observed von Mercy.

"No, it isn't," said Uriel, smiling. The Moravian Gate was the great pass between the Carpathian and Sudetes mountains that allowed easy access into Poland and the lands beyond.

"As to when . . ." Uriel shrugged. "There is really no great hurry. Two months from now would be ideal, but three months would be acceptable if you need that much time."

He made a little grimace. "The tricky question is by what route, of course. Given the unfortunate state of hostilities between Austria and Bohemia."

He glanced at Piccolomini.

"I'm afraid not," said the Florentine officer. "To allow Franz and his troops to pass directly from Austria into Bohemia would be just that little too blatant and obvious. So I'm afraid he'll have to take the longer route."

"That's time-consuming but not difficult," said von Mercy. "*Provided* I'm given free passage through the USE. I'll need to pass through the whole of the Oberpfalz and enter Bohemia at Cheb."

Uriel's good cheer was back in full force. "Not a problem."

Piccolomini and von Mercy both gave him skeptical looks.

"Johan Banér's in command of the USE Army in the Oberpfalz," pointed out Piccolomini.

"And he is, by all accounts," added Franz, "choleric to the point of lunacy."

"Banér." Abrabanel spoke the word much the way he might have named an insect. "Merely a general. Meaning no offense. Did I mention that my niece dotes upon me? And she, in turn, is doted upon by her husband?"

After a bit, his grin was met with two smiles.

"Well, then," said Piccolomini. "All seems to be well."

November 1634

Prague, capital of Bohemia

"You look tired, Melissa," said Judith Roth. She gestured to a luxurious divan in the great salon of the Roth mansion. "Please, have a seat."

Melissa Mailey went over to the divan, hobbling a little from the effects of the ten-day journey from Grantville, and plopped herself down. Her companion James Nichols remained standing, after giving the couch no more than a quick glance. Instead, his hands on his hips, he swiveled slowly and considered the entire room.

Then, whistled admiringly. "You've certainly come up in the world, folks."

Judith smiled. Her husband Morris looked somewhat embarrassed. "Hey, look," he said, "it wasn't really my idea."

"That's it," scoffed his wife. "Blame the woman."

The defensive expression on Morris' face deepened. "I didn't mean it that way. It's just . . ."

The gesture that accompanied the last two words was about as feeble as the words themselves.

"The situation," he concluded lamely.

Nichols grinned at him. "Morris, relax. I understand the realities, what with your being not only one of the king of Bohemia's closest advisers but also what amounts to the informal secular prince of Prague's Jewry. Of at least half the Jews in eastern Europe, actually, from what Balthazar Abrabanel told us."

Looking a bit less exhausted, Melissa finally took the time to appraise the room. And some more time, appraising Morris' very fancy-looking seventeenth-century apparel.

Then, she whistled herself.

"*Et tu, Brutus?*" Morris grumbled.

"Quit complaining," Melissa said. "You asked us to come here, remember? With 'Urgent!' and 'Desp'rate Need!' oozing from every line of your letter."

"Asked *you*," qualified Nichols. "Me, he just wanted to come here to give some advice to his fledgling medical faculty at his fancy new university. *I'm* just a country doctor."

"From Chicago," Melissa jeered. "South side, to boot—which has about as much open land as Manhattan."

James grinned again. "You'd be surprised how much open land there is in Chicago's south side. Vacant lots, I'll grant you. Nary a crop to be seen anywhere except the stuff handed out by drug dealers, none of which was actually grown there. My point remains. *I'm* here in Prague as a modest medical adviser. *I'm* not the one who just landed a prestigious position at Jena University as their new—and only—'professor of political science.' *I'm* not the one Morris asked to come here to explain to him how to haul eastern Europe kicking and screaming into the modern world."

Melissa made a face. "My knowledge of eastern European history is pretty general. But... I'd say your best bet is to hook up with whatever revolutionaries you can find. There's got to be some. Poland produced almost as many radicals and revolutionaries over the centuries as it did grain and layabout noblemen. For that matter, the nobility itself produced a fair number of them. Remember Count Casimir Pulaski, in the American revolution?"

James looked startled. "Is *that* who Pulaski Boulevard in Chicago is named after?"

"Doctors," scoffed Melissa. "Talk about a self-absorbed class of people. Yes, dear, that is who one of your hometown's main streets is named after. But don't get a swelled head about it. There must be a thousand Pulaski streets or avenues or boulevards in the United States, in just about as many towns."

"How the hell am I supposed to find Polish

revolutionaries?" demanded Morris. "I'm a *jeweler.* Fine, my family came from Kraków. That's ancient history."

"We're *in* ancient history," said Melissa. "Start with Red Sybolt. He's an old friend of yours and he's been a labor agitator for years. By now, if he hasn't run across some wild-eyed Polish rebels, I'll be surprised. Plant Red on a desert island in the middle of the Pacific, and he'd somehow manage to rouse a rabble."

Morris chuckled. "Well, that's true. Of course, first I'd have to track him down. He hasn't been in Prague for months."

"That's a manageable problem. Somebody will know where he is. Moving right along, you need to get Uriel Abrabanel—remember him? he works for you already—to start investigating the chances of cutting a deal with the Austrians. Now that that bigoted bastard Ferdinand II died, we're dealing with a new emperor in Vienna. He's a lot more capable than his father, by all accounts."

"Yes, we've heard that," said Judith. "He's not narrow-minded, the way his father was—and his sister Maria Anna just turned half of Europe upside down thinking for herself."

Morris scratched his jaw. "'More capable' could be bad as well as good, y'know. Still, it's worth looking into. In fact, if I know Uriel, he's already started." He eyed Melissa skeptically. "And how many more rabbits do you want me to pull out of a hat?"

"Well, here's one," said Melissa. "See if you can make an accommodation with the Cossacks. You'd have to find a suitable emissary, of course."

Morris' eyes widened. "*Cossacks?* For God's sake,

Melissa! They're the same murderous bastards who led the Chmielnicki Pogrom—which is named after their leader—in the first place! Not to mention such minor accomplishments as the pogroms at Kiev and Kishinev." His face grew hard. "Or the massacres carried out in the Ukraine during the Russian Civil War by the counter-revolutionary armies, half of which were made up of Cossacks or their hangers-on. The stinking swine murdered something like fifty thousand Jews before the Red Army put a stop to it. Fuck the Cossacks. Every one of them can rot in hell, as far as I'm concerned."

"I'm with Morris," said Nichols stoutly.

"Stick to doctoring," sniffed Melissa. "See if you can come up with a cure for excess testosterone, while you're at it." To Morris she said: "You're being childish, to be blunt. How is dealing with Cossacks in the here and now any different from what Mike Stearns has been doing with Germans? Compared to what they did to Jews in the Holocaust, the Cossacks are nothing."

"Well, yeah, but . . ."

"But *what?* Since when did you start believing in racial destiny, Morris? Nazi Germany was the product of centuries of history. Change the history, like Mike is doing, and you eliminate them before they even appear. So why can't you do the same with the Cossacks?"

"Because they're nothing but a bunch of—"

"Mounted hooligans? Thugs? For Pete's sake, Morris, in this day and age—early seventeenth century, remember?—the 'Cossacks' are barely even 'Cossacks' yet. They're just getting started. A lot of them are former serfs, in fact, who ran away from their masters. We're at least a century away from the time they started serving the Russian tsars as their mailed fist. This is the best time I can think of to stop that in its tracks, too."

Morris looked mulish. Melissa looked exasperated. "Dammit, you *asked*. At my age, I'd hardly have come racing to Prague on horseback of my own volition."

"You *rode* all the way?" asked Judith.

James grinned. "She rode on a horse for exactly one day. After that, she put her foot down and insisted we hire a carriage. One of those litter-type carriages, of course, not a wheeled one. Going over the mountains on a wheeled vehicle is best left to mad dogs and Englishmen."

It was Melissa's turn to look defensive. "I spent my youth waving a placard at demonstrations. I did *not* attend the kind of ladies' finishing school where Mary Simpson learned to ride."

"How's she doing, by the way?" asked Morris.

"Given her recent hair-raising adventures, quite well. It helped a lot, of course, that when she got back to Magdeburg her son was waiting for her along with her husband."

Judith peered at her. "I thought you detested the Simpsons. Well, except Tom."

"I did, sure, when John Simpson ran that godawful campaign against Mike three years ago." Melissa waved her hand. "But three years is ancient history, as fast as things have been changing since the Ring of Fire. I think quite well of them, these days."

She pointed an accusatory finger at Morris. "And there's a lesson for you. If I can make friends with Mary Simpson, why can't you do it with Cossacks?"

He threw up his hands. "They're barbarians, for the love of God!"

"Again, so what? Yes, they're not far removed from barbarism. What do you expect, from a society being forged out of runaway serfs and bandits on the borderlands? Nobody is *simply* one thing or another, Morris. It's always more complicated. To go back to Mary Simpson, she's still haughty as all hell—can be, anyway—and I don't think she'll ever really be able to see the world except through her own very upper-crust perspective. But that's not all there is to the woman, not by a long shot. The trick is finding a way—which is exactly what Mike did—to match her and her husband properly to the right circumstances. Bring out their best, instead of their worst. So do the same with the Cossacks."

"They don't *have* a 'best side,' that I can see," Morris groused.

"Oh, that's silly," said his wife. "Of course they do, even if it's only courage. If they hadn't been tough bastards, the tsars couldn't have used them in the first place."

A young servant entered the salon. "Dinner is ready, Lady Judith."

Judith rose. "Thank you, Rifka. Come along, folks. You must be starving by now."

Fortunately, they were hungry—or James might have spent half an hour instead of three minutes making wisecracks about Lord and Lady Roth and the way they bid fair to make pikers out of any European aristocrats barring maybe the odd emperor here and there. He didn't even make one wisecrack about the food being kosher.

Of course, he might not have noticed anyway. But Melissa did, and after the meal was over she gave Morris a little smile.

"I see even you can bend a little. Smart move, if you ask me."

Morris was back to being defensive. "I didn't eat pork in the old days, even if I never had any use for most of those silly kashrut rules. Here . . ."

His wife gave him a mildly exasperated look. "To start with," she said, "we didn't really have any choice. Things are changing in Prague, but there's still no chance of Jews, even very rich ones, hiring Christian servants. And even if you could, you couldn't trust them not to be spies working for somebody else. So all the servants in the house, including the cooks, are Jewish—and the only way they know how to cook is kosher."

She shrugged. "So, I persuaded Morris that it just made sense to make a virtue out of the business. You know how Jews are, Melissa, even if"—she gave Nichols a skeptical glance—"James is probably awash in goofy notions. Most of Prague's Jews, and certainly all of the rabbis, know that Morris' theological opinions are radically different from theirs. But Jews don't care much about theology, the way Christians do. They care a lot more about whether people maintain Jewish customs and traditions and rituals. And since we now do—"

"Not all of the customs," said Morris, half-snarling. "I was born Reform, raised Reform, and I'll damn well die Reform. No way I'll ever—"

"Husband, quit it," snapped Judith. "We follow most of them, and you know it perfectly well. And you also know that between that and the fact that all of Bohemia's Jews depend on you to keep them in Wallenstein's good graces, everybody is being friendly to us. Even the rabbis, most of them."

She gave Morris an accusing glare. "And don't pretend otherwise! You even *like* some of those rabbis."

"Well . . ."

"Admit it!"

"Fine. Yes, I like Mordecai and Isaac. But they're—they're . . ."

He made a vague motion with his hand. "Not exactly just orthodox rabbis. It's more complicated. More . . ."

"Many-sided?" asked Melissa. "Full of potential, not just limits?"

Seeing her triumphant look, he scowled. Then, transferred the scowl to the servant Rifka when she entered the dining room.

Timidly, seeing her employer's expression, she drew back a pace.

"Oh, stop it, Morris!" snapped Judith. "He's not glaring at you, Rifka. He's just glaring the way he always does when one of his pet peeves develops legs and starts walking around on its own instead of obeying his orders."

She added a winning smile to settle the young woman's nerves. "What do you need?"

"Ah . . . nothing, Lady Judith. It's just that some people have arrived and insist on speaking to you immediately."

"And that's another thing I miss," muttered Morris. "Doorbells, so you'd know when somebody was at the blasted door."

"House this size," James muttered back, "you'd need a foghorn."

Judith ignored both of them. "Please, show the visitors in. We've finished eating anyway."

When the newcomers entered the room, Morris' expression darkened still further. Melissa's, on the other hand, was full of good cheer.

"Well, I do declare. Red Sybolt, in the flesh. We were just talking about you, as it happens. Or rather, I was. Morris was trying to evade the subject."

"What subject?" asked Red. "But, first, some introductions." He gestured to the four men who'd come in behind him.

"You know this big fellow, of course." Pleasantly, the very large man standing just behind him nodded at the people at the table. That was Jan Billek, one of the central figures of the Unity of Brethren, the theologically radical church led by Bishop Comenius which, in another universe, would be driven into exile and eventually become the Moravian church in America.

Red's hand indicated the two men standing to his left. One of them was blonde and large, if not as large as Billek. The other was of average height and more dark-complected. "And these are Krzysztof Opalinski and Jakub Zaborowsky. My kind of guys, even if they're both Polish szlachta. Finally—"

He clasped the shoulder of the last man, a burly fellow wearing a rather exotic-looking costume, and pulled him forward. "And this here's Dmytro Fedorovych."

Sybolt grinned cheerfully. "He's a Cossack, of all

things. Well, sorta. They're not exactly Cossacks yet, you know. He tracked me down while I was in Lublin with Jan here, doing nothing we need to discuss at the moment. He heard I was connected to the Prince of the Jews in Prague, and insisted I take him there and make the introductions. That's you, Morris, if you didn't know."

Morris was practically ogling Fedorovych. The fact was, for all his belligerent talk on the subject, the Jewish jeweler had been born and raised in America. Melissa didn't think he'd ever actually met a Cossack in his life.

"Oh, my," said Judith. She indicated the many empty chairs surrounding the huge table in the dining room. "Please, gentlemen, have a seat."

Morris kept staring at Fedorovych. Wondering, apparently, if the savage Cossack even knew what a chair was in the first place. Melissa almost laughed.

As it happened, despite the rather outlandish outfit— she thought it was probably derived from Tatar or Mongol apparel—Fedorovych took his seat quite gracefully.

"And to what do we owe the pleasure of this visit?" Melissa asked them.

"What do you think?" said Red. "Word's out that Wallenstein appointed Morris to grab half of eastern Europe for him—"

"*Already*?" demanded Morris. "Dammit, who blabbed?"

"Could have been Wallenstein himself," said Red. "It's a tossup whether he's shrewder than he is vainglorious. Relax, willya? When I said 'the word was out,' I only meant in selected circles. Mostly Jewish circles. The most likely culprit for the leak is you, actually. Or rather, the servants who overheard you talking about it. They'd have passed the word into the Prague ghetto and from there . . ."

He smiled. "In case you hadn't figured it out already, what with you being the Prince of the Jews, all the Jewish settlements in the towns of eastern Europe are connected to each other. The point being, the word's out, and these gents want to dicker with you."

He turned toward the handsome young Pole named Krzysztof Opalinski. "You can start the dickering with these two. The reason they know about it is because I'd already gotten to know them while engaged in that business we don't need to discuss, and I told them myself."

"We don't care about Wallenstein's aims on the Ruthenian lands," said Opalinski. He gestured to his partner. "Jakub even less than I do, being as he is from the area himself."

Jakub Zaborowsky had a twisted smile on his face. "My family is szlachta like Krzysztof's. But his family is prominent and well-off and we are dirt-poor, as Red would put it." The term "dirt-poor" came in English, easily blended into the German they were all speaking. "I think we'd do better off back in Poland, if the situation was changed. The only ones who do well in Lesser Poland are the magnates, even if most of the szlachta there try to console themselves with the sure knowledge that they are of noble blood while they spend their days dealing with hogs and moneylenders like any peasant does."

Opalinski spoke again. "So we will not contest that issue with you. Indeed, you will have our blessing, even to a degree our active support. Strip away their Ruthenian estates, and half the magnates who have Poland and Lithuania under their yoke will lose most of their wealth and influence."

For the first time, he came into focus in Melissa's mind. The easy and effortless way he said "under their yoke" was the tip-off. In Melissa's experience—which had been quite extensive in her youth—the only people who could whip out phrases like that as naturally as most people talked of the weather were dyed-in-the-wool radicals.

"And who, exactly, is 'you'?" she asked.

The blond young Pole sat erect, looking stiffly proud. "We are members of the newly formed Spartacus League of the Polish–Lithuanian Commonwealth."

His partner Jakub, who seemed either less full of himself or simply blessed with a good sense of humor, smiled ironically. "We took the name from Rosa Luxemburg's revolutionary organization. She was a Pole, you know, and a Jewess. Even if the history books mostly talk about her in Germany."

James Nichols rubbed his face. "I swear, no virus or bacillus which ever lived is as contagious a vector as those fricking books in Grantville."

Melissa smiled back at Zaborowsky. "Out of idle curiosity, which unlikely tomes did you find in Grantville that said anything about Rosa Luxemburg and the Spartacus League? I wouldn't have thought the public library—much less the high school's!—would have carried any such books."

Both Poles looked at Red. For his part—very unusual, this was—the UMWA man looked almost embarrassed.

"Well . . ."

After a moment, Melissa's jaw sagged. "You swiped them! From *my* library."

"Oh, jeez, Melissa, I don't think loaded terms like 'swiped' are called for here. What the hell, you were locked up in the Tower of London for a whole year. Not as if you'd miss them any, until I got them copied and put them back."

Melissa glared at him. Then, glared at Nichols.

"Ease up, dear," he said mildly. "*I* didn't give him permission to come into our house and take the books. First I even knew about it."

The gaze he gave Red was every bit as mild as his tone of voice. "Odd, though. I never imagined you had second-story burglar skills."

"Me? Oh, hell no." Red was back to his normal cheery self, the momentary embarrassment having vanished like the dew. "But I know some guys who do."

To Melissa, he said: "And since you asked, the three books in question were a biography of Luxemburg, a collection of her writings, and a history of the German Social Democratic party." He coughed into his fist. "Among others, of course. I gotta tell you, for someone like me, you got far and away the most useful library in Grantville. Anywhere in this here world."

"You could have asked!"

"You were locked up in the Tower, like I said," he replied reasonably. He gave James a glance. "And since I figured he was likely to get stubborn about it, you not being around to say yes or no for yourself, and since he wasn't hardly ever in the house anyway what with spending every waking hour at the hospital, I figured it was just simpler all the way around to borrow them for a while until I could get copies made."

Melissa didn't know whether to swear at him or laugh. In the end, she did both. "You lousy fucking commie!" she exclaimed, gurgling a little.

He shrugged. "I prefer the term 'revolutionary socialist,' myself, although I certainly won't squawk at 'Bolshie.' But fair's fair. From now on, Melissa, you can borrow anything of mine without so much as a by-your-leave. What's mine is yours, as they say."

"You don't own anything, Red," said James, in that same mild tone of voice. "Except the clothes on your back, which wouldn't fit Melissa anyway."

"Well, of course not. What kind of agitator goes around hauling lots of trunks and suitcases with him? I got exactly what fits into a reasonable-sized valise. Still. The principle's the same."

Melissa had never found it possible to stay mad at Red Sybolt for more than a few seconds. First, because he was such an incorrigible sprite. Second, because she was something of a kindred spirit. She'd admit it was a little silly for her to be denouncing Sybolt as a commie, seeing as how she could remember the label being applied to her often enough.

"And what's Mr. Fedorovych's angle in all this?" she asked.

"Well, it's complicated," said Red. "And we'll have to have Jakub do the translating for us. Dmytro's German is lousy and my Ruthenian—which is actually about a jillion dialects—is even worse."

Everyone looked at the Poles. Zaborowsky began speaking to Fedorovych. After a while, the Cossack started speaking.

The first sentences translated were:

"He says he thinks—so do many people he's spoken to among the Zaporozhian Host—that they'd do better if they shifted their allegiance to Wallenstein. They're fed up with the Lithuanian and Polish boyars, and they don't trust the Russians at all. But first, he says, Mr. Roth has to agree to do something about the Jews."

"I knew it," hissed Morris. He scowled at the Cossack. "I suppose he expects me—God knows how I'd do it even if I were so inclined—to make all the Jews living in eastern Europe just somehow vanish. Stuff somewhere around a quarter of a million kikes into my kike pocket, I guess."

Zaborowsky translated. Frowning—he seemed more puzzled than anything else, from what Melissa could tell—Fedorovych shook his head and spoke. The translation came back:

"He doesn't understand why you think to move the Jews. It's impossible anyway, because there are far too many of them. Besides, they do lots of useful things. But he says they have to stay in their towns, or, if they move into the countryside, they have to do it like any other farmer. No more working for the boyars."

Morris stared at him. Then, glared at Melissa. "This is *your* fault."

"Huh?"

His wife looked exasperated. "Morris, that's absolutely childish!"

He slumped back in his chair. "Yeah, I know it is. It's

still her fault. I can remember her causing trouble since practically the first day she showed up in Grantville, way back almost forty years ago."

Melissa sniffed. "That is why I came here, after all. At *your* insistence."

"Don't remind me." Morris wiped his face. "I feel like I got somehow dropped into the set of *Lord of the Rings* right at the point when Tolkien conjured up an alliance with dwarves and elves." Gloomily: "And what's worse, some idiot cast me as Gandalf."

Krzysztof Opalinski was obviously puzzled by Morris' reference to himself as Gandalf. But, to Melissa's surprise, his companion Jakub Zaborowsky grinned.

"Not exactly, Herr Roth—at least, not from our viewpoint. You are more in the way of our Elrond. Perhaps Galadriel."

Morris gaped at him. Jakub made a modest wagging gesture with his hand. "I like to read. Although I must say that while I enjoyed *The Lord of the Rings,* the premises are preposterous. In that story, everybody loves the king except the forces of evil—and there are no rapacious great noblemen to be found anywhere. A fantasy, indeed."

Morris was still gaping at him.

"Close your mouth, dear," murmured Judith. She gave Zaborowsky a smile. "I'll admit the image of my husband as an elf is delightful, but . . . I don't really understand what you mean by it."

Jakub shrugged. "It is not complicated, really. Gandalf was the leader of the active struggle against Sauron. In Poland and Lithuania, at least—and certainly in the lands controlled by the Cossacks—Herr Roth cannot possibly play that role. The Poles are a fractious people, and the Lithuanians even more so. If Wallenstein makes the mistake of trying to encroach upon their territory, they will unite against him. And they will have Hetman Koniecpolski leading their armies. He is not a general any sane person takes lightly."

Morris had closed his mouth, by now. "Well. No, he isn't."

"As for the Cossacks," Zaborowsky continued, giving his companion Fedorovych a little nod that seemed half-amused and half-respectful, "I am afraid you cannot take Dmytro here as a valid sample of the lot. He has no animus against Jews at all, so far as I can tell. Not so, for the average Cossack. Even Jewish traders are at some risk in Cossack territory."

Naturally, that set Morris back to glaring. At the wall, however, since he couldn't very well glare at the only Cossack actually present.

Seeing the nod in his direction, Fedorovych asked for a translation. Once he got it, he grunted. Then, jabbered something that had to be translated back.

"What he says," explained Zaborowsky, "is that I am exaggerating some. Most Cossacks have no contact with the Jews in the towns and their villages. All they see are the Jewish rent collectors and estate managers who exploit the Ruthenian peasants. So they take those as representative of the lot, when in fact they are a small portion. Dmytro's been in the towns, and he knows that most Jews are just as poor as most peasants."

Having finished, he shrugged again. "What he says is true enough. But Dmytro is such a good Christian under the Cossack bandit exterior—you understand, I am being very generous with the term 'Christian'—that I think he underestimates the force of sheer bigotry. Especially when it is reinforced weekly, sometimes daily, by priests of the Greek faith."

Melissa couldn't help but make a face. "The Greek faith" referred to Orthodox Christianity, which, in this day and age, was lagging centuries behind both the Catholics and the Protestants. Where the Roman church and any one of the major Protestant denominations could boast many accomplished and sophisticated theologians, the Orthodox church could count none. The highest Orthodox prelates were usually under the thumb of either Istanbul or Moscow.

So, it was a church that relied almost entirely on ritual and custom. Good enough, perhaps, for the illiterate or semiliterate peasants of eastern Europe, and the Cossacks. But it had lost the allegiance of the native ruling classes of the vast Ruthenian lands. For all practical purposes, they had been Polonized. Ethnically still Ruthenian, they spoke Polish and practiced Catholicism or, in some cases, Protestantism. Very few of them even dwelt any longer on their Ruthenian estates. They left those to be managed by overseers—often Jewish—while they moved to Warsaw and lived in city mansions. The last of the great Ruthenian magnates still of Orthodox faith, Prince Władysław Zasławski—one of the richest lords in the entire Commonwealth—had converted to Catholicism in the summer of 1632.

The end result was a "Commonwealth of Both Nations" that was actually a commonwealth of *three* nations—but the third nation, the Ruthenians, had no voice or say in the affairs of state.

Nor did the Poles and Lithuanians bother to be polite about the matter. Just two years earlier, a Cossack delegation had shown up at the electoral convention which chose Władysław IV as the successor to the Polish–Lithuanian throne, following the death of his father Zygmunt III. They claimed the right to participate in the convention, pointing to their frequent and valiant role in Poland's battles with the Turks and Tatars as their credentials.

The response had been blunt, and as rude as you could ask for. It was explained to the Ruthenian roughnecks that, yes, they were indeed part of the Commonwealth's body—just as nails are part of the human body, and need to be trimmed from time to time. And they were not welcome in the convention.

Leaving aside the arrogance and bigotry involved, it was hard for Melissa to imagine anything more stupid on the part of Poland and Lithuania's rulers. Bad enough, that they treated their Ruthenian serfs like animals. But to do so when those serfs had living among them a large and ferocious warrior caste like the Cossacks . . .

They were practically begging for a social explosion, and, sure enough, it was on the horizon. In the universe she'd come from, the situation had finally erupted in the great Cossack Revolt of 1648, led by the Cossack ataman Bohdan Chmielnicki. The revolt had shaken the Commonwealth to its foundations, leaving it wide open to the foreign invasions that would devastate Poland and go down in its history as "The Deluge." And, in the end,

Poland would lose the Ukraine to Moscow. And with that loss, the power equation between the two great Slavic nations would shift drastically in favor of the Russians.

Morris was muttering something. She thought it was "I knew it."

"Stop muttering, husband," said Judith. "Say it out loud, if you have to say it."

"I knew it," he pronounced.

Krzysztof Opalinski frowned. "Knew what?"

Zaborowsky, whom Melissa had already pegged as the brighter of the two Polish radicals, gave him a sideways glance. "He means 'I knew the Cossacks would be useless. Probably enemies.'"

Fedorovych demanded a translation. Jakub gave it to him, and from the brevity Melissa was sure he pulled no punches. But instead of matching Morris' glare with one of his own, the Cossack just grinned.

He jabbered something. Jakub translated.

"He says he didn't mean to suggest anything would be easy. With Cossacks, nothing is easy. He says you should watch them quarreling over the loot. Worse than Jews in a haggling fury."

Morris looked to the ceiling. "Oh, swell."

Later that night, after they retired to their chamber—chambers, rather—James Nichols gave their surroundings another admiring whistle. Then, eyed the bed a bit dubiously, and the canopy over it more dubiously still.

"You realize that if that comes down and buries us, we'll smother to death. Damn thing must weigh a quarter of a ton."

"Oh, don't be silly," said Melissa. But her own gaze at the canopy was probably on the dubious side, also. The thing wasn't really a "canopy" such as you might find over a bed in a fancy hotel. It bore a closer resemblance to the unicorn tapestries she'd once seen at The Cloisters museum in New York. It certainly didn't weigh a quarter of a ton. That was just ridiculous. Still, it wouldn't be a lot of fun to wriggle out from under if it did come down.

Not that that was likely to happen, of course. The four-corner posters holding it up didn't bear much resemblance to anything you'd see in a fancy hotel either. They looked more like floor beams, except they were ornately carved.

There came a soft knock at the door. James turned and gave it a frown. The door was visible through the wide entryway connecting the salon with the bedchamber.

"Who . . . ?"

Melissa was already moving through the entryway toward the door. "That'll be Red, I imagine. At least, if I interpreted a look he gave me at the end of the meal correctly."

"Why would . . ."

Melissa paused at the door. As thick as it was, she wasn't worried about anyone standing outside hearing their conversation.

"Why? Because, knowing Red, I'm sure there are things he's not prepared to ask or say in front of anybody. Especially not someone like the Roths, whom he likes personally but are for all practical purposes in Wallenstein's camp."

The frown on James' forehead faded. "Ah." Then he grinned. "You don't seriously mean to suggest that a flaming commie like Red Sybolt isn't entirely trustful of the intentions of Albrecht von Wallenstein, mercenary-captain-in-the-service-of-reaction-*par-excellance* and nowadays a crowned king in his own right?"

Melissa smiled. "Not hardly."

She opened the door. Sure enough, Red Sybolt was standing there. To her surprise, though, he was accompanied by Jakub Zaborowsky. She'd expected him to come alone.

As she ushered them into the salon, Melissa pondered that for a moment. Why Zaborowsky and not Opalinski? She was quite sure there wasn't any mistrust involved. Having spent a very long dinner in conversation, much of it with the two Poles, she felt confident she had the measure of Krzysztof Opalinski. Allowing for the inevitable cultural variations you'd expect from the gap in time and place, Krzysztof reminded her of any number of student radicals she'd known in the 1960s. Sincere; earnest; filled with a genuine desire to Do The Right Thing. Whatever faults such people had, treachery was rarely one of them.

On the other hand...

As a rule, they *did* have faults. The biggest of them—which Krzysztof Opalinski certainly shared, from what she'd seen—was a tendency toward certainties. And, still worse, simplicities. Revolution was not a complex and turbulent episode in human affairs, filled with contradictions and confusion. It was spelled with a capital R.

Such people could be trusted not to be treacherous, sure enough. But they could usually be trusted to screw up, too, sooner or later.

Red Sybolt was a different sort of person altogether. He had the same strength of convictions—probably even stronger, in fact. But he was a man in his mid-forties, born and raised in a working-class family, who'd developed his opinions and his political tactics dealing with his fellow coal miners in the gritty reality of working lives. Not from speeches spouted on college campuses, or late-night talk sessions. And he'd held those convictions for many years, solid as a rock, where most student radicals shaded into comfortable liberalism within a short time after leaving the ivory halls.

So. If she was right, that meant that Red thought there was a lot more substance to Zaborowsky than to his companion. Which wouldn't surprise Melissa at all, since that was her assessment also.

Those calculations didn't take more than a few seconds, by which time they were all seated in the comfortable chairs and divans in the salon.

All except James, that is. He was still standing in the entryway that connected the salon with the bed-chamber.

Red flashed him a grin. "Hey, you're welcome to join us, James."

"Just a country doctor, remember?"

"Oh, cut it out." Red jabbed a thumb at Melissa. "I know damn well she'll tell you anything important, anyway. And leaving aside the 'country' bullshit, you're a black doctor from one of Chicago's ghettos, not some jerk

MD who grew up in a gated community and thinks manicured lawns are a natural growth."

James smiled thinly. "True. But I spent no time at all meddling with black-power ghetto politics in my youth, neither. Went straight from honest crime into the military." He waggled a finger at the three people sitting on the couch. "This sort of revolutionist caballing and cavorting is not my forte."

"Yeah, sure. But you're not given to blind trust in the good intentions of the high and mighty, either."

Nichols' smile grew even thinner. "True again. In those days, my opinion of Lyndon Johnson and Robert McNamara was unprintable. To say nothing of my opinion of Nixon and Kissinger after they took over." His shrug was as minimal as his smile. "You could print them today, but only because I picked up an education afterward. So, these days, I know there are alternative terms for 'lying motherfuckers.'"

After a pause, he said: "Well, okay. Why not?" And took a seat next to Melissa.

Red now looked at her. And then jabbed a thumb at Zaborowsky.

"I want to know if you agree with him. About the Ruthenians, I mean. We've been arguing about it. Well . . . maybe 'arguing' is too strong a word."

Melissa looked at Jakub. He was giving her a look that was far more placid than anything that really belonged on such a young man's face. "Placid," not in the sense of uncaring, but in the sense that he was quite willing to entertain notions that he suspected were wrong, but wasn't sure.

Impressive. Most political radicals that age were sure of everything.

"Well..."

She thought about the problem. It was quite a tricky one, actually.

"The thing is, Red, I think Jakub's *attitude* is the right one to take." She made a little face. "Although I'd recommend keeping the wisecracks about illiteracy and drunkenness to a minimum. The reason being, that any Polish revolutionary movement that isn't prepared to let Ruthenia go if that's what the Ruthenians want, won't be worth a damn. Sooner or later it'll most likely collapse. It's like..."

Jakub spoke up, for the first time since entering the room. "Here is what they would do. The leadership of the Cossacks, except perhaps the Zaporozhian Host, is not at all interested in eliminating serfdom. Their grievance is simply that the Polish and Lithuanian szlachta won't accept the Cossack starytsa as their social and political equals. But if they do so, the starytsa will be satisfied. And even stupid, stubborn Polish noblemen—even Lithuanians, who are more stupid and stubborn still—can face reality if their backs are against the wall."

He shook his head. "Besides, they wouldn't even have to carry it out. Those registered Cossack colonels and atamans are every bit as stupid. All the Poles and Lithuanians have to do is promise them they'll give them equality. And then we'll have thousands of Cossacks to deal with as well as the great magnates and their private armies. Whereas if we make clear from the beginning that we will let the Ruthenians decide their own fate, when we take the state power, we'll gain the support of many Ruthenians and the Cossacks will most likely spend all their time quarreling."

He jeered. "They're very good at that."

The sarcastic jeer bothered Melissa a little. There was a hard edge to Jakub Zaborowsky that she hadn't detected in his companion Krzysztof. It was understandable, of course. Unlike Opalinski, who'd been born into wealth and privilege and had the relaxed cheeriness that often came with such a background, Jakub had been born into a hardscrabble szlachta family. There was no way he could have arrived at the conclusions he'd come to if, probably at a very early age, he hadn't come to loathe and detest the bigotry and narrow-mindedness he saw around him.

In most ways, in fact, that hard edge would be necessary. In the years to come, if he survived, Jakub Zaborowsky would have to deal with Polish and Lithuanian magnates who were as savage and ruthless as any rulers in history. Their standard response to rebellion was a bloodbath. Treachery and double-dealing came as naturally to them as venom to a viper. No revolutionary leader who was soft and sweet could possibly defeat them.

Still, a revolution could turn very ugly, if the people leading it started crossing certain lines.

She shook her head, slightly. Such worries were very premature, after all. So far, from what she could see, the "Polish revolution" amounted to a small number of young szlachta radicals organized by an up-time labor agitator and allied only with a small sect of radical Christians and—maybe, down the road—with eastern Europe's Jewry, or at least a part of it. They were hardly on the verge of having to deal with the problems and temptations of triumph.

Red cleared his throat. "To get back to the point. Leaving all that aside—yeah, sure, I agree nobody should try to force the Ruthenians to do anything—what do you think about the rest of it? What I mean is, do *you* think Ruthenians would be better off if they were part of Wallenstein's empire in the making?"

Melissa hesitated. Partly, just to ponder the question. Mostly, though, because she was feeling a little guilty. Morris Roth had asked her to come here in order to help him figure out how to do precisely that—absorb the Ruthenian lands and peoples into Bohemia's realm.

Which she would do, and do faithfully, because *anything* was better than the situation that existed. But...

"Well, no, actually," she said. "Or, it'd be better to say, it depends. *If* the Poles straightened out their act, then I think the Ruthenians would probably be better off as part of the Commonwealth than as subjects of Wallenstein."

Zaborowsky was peering at her intently. "Why?"

"Because..."

She tried to figure out how to explain it, in a way that would make sense to a young man who came from this era and didn't have the benefit of being able to look back on it from her vantage point centuries later.

"Because the worst thing about Polish history is that it was such a tragedy, what happened. It *could* have turned out completely differently. The potential that was destroyed was incredible. In the Middle Ages, Poland was as advanced as any European country, at least in most respects. And much further advanced, in some. No other European country developed Poland's traditions of religious toleration and multi-nationalism, for instance."

Jakub grunted. "That was under the Jagiellonian dynasty. During the reign of Stefan Batory also. Those kings always favored the lower classes and the burghers, against the great lords. Just like the Vasas do in Sweden. But our branch of the Vasas, when they became Poland's ruling dynasty, did the exact opposite. Since they really only care about regaining the Swedish crown which they think belongs to them, they allied with the great magnates. It is ruining our country. Everything is now subordinated to the grain trade. The conditions for the peasants get worse every year, and the towns are shrinking. Even the richest burghers have no favor at all, any more, and while most of the szlachta—stupid bastards—bask in their official status as the equals of the magnates, the fact is they are becoming nothing more than lowly vassals."

That . . . was a pretty damn good summation of what had happened to the Commonwealth in the half century since the Poles and Lithuanians made the mistake of electing Zygmunt III Vasa to the crown.

The question was, could the situation still be turned around?

She returned Zaborowsky's gaze with one that was every bit as intense. And reminded herself, not for the first time since the Ring of Fire, what a terrible mistake it could be to underestimate the people of the seventeenth century.

"Yes," she murmured. *"Hell*, yes."

✥ ✥ ✥

The next morning, when Melissa and James came down to the dining hall for breakfast, they found Morris Roth standing at the window with a letter in his hand. He had a very peculiar expression on his face.

"What's up, Morris?" asked James.

"Huh?" Roth looked at them, a bit startled. Then, looked down at the letter.

"I just got some news from Uriel. And I'm trying to sort out how I feel about it."

His eyes went back to the window and his gaze seemed out of focus. "He's one of the great arch-villains of Jewish history, you know. Not up there with Hitler and Himmler, of course. No one is. But he's solidly in the second rank. So I'm wondering why I'm not dancing with glee."

"*What* are you talking about?" Melissa asked, a bit exasperated.

Morris lifted the letter. "Bohdan Chmielnicki. Today, of course, still a relatively young man and just a minor officer among the registered Cossacks."

"And . . ."

"He's dead. He was assassinated two weeks ago, at his estate in Subotiv. Three men appear to have done it. None of them were apprehended, because he was just a minor officer and wasn't surrounded by guards. The suspicion is that they were Polish, but no one really knows."

He gave James a wry little smile. "What was it you said last night? 'No virus or bacillus which ever lived is as contagious a vector as those fricking books in Grantville.' You sure had the right of it. Someone must have read the future history and figured they'd take out the leader of the

1648 rebellion before he got any further." He shook his head. "As if that'll really change anything."

Melissa took in a long, slow breath. "So. That means there's already at least one conspiracy afoot." She smiled wryly herself. "One other, I guess I should say."

Morris nodded. "Yes. It's starting."

December 1634

Red Sybolt, the two Poles and the Cossack Fedorovych left a few days later. Their destination: the Zaporozhian Sich, the great Cossack fortress on an island in the Dnieper. It would take them weeks to get there, in mid-winter, but Red didn't want to lose any time—and Dmytro Fedorovych was practically champing at the bit.

"You're sure about this, Red?" Judith Roth asked.

"Oh, hell, yes. In politics just like in war, Nathan Bedford Forrest's maxim applies, even if he was a stinking murderous racist bastard they shoulda hung after the Civil War. 'Get there firstest with the mostest.'"

Judith looked at him, then at his companions. "I count four of you. As in, 'fewer than the fingers of one hand.'"

Red grinned. "So we'll make do. Get there firstest.'" He shrugged. "Look, the Cossacks will be boiling mad. By now, even the Cossacks—well, some of them, anyway, even if Chmielnicki himself seems to have been in the dark—will know the gist of that future history too. They'll figure it just like we do. This was ordered by one of the Polish magnates. Or, most likely, a cabal of Polish magnates. And if they don't know, by some odd chance . . ."

He bestowed the grin on Melissa, now. "I just so happen to have some copies of the relevant passages, from those books of yours I borrowed for a time."

"Swiped for a time," she growled.

"Whatever."

Melissa was just as dubious about Red's project as Judith was. "Fine, fine. But . . ."

She looked at Jakub and Krzysztof. "*They're* Polish. And while nobody is ever going to confuse you with a nobleman, Red, you're not exactly going to blend right in with Cossacks. Has it occurred to you they're likely to chop first and ask questions later?"

"I figure Dmytro can run interference for us. If we even need it at all. Cossacks aren't actually mindless, you know. They're also not going to confuse any of us with great magnates, either. And there really isn't that big an ethnic issue, in the first place. A hell of a lot of Cossacks are former Poles, and a good chunk of their officers are former szlachta."

James' eyebrows lifted. "Really?"

"Oh, yeah." His grin seemed insuppressible this morning. Red always did love a fight. "It's a complicated world, you know. Or hadn't you noticed already?"

"Be off, then, Red," Melissa said softly. "I'd add 'Godspeed,' but I'm an atheist. Still, the sentiment's the same."

After they left, Morris shook his head. "Do you think we'll ever see the rascal again?"

Melissa had been wondering the same thing. After a pause, she said: "Yes, actually. Up-time American coal companies have—had, will have, whatever—the same mindset as great Polish magnates."

"And . . . your point is?"

She nodded in the direction Red and his companions had gone. "They really hated that man, Morris. But he's still here, isn't he?" She burst into laughter. "Three and a half centuries earlier!"

Part One

October 1636

From the east falls, from poison valleys,
A river of knives and swords

"The Seeress's Prophecy," *The Poetic Edda*

Chapter 1

Linz, provisional capital of Austria-Hungary

"Interesting idea," said Gustav II Adolf. The emperor of the United States of Europe—also the king of Sweden and the High King of the Union of Kalmar—rose up from his study of the map spread across a table in the chamber he used for private meetings. He looked at the two people standing on the opposite side of table.

"Which one of you thought of it?" he asked, smiling a bit slyly.

"Oh, Michael did, of course," said Rebecca Abrabanel. 'I am a diplomat, not someone versed in military—"

"She did," said Mike Stearns. With a grin on his face, ιe pointed with a thumb to his wife standing next to him. The basic political ingredients that are the heart of the cheme, anyway. I just came along afterward and fleshed ιut the military details."

"That *is not* true, Michael," protested Rebecca. What you dismissively call 'the military details' are in fact the essence of the plan." She sniffed. "Plan, not a 'scheme.'"

Mike's grin never wavered. Gustav Adolf's smile widened until he was grinning also. "Oh, come, Rebecca. Of course it's a scheme. Quite a charming one, though. I'm taken by it."

He turned his head to look at his future son-in-law, Prince Ulrik of Denmark. Looked down, as well. Gustav Adolf was a big man and the prince was no more than average size. "What do you think?"

Ulrik gave his shoulders a little heave; not quite a shrug. "Like Rebecca, I am in no position to gauge the military aspects of the plan—scheme, if you prefer. But I think the political possibilities are . . . intriguing, certainly."

He leaned over the map and placed his forefinger on the city of Beirut. He had to lean over quite a bit because Beirut was at the center of the map, and it was a big map which showed all of the eastern Mediterranean and the Near East from the coast to Baghdad.

"Assuming you can hold Beirut—"

"We'd actually be holding most of what we called Lebanon up-time," interjected Mike. He leaned over and pointed with his finger as well, although he kept the fingertip several inches above the map so it wouldn't crowd Ulrik's. "Everything between the sea and Mount Lebanon—including, of course, Mount Lebanon itself. Which is actually a range of mountains, not a single one."

Ulrik then moved his finger to Egypt. "And you think that will trigger a revolt in Egypt?"

Rebecca fluttered her hands by way of caution. "I would say 'hope' rather than 'think.' There are too many factors involved in Egypt's relationship to the Ottomans for us to be certain of any outcome. Officially, it is simply one of the empire's provinces. An *eyalet*, as they call them. But although the Ottomans seized Egypt from the Mamluks more than a century ago, the Mamluks are still a powerful and influential force there. The truth is that, under the surface, Egypt remains semiautonomous. If the Egyptians can be persuaded that our stronghold in Beirut shields them—even if only partially—from Ottoman power, they might well decide to revolt."

Ulrik then pointed with his chin toward the side of the map in front of Rebecca and Mike. "But you say the main target is the Safavids."

"That's the gold ring," said Mike, nodding. "If the Persians see that we're tying up Murad's forces in Lebanon as well as Austria, we're hoping they'll decide to resume their war with the Ottomans." He planted his finger on the spot marked *Baghdad.* "They've got to be holding a grudge over Murad's seizure of Mesopotamia from them, which happened less than a year ago."

Ulrik made a cautioning motion with his own hand. "Yes, they might. But it's also possible Shah Safi will view the Ottoman entanglements as an opening for him to finally settle accounts with the Uzbeks instead."

"Yes, that's possible," Mike admitted. "If Shah Abbas were still on the throne . . ."

Gustav Adolf chuckled. "If Abbas had still been alive, I don't think the Ottomans would have been able to take Baghdad in the first place."

He was probably right about that, thought Mike. There hadn't been much information in Grantville's libraries or computer records concerning the Safavid dynasty that ruled the Persian empire in the sixteenth and seventeenth centuries. But one thing that seemed clear was that the greatest ruler produced by that dynasty had been Shah Abbas I, whose reign had lasted from 1588 to 1629. His death had come just two years before the Ring of Fire.

· The man who had succeeded him, his grandson Shah Safi, did not appear to have the same ability. On the other hand, by all reports that came to Europe the man recently appointed as the Persian empire's grand vizier, Saru Taqi, was quite competent.

If Mike succeeded in his plan to open a second front against the Ottomans in the Levant, the Safavids might go any one of three ways. They might simply sit tight. They might renew the war with the Ottomans. Or they might use the preoccupation of the Ottomans to attack the Uzbeks in central Asia. The great strategic problem faced by the Safavids was that they were caught between two powerful foes, the Ottomans to the west and the Uzbeks to the east.

Mike and Rebecca were hoping for the second outcome. But there was no way to read the future. The same was true with their hopes that the Egyptians might revolt. There were a lot of factors working in favor of that, if the USE established a strong position in Beirut and the surrounding region. But those same factors made for a complex situation. There was no way to know in advance what might result.

The one thing Mike was confident about was his ability to hold Lebanon against the Ottomans, as long as two conditions were met. The first was that Gustav Adolf, the commander of the allied military forces, gave him permission to use his Third Division for the purpose. The second was that he and Rebecca could forge an alliance with the Druze who dominated Mount Lebanon and the Jabal al-Druze (Mountain of the Druze) area in southern Syria.

Forging an alliance with the Druze meant coming to an agreement with the leader of the Druze, Fakhr-al-Din, the emir of Mount Lebanon. And that meant going to Italy. Fakhr-al-Din had recently fallen out of favor with the Ottomans and had been forced to go into exile. Fortunately for him, the duke of Tuscany, Ferdinando II de' Medici, who had once before provided Fakhr-al-Din with sanctuary, was willing to do it again.

"You will need to go to Florence, of course," said Ulrik. "What about the Maronite Christians? Is there a chance they might be brought into the alliance?"

Mike looked at Rebecca, who shook her head. It was an indication of uncertainty, though, not negation.

"Very hard to tell," she said. "On the one hand, by all accounts we've received the Maronites chafe under Ottoman rule. On the other hand, insofar as they look to Europe for assistance, they look to France. And France . . ."

She shrugged. "Who can say what the newly crowned— and many believe to be a usurper—King Gaston will do? The man is . . . capricious."

She looked back down at the map. "We will certainly try to bring them in, of course. Working in our favor is the fact that the Maronites are on cordial terms with the Druze, currently. We will just have to see."

Ulrik went back to studying the map. "I am no expert

on military history," he said, "but I hope you do not expect your proposed expedition to the Levant to be another— what do you call it?—'D-Day,' I think. That coastal invasion during your second world war that enabled you to drive the Germans out of France."

Mike laughed. "Oh, certainly not! We're just talking about the Third Division, not the whole USE Army. There's no chance that we could do more than establish what amounts to a beachhead on steroids in Lebanon."

Ulrik frowned. "What are steroids?"

"Sorry. American slang. It means something larger or more powerful than usual."

Gustav Adolf chimed in. "The historic parallel Michael is thinking of happened during the Napoleonic Wars. When the English duke of Wellington turned the area around Lisbon into a bastion against Napoleon. The 'Lines of Torres Vedras,' the fortifications were called. The French never did succeed in taking Lisbon."

Mike wasn't surprised by the emperor's detailed knowledge of future military history—more precisely, the history of a future that would now never happen in this universe. In the years since the Ring of Fire, Gustav Adolf had spent a great deal of time studying that history. And for a wonder, not making the common mistake of so many rulers in the here-and-now of thinking that history could be duplicated.

Gustav Adolf stroked his short, blond beard. It was an unusual gesture for him, and one that Mike had only seen him use when he was seriously pondering something. After a minute or so, the emperor lowered his hand and nodded.

"We will do it," he announced. "Even if nothing else comes of it, seizing a portion of Murad's empire will boost morale." He gave Mike a look from under lowered brows that came close to a scowl. "Assuming that the sometimes reckless—perhaps that's too strong; let us rather say excessively bold—commander of the Third Division can keep Beirut and Mount Lebanon once he seizes them."

Mike smiled, as seraphically as he could manage, although he was pretty sure the effort was pathetic. He'd never heard anyone, not even his wife—especially not his wife—describe him as angelic. "I'm sure I can do that, whatever else," he said stoutly.

Gustav Adolf's near-scowl didn't fade at all. "Even without the Hangman Regiment?"

Mike frowned. "Why wouldn't I have the Hangman?"

"Because I want to send them to Silesia." Now, the emperor made a stab at assuming a seraphic smile. The result was even more pathetic than Mike's had been. "Come, Michael! It will take you months to arrange the prerequisites for your expedition to the Levant. Leave aside whatever obstacles you may face persuading Fakhr-al-Din to form an alliance. The only way you could move your Third Division to Beirut would be by sea, and you can't risk that without having Admiral Simpson bring his Baltic fleet into the eastern Mediterranean. And how long will that take?"

Mike had already given that matter a lot of thought. Not till next spring, at the earliest. Probably not until summer. There's a good chance the Spanish will try to block him, for one thing."

Gustav Adolf shook his head. "I doubt they will,

actually. They must realize by now that they can't stand up to Simpson in a naval battle—not if he brings his entire fleet into the Med. And they have enough trouble as it is, with that maniac Cardinal Borja stirring everything up in Italy."

"I think the emperor is right, Michael," said Rebecca. Now it was her turn to lean over the map and plant a forefinger on it. In her case, on the western coast of North Africa, which Europeans called the Barbary Coast. "The Spanish might, however, try to bribe the corsairs to do it. So might the Ottomans, since the corsairs are officially their subjects."

Officially was the right term, Mike knew. Though most of North Africa was formally under Ottoman control, of necessity the empire's pashas ruled with a light hand. They had no effective way of controlling the powerful corsair fleets except by persuasion—and bribery, of course.

"Even if Simpson can get into the Med without a fight," Mike said, "he still can't provide us with naval protection in the Adriatic until late spring or early summer. Let's say"—he did a quick calculation—"seven to nine months from now."

"I agree," said Gustav Adolf. "Which is why I want to send the Hangman Regiment to Silesia."

He held up his hand, forestalling Mike's protest—which, in point of fact, Mike wasn't inclined to make anyway. It hadn't taken him long to grasp the logic of Gustav Adolf's intentions. The Third Division was overstrength to begin with—the only division of the USE's army of which that was true—and the troops were now settled in for a long siege. Mike didn't really need all his regiments for that purpose, especially over the winter when Murad was bound to withdraw his forces back to Vienna.

"You do not need all your regiments, Michael," said Gustav Adolf. "You have too many regiments, anyway! Ten, when you are supposed to have no more than nine."

He made an attempt to scowl again, but this was a feeble one. The emperor was hardly displeased that one of his divisions was unusually adept at recruiting soldiers. "And the Lady Protector of Silesia just sent me a request to provide her with some troops."

Mike had to fight down a grin. The "Lady Protector of Silesia" was more commonly known—throughout Europe, not just in the USE—as Gretchen Richter, probably the continent's most notorious radical agitator and organizer. And just by coincidence, she was married to Jeff Higgins, the commander of the Hangman Regiment.

"Did she specify the Hangman?" asked Rebecca, who was making no attempt to hide her own amusement.

Gustav Adolf waggled his hand. "Not in so many words. But I'm sure that's the one she most wants." More seriously, he said to Mike: "I will defer to your judgment in the matter, however, since you know the man better than I do. Higgins is very young to be in command of a regiment, and this will be in many respects an independent command for him, if we send him off to Silesia. Is he ready for such a challenge?"

Mike had already been thinking about that, and it hadn't taken him long to reach a conclusion. "It'd be good for Jeff, actually. But..."

He glanced at the Danish prince. "I think I now understand why you wanted Ulrik to be present at this meeting." Mike had wondered about that. Ulrik was exceptionally shrewd, but most of his experience had been political, not military. True, he had a naval exploit under his belt, having badly damaged a USE ironclad during the Baltic War. But he was hardly an expert on such questions as fleet maneuvers, much less commanding large land forces. Why involve him in this discussion, then?

Judging from the expression on Ulrik's face, he was puzzled as well. Mike had to fight down another grin. It would be interesting to see how loudly Ulrik squawked once the emperor explained his intentions.

"If I'm right," Mike said, "you plan to put Ulrik in overall command of all Silesian forces. Which means Colonel Higgins has to be able to provide Ulrik with effective advice, as well as commanding his own regiment."

To his credit, Ulrik didn't actually squawk. He didn't even sputter. His eyes grew wide, though. Very wide.

"*Me?*" he said. "But I—" He seemed to brace himself. "Pardon me, Your Majesty, but I think your proposal—"

"It's not a proposal, Ulrik," said Gustav Adolf. "It's actually a command."

Ulrik's mouth clamped shut. If he'd been a lawyer, he might be inclined to argue the matter, since Gustav Adolf's military authority over him was rather dubious. However, since he was a prince rather than a lawyer he declined to pursue what would be, politically speaking, a monumentally stupid course.

Rebecca came to his rescue, in a manner of speaking.

"I am sure the emperor does not expect you to be the one to develop battlefield tactics, and such. If I am not mistaken, he is thinking in political terms, not military ones."

Ulrik looked at her, frowning. "I don't understand what you mean."

"Oh, but it is obvious!" exclaimed Rebecca. Thereby demonstrating again what Mike considered her only major personal flaw. Rebecca was so intelligent—she was smarter than he was, for sure—that her thoughts often raced ahead of others, and she could get a bit impatient over the sluggards' failure to keep up.

But he'd lived with the flaw for years, now. Quite cheerfully, in fact. And in this instance, his thoughts had caught up very quickly.

"One of these days, Ulrik, you will be effectively the emperor of the USE," Mike said.

"That's preposterous!" said Ulrik. "I will be Kristina's consort." He made his own hand-waggling motion. "Co-monarch, if you insist."

"Don't play the fool," said the emperor. His tone wasn't harsh, but there was the suggestion it could become so very quickly. "You know perfectly well that Kristina has neither the inclination, the talent—and certainly not the desire—to be a ruling empress. She will be delighted to leave those chores to you while she races about engaged in whatever whim or folly has engrossed her lately."

He waved a big, meaty hand. "Whatever. Horse racing is a given. And just the other day I caught her looking through an American magazine—an article on something called 'white water rafting.'" He gave Mike a glare. "It's *your* fault. You Americans. You should keep such things away from children. Under lock and key!"

Mike spread his hands. "There's no way to stop it, Your Majesty. You know Kristina will insist on learning how to fly. From there it's just a short step to the ambition of becoming the first woman—no, first person—to fly around the world. She might even insist on doing it solo."

"I'm sure I can keep her from doing anything so foolhardy," said Ulrik. "Well. Quite so foolhardy."

He looked back at Gustav Adolf. "Assume that I accept your premise, for the moment. I still don't see where that leads to me being in command of an army."

"I said, don't play the fool," growled the emperor. "You know perfectly well that nothing bolsters a monarch's prestige so much as being perceived as a capable military commander in his own right." He thumped his chest with a fist. It was a big chest and a big fist and Gustav Adolf was not holding back. It sounded like a drum. "The 'Golden King,' they call me! 'The Lion of the North!' You think anyone would call me those things if I hadn't commanded armies on a battlefield? And won most of my battles!"

"He's right, Ulrik," said Mike. "Nobody doubts your courage—not after you led a flotilla of cockleshells against ironclads and almost sank one of them. But that's not the same thing as being the commander of an army. For that, you need to do what the emperor proposes."

Ulrik made one last attempt to scuttle the idea. "But everyone will know perfectly well that I am simply following the advice of my advisers who *do* know what they're doing. Colonel Higgins, first and foremost."

"And what do you think *I* did, when I started this new trade of mine?" demanded Mike. He made a little gesture indicating the uniform he wore. "I didn't brush my teeth without checking with my aides first."

There was a brief silence while everyone else in the room gave Mike a very skeptical look. Especially his wife. But no one said anything.

Ulrik sighed. "Fine. When do I leave for Silesia?"

"Weren't you listening?" said Mike, displaying that famous grin of his. Inimitable, it was, if he said so himself.

"Go see Colonel Higgins. After you explain to him his new assignment, he will tell you when you leave for Silesia. When, where and how."

"And what to wear," added Gustav Adolf. "And while I think about it, isn't it time we promoted Higgins to a real colonel?" He gave Mike a glower, although it didn't have much heat in it. "Don't think I didn't notice that little trick you pulled with giving him the rank of 'Lieutenant Colonel' which doesn't exist in the USE Army."

"Well, it should," Mike replied. He'd learned long since that when dealing with Gustav Adolf, you had to stand your ground. Happily, while the emperor had a very dominant personality he didn't object to subordinates challenging him as long as they were respectful about it. In fact, he encouraged it—though not publicly, of course.

"Yes, I agree. I've instructed the army to add the rank to its—what did you make me call it?—table of operations, something like that."

"Table of organization," Mike supplied. "And nobody 'forced' you do it, Your Majesty. You thought it was a good idea."

"Why, yes. So I did."

In the event, Mike wound up being the one who gave Jeff the news. Ulrik spent his time in a fruitless search for the young American colonel in the regiment's headquarters, the barracks, the stables—even two of the taverns known to be frequented by the Hangman Regiment. Mike, who knew Jeff much better than the Danish prince did, went to Jeff's personal quarters.

Where, just as he'd expected, he found Colonel Higgins sitting in a comfortable-looking armchair, with his bootless feet propped up. He was reading a book and had a mug of beer on a side table.

Mike concluded his explanation of Higgins' new duties by saying: "You do understand, I hope, that Gretchen is the boss in Silesia. Until things change, her relationship to you is that of the Lady Protector of Silesia, not your wife. You'll be taking her orders."

By the time he finished, Jeff had his hands clasped behind his head and was laying back as far as he could in the armchair.

"I got no problem taking orders from my wife," he said. "Excuse me, the Lady Protector of Silesia who'll just happen to be in bed with me every night."

His expression grew positively serene. "Especially since I know what her first order will be." He began singing off-key:

"Happy days are here again,
The skies above are clear again."

Mike smiled. "Clearly, morale won't be a problem."

Chapter 2

Breslau (Wrocław), capital of Lower Silesia

In the chamber in Breslau's town hall that Gretchen Richter used as her headquarters, Jozef Wojtowicz was leaning over another map, also spread across a large table. And, by coincidence, was also singing a cheery song. Rather loudly, too.

"Sto lat, sto lat,
Niech żyje, żyje nam."

"Make him stop, Gretchen," complained Major Eric Krenz. "I can't think clearly while he's wailing that—"

He turned his head and glared at Lukasz Opalinski, who was standing next to him. Only half-glared, however. Not even someone as insouciant as Krenz wanted to irritate a big Polish hussar who was known—Gretchen herself had been a witness—to have cleaved a head with one stroke of his saber.

"What *is* he singing?" Eric asked. "An uncouth drinking song, I bet. Hardly suitable for these august

premises—and in the presence of the Lady Protector
herself!"

Gretchen was on her feet, leaning over the map with
her hands planted on the table to provide her with
support. She smiled but didn't look up from her own
scrutiny of the map. She'd reached the point in her
pregnancy where she economized her movements. Even
standing up straight was something of a chore.

"It's a birthday song," said Lukasz mildly. "The words
mean 'one hundred years, one hundred years, may she
live for us one hundred years.'"

"He started singing it as soon as he got up this
morning," said Denise Beasley, who was sitting in a chair
against one of the walls with a book in her hands. The
unlikely presence of a teenage up-timer at the meeting
was due to Denise's unofficial status as Gretchen's
unofficial liaison with Francisco Nasi. The Sephardic Jew
who had once been Mike Stearns' chief of intelligence had
moved to Prague after Mike lost his position as the USE's
prime minister. Since then, Nasi had been operating what
was probably Europe's premier private intelligence
agency.

When Denise looked up, she was scowling even more
than Krenz. "On account of my mother. She turned thirty-
eight today."

"Ah," said Eric. "Well, in that case . . ." Unlike Denise
herself, Eric approved of Jozef's liaison with Christin
George. He'd discussed it with Lukasz recently, and
found that Jozef's close friend since boyhood approved of
it also.

"It's good for Jozef to have a woman who's almost a

decade older than he is and not excessively charmed by his excessive charm. He usually cavorts with young girls whose breasts are considerably more substantial than their brains."

Gretchen now looked up from the map. "Lukasz, Jozef—whichever one of you knows the answer—how many volunteers have we gotten from the countryside? They're almost all Poles, yes?"

To Eric's relief, Jozef broke off from his singing. "As of right now—well, yesterday," said Wojtowicz, "we had three hundred and sixty-three men in the new infantry units. One of them was Czech, one was Hungarian, and two were German. The rest were all Poles."

"How good are they?"

"Not too bad," said Jozef, "although—"

"They stink," interrupted Opalinski.

"—I wouldn't want to use them for a while except fighting from defensive positions," Jozef finished. He gave Lukasz a look of reproof. "Ignore him. He's a hussar with absurdly lofty notions of what sort of training a soldier needs to fight like a hussar. Which these men will *not* be doing."

"Being sensible Polish peasants instead of idiot szlachta," Eric muttered.

"I heard that," said Lukasz. He was smiling when he said it, though. The big hussar came from one of Poland's most prestigious noble families. Did he care what some German ragamuffin thought of his lofty place in the world?

Gretchen had the distracted look on her face that people get when they're doing calculations in their head. After a few seconds, she said: "Then we add the Third

Division regulars—that's what now, Eric? Two hundred and fifty?"

"More like two hundred and twenty," said Krenz. "Sickness, desertion, the usual."

Gretchen nodded. "Add Bravnicar's cavalry, that's another one hundred and fifty. I asked him this morning before he left on patrol. Then the Vogtland irregulars add another five hundred—that's men, I'm not counting the women and children although some of the women can fight—"

"Behind defensive positions," Eric interjected.

Gretchen made a hand motion as if brushing away insects. "Don't quibble. That's mostly what we plan to do anyway. That brings us up to eight hundred and seventy combatants. Then we can add the German town militias that are willing and able to fight in the field. I figure that's about six hundred more men. For a grand total of just under one thousand, five hundred soldiers."

She pursed her lips and made a faint whistling noise. "That means that once Jeff arrives—Prince Ulrik arrives—we've almost doubled our fighting strength."

"More like tripled it," said Eric. "Maybe even quadrupled it. The Hangman Regiment are elite soldiers, Gretchen. Veterans, almost all of them."

"In this instance, I have to say I agree with him," said Lukasz. "There's really no comparison between the soldiers Prince Ulrik is bringing and the forces we already have here in Silesia." He nodded toward Eric. "With the exception, of course, of the men under Major Krenz's command, who are detached from the Third Division of the USE Army."

Gretchen ran fingers through her blonde hair. Her still-long blonde hair. She'd been planning to cut it, but once she discovered her husband was coming to Silesia she decided otherwise. The length wasn't that much of a nuisance and she knew Jeff adored it.

Thoughts of her husband distracted her for a moment. It had been half a year since she'd seen him. She glanced down at her belly, which was now providing full evidence of the condition that last encounter had produced. She was somewhere between seven and eight months' pregnant, she figured, probably closer to eight. Even for a woman as strong and robust as she was, moving around was getting a bit difficult.

On a bright note, Jeff would be here not long after their child was born.

She turned and took a few steps so she could look out of a window. It was a clear, sunny day, which was not unusual for Poland at this time of year but not something you could count on, either. Even in midafternoon, the temperature was cool, though not uncomfortably so. Fifty-five degrees Fahrenheit, according to the thermometer hanging on the wall next to the window.

The Europe of her day had no standard system for measuring temperature—or distances, or weights, or anything else. One of the effects of the Ring of Fire had been the swift adoption of the American system of measurement in many parts of the continent, especially those most heavily influenced by the up-timers. Steadily, if not evenly, universal standards were emerging.

Ironically, the only vociferous opposition to the trend came from Americans themselves, led by the indomitable

Melissa Mailey, who advocated adoption of what was called the metric system. *Why are we inflicting this idiotic English system of measurement on a whole new world?* she would demand. *It caused enough headaches in the one we came from. Measuring distance by the length of a king's thumb, for Pete's sake!*

But she had few followers. Americans were accustomed to their antiquated system—and more to the point, so were most of their tools and instruments. When a down-time craftsman built a thermometer—such as the one hanging on the wall less than three feet from her, which had been made in Dresden—they copied an American design. Which came in sturdy Fahrenheit, thank you very much.

The window overlooked Breslau's central square, what was called the Market Square. The town hall itself was called either the Stary Ratusz, if the speaker was Polish, or the Rathaus by those who spoke German. Since most of Breslau's inhabitants were Germans, as was true of most of the bigger towns in Silesia, the word Rathaus was the one most commonly used.

From the outside, the town hall was an impressive sight. It had been built four centuries earlier, in the Gothic style. More precisely, the construction had *started* in the thirteenth century. The work had continued off and on for the next three hundred years or so. The building as it now existed had been more or less completed by 1560.

Only more or less, though. Gretchen could hear the faint sounds of workmen as they installed another modern toilet. The new facility was on this upper floor, not far from her own living quarters, thankfully. In her condition waddling up and down two flights of stairs to use a toilet in the middle of the night was a nuisance. Gothic grandeur be damned, especially in the winter. As far as Gretchen was concerned, "medieval" was just a synonym for "cold."

She could hear the clatter of horses—quite a few of them—arriving in the square below, but they were out of sight of the window she was standing at. Some large party had arrived in Breslau, apparently. She wondered who it might be, since she knew of no delegation scheduled to appear today.

But she'd find out soon enough, when they were ushered into this chamber. In times past, she would probably have gone downstairs to see for herself. Today?—as pregnant as she was? No, thank you. Let others do the stair-climbing.

She turned away from the window and went back to her study of the map. Krenz and Wojtowicz and Opalinski were still gathered around the table.

"So what do you think?" she asked. "Can we defend all of Lower Silesia with the forces we have?"

Krenz shook his head. "Not without help from Roth's Bohemian troops. And those will come at a price."

Eric was talking about a political price, not a monetary one. Morris Roth had assembled an army in Brno for Wallenstein—King Venceslas V Adalbertus of Bohemia as he was formally and officially called, but he preferred his close advisers and confidants to keep using the name he'd gone by most of his life. Wallenstein had put Roth in charge of conquering as much territory to the east as he could. Most of that territory would come from the Ruthenian lands controlled by the Polish–Lithuanian Commonwealth—the area that in a future world would be known as Ukraine—but at least some of it would have to consist of portions of southern Poland. Between those portions and the northern part of Royal Hungary, which Wallenstein had already obtained through the recent treaty he'd made with Austria, he'd have a corridor connecting Bohemia and Moravia to Ruthenia.

In short, if Roth brought his army to assist Lower Silesia, he'd insist on getting something in return.

Gretchen now looked at Lukasz and Jozef. "How much of the Polish–Lithuanian Commonwealth's territory can we let him have without stirring up too much resentment among Poles? Commoners, I'm talking about, not szlachta and certainly not magnates. I don't care what they think." She waggled her hand. "The upper ranks of the szlachta, anyway."

The *szlachta* was Poland's nobility. It constituted about ten percent of Poland's population, a much higher percentage than the aristocracy of most European realms. Despite their prestigious social status, the majority of the szlachta were not much, if any, richer than their peasant neighbors.

Lukasz planted a big forefinger on a part of the map. "As long as Roth stays south of the Vistula River and, if he gets that far, south and west of the Dniester, his quarrel will only be with the magnates. The population is mostly not Polish. But it's very important that he make no attempt to seize Kraków."

"Why?" asked Krenz. "From what I've heard, most of

the people living in Kraków these days are either German or Jewish."

Jozef shook his head. "It doesn't matter. Lukasz is right. There's no city in Poland that has more sentimental importance. It's still the official capital of Poland, you know, even if the real capital has been in Warsaw for the past few decades. And Poland's oldest and most famous university is there: Jagiellonian University, founded by Casimir the Great almost three centuries ago. If Roth tries to take Kraków he'll stir up a hornet's nest."

"Don't worry about it," piped up Denise Beasley. She didn't bother looking up from her book. "I know Morris Roth. He's as shrewd as they come. He won't do anything stupid."

"I know the man also," said Gretchen. "From my time in Grantville, before he and his wife Judith moved to Prague. As Denise says, he's a sensible man."

Her attention was distracted again, this time by the sounds of voices coming from below. Several voices; but they were simply engaged in discussion, not shouting. She couldn't make out the words, but it was obvious that the guards weren't challenging their credentials. The party she'd heard arriving at the town hall would be on their way up soon.

"We're about to be interrupted," she said. "For the moment, I have one last question. Assuming Roth and his Bohemian forces are here with us, can we then hold all of Lower Silesia?"

"That depends on who attacks us," said Lukasz. "That there *will* be an attack is certain. The Polish and Lithuanian powers-that-be can't just let Silesia go without a struggle. But it'll make a big difference who comes. If it's the Polish army, led by Koniecpolski..." He grimaced. "There'll be no chance we could do more than hold Breslau and maybe Lignitz. But I don't—"

"There's no chance at all the king and the Sejm would send Koniecpolski," said Jozef. He sounded very confident. "The real threat to Poland comes from Torstensson's two divisions besieging Poznań. They need the grand hetman up there."

"He's almost certainly right, Gretchen," said Lukasz. "It will be an alliance of several magnates."

"How big an army can they put together?" asked Gretchen.

"Hard to say." Lukasz looked at Jozef. "I'd guess ten thousand men, all told. You?"

"I think they can put together more than that," said Jozef. "How many more? That would depend on which magnates are involved and—most importantly—which one of them is in command." The smile that came to his face was thin and derisive. "Polish and Lithuanian magnates are not exactly famous for their cooperative spirit and self-effacement for the greater good."

Lukasz barked a laugh. "To put it mildly!"

The sound of boots clattering up the stairs was getting louder.

"Someone's coming," announced Eric Krenz. "Who is it?"

"I have no idea," said Gretchen. She was already rolling up the map as a security precaution. Given the swiftness with which the guards below had let the party pass through, they couldn't be unfriendly. Still, there was no point letting people see what she and her aides had been studying.

She'd just finished when the door swung open. One of the guards came through first. He was holding a musket but clearly wasn't expecting to use it.

"Lady Protector," he announced, "a delegation has arrived from the"—he stumbled over the next words a little—"Galician Democratic Assembly. May I present—"

But he got no further. The first person in the delegation had already passed through the door and needed no introduction.

"Red!" exclaimed Gretchen. "Red Sybolt!"

The up-timer who was, with the possible exception of Melissa Mailey, Grantville's most notorious political agitator, was grinning widely. "Hey, Gretchen. Long time no see."

Another man came into the room, followed by two more. These were all clearly down-timers, but Gretchen didn't know any of them. The fellow in the lead was as big as Lukasz, and like him had blond hair—in fact . . .

She looked back and forth between Lukasz and the newcomer. "Are you by any chance related?"

Lukasz ignored her. His expression was oddly stiff. "Hello, Krzysztof," he said.

The newcomer nodded. "Brother. You're looking well." But his attention was riveted on Wojtowicz, not Lukasz. "What is *he* doing here? And why isn't he manacled?"

Startled, Gretchen looked at Jozef. His expression was even stiffer than Lukasz's.

"What do you mean?" she asked. Krzysztof glanced

quickly from Jozef to her to Lukasz and then back to her.

"My pigheaded younger brother didn't tell you who Wojtowicz is, did he?" Krzysztof shook his head, in a gesture that somehow managed to combine disapproval with grudging respect. "He's always been loyal to a fault."

"They're friends," said Eric Krenz. He had a frown on his face and had his hand placed on the pistol at his waist. "Aren't they?"

"Oh, yes. Best friends since they were little boys. Whenever we visited Koniecpolski on one of his estates, they were inseparable." He planted his big hands on his hips. "But apparently my brother didn't tell you what *else* is true about Jozef Wojtowicz. He is Grand Hetman Koniecpolski's nephew as well as his chief of espionage in the United States of Europe. Very good at it, too, by all accounts. In short, one of your mortal enemies."

Eric's pistol came out of the holster. The guard at the door now had his musket at the ready.

"*Stand down!*" Gretchen barked.

Everyone in the room froze at that commanding voice. Except for Denise Beasley. She was on her feet and racing for the door.

"I knew you were no good!" she yelped. "Wait till I tell Mom! You're in for it, buddy!"

Chapter 3

Wiśniowiecki town house
Warsaw, Poland

After the servant poured the wine, Prince Jeremi Wiśniowiecki waved his hand dismissively. The servant, whose name Wiśniowiecki didn't know—it had never occurred to him to ask the man—quietly took his stance by the door to the salon, ready in case his services were needed further.

Which they would be, judging from the consumption of wine by the two noblemen sitting in front of the fireplace, enjoying the heat produced by it. The fire was not a big one, though. It was autumn, not winter.

"It's done," Wiśniowiecki said, after taking a gulp of wine. His voice was full of satisfaction. A hefty portion of smugness, as well—the sort of smugness that comes to rich, powerful and capable young men after they've completed a task well. A middle-aged man will invariably have suffered his share of misfortunes and setbacks by the time he's in his forties. At the age of twenty-six, Wiśniowiecki had known nothing but success.

Of course, he'd started off with many advantages. To begin with, he'd been born into one of the wealthiest families in the Polish–Lithuanian Commonwealth. He was an orphan, his parents having both died by the time he was seven. His uncle Konstanty was now the formal head of the family, but Jeremi had taken over control of the family's huge estates in 1631, after he returned from a sojourn in western Europe.

The estates were centered on the Ruthenian town of Lubny, about one hundred and twenty miles southeast of Kiev. The estates were so enormous that they were sometimes called the Łubnie state, being larger than most European realms and having a population of almost a quarter of a million people. Wiśniowiecki could field a private army of several thousand men.

But, as was typical of most young men of his lofty rank, he took all that for granted; nothing more than his proper due. The Americans had an expression for his attitude: *He was born on third base and thinks he hit a triple*.

Wiśniowiecki himself had never heard the expression, though. While still a teenager, he'd spent time in western Europe; first, attending a Jesuit college and then gaining some military experience in the Netherlands. But he returned to the Commonwealth before the Ring of Fire, which he only heard about many months later. He'd never had any personal contact with the up-timers. That was not surprising. Like almost all Polish and Lithuanian magnates, Wiśniowiecki despised the political notions that the Americans had brought with them. He had no desire to see one of the insolent creatures unless he was hanging from a gibbet.

"You're sure of that?" asked his companion, Mikołaj Potocki. "There's been no news from Poznań."

The self-satisfied expression on Jeremi's face remained in place. "Not yet, no. But that's to be expected. Those men know their trade. They'll make it look like something resulting from natural causes. Food poisoning, most likely. I didn't want to know the details, of course."

He took another quaff of wine. "Relax, Bearpaw," he said, using the nickname that his close associates used for Potocki. Despite their difference in age—Potocki was forty-one, fifteen years older than Wiśniowiecki—the two men were on close terms. They'd both participated in the Battle of Paniowce in 1633, where Grand Hetman Stanisław Koniecpolski had defeated the Ottoman Turks, and had been friends ever since.

"I've used these men before," he continued. "They were the ones who took care of that would-be upstart Bohdan Chmielnicki for me, two years ago. They're Lisowczycy."

"Ah." The name referred to men who'd fought under Aleksander Józef Lisowski, a Lithuanian military adventurer. After his death in 1616, many of his followers had continued Lisowski's banditry-in-all-but-name.

The older man took a sip of his own wine. Unusually for a Polish nobleman, Potocki was abstemious with liquor. In truth, he'd only accepted the wine out of politeness. From past experience, he knew that the prince would outdrink him by three or four cups to one.

That same caution was what had led him to allow

Wiśniowiecki to be the leader of their cabal, despite being young and inexperienced. If the plot should go sour, Potocki was sure he could still slide out from under whatever repercussions might follow.

"Assuming the ploy works," he asked, "what do you plan to do then?"

Wiśniowiecki frowned. "That's become something of a problem. I'd thought we could concentrate our attention on Lower Silesia. Driving out that German bitch with the ridiculous title of Lady Protector—hopefully, we'd kill her in the doing—would do more to enhance our status and gain adherents to our cause than anything."

Potocki nodded. "Yes, it would. But you said 'I'd thought,' implying you've changed your mind. Why?"

"It's those rebels in Galicia. They're now calling themselves the Galician Democratic Assembly and are claiming they're a konfederacja."

"That's ridiculous!" exclaimed Potocki.

A *konfederacja* was a unique tradition of the Polish–Lithuanian Commonwealth, not found in any other realm in Europe. It amounted to an armed rebellion, but one that had semi-official status; an extraordinary form of direct democracy, you might call it. But it was a custom reserved for noblemen, not something any serf or guttersnipe could adopt.

"Indeed it is," agreed Wiśniowiecki. "But they can't be ignored any longer. They've brought much of Galicia under their influence—and just recently they've seized Lviv."

"*Lviv*? You're joking!"

The prince shook his head. "I wish I were. They're

not—yet—making formal claim to it as their capital, but for all intents and purposes they now control the city. One of the largest in Ruthenia—and which puts them in position to threaten not only my own estates but those of many other magnates as well."

Potocki replied, "Just to name one, Prince Władysław Zasławski. He's still very young, though."

"Only twenty. But there's also Janusz Łohojski. He's not a great landowner but he is the voivode of Kiev and the starost of Śniatyń and Żytomierz. He's both alarmed and enraged by the developments in Galicia, which is not far from him. In fact, he's the one who sent me this latest news—along with the clear suggestion that he'd be willing to form an alliance."

That called for a bit of celebration. Potocki drained his cup of wine. From his point of view, what was most important about the prospect of Łohojski joining them was that the voivode of Kiev was also a man in his forties—just a bit older than Potocki himself—who had considerable military experience. He'd participated in the Battle of Chocim fifteen years earlier where armies assembled by Polish–Lithuanian magnates had driven off the Ottoman invasion of Moldovia led by Sultan Osman II.

Potocki suppressed a smile. What had worried him the most about his participation in Wiśniowiecki's plot was that, if—no, it would almost certainly be *when*—it became necessary to engage in military action, he would be one thrust forward into the limelight. Wiśniowiecki was simply too young to assume command of their forces. Now . . .

Potocki had no problem with allowing another man to be the official military leader when the time came. No problem at all.

"So we'll be heading to Galicia, then," he said. "I can bring an army of three thousand men. Added to yours—"

"We'll have at least seven thousand men, which is probably enough but I'd like to be stronger."

"That shouldn't be a problem. Zasławski can field three thousand—maybe four—and now that Lubomirski's thrown in with us that'll be another two or three thousand. That leaves the voivode of Kiev. I imagine Łohojski's good for another two thousand, especially since he'll be in command."

Wiśniowiecki smiled thinly. He knew his friend's cautious manner. "Yes, he will. More wine?"

Without waiting for an answer, he waved a hand to summon the servant. His own cup was empty, whether or not Potocki wanted any more.

"It's a pity, really," said Potocki. "He was a great man, in his way."

The prince shifted his shoulders; a minimalist shrug, you might call it. "Yes, he was. But the Ring of Fire changed everything. You and I both know we can't continue as before—but he never would have agreed. And as long as he was there, he was like a fallen tree across a road, impeding all forward movement."

The servant arrived and Potocki held up his own cup. "True," he said.

After the servant resumed his place, he began pondering the possibilities. The man's name was Andrzej

Kucharski, and despite his humble ancestry—his last name meant "cook"—he had very good hearing. He'd been able to follow the conversation between Wiśniowiecki and Potocki. As was typical of men of their class, they'd simply been oblivious to the servant's presence in the room.

Kucharski was bolder than most servants, but that didn't make him very bold. Passing this information on to whoever might wish to buy it was bound to be dangerous.

But *dangerous* also meant *worth a lot* and Kucharski was ambitious, insofar as that term could be applied to men of his class. He wanted to get a wife, and for that he needed enough money to set up a household—which would take him another five years on the miserable wages he got paid by Wiśniowiecki. "Prince" or not, the man was a miser when it came to his servants.

The conversation between the two noblemen had drifted over to personal affairs. Kucharski stopped listening. He was too intent on considering his possible market.

Chapter 4

Breslau (Wrocław), capital of Lower Silesia

By the time the guard got the door to his room open, Jozef Wojtowicz had moved from the bed to the armchair. He'd placed it in the corner that got the most light so he could read easily. Once seated, he considered picking up the book from the side table next to the armchair and opening it just to show his captors that he was nonchalant about his situation. While he'd been staying in Grantville he'd run across a couple of appropriate American slang expressions, one of which they'd stolen from the French.

Sang-froid. Calm, cool and collected.

But he decided not to. There would be something a bit rude about it, he thought.

He'd always considered rudeness to be a display of anxiety—inferiority disguised as arrogance; a sheep in wolf's clothing. He'd gotten that attitude from watching his uncle Stanisław Koniecpolski. The grand hetman of the Polish–Lithuanian Commonwealth, one of the continent's half-dozen most prestigious military commanders, was never rude to anyone, from the king of Poland to his own servants and the peasants on his estates. To behave so would be beneath his dignity.

Jozef had plenty of time to make the decision, since it took the guard a ridiculous amount of time to get the door unlocked.

Unlocked? Say better, unlocked, unbarred, unbolted, unlatched, all padlocks removed—there might even be a barricade on the other side of that door which had to be manhandled aside.

His arrest had been . . . comical.

Gretchen had ordered that he be placed in one of the many rooms set aside for visitors in the town hall, rather than in the dank and cramped cells in the basement set aside for common criminals.

But he's a traitor! Eric Krenz had argued hotly.

He can't be a foreign spy and a traitor at the same time, Gretchen had pointed out. *Make up your mind.*

He's a foreign spy, then. Spies are hanged! Or stood up against a wall and shot!

Do I need to remind you that this evil spy once saved my life? And also led the sortie against General Banér at the siege of Dresden.

That had shut Krenz up for . . . maybe three seconds.

Fine. That's the one thing—okay, two things—that saves him from being summarily executed like he deserves.

Gretchen's tone of voice had remained mild. *Actually, there's a third thing that keeps Jozef from being summarily executed.*

What's that?

The fact that I'm the Lady Protector of Lower Silesia and you're not.

That shut Krenz up quite nicely.

When the emperor bestowed that silly title on me, I insisted he had to specify what my powers were as well as my duties. He did so promptly and in considerable detail. It's a bit fascinating, really—as well as being another example of the need for a democratic republic. Talk about arbitrary and capricious powers! Do you know that as Lady Protector I can have anyone *summarily executed? Even for such a trivial offense as quarreling with me. It's true—I'll show you the emperor's letter.*

Later. For now, Eric, take Jozef to one of the guest rooms.

Krenz had managed a final rally.

At least the door has to be locked! And barred!

Oh, certainly. Whatever you think is needed.

What had been needed, in Eric Krenz's opinion, were enough devices to have sunk a good-sized rowboat. It had taken the detachment of soldiers who'd accompanied Krenz and Jozef more than an hour to fix in place all the ways Krenz could think up to keep Jozef from escaping. Apparently he was not just a spy, but a Super Spy.

When the guard finally came through the door he had his pistol firmly in hand and pointed right at Jozef. On his heels came . . .

Jozef hadn't been expecting *this*. "I didn't think you'd visit me," he said, then gestured at a small divan next to his armchair. "Please, have a seat."

Christin George did so. She had a twisted smile on her

face, but didn't say anything until the guard left and finished the process of locking the door. Then she said: "You think this is the first time I've had to visit my man in jail? Hell, I had to bail Buster out more times than I can remember."

She cocked her head a little, examining him as if he was some sort of peculiar animal in a zoo.

"I'll say this much, though. You've definitely got style. Buster was mostly just locked up for barroom brawling. Not you! 'High crimes and misdemeanors,' no less." She issued a whistle. "I gotta admit that's a new one for me."

She cocked her head the other way. "So. Did you do it?"

"Do what? Spy or commit treason? Some people seem to be having a hard time deciding which it is."

She chuckled. "Oh, I don't figure you're a traitor, seeing how you didn't betray your own country. Which is Poland, the last I heard. How about the spy business, though? Is it really true that you're Poland's head spy in the USE? 'Chief of spy operations,' I think Denise called it. She's really pissed at you, by the way. But I think the real reason's not that you screwed our nation but that she still hasn't gotten over the fact that you're screwing me. She really adored her father, you know."

Jozef heaved a sigh. "Yes, I know she did. 'Head spy' is a muddled term. More often than not I hired someone to do the spying. I was 'chief of espionage operations.' But I worked for my uncle, not King Władysław—be damned to him—and certainly not the stinking Sejm. Leave that aside. It was your country that invaded mine, not the other way around. So you can't accuse me of aggression, the way I look at it. Just righteous self-defense."

Christin's eyes widened. "It's really true then? You're Grand Hetman Koniecpolski's nephew?"

"Bastard nephew. He acknowledged me as his brother Przedbór's son, but I was never a legitimate member of the family."

"Did that hurt?" she asked.

He didn't answer for a few seconds. "Yes. It did."

Christin nodded. "Okay. So now what happens?"

He shrugged. "I have no idea. If Gretchen keeps me here in Silesia—or Saxony—I'll probably stay alive. If she turns me over to the emperor or the prime minister of the USE . . . Maybe not. I don't know either man well enough to guess what they might do."

"Oh, you'll be staying in Breslau. Gretchen was inclined that way anyhow, and when I told her I wanted you here that clinched the deal."

"Why?" he asked. "I'm pleased to hear the news, of course, but it doesn't make a lot of sense. Gretchen Richter is hardly what you'd call a sentimentalist."

"Not hardly," Christin agreed. "What she is, though, when it comes to her enemies, is one coldhearted, ruthless bitch. All I had to do was point out that I'm her Number One Premier Bombardier—got a proven track record, which nobody else does around here—and it'd be a real shame if on my next combat sortie I dropped the bomb into a river instead of on top of the evildoers. On account of I couldn't see well, my eyes being all teared up with grief."

It was his turn to cock his head quizzically. "And would they be? Teared up, I mean."

She didn't answer for a bit. Then said quietly: "Some, yes. I don't know how much yet."

"Yet?"

For the first time since she'd come into the room, a big smile came to her face. That dazzling smile was something Christin and her daughter had in common. There was more than a hint of challenge in it, to go with the friendliness.

"I'm not what you'd call a casual person, Jozef. I hadn't come to a decision about you, but I did know that I wanted to keep working at it." She shrugged. "If you'd been guilty of treason, it'd be a different story. But I got no real beef with someone who's loyal to his own."

Again, the smile came. "Might have to shoot you some day, of course. But in the meantime . . ."

She eyed the bed. "I checked with Gretchen before I came over. She's okay with conjugal visits, as long as I don't help you escape."

That was an English term he'd never heard before. "What kind of visit is a conju—oh."

In another comfortable room on the same floor of the town hall—a considerably bigger room, though—Gretchen Richter leaned back in her own armchair and gazed approvingly at the three men sitting across from her, two on a couch and one on another armchair.

"I didn't think you'd accomplish so much in so short a time, Red," she said to the up-timer sitting on one end of the couch. "I'm impressed."

Using a thumb for the purpose, Red Sybolt pointed to the man next to him. "It's mostly thanks to Jakub, being honest about it."

She shifted her gaze to the down-timer on the couch.

There was nothing particularly striking about him to the eye. He was an averaged-sized man with a rather dark complexion for a Pole. The skin color went well with the black hair and was in marked contrast to his bright blue eyes. The fellow went by the name of Jakub Zaborowsky, and hadn't said very much since the arrival of the delegation from Galicia the day before.

"Tell me," she said.

Zaborowsky frowned. "Tell you what?"

"Don't play the innocent. No one just stumbles into a situation and conjures up a popular rebellion in less than two years unless they knew they could hit the ground running."

From the puzzled expression on his face, she realized her last phrase had been a spill-over from Amideutsch that Jakub wasn't familiar with. They'd been speaking standard German in deference to Zaborowsky and Opalinski—insofar as the term *standard German* meant anything in the seventeenth century. It would be more accurate to call it the Saxon dialect.

Before she could do so, Red translated. "'Hit the ground running' means you could start right off without having to get oriented."

"Ah." Now it was Zaborowsky who leaned back. "I had not thought of it that way, but I suppose you're right. I spent much of my childhood in Galicia and I have many family members there to this day. Every one of them down to the mewling babes is a hardened revolutionist except great-aunt Klara. Hopefully we won't have to shoot her."

Gretchen couldn't tell if the last bit was a joke. It

probably was, but... Maybe not. There was a hard edge to Zaborowsky that she didn't detect in Opalinski or Sybolt.

Being fair about it, she had a hard edge herself and knew that people often had trouble determining if she was joking or not when she said similar things. Some people, for instance, thought that she'd been joking when she named the revolutionary council in charge of the Dresden uprising the Committee of Public Safety.

Wiser folk knew the truth.

"Without my family—and it's a big one—it would have taken much longer," Jakub continued. "It's the reason I urged Krzysztof and Red to go to Galicia in the first place."

"And Galicia's not too far from the Zaporozhian Host where our Cossack comrade Dmytro Fedorovych comes from," Opalinski added.

By now, from her long hours poring over maps, Gretchen was quite familiar with the geography of eastern Europe. The big Cossack settlement known as the Zaporozhian Host was located on the lower reaches of the Dnieper River in what would someday be central Ukraine. Whereas Galicia was very far to the west, parts of it in Poland proper.

"That's hundreds of miles away," she protested. "How is that 'close'?"

Red grinned. "About six hundred miles, I figure. But you gotta remember that we're talking Cossack miles. Those people have a whole different attitude about distance than normal people do."

Jakub grinned as well. "Cossacks have a different

attitude on most subjects than normal people. It's why I'd just as soon let the Bohemians deal with them."

Gretchen stared at him. "You are familiar with Wallenstein's scheme, then."

"Oh, yes. We"—Zaborowsky gestured to all three men in the room—"visited Morris and Judith Roth in Prague almost two years ago. We found out about the plan from Morris."

"He calls it the Anaconda Project," said Opalinski. His countenance was serious, unlike that of his companions. But Gretchen had already deduced that Krzysztof didn't have much of a sense of humor. Quite different, in that regard, from his younger brother Lukasz.

"It should work out well—if all goes well," said Jakub. "We'll keep the westernmost Ruthenian territory in the Commonwealth. Those lands are already heavily Polonized, and they have many settlements of Jews and Bohemian Brethren, with whom we've established good relations. Once we get rid of the magnates, everything should be fine."

"Better, for sure," chimed in Red.

"Let the Bohemians do what they can in the rest of Ruthenia," Jakub concluded. "I wish them luck. They'll need it."

Again, his sharp edge showed in the derisive way he smiled when he said that last part.

"And you want what, exactly, from us here in Lower Silesia?" Gretchen asked.

The three men glanced back and forth at each other, in a silent way of deciding which one of them was going to bell the cat. So to speak.

In some manner Gretchen couldn't detect, Opalinski got elected. "It's inevitable that even if King Władysław does nothing—he's good at that; if for no other reason than he's always preoccupied with his whores—the great magnates will not long tolerate the situation that's developed in the south of the Commonwealth. The 'south' meaning you here in Lower Silesia and we in Galicia."

"And the Bohemians, if Roth finally gets his army moving." That came from Zaborowsky.

"You want a military alliance."

"Got it in one," said Red Sybolt.

Gretchen didn't need a translation of that American idiom. There were advantages to having an up-timer for a husband.

"We accept," she said.

Zaborowski's eyes widened a bit. "Just like that? You don't need to convene some sort of council?"

"No, I don't," said Gretchen. She tried to keep any trace of derisiveness out of her own smile, but was pretty sure she was failing. "There are advantages to having the title 'Lady Protector.'"

"I just gotta face it, Eddie," said Denise Beasley. Glumly, she stared down at the beer in her mug. Most of it was still there, half an hour after the barmaid had brought it to her. Denise didn't really like alcohol that much. She just insisted on being served in a tavern as a matter of principle. She was eighteen years old—by her own somewhat idiosyncratic reckoning, anyway—and so she was damn well entitled to drink publicly. Never mind that "eighteen" was only a magic number to up-timers.

Any down-time bartender would have been perfectly happy to serve her alcohol if she'd been fourteen. Beer, at least, which seventeenth-century Germans—Poles and Czechs, too—considered a soft drink.

"I gotta face it," she repeated. "My mom's a slut. Right now—as I speak—she's probably humping that rotten traitor."

From across the table, Eddie Junker studied his not-yet-formally-betrothed. He and Denise were what Americans called "going steady." That had no legal status down-time, but no officials or clergymen in the area were going to object to their relationship. Partly, because Denise had a truly ferocious reputation; partly, because she and Eddie were both suspected to be agents of the notorious Francisco Nasi; mostly, though, because five and a half years after the Ring of Fire most people in central Europe figured there was no point in quarreling with Americans or their down-time associates over matters of proper social protocol. The folk were known to be daft—and quite willing to fight over the issues.

In the world they'd come from, there'd been a saying about "mad dogs and Englishmen." In the here and now, it was "mad dogs and Americans."

Eddie wasn't quite sure how to approach this ticklish situation. His immediate and natural inclination was to say: *Oh, don't be silly.* With Denise, though, that would pretty much guarantee a fight.

Appealing to reason was always a better alternative, but it had its own risks. Depending on her mood, Denise could respond by taking offense at being patronized. She was normally in a good mood, at which times she was as rational as anyone and more rational than most. But if her mood was bad—and right now it was sour, sour, sour—she was what Americans called "prickly."

He decided the best course was to make an implicit criticism of Christin George. That would rouse all of Denise's protective instincts, which were as deeply rooted and fierce as any she-bear defending her cubs—or, in this case, she-cub defending her mama.

"You can't call Wojtowicz a traitor, Denise, because he never swore fealty to the USE. Whether you like it or not, he's actually a Polish patriot." He drained what was left in his own mug. "If the term 'traitor' has any relevance in this situation—which I, for one, don't believe it does—the only person it could be applied to is your mother. Given that she is—as you said, probably at this very moment—providing aid and comfort to the enemy. Well, comfort, at least."

"*What?* Hey, buddy, you better watch your mouth! Don't you dare call my mom a traitor!"

Courage, courage. Never show fear. "How is that any worse than calling her a 'slut'?"

"Are you really that dense?" Denise drained her own mug—almost all of it, not the pitiful amount Eddie had drunk—and then waved furiously at the barmaid, in a summons for another beer. Whether she liked beer or not was irrelevant. She was in a barroom argument now. Principles were involved.

"Being a slut is just a personal peccadillo," she continued, as she waited for the beer to arrive. "People throw that accusation around like confetti. Hell, I once got called a slut."

"Really? Why?"

"Stupid bastard was hitting on me and I made clear I wasn't the least bit interested—and wouldn't've been even if he'd been my age instead of thirty or so. That's when he called me a slut. I figure he was just engaged in wishful thinking."

The barmaid arrived and set two more mugs of beer in front of them. Denise immediately lifted hers and drained half of it in one long swallow.

When she finished, she set the mug back down on the table and wiped her mouth with a sleeve. Principles, again, in a tavern argument.

"So what did you do?" Eddie asked.

For the first time that day, a grin came to her face. It was like the first ray of sunshine on a dismal, rainy day. Eddie loved that grin.

"I didn't do anything. Didn't need to. I said the guy was stupid, didn't I? One of the definitions of which is you call a fifteen-year-old girl a slut within hearing range of her biker father."

Eddie winced. He hadn't really known Buster Beasley, although he'd occasionally encountered the man on the streets of Grantville before he was killed in the Dreeson Incident. But he'd known his reputation.

Denise came close to giggling, then—which she insisted she *never* did. "Oh, yeah, he came to repent his wicked ways, he surely did. People think being 'beaten to a pulp' is just an expression. Trust me, it isn't."

Eddie judged that Denise's mood had improved enough. "I didn't tell you why I came here." He didn't see any need to add: *because you started right in denouncing your mother and never let me get a word in edgewise.*

"You flew in," said Denise. "I just assumed you came to visit and would be leaving again in a day or two."

Eddie shook his head. "I'm on what you can call a detached assignment with no set time limit. Francisco agreed to Gretchen's request that he provide her with a private air force." He slapped his chest. "Which would be me. I could be here for months. Anywhere Gretchen goes—which means anywhere you go, since you're on detached assignment also."

Denise clapped her hands. "*Wheeeeeeeeeeee!*"

Later that night—much later—Denise caressed Eddie's right shoulder while her head was nestled on his left. "I miss Minnie," she said softly. "I really, really do."

Minnie Hugelmair was Denise's best friend. The two of them had been like sisters.

Eddie stroked her hair. "I know." He tried to think of something more to say, but couldn't find the right words. The problem was that Minnie—

"I don't even know if she's still alive." Denise did her best to stifle a sob, but her best wasn't good enough.

Minnie had not been able to get out of Vienna before the Turks took the city. No one had any idea what had happened to her.

"I know," he said, continuing to stroke her hair. He could do that all night.

Chapter 5

Vienna, official capital of Austria-Hungary
Now under Ottoman occupation

"I can't play another word game today," said Judy Wendell—Judy the Younger, as she'd been called in a previous existence, since she had the same first name as her mother.

That existence seemed almost a fantasy now, after two months living in cellars lit only by a few candles. Fortunately, since the cellars beneath an unused wing of the Austrian royal palace had been designed as a secret shelter, there had been a big supply of candles. Judy didn't want to think what it would have been like if they'd had to hide down here in darkness. Day after day after day— which would have seemed like night after night after night.

"I just can't do it," Judy said. She tried to glare at the young woman leaning back against a nearby pile of grain sacks, comfortably nestled inside the arm of a man not much older than she was. "Minnie, when you went out there with your cart whose contents I will not get into, why didn't you bring back a deck of cards instead of that stupid radio?"

Minnie just smiled in response. The accusation was wildly unfair as well as ridiculous, and the four people present knew it including Judy herself. Minnie had risked her life for all of them weeks earlier, when she'd sortied from the cellar disguised as a night soil worker in order to bring back the radio she and Denise Beasley had hidden. Hidden halfway across Vienna. It had been a harrowing journey.

The man who had his arm protectively around her did not share Minnie's blithe indifference.

"You should be ashamed of yourself for saying such a thing, Miss Wendell! That stupid radio, as you call it, is the only thing that might someday save our lives."

"The two operative words in that statement are 'might' and 'someday,'" Judy retorted. "In the meantime, I'd give my right arm—okay, left arm—to be able to play hearts, spades or whist instead of Ghost and Botticelli. Hell, I'd even be happy to play Old Maid."

The man who'd chided her bore the august title and name of Archduke Leopold Wilhelm of Austria. He was the youngest of Austria's four royal siblings. Since the death of their father two years earlier, his older brother had assumed the even more august title of Emperor Ferdinand III of Austria-Hungary.

"My brother's right, Judy," said Cecilia Renata, the fourth of the people in the cellars. She was Leopold's sister and bore the title of an Austrian archduchess. "Like he says, you should be ashamed of yourself."

There was no great energy in the words, though. Despite being, at the age of twenty-five, considerably older than Judy, the two women had become good friends in the course of their adventures. As much as anything else, Cecilia Renata had only said it to give herself something to do.

Yes, they were all in a very perilous situation, hiding from ruthless janissaries in a city occupied by one of the world's greatest powers. But that had only lifted their spirits for a short time. They'd been in the cellars long enough by now—more than long enough—to be forced to confront the greatest horror of all.

Boredom. Judy thought of it as a dentist's waiting room on steroids. Tedium cubed. They were adrift on a great ocean in the lifeboat *Ennui,* with no land in sight.

"It *would* be nice to have a deck of cards, though," Cecilia Renata admitted.

"Be nicer still to have one of the up-timer board games," said Minnie. "I don't think you two royals have ever played them. I learned when I was in Grantville."

"Which one?" asked Judy. "I'm partial to Monopoly, myself. But I'd settle for Clue."

"Monopoly and Clue are okay. But if I had to pick one for the desert-island scenario, I'd either go for backgammon or Parcheesi. Preferably backgammon."

Judy frowned. "That'd be antisocial. Backgammon can only be played by two people."

"Two people *at a time*," Minnie qualified. "All the better. While two of us played, the other two could be doing the exercises that we've all agreed we ought to be doing."

"You're not doing them either, Minnie," Leopold pointed out.

"'Course not. Exercise is boring. Just what I don't need. More boredom."

"You've got a lot of nerve complaining," said Judy. "You and Leopold get to . . . Well, you know."

"They do it a lot, too," said Cecilia Renata. "It's quite reprehensible."

Silence followed for a minute or so. The topic they'd wandered into was one they normally tried to avoid.

That was not due to ethics, though. When it came to sex, Minnie Hugelmair was the embodiment of hard-boiled seventeenth-century pragmatism. Judy had the usual romantic attitude of up-time teenage girls, but the attitude had been tempered by the fact she was so good-looking that teenage boys—adult men, too, plenty of them—had been buzzing around her since she was thirteen. She'd become so distrustful and cynical that she'd held onto her virginity to the present day—not out of any deep moral concerns but simply because she was damned if she'd let some lying slob get it from her.

As for Leopold and Cecilia Renata, their sexual mores were the inevitable result of knowing since they were children that they'd eventually be married off to someone for purely political reasons. A complete stranger, often enough. Or, which could be even worse, a close relative. Their older sister Maria Anna had been shipped off to Bavaria not long ago to get married to her uncle Maximilian I. She'd been twenty-four and he'd been in his sixties. In the event, Maria Anna had decided not to go through with it and had fled to the Netherlands, thereby precipitating what had become known since as the Bavarian Crisis. But in the history of the world the up-timers came from, she *had* married her uncle—and borne him two sons.

Although they looked at the matter from the top down instead of the bottom up, as Minnie did, the two Austrian royals were just as cold-bloodedly practical as she was.

Or . . .

Had been, at any rate. To his surprise and his sister's outright shock, Leopold had developed a genuine attachment to Minnie, never mind her low birth, orphan status, and glass eye. He'd never used the word "love," but he had declared that after they were rescued he'd insist his brother keep him as a bishop so he couldn't marry anyone and could maintain his liaison with Minnie.

She had also developed an attachment to him—but thought his plan to remain a bishop was foolish sentimentalism. There was no reason he couldn't get married to someone of suitable lineage *and* maintain his relationship with her. As had been royal custom from time immemorial.

After allowing the silence to last just long enough to restore propriety, Judy rose to her feet and beckoned to Minnie.

"Come on, girl, let's go. I'm pretty sure it's time for our weekly radio message."

Minnie rose from her pleasant snuggle. "I think it's probably still too early, but maybe you're right. It might even be later than we think. It's too bad you brought one of those clever up-time battery watches instead of an old-fashioned manual wind-up one."

Judy raised her arm and glanced down at the watch on her wrist. "Yeah, I just wear it out of habit, these days. The battery died almost a year ago."

Leopold brought forth a large pocket watch. An impressive one, too—it had jewels embedded it. "I have one!" he pronounced. "Just wound it not two hours ago."

Minnie and Judy made no effort to consult the archduke's watch. "And when was the last time you calibrated it?" asked Judy.

Leopold made a face. "Well ... It was before we had to come down to the cellars. How am I supposed to calibrate it here, with no way to gauge the sun properly and no functioning up-time watch to check it against?"

"What I thought," said Judy. "And what time does it claim to be now?"

Leopold studied the dial. "Two and a quarter hours past noon. Or maybe midnight."

"Or maybe any time of the day and night," said Minnie. "Leopold, you know perfectly well that watch loses at least ten minutes every day—and we've been here—I keep a record, you know—for exactly—"

"Don't say it! Don't say it!" exclaimed Judy and Cecilia Renata simultaneously.

The time turned out to be just about what Judy had figured. At this time of year, sunset came around six in the evening. The sun was clearly below the horizon, although they couldn't see it directly through the narrow window in the tower that rose above the cellars. But it was still twilight.

"We should probably wait till it gets a little darker," Judy whispered.

Minnie nodded her agreement. They'd have to extend their antenna out of the window in order to send or receive a signal. At this time of day, it was unlikely that anyone would observe the antenna, but it wasn't impossible. Once darkness fell, no one would spot it.

So, they waited another half hour. Two floors below them, Leopold and his sister watched in case someone came into this detached wing of the palace. Which was just as unlikely, since it was only being used these days for storage—and not storage of anything fancy or expensive. The wall opposite the entrance to the tower that the two young Habsburgs were watching from was covered with suspended saddles. Used, worn saddles. Just barely functional enough not to get pitched.

"Okay," Judy said, when she judged the time was right.

Slowly, carefully, Minnie extended the antenna. She did so mostly because the antenna wasn't all that sturdy and they couldn't afford to take the risk of damaging it.

Finally, she was done. Judy moved back into the narrow staircase leading down to the cellar and lit the candle she'd brought with her. Then, carefully shielding it with her hand so no significant amount of light would escape through the narrow window, she brought it close enough to enable Minnie to operate the radio.

Minnie found the right frequency and began the transmission. It was well-established protocol that the hideaways in the cellars would always initiate radio contact, since they could only come out of hiding on infrequent occasions while the USE Army's operators could maintain their watch twenty-fours a day, every day of the year.

Even using manually transmitted Morse code, she was done soon. The message had been short and simple:

LISTENING STOP

About fifteen minutes later, the answer came back:

CHEER UP STOP RESCUE MISSION IS BEING PLANNED STOP MESSAGE ENDS STOP

Minnie began drawing the antenna back in. "That's exactly what they said last time," Judy complained. "Word for word."

Minnie made no reply. There was nothing to say other than *so yet another week of monotony awaits us. Yippee.*

Chapter 6

Brno, capital of the Margraviate of Moravia
Kingdom of Bohemia

"I still say it would have been smarter to just buy some of the new rifles Struve-Reardon is making." His brow creased with disapproval, Paul Santee gazed down at the rifle on the table before them. "This thing is just a copy of a Sharps, like the French Cardinal. A crude one, to boot. Hell, they've had it for two years already. In time of war, you know, the pace of gun development—"

"Rises rapidly," said Morris Roth. "Yes, Paul, I know. You've said it about two thousand times already. But what's involved here is a political issue, not a practical one. I'd have preferred it myself if we'd taken the same money we shoveled into SZB's coffers and just bought the SR-1s from Struve-Reardon. But the problem is the 'S' in SZB. That stands for *státní* which, since you still don't speak or read Czech very well—I'm not criticizing, you haven't been here all that long—means 'state.' As in *Státní zbrojovka v Brno*, 'State Armament Works of Brno.' Guess who has the controlling interest in the company?"

"Wallenstein," said Paul sourly. "AKA King Venceslas V Adalbertus of Bohemia. Is the man really that greedy?"

Morris shook his head. "Actually, I doubt if Wallenstein made much if any money on the ZB-1636. His motives aren't pecuniary. They're political. First, he wants the prestige of Bohemia's having its own major gun manufacturer. Secondly and more importantly, he thinks that his kingdom's having its own armaments works will be important in the long run. I have to say I think he's probably right about that."

The third man standing in the small show room of the SZB's armaments plant drew a pistol from a holster and held it up for display. "Besides, Mr. Santee, if you'd been devoting your efforts to designing a new rifle you wouldn't have had the time or money to develop this marvelous weapon."

General Franz von Mercy gazed at the pistol admiringly. "The infantry will do well enough with the ZB-1636, as clumsy—no, what's that word you Americans use? Clanky?"

"Clunky," Morris provided.

"Yes, that one. As clunky as it may be. It's the cavalry that truly needs the more advanced weaponry."

Morris was amused to see the new expression on Santee's face. Despite the man's determination to be morose, Paul couldn't help but enjoy von Mercy's praise. The weapon the general was holding up was also being made by the State Armament Works of Brno, but unlike the rifle the pistol had been designed by Santee himself.

He'd modeled it on a little-known Italian pistol made in the early twentieth century, the Pedersoli Howdah. To modern-day Americans, the gun looked like a double-barreled sawed-off shotgun with a pistol grip. Like a shotgun, the weapon had an unlocking lever which allowed the barrels to be tilted down so the gunhandler could reload by simply sliding in the premade cartridges. Santee had designed the pistol so that it could fire paper cartridges, since that was the most common ammunition, but could be converted to brass cartridges whenever those were finally being made in sufficient quantity.

The original Pedersoli Howdah had been chambered either for a .45 caliber round or a .410-bore shotgun shell. Santee had chosen to design his model for a .58 caliber round. He'd made the barrels a bit longer also—twelve inches to the original ten and a quarter. It was a heavy pistol, by up-time standards, but down-timers accustomed to the wheel-locks of the day found it to be less weighty than they were accustomed to.

Every cavalryman who had been issued one of the pistols adored it. The official designation for the gun was the ZB-2, but the soldiers themselves called it the Santee. So far only five hundred cavalrymen had been provided with ZB-2s, partly because the pistols were time-consuming to make but mostly because every cavalryman wanted at least six of them—two holstered at the waist, two in boot holsters, and two more in saddle holsters. This wasn't a capricious demand on their part. Reloading such weapons in the middle of a cavalry charge was effectively impossible, so cavalrymen of the era typically carried multiple pistols.

But Morris figured he still had a few weeks before he had to order his army into action. By then, the entire cavalry should be equipped with the new pistols. The reason he'd decided to devote most of their resources to developing pistols instead of rifles was simple. His little army had only four thousand men—which to his way of thinking made it all the more absurd that Wallenstein insisted on calling it the Grand Army of the Sunrise. Fully half of them were cavalry, and they were by far the most experienced half of his army. The core of them were the professional soldiers von Mercy had brought with him when he entered Bohemia's service, and most of the ones who had joined later were also veterans.

The infantry, on the other hand . . .

Six hundred of them were Jews, for starters. Having *any* Jewish soldiers was unheard of in Europe of the seventeenth century. Openly self-identified ones, at any rate. It was not uncommon to have Jews serving in naval forces, but they kept their religious affiliation to themselves. These soldiers, on the other hand, had been recruited mostly from Prague, which was hundreds of miles inland.

Add to that the fact that the official commander of the Grand Army of the Sunrise was a Jew, which was widely known. Morris wasn't just "a" Jew, either. A lot of people in Bohemia, gentile and Jewish alike, called him the Prince of the Jews because of the leading role he'd played three years earlier in driving the mercenary army of General Holk out of Prague at the now famous Battle of the Bridge.

None of the gentile soldiers in the Grand Army of the

Sunrise objected openly to serving with Jews, whatever prejudices or anxieties they might mutter among themselves. Still, it was not something that instilled confidence in the army's infantry—even among the Jewish soldiers, who were well aware that they weren't veterans.

There were about half as many Bohemian Brethren in the army as there were Jews. Three hundred and eight, to be exact. Most of them actually were veterans, having also fought Holk when he invaded Prague. But their religious views seemed outlandish enough to the other Christian soldiers that their status as veterans was largely irrelevant. It didn't help that many of the more orthodox soldiers confused the trinitarian Bohemian Brethren with the unitarian Polish Brethren—the Socinians, as they were often called, after their founder Faustus Socinus. Who knew what men who denied the Trinity would do when they came under fire? Run? Vanish in smoke?

So, almost half of the infantry was made up of heretics (or possible heretics, to the more broad-minded of their comrades). And not very many in the other half were veterans. Some were idealistic youngsters motivated by excitement at what they sensed to be a new age in Bohemia, but most of them were the same type of men who'd volunteered to serve in mercenary armies since ancient times: paupers, adventurers, criminals hiding from the law, and men hiding from their wives' families. Until they'd had some real fighting under their belts, not the sort of fellows any sensible man put much confidence in.

As soon as von Mercy had arrived in Brno, Morris had put him in overall command of the army. Despite his formal status as the "commander" of the Grand Army of the Sunrise, Morris had no illusions that he was any kind of general. His military experience up-time as a draftee had consisted of a one-year tour of duty in Vietnam. Officially, he was a "Vietnam war veteran" but the truth was he'd never seen any combat at all while he'd been there because he'd been a supply clerk at the big army base at Long Binh.

"Life is weird," Morris muttered.

Linz, provisional capital of Austria-Hungary

"So how far is it?" Mike Stearns asked Jeff Higgins. "I've been completely preoccupied planning our own—well, never mind; need to know and all that. I didn't think to look into it myself."

"You mean from here to Breslau?" Jeff asked. "About three hundred and fifty miles, I figure. A fair amount of it's even on decent roads, at least by seventeenth-century standards of 'decent roads.' I figure we ought to make it in three weeks, thereabouts. Moving a regiment's nowhere near as complicated as moving a whole division."

Mike's Third Division had actually become rather famous in military circles for its ability to move quickly. Some people had even been known to refer to the Third as "foot cavalry," a term Mike himself considered a particularly idiotic oxymoron. Nothing put him in a foul mood as quickly as the headaches of getting ten thousand or more men to move in one direction fast enough not to be outrun by a tortoise.

Jeff eyed him sideways. "That's *assuming*, mind you, that we don't have to forage."

Mike shook his head. "You won't have to worry about that. I've been in touch with Wallenstein and he assures me that he'll have provisions ready for you all the way through Bohemia. After that..."

Jeff grinned. "After that, I'll be in Silesia and I've been in touch with the Lady Protector and she assures me that she'll have provisions ready by the time we get there."

The young colonel seemed to turn a little pink. Mike suppressed a grin of his own. He wouldn't be surprised if the Lady Protector of Silesia had appended *Including me* to one of her radio messages. Gretchen could be... forward.

Mike slapped Jeff on the shoulder. In the years since the Ring of Fire, those shoulders had become quite solid, in the meaty way that a man running toward fat puts on muscle. Between his belly, which had slimmed down some but had never vanished since Jeff had been a child, and the glasses on his nose, and the sometimes distracted expression on his face, Jeff still had more than a passing resemblance to a geek. But nobody in the Third Division thought of him that way, especially not the men under his command in the Hangman Regiment.

The "DM" they called him. That was because of the calm, unflappable and seemingly all-knowing way he issued orders under fire. The reputation wasn't diminished at all when a stranger or newcomer asked what the initials stood for.

The Dungeon Master. Let them make of that what they would.

"Good luck, Jeff," Mike said quietly.

"Same to you, Mike."

Ottoman siege lines southeast of Linz
About three miles from the confluence of the
Danube and Traun rivers

"They're certain?" demanded Murad IV. "Just one regiment?"

"Yes, My Sultan," said Süleyman. "Those are good men, too; not ones to confuse a kâfir regiment with a division."

The young sultan nodded. He had confidence in Süleyman. The man commanded the army's akinji, irregular light cavalry who also served as scouts and spies.

"One regiment..." Murad mused. "And a big one, they say?"

"Yes, My Sultan. Bigger than the usual." He ventured to add his own opinion, which Murad would tolerate if he wasn't in a bad mood. "I believe it to be the one the kâfirs call 'the Hangman.'"

Murad stroked his beard. It was a full beard but one he kept fairly short. Long, uncut beards were fine for religious leaders, displaying their piety. But a warrior with a long beard was just a fool. "I think you are right. Which means two things, since the Hangman is reputed to be their fiercest infantry. First, the USE's emperor is confident he can hold Linz, with winter coming upon us too soon for our sappers to undermine their defenses."

Süleyman nodded. They were well into autumn now,

and the defenses of Linz were still too strong to be overwhelmed by sheer force. If Murad waited too long before ordering the army to retreat back to Vienna, where they could winter over safely, he ran the risk of suffering the same disaster that had befallen Suleiman the Magnificent when he tried to seize Vienna the century before. Winter had come early that year, and his army had been caught in the heavy snowfalls. Many of his soldiers died in the retreat and the Ottoman army had to leave much of their baggage train and their artillery behind.

"And the other reason, My Sultan?"

Murad smiled. It was a thin smile, with a hint of savagery in it. "It also means that one kâfir ruler plans to attack another—or add to the attack, I should say. That regiment is headed toward Poland; probably the district they call Silesia, where they already have forces. Between those reinforced units and the large army they have besieging Poznań, they will have the Poles in a vise."

"Do you think they can conquer Poland?"

"No," said the sultan, shaking his head. "They are not strong enough for that, not when they have to devote so much of their army to facing us here in Austria. But they can make the Poles sweat heavily"—here his smile became a grin, and one that was obviously savage—"and a heavily sweating kâfir is a more reasonable kâfir, when—"

He broke off there. Murad trusted Süleyman, but there was no point in telling him things he had no need to know.

When my agents arrive in Warsaw, and explore the possibilities for a hidden alliance. Perhaps with Kin,

Władisław, but more likely with ambitious magnates. Which Poland produces like they produce wheat.

"Go now," he said. "I have no further need for you today."

Part Two

November 1636

Axe-age, sword-age, shields are cleft asunder,
Wind-age, wolf-age, before the world plunges headlong

"The Seeress's Prophecy," *The Poetic Edda*

Chapter 7

Breslau (Wrocław), capital of Lower Silesia

Gretchen Richter distrusted airplanes. Deeply. In part, that was because the first time she ever flew in one it crashed upon landing, but for the most part it was due to her idiosyncratic theological views. Those stemmed from her life experience, which precluded the possibility that the Almighty Lord was a just, kind and benevolent God. While still a teenager, much too young to have committed any serious sins, she'd seen her mother abducted, her father murdered and she herself subjected to gang rape followed by forced concubinage.

The most benign term that could be applied to any deity who allowed such things—even ordained them, if the claims that he was omnipresent and omnipotent were to be believed—was "capricious."

She'd ridden in airplanes since that first flight, several times. And from the moment her aircraft lifted into the air until the moment it taxied to a halt after landing, the thought that God was capricious never once left her mind.

Her misgivings were not ameliorated at all by the most common explanation of the presence of evil in a universe created by an omnipotent Creator: *God moves in mysterious ways.* To Gretchen, that truth was self-evident. Which meant that at any moment one was riding through the sky in an airplane, God might very well muse to Himself: *Oh, this is silly. People can't fly*—and down you went.

Nor were the unnatural machines safe once they had landed. No one could say when God might decide that a propeller should start up again just when someone walked by—and off went their head.

Her head, to be specific. So after Eddie Junker brought his plane to a standstill and shut off the engine, she not only waited for the propeller to stop moving but waited until the passenger had emerged and had walked safely past the possibility of decapitation.

She had nothing against Noelle Stull—indeed, her few encounters with the woman had left her favorably disposed toward her—but if anyone was going to suffer God's mysterious ways on this clear, bright and chilly November morning, let it be the woman who had so rashly tempted Him rather than her.

When Noelle reached her she said, smiling: "I'm flattered. I didn't expect the Lady Protector of Silesia herself to come out to the airfield to greet me."

Gretchen smiled back, but did so while shaking her head. "Actually, I didn't." With her chin, she gestured toward the pilot, who had just come out of the cockpit and was now on the ground. "I came to see Eddie. He's got—should have, anyway—information I need immediately."

Noelle's brow was creased with a little frown. "You still didn't have to come all the way out here. I'm sure he'd bring it to you right away."

"Probably, but he might not, too. Denise is in town, don't forget."

Noelle's brow smoothed out again. "Ah. I hadn't considered that. You're right."

Gretchen slapped her stomach, reveling in the restoration of its normal flat and firm state. "Besides, I enjoy moving around easily again. I just gave birth recently."

"I heard. And the baby is fine, I take it?"

"Oh, yes," Gretchen replied casually. Then, smiled. Noelle had the half-quizzical, half-worried expression on her face that women who'd never yet given birth had when discussing the matter. Some women, anyway.

Eddie had almost reached them. Glancing back at him, Noelle said: "I'll be on my way then, since I assume you'll be wanting to talk to him privately. Am I correct that that's our transportation into town? If so, I'll wait for you there."

The vehicle she was pointing to was a large carriage—more like a wagon putting on airs than a real carriage—standing just off the airstrip. The teamster driving it was slouched in his seat; clearly a fellow who saw no reason to let an idle moment go to waste when he could be napping. The four horses attached to the carriage were like-minded, except for the one who was shortening the grass in the vicinity.

"There's no reason you can't hear what Eddie and I will be talking about," said Gretchen. "In fact, it's probably good idea, since it may have a bearing on whatever mysterious mission brought you to Breslau."

Noelle tried to look innocent. "Mysterious mission . . . ?"

Gretchen sniffed. "Why else would you be here?"

Eddie came up. After glancing back and forth from Noelle to Gretchen to assure himself that Noelle would be privy to the conversation, he said: "Francisco agreed. Any mission you want, including combat sorties."

"Still with no time limit?"

"None. Understand, though, that he might recall me from time to time for a mission of his own. But he said he'd try to use commercial air transport if he needed it." Eddie smiled. "My boss isn't much fonder of flying than you are. Although he disguises his unease a lot better."

Gretchen saw no reason to dignify that with a comment. She just used her chin again to point to the carriage. "Let's be off, then."

Within an hour after they arrived at the town hall, everyone whom Gretchen thought needed to hear whatever Noelle had to say was present—and one whom she didn't think was needed at all.

That was Denise Beasley, who vigorously pressed her status as Francisco Nasi's agent to shoehorn her way into the meeting room. Gretchen thought her arguments were flimsy, given that Nasi already had an agent present—Noelle Stull, who was the very person at the center of the affair.

But . . . She didn't feel any great need to exclude Denise, either, so she let her stay. When she told Noelle she was doing so, Noelle pursed her lips for a moment and then shrugged her shoulders. "Sure, why not? I always felt bad anyway that we hadn't—" She shook her head. "Never mind that."

Eddie was with Denise. He had enough grace to claim he should be present since it was likely his pilot's skills would be needed for some portion of Noelle's proposal, instead of presuming on his status as another of Nasi's agents.

"All right, everyone," Gretchen said loudly. "Settle down. Noelle, you have the floor."

The slender American-cum-Bohemian-noblewoman-though-still-an-Austrian-resident rose and stepped forward where everyone in the room could see her. Noelle hadn't decided yet whether she'd become a citizen of the Austrian-Hungarian Empire. Cold-blooded political considerations propelled her in that direction, but habit and sentiment were holding her back.

She was an American, dammit. Had been all her life until that preposterous Ring of Fire had put her in a fantastical situation. True, she'd gotten a husband out of the deal. Still . . .

"What I'm about to say has to remain a secret. No one in this chamber can repeat any of it to anybody not here already."

She swiveled her head slowly, taking a few seconds to give everybody present a stern look.

Until she got to Red Sybolt, who was rising to his feet. "In that case, Noelle, I don't see any reason for me and Krsysztof and Jakub to stick around. Not that any of us has any trouble keeping our mouths shut when it's necessary, but this won't be any of our business, so—"

"Red, please sit back down. This matter does concern you. That's why I asked Gretchen to summon you here."

Gretchen had wondered about that, but she'd done as

Noelle bade her. This was getting more interesting by the moment.

Red shrugged and sat back down.

"I need to start by giving you all some information. The two youngest of the Austrian royal siblings—Archduke Leopold and Archduchess Cecilia Renata—never got out of Vienna before the Ottomans seized the city. Their fate and whereabouts have remained unknown since."

She paused dramatically. Gretchen was a little amused since Noelle was not naturally suited to dramatic pauses. She looked more embarrassed than anything else.

"Except to a few people. Of whom I am one. They are still ... Well, you can't say they're 'free,' since they're trapped in Vienna. But they're not captives. The Ottomans have no idea they're still in the city."

"How did they manage that?" asked Eric Krenz.

"There are secret cellars beneath a detached and no-longer-inhabited wing of the royal palace," Noelle explained. "They managed to get there before the palace was overrun by Turkish troops. They've been in hiding there ever since."

Again, she paused. She seemed to brace herself, as well. *For what?* Gretchen wondered.

"They are not alone, thankfully," Noelle continued. "They have two companions with them. The American girl Judy Wendell and one of Francisco Nasi's agents, Minnie Hugel—"

"*EEEEEEeeeeeeeeeeeeeeeeeeeeeeeeeeeeeeeeeeeeeeeeeeee eeee!!!*"

It was no wonder Noelle had braced herself. Gretchen's ears were ringing from Denise Beasley's shriek of joy and excitement. She might have suffered a permanent hearing loss.

Denise leapt to her feet. "You're planning a rescue mission! That's why you're here, isn't it? I'm going! I volunteer! I'm going!"

"No, you're not." That came simultaneously from Noelle and Gretchen.

"*Why not?*" Denise demanded.

"You can't pass as a down-timer," Noelle said. "Your teeth are too good."

"Oh, bullshit! It's a myth that all down-timers have crooked teeth. They don't. Hell, Noelle, your own husband has good teeth."

Gretchen weighed in. "That's beside the point, Denise. Leave the teeth aside—yes, you're right that not all down-timers have bad teeth." She left unsaid the fact that her own teeth were actually in better condition than those of most up-timers.

Which turned out to be a waste of modesty, since Denise immediately pointed at her and said: "Yeah, no kidding, Gretchen. Your own teeth look great. Especially to men. 'Course, that's partly 'cause they're preoccupied ogling the rest of you or trying not to."

Gretchen liked Denise—quite a bit, in fact. But, dear God, the girl could be exasperating.

"Yes, and *that's* the problem," Gretchen said. "You have a lot of nerve, Denise, accusing another woman of being too attractive to men. *You?*"

Denise scowled. "Hey, it's not my fault most guys can't think with their brains instead of their dicks."

"I didn't say it was. Nonetheless, the fact remains that

the moment you enter Vienna you'll be drawing the attention of every janissary in the city. Half the court eunuchs too, probably. You'll be jeopardizing—"

She broke off abruptly. Everything had just come into focus.

She looked at Denise; then, at Red Sybolt and his companions. Mostly, she looked at Krzysztof Opalinski.

Who was in every measure and respect a perfect specimen of the Polish and Lithuanian szlachta. Tall, ruggedly built—no one would have any trouble picturing Krzysztof as a winged hussar—even moderately handsome. More importantly, he carried himself with the indefinable air of someone who'd been born to a high station in life, even though he was now a political radical who had eschewed all such aristocratic pretensions. Done so in his conscious mind, at least. But he couldn't help maintaining habits which were so deeply ingrained he wasn't even aware of them.

"That's why you wanted them to stay, isn't it, Noelle?" Gretchen said. "You want to send a delegation from the Galician rebellion to the Ottoman court. With Krzysztof Opalinski as the leader of it. No one will think that's unusual. Every realm in eastern Europe, no matter how small or shaky or haphazard, sends an embassy to the Turks. And they almost always accept them, even if they don't take them very seriously. If the Ottomans check—which they might since they have good intelligence services—they'll soon find out that Opalinski is a notorious radical even though he was born into one of Poland's most prestigious noble families. In which case . . ."

She looked back at Denise. "It would actually make sense for Denise to be part of the mission. Someone like Opalinski would very likely bring a beautiful concubine with him—"

"Hey!" Denise protested. "No fucking way!"

"And the fact that she'd distract Ottoman officials and soldiers would be entirely to the good."

Denise's mouth had been open, ready to issue further objections. But by the time Gretchen had finished, her mouth was clamped shut. Then, after perhaps two seconds had elapsed, she said: "Well, okay then. I'm for it."

She glanced at Krzysztof. "As long as it's just for show. No funny business."

Throughout, Noelle had been staring at Gretchen, with a deep frown on her face. Clearly, she hadn't thought of that angle.

"Gretchen, are you sure...? I'd been planning to go myself. Posing as Krzysztof's wife. I'm a reasonable age for it—a few years older than he is but that's not unusual—and unlike Denise"—here Noelle smiled, a bit ruefully—"men usually don't have any trouble not noticing me."

She opened her mouth and pointed into it with a finger. "Even got crappy teeth."

Actually, they weren't that bad, certainly not by downtime standards. Her parents hadn't had the money to pay for orthodontic work, so Noelle's teeth weren't all even and straight the way the legends proclaimed up-time dentition to be. But she'd still gotten reasonably frequent care from a dentist. None of her teeth were missing or badly colored.

Jakub issued a sarcastic-sounding snort. "Not a problem. You go as the wife and she"—he nodded at Denise—"goes as the concubine. Sitting on either side of His Exaltedness in his carriage. You think a great magnate of the Polish–Lithuanian Commonwealth has any shame or scruples regarding such matters?"

Sitting next to him, Krzysztof shook his head. "I agree that's not a problem, but it's still not possible."

Red had started shaking his head at the same time. "Sure as hell isn't. Noelle, your plan overlooks a critical problem, which is that we—especially Krzysztof—need to get back to Lviv. Pronto. This fancy-titled 'Galician Democratic Assembly' of ours is still rickety. A lot of what holds it together is just the prestige of having an Opalinski in the leadership." He glanced at Jakub. "Sure, me and him have good organizational skills, but . . ."

By now, Jakub had joined the head-shaking. They were like a little a cappella chorus. "He's right, Noelle. People back in Galicia are willing to bide their time until we get back, given the nature of our mission here. But if they find out that Krzysztof's gone off on what you up-timers call a wild-goose chase, many of them will conclude he's given up on the revolt and almost all of them will be disheartened."

Noelle stared at him. Clearly, she hadn't anticipated this problem. She must have thought the prospect of getting on very good terms with the Austrian-Hungarian dynasty would be enough to persuade them to join in.

But Gretchen had been thinking ahead and the solution was obvious to her.

"We just need to get Lukasz to agree to do it," she said.

"He looks enough like his brother to fool the Ottomans unless they have an agent in Vienna who's personally familiar with Krzysztof. Which I think is very unlikely."

Noelle looked at Krzysztof. Who nodded his agreement.

"The truth is, Lukasz could do it better than I could," he said. Then, with a little smile: "You should see him when he puts on what we called 'the Opalinski Bravura' when we were boys. No magnate is more magnificent, at least in his own mind."

Jakub and Red both nodded as well, continuing the chorus. It was all Gretchen could do not to laugh.

"Okay, then," Noelle said. "But will he agree to do it?"

Gretchen shrugged. "I don't know. I'll ask him."

She came back a half-hour later. "Lukasz says he'll do it—but he's got one condition. We have to drop the charge of espionage against Jozef and let him go."

"No goddamn way!" That came from Eric Krenz.

"Goddamn blasphemer!" Denise exclaimed. "You ought to be ashamed of yourself!"

Thereby exhibiting the very first sign of religious sentiment Gretchen could ever recall coming from the girl.

"You just want to get Minnie out!" chided Krenz.

"Well, yeah, of course I do. She's the best friend I ever had. You still committed blasphemy and nobody should take the advice of a blasphemer."

She turned to Gretchen. "So let him out."

A struggle ensued, between the girl's mind and her

heart. It was the most amusing thing Gretchen had encountered that day.

"Please," Denise added, looking like she was sucking on a lemon.

Chapter 8

Ottoman airfield
Formerly Racetrack City
Just east of Vienna

Murad IV was a big man, so he satisfied himself with looking into the narrow, armored space rather than trying to climb into it. "And it will withstand the Jooli?" he asked the engineer at his side.

The engineer's name was Özil Demirci. He belonged to the Ottoman Empire's Cebeci Corps, one of the branches of the Topçu Ocaði, their corps of gunners. It was being expanded by Murad to support the new weapons. The *cebeciyan* were the armorers who made and maintained guns as well as almost everything else used by the artillery.

Özil had been in Murad's service long enough to learn that whatever anxiety he might have about the young sultan's reaction, the most foolish thing to do was to lie to him—or even fudge the truth too much.

"The problem is not the Jooli, My Sultan. It's the type of gun she will be using." He leaned into the gun turret and apped his knuckles against the steel sheet that formed one of the walls. The sound produced was tinny, not solid. "I am confident that if she uses the same type of gun I believe she used at Linz—*and* her shot does not strike the armor head on—that this will be enough to deflect the bullet. But if she uses a more powerful gun . . ."

He spread his hands as if making a presentation of something. "Our airships will only carry so much weight, My Sultan. As it is, this light armor leaves only enough lifting power for a skeleton crew, one janissary and an assistant, two guns and some ammunition. Adding thicker armor would only deduct from the mission's very purpose."

Now he pointed to the firing port at the front of the turret. Like everything about the turret, the design was simple, even crude. The two thin steel sheets that formed the walls of the turret were angled toward each other but they did not join. Instead, a gap of about fifteen inches— what the Ottomans called an *ayak*—had been left, allowing the shooter enough space to aim his rifle. "And you understand that even with a normal rifle, if the Jooli's aim is good enough, and she fires from the right angle, she will be able to kill our man."

"And by all accounts, the monster's aim is that good," said Murad, nodding. He looked at Özil and smiled. It was a thin smile but not an unfriendly one. "Do not call her 'she,'" he commanded. "The Jooli is just a monster. My janissaries will be disgruntled if I order them to go into battle against a mere woman."

"Yes, My Sultan." Özil thought most janissaries were idiots, so he was not surprised that they would not care to hear the truth. So be it. They would be the ones to have

their brains spilled by the woman-who-was-not-a-woman
not he. Özil designed the gun turrets. He was not the on
who would be manning them in a vessel no one had eve
dreamed of until a few years ago.

Why should it be a wonder that such a vessel woul
have a woman as its jinni?

"How soon can you finish the rest of the turrets?
asked Murad.

"They should all be ready within twenty days, M
Sultan." He nodded toward the hangar entrance. "Soone
if I could have more workmen."

"No. Building as many hangars as possible is th
priority, or we will lose too many airships over the winter.
Murad straightened up from his examination of th
turret's interior. "It is too late in the year to launch a majo
assault on Linz, so there would be no great advantage t
destroying the Jooli now. We will deal with her—deal witl
the monster—come the spring."

Özil had expected that answer. There had already bee
a snowfall three days before. Just a short flurry that soo
melted, but it was a portent of what was to come. The sulta
would need to order his men out of the siege lines soon, s
they could retreat to Vienna before winter really set in.

The assault on Linz would have to wait until spring. B
then, even with just the two workmen Murad ha
provided him, Özil could have all the Sultan's airship
fitted with the gun turrets.

All the ones that survived the winter, at any rate. Th
hangars were so huge that no matter how many me
Murad threw at the work, they couldn't possibly ge
enough of them built for all the airships. Some of th

irships would have to make it through the winter—try, nyway—just tethered to masts.

Some would fail to do so, that was a surety. Even the irships sheltered in the hangars were at some risk. The angars were sturdy enough not to collapse after a heavy nowfall, but they had no doors. They were shaped like he top half of giant cylinders planted on the ground, with oth ends open to the wind and the elements. That should e fairly safe given the mild winds in this part of Europe, ut . . .

The winds were *usually* mild. There could always be n exceptionally powerful storm, and if it was mighty nough some of the airships would be battered apart nside the hangars.

But that was not Özil's problem. He just had to have he gun turrets ready for the assault, and he had months o do it in. From there, come spring, it would be up to the irship crews and the janissaries in the turrets to destroy he monster so an aerial bombardment could clear the vay for the sultan's army.

He fully expected several of those janissaries to die in he opening battle. He'd heard depictions of what the ooli had done to the fleet that had tried to bombard Linz wo months earlier. But he didn't like janissaries anyway. Arrogant bastards, they were.

Airship hangar
Chiemsee (Bavarian Sea)
Bavaria

ulie Mackay (*née* Sims) was not a particularly big woman.

Somewhat on the stocky side, muscular—but she was no more than five and half feet tall. So she had no trouble at all clambering into the newly installed gun turret on the *Magdeburg* and giving it a slow and careful inspection.

It helped, of course, that the turret was a lot bigger than the ones the Ottomans were retrofitting into their airship gondolas. The *Magdeburg* was a much bigger airship than anything the Turks had built—or even could build, for the moment. It never paid to underestimate the industrial capacity of the enemy empire. The Ottomans had great resources, personal as well as material and financial. But it was just a fact that their technology was in most respects less advanced than European technology—and had been even before the Ring of Fire.

The Turks handled that challenge much the same way the Soviet Union in World War II had handled the disparity between its level of technological development and that of its enemy, Nazi Germany. The USSR had concentrated on making crude but workable—above all, reliable—machines and weapons of war, and then making a *lot* of them.

Julie was well aware of the Ottoman approach, and it guided her in her assessment of the gun turret she'd be fighting from when the aerial war resumed. No one expected that to happen for a few more months, however. Not with winter coming. So there was still time to make whatever modifications were felt to be necessary and she wasn't about to get sloppy.

"I can't say I'm real happy with these welds, Dell," she said, running her finger down the seam between two steel panels. "I mean . . . *tack* welds?"

The man who'd crowded into the turret with her hook his head. He had an aggrieved expression on his ace. "Julie, give me a break. Those are just temporary. Don't worry, we'll have 'em replaced with full welds within a couple of days. We weren't expecting you here his soon."

"I *told* you I was coming out this week."

The aggrieved expression on Dell Beckworth's face got replaced by one of exasperation. "Julie, when most people say 'this week' they don't mean Monday morning."

"Alex's birthday is Thursday," Julie said defensively. "I wanted to be sure I could get back in time."

"How's he doing these days?"

"You want the official opinion or the wife's opinion?"

"Let me have both."

Julie went back to studying the seams. "The official opinion is that he's the best thing in the cavalry department since hay was invented. Ever since he got promoted to colonel it seems he can do no wrong. There's already noises being made about promoting him to brigadier. If they actually do it, he'll have to start sleeping outside 'cause his head barely fits through the door as it is."

Beckworth chuckled. "Sounds like I got the wife's opinion already."

"Oh, hell, no. The wife's opinion is that if he keeps thinking his expertise on galloping around on a horse and waving a saber makes him an expert on every subject under the sun—including gunhandling, if you can believe it—then he won't have any trouble at all fitting his head through the door because he won't have one left."

She turned away from the seam she'd been inspecting and gave the five gunports an intense scrutiny. "Bit wide, aren't they?"

"Not given your normal firing position, which"—he slapped a flat, wide rail that ran around the center of the chamber—"will be using this as your gun rest. That way you don't have to expose yourself so much and the enemy will have a hard time spotting which gunport you're using. But the gunport can't be too narrow or you won't have a wide enough angle of fire."

Julie thought about it for a moment, and nodded. "Okay. That makes sense. I'll always be staying two to three feet back from the ports."

"Well, unless you have to start using the Lahtida. Which you won't be able to do until the spring, because I won't have it finished for a few months." He cleared his throat. "Uh . . . it'll have to be permanently fixed into that forward firing slot, since you won't be able to move it."

"Why not?"

"Well . . . it weighs about one hundred and twenty-five pounds."

"Jesus H. Christ, Dell! That's almost as much as I weigh."

"Relax, willya? It'll rest on a solid tripod and have a muzzle brake and a padded recoil pad. Think of more like a cannon than a rifle."

"You're not really planning to call it the 'Lahtida,' are you?"

He grinned. "Sure. We gun nuts have a reputation to maintain."

"For what? Having the world's stupidest sense of

humor? Who the hell calls a twenty-millimeter rifle a 'Lahtida'?"

Beckworth's grin didn't so much as flicker. "A gun nut screwy enough to design a seventeenth-century airship gun based on a World War II Finnish anti-tank gun. That'd be the Lahti L-39."

"Is it a requirement to be an official gun nut that you have to win some sort of obscurity contest? 'Hey, guys, betcha I know about a gun none of you dilettantes has ever even heard of.'"

Beckworth was *still* grinning. "Yup. We hold the contest every year in Ruso, North Dakota."

"Where?"

"Smallest town in the state. At last count, the total population was four. One of those towns nobody's ever heard of."

"How do you know about it, then?"

"One of those four people happens to be my cousin."

Julie tried her best to frown disapprovingly at Beckworth's low sense of humor, but gave it up after a few seconds. Actually, she thought the joke was sort of funny. Sort of. "If you're done with the stand-up routine, are you going to show me a heavy rifle I can use?"

"Follow me. I've made an anti-tank rifle modeled on a Polish design. It's a lot lighter than the Lahtida. It only weighs a little over twenty pounds and fires an eight-millimeter round."

Beckworth climbed out of the gondola onto the deck below. The hangar holding the *Magdeburg* was still under construction but the basic framework was in place. The huge wooden structure floated on the lake, supported by pontoons. That way it could be turned to face into or away from the wind whenever the airship was entering or leaving.

Once Julie had joined him on the hangar deck, Beckworth headed for the entrance where the boat that had brought them to the hangar was tied up. "The gun's in my shop on shore," he explained.

"So what silly name did you give this one?"

"I just call it the 'Karabine.' On account of I can't begin to pronounce the full name the Poles gave it. Talk about a language with screwy spelling! They could give the Welsh a run for their money."

It was quite a name, all right. Dell had copied it from one of his books across the diagram he'd used to design the weapon.

Karabin przeciwpancerny wzór 35. Julie wasn't even going to try to figure out how to pronounce it. "Karabine" it was, "Karabine" it would be.

It was quite a gun, too, truth be told. A pure bitch to lug around or even shift a little to aim properly if you had to lift the tripod holding up the barrel. On the other hand, that same weight made the recoil something an average-sized woman could withstand.

The Karabine was more accurate than she'd expected, although it didn't measure up in that respect with the rifle she normally used, which was a Remington 700.

"Okay, I forgive you," she said, after she was done test firing it.

Chapter 9

Linz, provisional capital of Austria-Hungary

Julie returned in time to celebrate her husband's birthday. The festivities went well, but they would have gone better if, after one too many alepots, Alex hadn't ventured to explain to Julie the inadequacies of a measly 8mm rifle against an armored Ottoman airship.

"You should have insisted on at least ten millimeters," he pronounced.

Approximately 7,000 feet in the air
over the Tuscan countryside
Italy

First Lieutenant Laura Goss was proud of herself. She'd managed to keep a grin off her face—not even a smile—ever since they'd lifted off from the airfield at Linz. The straight face had lasted all the way to their landing at the Venice airfield on the Lido sandbar. Once her passengers had deplaned and gotten on the boat that would take them over to Venice for their various diplomatic and other meetings, she'd finally broken into laughter.

Nothing uncouth; more of a giggle, really. She'd then enjoyed herself for the next three days, staying in the small tavern that serviced the airfield and (mostly, because there still wasn't much air traffic) the local fishermen.

Now they were on the second and final leg of the journey, which would end at the newly built airfield at Florence, capital of the duchy of Tuscany. She'd put the straight face back on when her passengers returned from Venice and had kept it on ever since.

For someone with her insouciance about flying, it was a bit of a struggle. All pilots tended to be relaxed about the so-called perils of aviation, but Laura was carefree even by those standards. Quite unlike the man sitting in the aircraft's right front seat next to her, whose white-knuckled grip on the armrests and face woodenly devoid of any expression at all were sure signs of acute aviophobia.

You'd think a former prizefighter, former prime minister, current commander of an army division, a man who'd gotten into a gunfight the same day as the Ring of Fire, and had been in several pitched battles since, would be casual about something as comparatively safe as air travel. (Okay, it wasn't as safe as flying had been up-time. But it was still pretty safe, as far as Laura was concerned. She'd never crashed once. Never come close.)

Fear of flying wasn't rational, of course, which she knew perfectly well. In a moment of empathy, she smiled and said: "Hey, Mike, relax."

She pointed with a forefinger at the window on the passenger's side. Beyond, clearly visible, was one of the Dragonfly's two engines, securely attached to the lower wing of the biplane. "This plane's got two engines, you know, and it can fly just fine if either one of them goes out. It's quite a bit safer than the single-engine planes Colonel Wood's put you on before."

Mike Stearns pulled back his lips in a rictus that bore precious little resemblance to a smile. "Correct me if I'm wrong, but I believe this plane is a new model, made by an upstart manufacturer whose owner is a down-timer— that is to say, has hardly any experience building airplanes."

"Oh, hell, it's not *that* new. The first Dragonfly came into service a year and a half ago. This is the fifth one they've made."

From the rear came Rebecca's voice: "It's slightly new, because it was modified for the needs of the State Department. But Lieutenant Goss is right, Michael. You really should try to relax a bit."

"As far as the rest of it is concerned, General," said Laura, "it's true that *Ziermann Flugzeugwerke* was founded by a down-timer, but the aircraft itself was designed by Kitt and Cheng Engineering—and they didn't suck it out of their thumbs. This beauty's closely modeled on an up-time airplane that saw a lot of service, the de Havilland DH90 Dragonfly. They even named it after her."

Mike Stearns glanced out the window. "I noticed right from the start that it was a biplane. That is to say, an antique. When did the original see service?"

"Mid-thirties. Mind you, that's the mid–*nineteen* thirties. Three centuries from now."

Mike's tight lips tightened further. "Swell. Three hundred years from now means it was built thirty years before I was born. Like I said, an antique—and this particular one was built three centuries before that."

He closed his eyes. "I appreciate the effort, Lieutenant Goss. But I didn't even like to fly in Boeing 737s."

Behind him, his wife clucked her tongue reprovingly. "You really should try to keep up with the times, Michael. The days when you could count the number of aircraft in the world on the fingers of one hand—even two hands— are long gone."

"Two years gone, anyway," said Goss. "These days you'd need all your toes also. Even that might not be enough."

The only response made by the former prime minister of the United States of Europe, former professional boxer and now Major General Stearns, was: "How soon will we be landing, Lieutenant?"

Sitting in one of the back seats next to Rebecca was Mike's quartermaster general, David Bartley. He hadn't been paying much attention to the conversation because he'd been engrossed studying the landscape below. They were passing over the Apennines now, and the scenery was pretty spectacular. Unlike up-time commercial jets, which typically flew at an altitude between thirty and forty thousand feet, far above the land they were passing over, the Dragonfly seemed to be grazing the mountains.

That was mostly an optical illusion, David knew.

Mostly.

"What's the ceiling for this aircraft, Lieutenant Goss?" he asked.

"Twelve thousand, five hundred feet. But there's nothing to worry about, Major Bartley. The northern Apennines aren't very high. The tallest peak is Monte Cimone, but that's sixty miles northwest of us—and it's only seven thousand feet or so."

She tried to keep the smile on her face seraphic rather than sly, but suspected she was failing. It didn't really matter, though, because Stearns still had his eyes closed. "The reason it seems we're flying pretty close to the ground is because we are." She glanced out of her window. "About half a mile, thereabouts. I'm doing that because we're not too far out from Florence. We'll be landing soon."

"How soon?" asked Mike, without opening his eyes.

The Dragonfly was a six-seater. The two men in the very back were both radio operators—and repairmen, if need be—who'd be staying in Florence along with the equipment they were bringing. Both of them were down-timers, but their disparate reactions to the experience of flying for the first time showed once again that fear of flying had little rhyme or reason. The one on Mike's side, like Mike himself, had his eyes closed and a death grip on his arm rests. The one on the other side shared all of David's interest in the view—and then some.

"Oh, look, Heinrich!"

But Heinrich kept his eyes closed.

Florence, capital of the Duchy of Tuscany
Italy

"My hosts keep urging me to move into one of their bigger and newer palaces. I lived in one of them for a time, in my first exile. The Palazzo Medici, they call it."

Fakhr-al-Din waited for the translator to finish, before continuing. The emir's Italian was excellent, but unfortunately Mike's was mediocre. If Rebecca had been present, she could have done the translating. But the customs of the Levant were such that his host would have deemed it very improper for her to be present.

As Fakhr-al-Din proceeded to demonstrate. "But I much prefer this older palace, the Palazzo Vecchio. Yes, the rooms are small, as you can see"—he waved his hand about—"but there is much more privacy. That is very important for the women. Here, they can move about outside, because there is an enclosed garden. In the larger and more recently built palaces—"

His expression grew stern. "It is quite scandalous, the way the Florentine boys try to get a glimpse of our women. It is very hard to prevent them from doing so, in a place like the Palazzo Medici."

Mike kept his expression as bland as possible. He couldn't quite bring himself to nod in a gesture of agreement, though. Some impish part of him was tempted to explain to the emir that the customs in the German lands he now called home included public baths, which were not segregated by gender. So far as he could tell, there was no significant moral decay caused by this practice, compared to that which prevailed anywhere else in the world, including the Near East.

He glanced at David Bartley, who was sitting next to him. The young man's own expression indicated a certain degree of reproof. Hopefully, Fakhr-al-Din would interpret that as David's disapproval of young rascals rather than his disapproval of old male chauvinists.

"But I grow tiresome, I fear," said the emir, after another pause for translation. "You did not come all this way to hear an old man grumble about the sinfulness of young men."

He smiled, and his face seemed to lose about twenty years of age and forty years of disapprobation. "I fear I was no angel myself when I was young."

Fakhr-al-Din wasn't particularly old by up-time standards, being only in his early sixties. But down-timers gauged these things differently. Any number of them could and did live into their seventies and eighties; and some into their nineties. But as they drew near to the Biblically stipulated lifespan of threescore and ten, they tended to become fatalistic on the subject of age.

"We wish to propose an alliance, Emir."

The years of age returned. "For what purpose?"

Mike began to explain.

Rebecca's meeting with the rulers of Tuscany was a relaxed affair. Perhaps that was due to the fact they were meeting in the open air, in the spectacular Boboli Gardens adjacent to the Palazzo Pitti, which served as the residence for Florence's ruling family. More likely,

Rebecca thought, it was because for all practical purposes the meeting was between women.

Yes, a man was present at the meeting—no less a figure than the grand duke himself, Ferdinando II de' Medici. But Ferdinando's great passion was not politics but new technology. That had been true even before the Ring of Fire and had become something of an obsession since. The moment he learned that the diplomatic delegation from the USE had brought a radio to give to the Tuscans and Rebecca handed him the manual of operation—already translated into Italian, conveniently— he'd had no interest in anything else. So while he stayed in his seat with his nose in the manual, Rebecca discussed affairs with his wife Vittoria della Rovere. And they did so in the course of a stroll through the gardens.

The grand duke's wife had considerable influence in Tuscany's political affairs, though in her case it was tightly focused. Vittoria was a devout Catholic, and she had been determined to attach Tuscany as closely as possible to the church. When Cardinal Borja had carried out his coup-in-all-but-name and Pope Urban VIII had barely escaped Rome with his life, Vittoria had become a partisan for the pope in exile. That partisanship had only increased and become fiercer after Urban was murdered.

But that was something she and her husband, who sided with her although he didn't share the same fury, had to keep hidden for the time being, as much as possible. Borja and the Spanish who ruled half of Italy had enough on their plate already to want to avoid a war with Tuscany. But if the Medicis made too much trouble, that could change. In the meantime, the grand duchess was keenly interested in forging good, if discreet, relations with the United States of Europe.

Hence the very pleasant reception she gave Rebecca. If Vittoria was dismayed that her guest was Jewish, she kept it to herself. Rebecca suspected the grand duchess found that reassuring, actually, since there was little chance Rebecca could be an agent of another faction within the Catholic church.

"I will need to consider your proposal," said Fakhr-al-Din. "It is not something I can give you an answer to immediately."

Mike nodded. "Of course, Emir."

"How long can you stay in Tuscany?"

"There is no set time by which I need to be back. The siege will be lifted for a time, since Murad will need to winter over his forces in Vienna."

With a finger, Fakhr-al-Din summoned one of the servants standing next to the door. "Make ready a suite for the general," he commanded. Then, eyed David Bartley.

"He does not need to remain in Florence," Mike said. "We've discussed enough of Major Bartley's logistical plan already."

Given the small dimensions of the room, there was no chance the servant hadn't heard their entire conversation. That had made Mike uncomfortable, but by now he was accustomed to the habit which seventeenth-century grandees almost invariably had of ignoring the presence of servants when important matters were being discussed. When he'd been prime minister, his chief of intelligence

Francisco Nasi had taken full advantage of that careless practice.

The Druze emir must have sensed Mike's discomfort. After the servant left, he said: "You need not worry, General Stearns. All of my servants belong to Druze families closely bound to my own Ma'an family."

As if treason isn't something done by insiders. But Mike kept the thought to himself. So far they'd only discussed the broad elements of Mike's proposal, including the part David Bartley would be playing. He'd said nothing at all, for instance, of bringing Admiral Simpson and the Baltic fleet into the Med.

They were still at a political stage of the negotiations. When and if it became time to discuss operational matters, he'd insist that the meetings be kept completely private.

"We can have a suite prepared for you," Vittoria said to Rebecca, as they concluded their stroll through the gardens. They were approaching the figure of the grand duke, who was still sitting on the same bench and still had his nose in the radio manual.

"One of the ones with a private bath," she added, smiling.

The smile seemed quite innocent, diplomatically speaking. As if the woman who was pointing out the amenities was not fully aware that Jewish custom was to bathe more frequently than Christians generally did. Rebecca wouldn't be at all surprised if they had dinnerware in the palace appropriate for kashrut as well. The Medicis were nothing if not sophisticated, and while much of Italy was hostile to Jews, Tuscany was more liberal. Some Jews were politically prominent and a larger number were important to the duchy's financial affairs. Rebecca would not be the first Jew who'd enjoyed the dynasty's hospitality.

The Catholic church was just as powerful in Italy as it was in her native Spain, but Italians did not share the typical Iberian obsession with "Judaizers," also known as *marranos*, "Secret Jews." That was because the Italians had been more humane—or simply smarter—and had not emulated the mass forced conversions that the Dominicans had carried out in Spain and Portugal at the end of the fourteenth century.

If you don't force Jews and Moslems to hide their religion, then you don't have to be worried about secret Jews and Moslems, do you? *It ain't rocket science*, as her husband Michael would say. But he had a much greater aptitude for politics than most people did, including most rulers.

"No, thank you," she responded. "I need to get back to the USE as soon as possible. The radio operators will stay, of course. But I do have one favor to ask . . ."

If there had been anyone watching the day the USE delegation arrived—which there probably had been—they would have seen five people leave the airfield along with their luggage and equipment of some kind. Four of them would have been men, all of them in uniform. The big man who seemed to be their leader wore a particularly floppy hat that made his face difficult to see, but was obviously the famous Michael Stearns. Obviously, if for no other reason than the proprietary manner in which his beautiful wife held onto his arm as they walked away from the plane.

Very beautiful wife, as said all the tales about the famous Jewess, Rebecca Abrabanel. If any watching spies had been male—and most spies were male—they would have spent most of the time they had available to study faces studying hers.

If there was anyone watching on the morning the delegation left—and there probably was—they would have seen only three people return to the airfield. The same beautiful woman—no doubt about it, since she wasn't wearing a veil of any sort—and the same two men in uniform. One, slender and quite young. The other, the big fellow in the floppy hat. That would be General Stearns. Had to be, for his wife had the same proprietary grip on his arm.

Once in the air, the Florentine nobleman who'd been posing as Mike Stearns proved to have none of the up-timer's anxieties—and had the privilege of riding in the front seat, as Mike had done himself. He'd have to make his own arrangements for returning to Tuscany, but he wasn't worried about that. He was a self-confident man who'd traveled a lot, and the grand duchess had provided him with ample funds for the purpose.

For the moment, he was just enjoying himself, looking out the window.

"Oh, look!" he exclaimed.

Chapter 10

Prague railroad station
Bohemia

Colonel Jeff Higgins finished his scrutiny of the train drawn up to the new station the king of Bohemia had built in his capital. Wallenstein had situated it in that part of the city that would have someday in another universe been called "Wenceslas Square." In this universe, it had been named Wallenstein Square—which Jeff thought was a little ridiculous since there was no square there yet.

The section of Prague where the train station was located did exist by this time. It was called *Nové Město*— New Town—and had been established by Charles IV almost three centuries earlier. Protected by a fortified wall, New Town had grown rapidly, partly because the king decreed that all noisome trades had to be located there. The banks of the Vltava River in the area were soon lined with structures suitable for tanners, dyers, fishermen, carpenters and woodworkers of all sorts, brickmakers—you name it and if it was practical and/or loud and smelly, it would be in New Town.

The area that was now Wallenstein Square had been known as the Horse Market, and was still used for that purpose. The only large building yet constructed was the train station at the southeast end of the square, abutting the Horse Gate which led out of the city.

The train station was called—what else?—Wallenstein Station. Jeff was a little puzzled that Wallenstein kept naming things using his original cognomen, when he now had much more prestigious ones he could use, such as *Venceslas V Adalbertus*. But he was pretty sure Prince Ulrik's analysis was correct: "Wallenstein has read the famous-in-another-world poet Schiller's play about him, which Schiller titled *Wallenstein*. He probably thinks the name is some sort of lucky charm. He's very superstitious, you know."

As the years passed since the Ring of Fire, Jeff was finding that "other universe" to be increasingly fantastical. He still had moments when he deeply missed his parents, but not many of them anymore. He had a wife and family of his own now. Perhaps most important of all, he had a *life*—and not one he could ever have had in the world of his origin.

As for the lucky-charm business . . .

"Good luck with that," Jeff muttered. Ulrik was standing close enough to him to overhear and cocked his eye quizzically.

"I was just thinking that Wallenstein's looking pretty bad these days." Jeff and the prince had had an audience with Bohemia's ruler the day before, right after they arrived in Prague city. Most of the Hangman Regiment was camped outside the city, of course, since no ruler in this century—well, any century—wanted a lot of foreign troops stationed in his capital.

Wallenstein had been quite cordial and pleasant. But only Jeff and Ulrik had been allowed to see him, since he was now more or less permanently confined to his bed. He'd looked . . .

Awful. *At death's door,* as the saying went.

"I don't think he has much longer to live," said Ulrik, nodding his agreement.

"And then what'll happen?"

The prince shrugged. "Nothing too dramatic, unless I'm greatly misreading the situation."

"And your reading is . . . what?" Jeff was genuinely interested. Over the past few weeks in Ulrik's company, he'd come to have a lot of respect for the Danish prince's political acumen. That boded well for Ulrik's ability to absorb military lessons in the future.

"The key is that Pappenheim seems to have no political ambitions of his own and he seems genuinely attached to Wallenstein. Without Pappenheim leading or at least lending his support to a coup attempt, I see no way it could succeed."

Jeff grunted. "Yeah, no kidding." Pappenheim was the commander of Bohemia's army and was utterly ferocious in battle. He was universally considered one of the premier generals of the day.

"So I think a regency would be—will be—set up, given that the king's son is still a small child. Queen Isabella Katharina will be the official regent, but the power will actually be wielded by a privy council. Say this much for

Wallenstein, he's a good judge of talent and has picked capable subordinates and advisers."

"None of whom are going to be stupid enough or rash enough to piss off Pappenheim. He'd be part of the council but mostly there as the queen's watchdog."

"Precisely so." Ulrik gave the train another quick examination—which really didn't take long given its modest dimensions.

"What's your conclusion, Colonel?" he asked. Whenever their discussion ventured onto military issues—which Ulrik defined quite expansively—he was punctilious about getting Jeff's advice.

"Forget it," said Jeff. "It sounded like a great idea in the abstract, but now that we've been able to see the actual reality..."

He gave the train a look that wasn't quite disgusted but was certainly wading into those waters. "There is no way this rinky-dink barely-more-than-a-Lionel-toy-train is going to move an entire regiment with all of its horses, weapons, ammunition and equipment from here to Breslau without taking weeks and weeks to do it. One little shuttle at a time, carrying a relative handful of soldiers"— he eyed the locomotive—"and doing it none too swiftly."

The locomotive was newly built, but to Jeff it already looked like an antique, something that belonged in a museum.

"Assuming it didn't break down—and I wouldn't bet a lot of money on that—it'd still take longer than the tried-and-true old-fashioned method. What's called 'marching.'"

Ulrik smiled. "I suspect the men would give me a different opinion."

"Sure. Lazy buggers. That's why officers were invented."

Ulrik stroked his beard. Like his father and Gustav Adolf, he favored a Vandyke, but he kept his cut shorter than usual. Quite a bit shorter than Jeff's own, for that matter.

"There's no reason *you* couldn't take the train, though, Colonel," he said, "along with a bodyguard detachment. I'm sure I can manage overseeing the regiment while it's just marching through friendly territory. I wouldn't really have to do much, since you have such good officers."

Ulrik left off the beard-stroking and swept his finger down the length of the train. "There's room for at least thirty men and their horses and equipment."

Jeff frowned. "What would be the advantage of my going ahead?"

Ulrik smiled again. "Aren't you the one who keeps stressing to me the importance of having your soldiers end a long and tiring march with good quarters?"

"Well, yeah. Troops get cranky when they finish plodding along carrying a third of their body weight in backpacks and discover they're supposed to sleep in a hole in the ground or a tent made of scraps and held up by a couple of twigs." He stroked his own beard. "It's true that if I got to Breslau a week or so before the regiment did that I could probably wrangle us some decent quarters."

Ulrik's smile widened. "Especially since you'd be wrangling with your own wife. Whom you'd be seeing earlier than either of you expected."

The beard-stroking got more vigorous. "Yeah, there's that too."

✛ ✛ ✛

Jeff left the next morning, with one of the regiment's platoons. The train didn't take them the whole way, since the line ended at Ostrava, which was becoming a major coal and steel center for the kingdom. In terms of pure distance, they hadn't actually gained much since they'd traveled east instead of northeast. But the train got them across the Sudetes mountains and put them on the Amber Road. That ancient trade route would take them straight to Breslau. Men on horseback could handle it easily.

Jeff still wasn't all that impressed with the train. But it had done its job well enough—and he would allow that it had a dandy whistle.

The Amber Road had a reputation for being plagued by highwaymen, but Jeff wasn't concerned about that. In fact, he was hoping some robbers would be foolish enough to attack them. The Hangman Regiment had just recently been equipped with the USE Army's new rifle, the Hockenjoss & Klott Model C, shortened to H&KC, but which the troops themselves were starting to call the Hocklott. It was a .406 caliber breech-loading bolt action rifle and had been modeled on the Chassepot rifle which the French used to great effect in the Franco-Prussian War. (Which explained the "C" in "Model C.")

It was probably the most advanced rifle anywhere in Europe for the moment, but it had never been used in action. Not by the Hangman Regiment, at any rate.

"C'mon, brutal bloodthirsty robbers," Jeff would mutter from time to time. "Do your thing."

But if the train hadn't failed him, the highwaymen of

the Amber Road certainly did. They never made an appearance.

One of his soldiers did shoot a bear which he claimed was looking at him in a threatening manner. Jeff was dubious of the claim but didn't make an issue about it. In the seventeenth century the concept of "endangered species" was about as familiar to the average person as "quantum mechanics." And bears wouldn't qualify anyway. In the year 1636, the critters were as thick as thieves. Thicker, actually, judging from appearances.

The Hocklott did a fine job on the bear, though. That was a good sign.

Breslau (Wrocław), capital of Lower Silesia

"So, have you cracked the code yet?" Gretchen asked.

Major Eric Krenz looked sulky. "Well...no. But it's just a matter of time."

Gretchen shook her head. "I doubt that. You've had weeks already." She rose from the big table she used in lieu of a desk and picked up the sheaf of papers lying there. It wasn't a thick sheaf—not more than a dozen pages.

"Follow me," she said. "I will show you the proper way to decode secret messages sent and received by a spy."

It didn't take them long to get to their destination. Down one corridor in the city's town hall, down one flight of stairs, then a short distance to a door.

The door was guarded by two soldiers, one on either side.

"Unlock the door," Gretchen commanded.

One of the soldiers set about the task. That was going to take a while, given the number of locks, padlocks, bolts and bars. If Gretchen didn't know better, she'd assume some sort of slavering monster was being held there.

"About time!" said Eric. "I told you long ago we should just beat it out of him."

Gretchen didn't bother to respond to that. Once the door was finally open, she strode through.

If Jozef Wojtowicz had been sleeping, he wasn't by now. But he'd almost certainly been awake already, this late in the morning. He was fully dressed and sitting in the small room's armchair with a book in his hands.

Gretchen held up the sheaf of papers and said: "I need you to tell me what these say, Jozef. If any of the messages involve military operations, you can keep those to yourself. But I want to know everything else."

Jozef studied her for a moment. "That provision's meaningless. If I decipher some of the messages for you, that will give you what you need to decipher the rest."

"Good point. I will let you burn any messages you don't decode."

"How am I to know you don't have copies?"

She swiveled her head to look at Krenz. "Do we have copies?"

"Uh . . ."

"We do. Get them and bring them here—and don't dawdle. The radio room's just up the stairs. Now, Eric."

Off he went.

Gretchen turned back to Wojtowicz. "He won't have

time to make more copies. You can judge that for yourself."

Jozef was starting to look like a cornered mouse. His mustache was actually twitching a little. "But . . . how do I know . . ."

"Because I give you my word," Gretchen said. She handed him the sheaf of messages. The lettering on them was just the dots and dashes of Morse code.

DOT DASH DASH DASH DOT DOT DOT
DASH DASH

"What do they say?"

Jozef took the papers as if they were so many hornet's nests. He started to read through them, although he hadn't started translating yet. That wouldn't be quick. First he had to translate the Morse into actual letters and then he'd have to translate the code itself.

Gretchen pulled out the chair at the small desk—just a side table, really—that was part of the room's spare furniture and sat down.

She waited.

"I see you found my radio," Jozef said.

"Of course we found it. Did you think we wouldn't search your quarters once we discovered you were a spy? You didn't have it hidden that well, anyway."

"I didn't keep written messages. And this isn't my handwriting."

"Of course you didn't. You're not stupid." She nodded toward the papers in his hand. "We moved the radio here and we've had one of our operators on duty around the clock. Any messages that came in, we copied what they said. Copied the Morse, rather. We still haven't cracked the code."

Jozef smiled. "It's a good code, I always thought. Nice to see that confirmed."

Krenz came back through the door, with a thicker sheaf of papers in his hand. His expression was sulkier than ever.

"Here are the copies," he said, thrusting them at Gretchen. "All of them. Ah, Lady Protector."

She took the papers and immediately handed them to Wojtowicz.

Or tried to, rather. He was paying no attention to her now. He was staring at the next to last message, his eyes wide.

Then, quickly, Jozef read the last message. By now, Gretchen thought his face was getting pale.

Wojtowicz lowered the messages until he had his hand resting on his lap. He looked out the window for a few seconds.

"Where's Lukasz?" he asked abruptly.

"I don't know." Gretchen looked up at Krenz. "Do you, Eric?"

He shook his head. She looked back at Jozef.

"Do you want me to have him brought here?"

"Yes. Please."

She looked back up at Krenz. "Find him. If he's not in the town hall—look in the Ratskeller first—he'll be in one of the nearby taverns."

Off he went.

"It shouldn't take long. Opalinski doesn't actually

drink very much but he spends most of his time these days in the taverns, talking to soldiers who do. I'd suspect him of being another spy, except..." She shrugged.

A wan smile came to Jozef's face. He was still looking out the window. "Lukasz has about as much natural inclination to spy as a... Hard to find an analogy. Lamppost? Pile of bricks?"

"He's a hussar."

"Yes. That's the analogy I was looking for."

"I'm not sure that's an analogy."

"Neither am I." He was still looking out the window. There was not much to see out there, since this window didn't look out over the square. Just a lot of tightly packed rooftops.

Something had him upset, Gretchen realized. *Really* upset.

It took longer than she'd expected, but eventually Eric returned with Opalinski in tow.

The big hussar didn't look for anywhere to sit, since the only space still vacant was the bed. Hussars don't sit on other men's beds. It just wasn't done.

"Why did you call me here, Jozef?" he asked.

Wojtowicz held up the sheets of paper. "They've been keeping records of the radio messages that came in."

"Of course. Did you really think they wouldn't, once they found your radio?"

Jozef shook his head. "No, I expected it. What I didn't expect..."

He sorted through the papers and withdrew the last

two messages. "My uncle is dead, Lukasz. That's what this one says."

He then held up the last one. "And this one says—it's just a few words—*Suspect poison. Return immediately to Poznań.*"

He lowered the paper. "I'm sure the last two were sent by one of the radio operators on his own volition. Czesław Kaczka, probably. He's a good man. Very loyal."

Lukasz's face also seemed to be pale, although it was hard to tell since it was naturally pale. Slowly, he went to the bed and sat down on it.

"The grand hetman is dead? *Dead?*" He shook his head. The gesture was not so much one of denial as disbelief.

"He always seemed indestructible to me."

Jozef's face tightened. "No one is indestructible, Lukasz. Especially not against poison."

He looked over at Gretchen. "I would like to talk with Lukasz alone. Please."

Gretchen didn't say anything. She just got up and left the room, with Krenz trailing behind.

Once outside, Eric lapsed into blasphemy. "Jesus," he said, almost whispering. "Koniecpolski's dead?"

Gretchen drew him by the arm further down the hall, out of the hearing of the two guards.

"He isn't just 'dead,' Eric," said Gretchen. "He was apparently murdered. There's a difference. Big difference."

He stared at her.

She suppressed her impatience. Eric was a smart man, but his mind just didn't run down certain channels.

"Eric, *think*. The only thing that really held the loyalty of the two men in that room"—she nodded toward the door they'd come out of—"was their attachment to Grand Hetman Stanisław Koniecpolski. If he'd simply died of natural causes, they'd probably retain their loyalty to the king, if not the Sejm." She smiled thinly. "Both of them, especially Lukasz, are still medieval in some ways."

Eric had finally caught up with her. "But with the grand hetman murdered . . . by whom, though? I can't see why the king—"

"It wouldn't have been Władisław," Gretchen said firmly. "He would have no reason to—quite the opposite. As long as Koniecpolski was the grand hetman, Władisław had no fear of being overthrown. Which is the reason I think Koniecpolski was actually killed."

Krenz frowned. "Someone is planning to overthrow Władisław?"

"Not necessarily. By all accounts, the king of Poland can be manipulated rather easily. Just wave some new whores under his nose. But the great magnates of the Commonwealth chafe under any sort of regulation or oversight. With Koniecpolski gone, their leash is gone as well—or it's a lot longer, anyway. Whatever schemes they might have can now be advanced boldly."

"What schemes?"

Gretchen shrugged. "How should I know? I'm not a master spy."

Now it was she who nodded at the door. "But one of Europe's great master spies is sitting in that room. And those arrogant bastards just cut his leash too."

"Oh." Eric's mouth dropped open a little. His mind just didn't run down certain channels.

The door opened and Lukasz stuck his head out. "Gretchen, could we talk to you?"

"Certainly." She headed for the door.

Behind her, Eric's mouth closed. He wasn't stupid. "Ah," he said.

Chapter 11

Pescia, grand duchy of Tuscany
Italy

"I assure you we will be undisturbed here," Fakhr-al-Din said to Mike Stearns. "I have used this villa before, both as a retreat and a refuge from Florence's noise and disquiet. Furthermore, it belongs to me personally. It is not a gift from the Tuscans. I purchased it through an intermediary, so no one here knows who I am."

After the translator passed that on, Mike was careful to keep the expression on his face from reflecting his true reaction. Mike was skeptical of the last claim. Fakhr-al-Din had insisted on keeping his wife Khasikiya clothed in what he considered a properly modest manner. If she'd stayed in their carriage the whole time, no one might have noticed, but she'd gotten out every time they stopped in order to sleep in the more comfortable rooms of a tavern. People who saw her wouldn't have known who she was, because of the veil and the very unrevealing garments, but she'd certainly drawn attention—not only to herself but to the husband who accompanied her. Fakhr-al-Din himself wore Italian clothing, but, unlike his wife, his face was not covered.

As security precautions went, those of the Druze emir were pretty wretched, in Mike's opinion. Three of Fakhr-al-Din's bodyguards had accompanied them on their trip from Florence to Pescia. The guards had the bearing of men who knew how to fight and would almost certainly be able to handle one or two assassins. Highwaymen wouldn't even think of attacking their party. But in the turmoil that raged in Europe in the middle of the 1630s, it was not unheard of for assassination attempts to be mounted by large parties of men. That was how Pope Urban VIII had been killed, and Julie and Alex had come close to losing their own lives in Scotland from such an assault.

Mike was now regretting his decision not to bring bodyguards on this trip to Italy. But he'd assumed they'd be staying in Florence, where Fakhr-al-Din not only had a well-guarded palace of his own but where there would be plenty of Tuscan troops available as well.

What he hadn't taken into account were the foibles of Levantines, because he wasn't familiar with them. Privacy ranked very high on their list of *things to be greatly desired*. And unfortunately, the patience of the emir and his wife had been badly frayed in the weeks prior to Mike's arrival. The dowager grand duchess of Tuscany, Ferdinando's grandmother Christina of Lorraine, had died not long before. She'd been the regent of the grand duchy for years after the death of Cosimo II in 1621, and even after Ferdinando came to maturity she continued to be immensely influential. She'd played in Tuscany much the same role that the formidable Archduchess Isabella had played—continued to play—in the Low Countries.

Christina's funeral had been a major affair of state, and Florence had been filled with visitors before and since. Eventually, Fakhr-al-Din had decided he and Khasikiya needed a break. And what better place to do it than his little-known villa in the town of Pescia, right on the border with the Republic of Lucca? The republic had good relations with Tuscany, so it was not as if they'd be near any of the potentially hostile Papal States.

Despite his misgivings, Mike had agreed to the relocation. The negotiations he'd started with the Druze leader looked very promising and this was no time to be breaking them off.

He accepted the cup of tea offered to him by one of the servants Fakhr-al-Din and his wife had brought with them. (There were only four, which was the emir's notion of "roughing it.") It was still too hot to drink, so he set it down on the small round table in front of him. He'd hesitated to do so when they first arrived at the villa, since it was a work of art—beautifully polished brass with intricate designs etched into it. Mike wasn't certain, because he wasn't familiar with Arabic, but he thought the design of the etchings derived from calligraphy. Whether they did or didn't, they were gorgeous. It hadn't been until the third time he accepted tea from Fakhr-al-Din after they arrived in Pescia that he accepted the emir's assurance that the table was "just an old family piece, intended for practical use."

"It is unfortunate that Borja has taken the papacy," said

Fakhr-al-Din, after Mike set down the cup. The emir had started drinking from his own cup immediately, and now used it to indicate a window that looked to the south. "Whatever the Spanish usurper claims, he has made himself a pope in all but name. Which is a pity, since I got along quite well with Urban. With the archbishop of Florence also. Pietro Niccolini, that was. But he was one of those murdered in the Spanish coup, and the man who replaced him—".

The emir made a face and drank again from his cup. When he lowered it, his expression was one of distaste. "He's an Italian, not a Spaniard, but he's still a swine."

Mike had understood most of that without translation. His Italian was improving rapidly, partly due to his natural linguistic skill and partly because he was now immersed in the language.

Still, he waited for the translator to finish before speaking, to make sure he'd understood everything. "Which means you can't get any help from the papacy in approaching the Maronites," he then said.

"I am afraid not. But I don't believe that's a critical problem. My relations with the Maronites are already very cordial. They, too, chafe under Ottoman rule."

Mike didn't think he was boasting. He'd heard from several reliable sources that in this day and age the Druze and the Maronite Christians generally got along quite well. Rebecca had heard the same thing, before she left. The savage wars between the Druze and Maronites of which there'd been some mention in Grantville's records were two centuries in the future—and a future that would now never happen, anyway.

All in all things were looking good. Put together an alliance of Druze and Maronites, each of whom could probably field an army of ten thousand men, add to that Mike's own Third Division...

That was enough to hold Mount Lebanon and the cities cupped along the coast in its shelter. Of course, there was still the issue—hardly a small one!—of getting Simpson's fleet into the Med, without which a seaborne seizure of Beirut would be too risky. And there was also the question—no small one, either—of whether David Bartley's logistical plan could be made to work.

Still, things were looking good. Very good.

Breslau (Wrocław), *capital of Lower Silesia*

The first word Rebecca got of Koniecpolski's death was after she landed at the airfield in Breslau. Both Gretchen and Noelle were there to greet her, which didn't surprise her that much. It was taking her a while to get accustomed to her new status in the world. Her life until the Fourth of July Party won the election and Ed Piazza became the new prime minister and she became the secretary of state had been—or so she thought, at least—one of circumspection. She was just Michael Stearns' wife. True, she'd held a position for a time in the legislature, but she'd been one of many legislators. True also, she'd been an envoy extraordinaire to France and the Netherlands. But she thought of that as a temporary and provisional position.

In point of fact, she'd long been one of the most famous women in Europe. Notorious, in many circles.

The anti-Semites had hated her with a passion. But Rebecca had been able to dismiss most of her fame as silliness—what Americans called "celebrity," a concept she found utterly absurd. In essence, it meant you were famous because you were famous, a form of tautological reasoning that any reputable school of philosophy could dismantle easily.

But over the past three months, since she'd become the secretary of state, Rebecca had been forced to admit to herself that her days of being out of the public eye were now gone—and probably gone forever. That unsettling state of affairs was about to get worse, too, she was pretty sure. She'd passed through Magdeburg on her way from Tuscany to Silesia. Most of the time she'd spent there had been with her latest child, Kathleen, who had been born just two months earlier. She'd also had meetings with Ed Piazza and other top government officials, and she'd taken the opportunity to visit her publisher, who had excitedly informed her that the first-print run of her new book, *The Road Forward: A Call to Action*, had sold out in less than a week.

"Of course, almost all of the sales were right here in Magdeburg," the publisher told her. "But I was surprised by how many orders I got from other provinces, too. The landgravine of Hesse-Kassel ordered fifty copies, can you imagine that?"

Rebecca could, actually. She knew the woman. Amalie Elisabeth, the widow of Wilhelm V who was now the regent of that province, was one of the most astute political figures in the USE. Rebecca knew that the landgravine had required all of her top officials and advisers to read Alessandro Scaglia's *Political Methods and the Laws of Nations*. Rebecca's book had been written in part as an analysis and rebuttal to some (not all) of Scaglia's arguments. It would be very much like Amalie Elisabeth to require her advisers to read it as well.

One aspect of the news was very pleasant to hear. "Big sales" meant a lot of royalties, and she and Michael could certainly use the money. They'd piled up quite a bit of debt and their family kept expanding.

But "big sales" also meant more fame—or notoriety. Rebecca sometimes found it hard to tell the difference.

So, she wasn't particularly surprised to see that the Lady Protector of Silesia and the new Countess of Homonna—Noëlle Stull, in a former life—had come out to the airfield to greet her personally. What *did* surprise her was the presence of the two Poles who'd come with them. One of whom, the last she'd heard, had been imprisoned for espionage.

Gretchen was never one for "beating around the bush," as Rebecca's husband would say. "Grand Hetman Koniecpolski's dead," she told Rebecca, as soon as she deplaned. "Murdered, apparently. Poison."

Rebecca stared at her. Then at Jozef and Lukasz.

"I see," she said. She had the bizarre sensation of simultaneously feeling her spirits rising and her stomach sinking. The rising spirits were due to the obvious possibilities that might now open up; the sinking stomach because she'd hoped to make this a quick visit so she could return home to her infant daughter.

Rebecca was a down-timer and didn't share the obsessions of up-timers over the proper care of babies. As long as they didn't get sick, the creatures were quite sturdy. The up-time terror that any slight disturbance in an infant's life—a mother gone for a few weeks here and there, for instance—would mutilate their dispositions, was just nonsense.

Still, it had been disconcerting to realize that Kathleen had really had no idea who Rebecca was. The important attachment she'd made in her first weeks of life had been to her wet nurse.

But her newborn daughter would just have to wait for a bit. *Koniecpolski dead . . .*

No, not just dead—*murdered.*

"We need to talk," she said to Jozef and Lukasz.

Pescia, grand duchy of Tuscany
Italy

It really was a lovely town. As he leaned slightly out of the window, Mike's gaze wandered randomly over the surrounding countryside. He wasn't looking for anything in particular, just enjoying the view.

Pescia was situated on a river—the Pescia River, which presumably gave the town its name—which meandered through a valley in the foothills of the Apennines. There were some architecturally interesting buildings, a couple of palazzos and a cathedral that obviously dated far back into the Middle Ages. All of the stone structures would probably be freezing cold before long, but so far the autumn had been quite mild, especially for November. There was still no snow on the ground.

The town was attractive enough that he wished he could take a couple of days to just sightsee. But that simply wasn't possible.

The problem wasn't that his host would grow impatient at his absence. Whether because of his cultural upbringing or simply his age, Fakhr-al-Din had very leisurely notions of the proper pace of political negotiations. The problem was a crude and simple one. As pleasant as his stay here was proving to be, Mike was still not happy at what he considered the emir's lackadaisical, almost nonchalant, attitude toward security. The least he could do was not add to the problem by parading himself around the town in plain view.

He wasn't worried that he'd be recognized. This was an age of woodcuts, not photographs. The likelihood that the inhabitants of a town in seventeenth-century Europe—even in the USE, much less Italy—would recognize Mike from having seen a woodcut of him was miniscule.

But he wasn't concerned about casual passersby and inhabitants. The real risk came from spies who were following them, even if they were only guided by rumor.

"You worry too much," the emir had told Mike, just the day before. That hadn't been a reproof so much as a tease, since Fakhr-al-Din had been smiling when he said it. "Who would attack us here? And why?"

He'd waved his hand, as if brushing away an annoying but harmless insect. "The Ottomans? No, they're accustomed to restive provinces. They made no attempt on me during my first exile in Italy. Why should they do it now?"

Because of the Ring of Fire, Mike was tempted to say. *Everything is different now.*

It was ironic, in a way. Mike's usual criticism of the reaction of down-time rulers to the Ring of Fire was that they developed the delusion that they could use knowledge of the future—no, *a* future—to unerringly guide them in the present. What they failed to understand was that *this* present, the one created by the Ring of Fire, was a historical reality of its own. The future of another universe could serve as something of a guide, but only in the broadest possible sense. It was not a blueprint.

But that didn't mean that the Ring of Fire had been irrelevant. No, it really had changed all of the world, especially its political affairs. This world's rulers often raced about hysterically, thinking they could control the future. That belief was a delusion—but the hysteria was real and was a danger of its own.

Fakhr-al-Din came into the room and joined Mike at the window. "A beautiful day, isn't it?"

"Yes, it is," said Mike.

Magdeburg, *capital of the United States of Europe*

The first thing Rebecca did when she returned from Breslau was go to her home and make her way to her new daughter's room.

Kathleen was awake, happily. Her wet nurse, Sibylle, handed her to Rebecca as soon as she came into the room.

Rebecca cradled her infant and gazed down at her, with a big smile.

Kathleen stared up at her mother. Her mouth was open, as if she was trying to figure out a mystery.

She couldn't speak, of course. She was only two months old. But Rebecca had no trouble interpreting her daughter's expression.

Who are you?

Chapter 12

Breslau (Wrocław), capital of Lower Silesia

"We're agreed, then?" asked Gretchen. She pointed at Lukasz, who was sitting against one of the walls of the room close to the entrance. "He will head up the diplomatic mission to Vienna and Jakub will go with him. Meanwhile, Krzysztof and Red will return to Galicia."

"Early tomorrow morning," Red said. He was sitting against the same wall, along with the two Polish szlachta who had come with him to Breslau. "We've got to get back as soon as possible."

He closed his mouth, opened it, then closed it again. Gretchen knew he'd wanted to argue once again that they really needed Jakub to go back with him and Krzysztof, but he'd already lost that argument the day before. Red Sybolt was a stubborn man, but he wasn't outright pigheaded. Noelle had insisted that at least one of the three people from Galicia had to accompany the diplomatic mission—the *fake* diplomatic mission—to the Ottoman court.

Eric Flint

"Face facts, Red," she'd said forcefully. "Sure, Lukasz can head up the mission—but that just means he swaggers around looking very Polishy szlachtish."

Several people had winced at that expression. They were speaking Amideutsch but even by the mongrel standards of that still-emerging language "Polishy szlachtish" was something of an abomination.

"But he doesn't really *know* anything about what's happened in Galicia over the past year and a half. If the Ottomans question him at all—and they're almost sure to—he'll fumble around and they'll start getting suspicious."

"We can brief him—"

"Red, cut it out. Aren't you the one who just got through saying you had to leave immediately? You can't possibly teach Lukasz everything he has to know in a short time."

"She's right," Krzysztof said. He smiled at Lukasz. "Even if my brother were as smart as me—"

Lukasz smiled back. So might sibling tigers have exchanged toothy yawns.

"—he'd need days—a week at least—to have everything he needed to know fixed in his mind."

"I agree," Jakub had chimed in. That had pretty much settled the argument. Red still wasn't happy about it, but he understood the old saying *what's done is done.*

Gretchen's finger moved to indicate Noelle, who was sitting at the table to her left. "She will go with Lukasz posing as his wife."

Red had argued about that, too. *What's the point of bringing* another *person who doesn't know squat?*

The term "squat" then had to be explained to several of the people present, since it hadn't yet worked its way into standard Amideutsch. (Insofar as "standard Amideutsch" wasn't an oxymoron.)

Gretchen had gotten a little exasperated at that point. "Red, how many times do we have to keep trampling over the same ground? Noelle's going for two reasons. First, she's probably smarter than any of you. She's got the advantage of being a woman. So listen to what she tells you."

Gretchen wasn't exactly what up-timers meant by a "women's libber." She thought a lot of that philosophy was questionable and some of it was downright preposterous.

"She'd have driven second wave feminists nuts," Melissa Mailey once said to a friend. "Gretchen thinks the differences between men and women are deep and profound. The problem is that people have screwy notions about which gender is really superior. Think of her as a female chauvinist and you won't go far wrong."

With a jerk of her head, Gretchen indicated the beautiful teenager sitting to her right "Secondly, Noelle's going along because in combination with Denise that's bound to reassure the Ottomans concerning Lukasz's bona fides. Who but a swollen-headed szlachta would bring his wife and mistress on a diplomatic mission?"

Denise didn't look very pleased at that depiction of her role in the expedition, but she didn't say anything. She *really* wanted to see Minnie again.

"What about bodyguards?" asked Lukasz. "I'm not particularly worried about being attacked by highwaymen, of course."

So might a crocodile announce that he wasn't too worried about being attacked by catfish. A couple of the people in the room snorted.

"But if I don't show up in Vienna with a cavalry escort—at least ten men—the Ottomans will get suspicious. Even the scruffiest Cossack chieftain would be accompanied by some bodyguards. And I can't take the men who came here with my brother and Red Sybolt because they need them as an escort back to Galicia. Some of that territory they'll be crossing is lawless and infested with bandits."

Gretchen had already considered that problem. She'd consulted with Eric Krenz, who'd then discussed it with Lovrenc Bravnicar.

"The Slovenes have agreed to send a detachment," she explained. "True, they're not Poles, but . . . " She shrugged.

Jakub chuckled harshly. "As if Turks are going to worry over the fine distinctions between Slavs."

Lukasz shook his head. "Don't forget how many Ottoman officials aren't Turks themselves. They're from the Balkans. They'll know the difference between Slovenes and Poles—and Bulgarians and Albanians— especially if they hear them talk."

He shrugged. "I'm not worried about that, however, because those same officials won't care. It won't strike them as odd. Why should it? The Ottoman Empire itself is a mixed-up jumble of tribes and nations."

Gretchen waited to see if anyone else had a comment to make. When she was satisfied they didn't, she looked at Jozef Wojtowicz. The former prisoner was sitting at the same table as she, Noelle, Denise and Eric, but he was opposite Gretchen and had his chair pushed back a foot or so. As if he was not quite part of the discussion.

What was odder was that Christin George was sitting next to him. Not quite, rather. She was sitting forward with her elbows propped on the table and her chin resting on cupped hands. She hadn't been part of the planning, so her presence was something of a mystery. But just before the meeting Jozef had told Gretchen he wanted Christin to attend and she'd acquiesced readily enough. Denise had frowned at her mother's presence but had raised no objection either.

Jozef spoke up for the first time since the meeting began. "Meanwhile, I will go to Poznań to find out what happened to my uncle. And, if possible, to see if we might find sympathizers among the Polish troops in the city. The Grand Hetman was very highly thought of. And plenty of them know who I am."

"Won't anyone be suspicious?" asked Eric.

"Why should they be? If anyone knows of my presence here, they'll also know I had been captured. How did I escape?" He raised his hands and spread them, in an insouciant gesture. "I am a master spy. Such men make escapes. It is well known."

When he lowered his hands, he turned slightly toward Christin. "But to further allay anyone's suspicions, I have asked Christin to accompany me and she has agreed."

"Hey!" Denise squawked.

Gretchen ignored her. "Posing as your wife also?" she asked.

For the first time since she'd made Jozef Wojtowicz's

acquaintance, the man seemed somewhat abashed. "Ah... Well. No," he said.

"That's what I thought!" Denise rose and pointed a stiff forefinger at Jozef. *J'Accuse!*

"Mom, he's just trying to take advantage of you! He's a lech!"

Without lifting her chin out of her hands, Christin swiveled her head to gaze upon her irate offspring. "Honey, let me get this straight. My seventeen-year-old daughter—"

"Eighteen! Almost nineteen!"

"Only by your New Math. My seventeen-year-old daughter is warning me that my boyfriend is a rotten bastard and I have to stay away from him? Talk about a role reversal."

Denise looked sulky. "Well... You and Dad did it to me."

"Ted Hancock *was* a rotten bastard and you know it. You said so yourself less than a year later. Besides, the real issue was that you were fourteen and he was twenty. That's why Buster warned him off."

"That's what you call it? 'Warned him off'? Dad threatened to kill him!"

"No, he didn't. He told Ted that if he came near you again he'd beat him within an inch of his life." Christin shook her head, still keeping her chin cupped. "Not a murder threat. And to get back to the point, I'm almost ten years older than Jozef. An impartial observer would accuse me of taking advantage of him, not the other way around."

Lukasz intervened in the family quarrel. "It's a good

idea, I think. It's true that Jozef has a reputation. If he shows up in Poznań with a beautiful woman whom he seems genuinely attached to—especially an older one—people will be too bemused to suspect him of evildoing." He lifted his chin to point at Denise. "His usual girlfriends are closer to her age. My one concern is that Christin is an up-timer."

He gave Denise's mother a look that wasn't skeptical, just questioning. "This is not a big problem for the people going to Vienna, because Noelle and Denise just have to be seen, not heard—and then, seen from a distance. But, up close, it's usually hard for an up-timer to pass as a down-timer."

He made a slight brushing motion with his hand. "Don't ask me why, because the differences are subtle. Just take my word for it."

"Or take mine," said Jozef. "He's right. I can almost always tell if someone's an up-timer. On the other hand, I have a lot of experience dealing with Americans and being around them, which is not true of almost any down-timers. So they won't know they're American, but they will know they're not what they claim to be. They'll smell a rat, as you would say."

He looked at Christin. "So, can you do it? Pose as a down-timer, I mean?"

"Don't see why not. I'll be a stranger in a strange land, don't forget. I'll be posing as a German, not a Pole, and my German—regular German, I mean, not Amideutsch—is pretty damn good." She shifted languages: "Even got a Thuringian accent, people tell me."

She opened her mouth and peeled back her lips, still

with her chin cupped in her hands. The teeth thus displayed were not in bad shape, by down-time standards. They were white and none were missing. But it was obvious that unlike her daughter Christin had never gotten orthodontic care as a child.

"Even got lousy teeth."

"As long as you don't let anyone look into your mouth," said Gretchen. The teeth of up-timers differed from those of down-timers in several respects. One of them was the number of fillings they had. Up-timers typically had a lot, especially if they were Christin's age, where down-timers usually had none.

But that was something that could be kept hidden, well enough. And if Christin were captured and her mouth subjected to that sort of inspection, she was probably doomed anyway.

"All right," she said. "I have no objection." In truth, she was rather inclined to support the proposal. Gretchen thought Christin George was a good influence on Jozef. Maybe he'd be smarter than most men and listen to his woman.

Still looking very irked, Denise resumed her seat. "Okay," she said—as if she were the suspicious mother barely agreeing to her daughter's proposed outing.

Again, Gretchen waited to see if anyone had anything further to say.

Apparently not. "All right, we're adjourned. Jozef, you and Christin stay. We need to discuss how we will stay in touch."

"Radio."

"Obviously. But what code do we use? That one you

used was good but we have to assume it's been compromised. And I'd be happier anyway with—"

Christin rose and headed for the door. "This is going to get technical, I can tell. Make my brain hurt. Jozef, I'll see you at home."

Christin didn't actually have any problem with "tech stuff." The real reason she'd left the room was waiting for her in the corridor outside.

"Okay, Denise. Spit it out."

Her daughter had had enough time to be reasoned with. Christin had figured she would be. She knew Denise better than anybody, even Minnie. The girl got excited easily but she also settled down quickly.

Denise's frown was now one of puzzlement rather than disapproval. "I don't understand why you're doing this, Mom. Do you really have the hots for Jozef that much?"

"I'm getting pretty damn fond of him, as a matter of fact. But no, that's not why I'm doing it." She waved her hand briefly. "Well, some of it's him. Mostly, though, I'm doing it for Buster."

Her daughter's frown was now joined by wide eyes. "Huh? How does Dad figure into this?"

"What killed him, Denise?"

"Those stinking anti-Semites. You know that."

Christin shook her head. "I didn't ask 'who.' I asked 'what.'" She didn't wait for an answer. "I'll tell you what killed him. The seventeenth century killed him. And all the centuries that went before it, except maybe the one when Christ was around. What killed him was a world where people think they can kill anybody they hate and they hate almost everybody who isn't like them. And there are no governments that'll stop them—hell, most of the governments put their stamp of approval on it."

She paused, and placed her hands on her hips. "Isn't that why you started working for Francisco Nasi? Sure, I know some of it was the excitement of what you're doing. But I know you, Denise. You don't approve of this crap anymore than I do and you figure Francisco's working to end it."

"Well. Yeah."

Christin nodded. "Your dad was a patriot. Most people didn't think of Buster that way, because he didn't talk about it much and he never had any use for people who waved the flag all the time. He thought they were mostly phonies. But he approved of the country we had. The United States of *America*, I mean. He didn't think it was perfect—not even close—but he figured it was way better than most of what the human race had come up with before. After the Ring of Fire, he supported what Mike Stearns was doing right from the start because Mike was trying his best to recreate that country here."

She waved her hand again, more expansively. "Not exactly the same, of course. But close enough so everyone can have a life of their own and vicious bastards like the ones who killed Buster don't dare raise their heads."

Her eyes had gotten a little teary, so she paused to wipe them with the back of her hand.

"Anyway, honey, that's why I'm doing it. I'm in favor of what these Polish people are trying to do, and I'm going to help. If Buster were still here, I think he'd approve." A grin appeared, which was very much like the one Denise got so often. *If the world don't like it, the world can jump in a lake.* "Well, he wouldn't approve of me screwing Jozef, of course. But since he's gone, that's neither here nor there."

It took a few seconds, but eventually Denise's frown was gone. She linked arms with Christin and the two of them started walking down the hall toward the stairs that would take them out to the square.

"I love you, Mom."

"I love you too, honey. We've got some Polish ancestry, you know. That's maybe a little of why I'm doing it also."

"I didn't know that."

"Well, I've never been big on tracing family trees and Buster cared even less. But, yeah, my mother told me about it once. Turns out her grandfather came over here—there, I mean, back in the USA—from somewhere around Warsaw. Mom thought I'd be interested because he stuck out like a sore thumb—the only Pole at family reunions that were otherwise totally Lebanese. That was sometime in the last century, toward the end. The nineteenth century, I mean." She smiled. "Think of it as two hundred and fifty years from now."

"Mom, that's ridiculous. The past is the past and the future is the future. Stop mixing them up."

"Says the girl whose boyfriend was born almost four hundred years before she was."

"Mom, that's *sick*. Eddie's only twenty-four."

They reached the stairs and started down, still arm in arm.

"What was his name?" Denise asked. "Your great-grandpa's, I mean."

"His last name was Smolarek. I think I'm pronouncing that right, but I'll check with Jozef. I'm not sure about his first name. It was a long time ago when my mother told me about him and, like I said, I'm not real big on family trees. Boguslaw, something like that. Boleslaw, maybe?"

"You don't know our own ancestor's *name?*"

"Hey, smarty-pants. You didn't even know he existed until I just told you."

"Not my fault. You didn't tell me until just now. But I bet I would have remembered his first name."

They'd reached the ground floor and headed for the exit to the square. Still arm in arm.

"Well, sure. You've still got a youngster's memory," said Christin. "You're only seventeen."

"Eighteen! Nineteen next month!"

"Your math really sucks, though."

Part Three

December 1636

There comes the dark dragon flying,
In his wings he carries corpses

"The Seeress's Prophecy," *The Poetic Edda*

Chapter 13

Breslau (Wrocław), capital of Lower Silesia

Gretchen stared out the window of the town hall at the market square below. She'd been drawn to the window by the sounds of a large group of horsemen. She was puzzled since, so far as she knew, Lovrenc Bravnicar and his Slovene cavalrymen were still out on patrol and weren't expected to return for several more days.

Her eyes were drawn to the stone pillory to the southeast, where people convicted of crimes were subjected to public flogging. Probably because she was tempted to order the commander of the troops below, who was just now dismounting, to be dragged over there and whipped for—for—

However many times a Lady Protector could have her own husband flogged. There might not be any limit at all. The legal authority of a Lady Protector was . . . vast.

Accompanied by a wordless squawk made up of equal parts glee, anticipation and fury, Gretchen raced out of her headquarters office. Within seconds she was pounding down the stairs, two steps at a time. Some part of the brain reveled in the fact that she could do so again. She'd given birth to her new son recently.

She reached the entrance just as Jeff came through. He was a big man, but she almost knocked him over from the force of her embrace.

"Why didn't you—" She broke off for a kiss. A long and fierce one.

"—tell me you were coming this soon?"

Jeff was trying to breathe. The impact of Gretchen's hurtling form had knocked the air out of him, and she'd been hugging him too tightly for his lungs to work properly. Not that he was inclined to complain.

"Op—ratio—nal. Curity," he managed to get out.

"Security!" she scoffed. "Who would be listening to a radio message?"

She knew the question was stupid the minute she asked it.

"Poles, for sure," came the answer. "By now, probably the Turks too. Those people are no slouches."

Still holding her in his arms, he looked around the square. "I only brought this detachment with me. But within a week—two, at the outside—Ulrik will be here with the rest of the regiment. All told, a little under twelve hundred men. And around four hundred horses."

She smiled. "You rode all the way, I take it. Have you finally made peace with the creatures?"

"Horses are brutes. Always will be. I don't trust them any farther than I can throw them." He heaved his shoulders in what would have been a shrug if he weren't still holding her tightly. "But it beat the alternative, which would have been to walk the whole way from Ostrava."

Finally, their mutual clasp relaxed a little and she pulled away from him. An inch or so. "Ostrava? Why take that route? I would have thought you'd go through Saxony."

"Most of the army will. But Wallenstein finished the train route from Prague to Ostrava—just three weeks before we got there. I wanted to get here ahead—well, Ulrik talked me into it—so I could get billets ready for the troops."

He looked around again. "Have you got room for them in Breslau? If need be, they can camp outside the city, but I'd rather have them in better quarters."

"Yes, of course. It might be a hard winter."

She could feel Jeff tense up a bit. Anyone other than she wouldn't have noticed it, but she knew her husband very well by now. They'd been together more than five years.

"What is it?" she asked. Not *what is wrong?* because she could tell the difference between Jeff being concerned by something and being worried about it. He was a thoughtful man, but not one much given to anxiety.

He didn't answer immediately. Just pursed his lips.

"If you tell me again that operational security is involved..." Gretchen pulled back her head and jerked it in the direction of the pillory. "I have immense and arbitrary powers here, you know."

Jeff grinned. "Hell hath no fury like a Lady Protector told she doesn't have a need to know."

Finally, he broke off their clasp and took her by the arm, heading toward the entrance of the town hall. "It's a secret but you have to be in on it anyway. Let's wait till later, though. Right now, I want to see Larry. He's okay, right?"

Gretchen shook her head. "Up-timers! The way you worry about babies is ridiculous. We down-timers don't, even though we have—had—much more reason to be."

That wasn't really fair on her part, and she knew it. When it came to children, Gretchen had the fatalism of people born in an era of fifty percent child mortality. Her brother Hans had survived until adulthood, before being killed in combat. And her sister Annalise was alive and well. But by the time she was fourteen, Gretchen had seen a younger sister die at the age of four and a baby brother who'd never made it through his first year of life.

As a mother herself, though, she had never had to live through the experience of watching one of her children die. The death rate for small children had started dropping as soon as American medicine and—even more importantly—sanitation practices had started taking hold. Her first child had been only one year old when she and her family were taken in by the newly arrived Americans of Grantville. Since then, she and her children had been shielded by the medical knowledge of the up-timers.

"I told you he was well," she said a few minutes later, watching Jeff cradle his son. Lawrence Higgins, he was, but they'd call him "Larry." They'd named him after Jeff's best friend Larry Wild, who'd been killed in the Battle of Wismar three years earlier.

"I didn't doubt you, love," Jeff said softly. "For my money, you're the best mother in the world."

He looked around Gretchen's quarters—his quarters too, now, at least until the regiment had to move out. The quarters were . . .

Odd.

"Who used to live here?"

"Nobody, exactly," was her reply. "The town's notables used it as a place to put up visiting dignitaries. There weren't many, of course, and they usually didn't stay long. If they were Polish or Lithuanian, they'd want to stay in Kraków, not here."

That explained the fancy four-poster bed and even fancier armoire and the really fancy freestanding copper bathtub in one of the corners—and the absence of anything else except Larry's crib, which was obviously a later addition and much more cheaply made.

He grimaced. "There's no way I'm going to fit in that bathtub. I'm surprised you can."

She shook her head. "I've never tried. Leaving aside whether I'd fit or not—and I certainly wouldn't fit comfortably—it would be too much work to haul hot water up from the kitchens on the ground floor." She nodded down at Larry. "I use it for him, not myself. I just use one of the showers I had built in a room next to the kitchens."

Jeff set Larry down in his crib. "We can have a bookcase made for you," said Gretchen. "I'm always amazed at how many books you insist on traveling with."

Jeff chuckled. Gretchen was a printer's daughter, so she was not only literate but well read, at least by the standards of her time. But Jeff was an up-time geek who'd been devouring books since he first learned to read. There was just no comparison between the way each of them looked at the necessity of bringing books along when you traveled.

For Gretchen that meant one or two books. None at all, if she wasn't going to be gone long. Jeff measured his necessary reading material when he left home in terms of chests and crates.

"There's no point," he said. "I won't be staying that long."

She frowned. "Why not? Surely you're not planning to march your regiment about in the countryside in midwinter."

"No, of course not. But that brings us to the Secret Plan."

She could practically hear the capital letters. She took a deep breath, but suppressed the sigh that would normally have followed. "Let me hear it, then."

By the time he finished, Gretchen was at the window, staring down into the market square below.

"You can't possibly hold Kraków with just the Hangman Regiment," she said. "I'm not sure you could take the city in the first place, even as poorly guarded as it is now. By the accounts we've collected, at any rate. The garrison is not big, and its soldiers are hardly what you'd call an elite unit. Still, it's a fortified city and by the time you could get there at the earliest . . ."

She paused, doing some quick calculations. By now, after the sieges of Amsterdam and Dresden and the seizure of Silesia, Gretchen was quite well versed in military affairs. "The soonest you could invest Kraków would be toward the end of next month, husband—and that places you in full winter."

"December winter," Jeff said. "Not January or February. And the march isn't really that big of a risk, Gretchen. If the weather's really rough, we just won't do it. But December's not usually too bad and the distances involved aren't bad either. It's a little less than one hundred and twenty miles from here to Bytom, as near as I can figure it. The Hangman Regiment can make that in a week. And we've still got all of our winter gear from the assault on Dresden."

That much made sense. It was true that the Hangman—all the regiments in the Third Division—had a reputation for marching quickly. And Bytom was within that part of Silesia which the Bohemians had seized. According to Bravnicar, there was even a small Bohemian garrison there. The Hangman wouldn't have to fight to take the town and if winter did then close in on them, Jeff and his men could shelter in Bytom. The residents would hate it, of course, having to billet troops in their own homes—especially since it was not a big town. But the population was mostly German, not Polish, so there wouldn't be any armed resistance.

"All right," she said. "Go on."

"From Bytom, it's only sixty miles to Kraków. Unless the weather is bad, the Hangman can make it there in two days."

"That's awfully fast, even for a forced march. There is almost bound to be snow on the ground by them."

Jeff shrugged. "You might be surprised at how much ground the Hangman can cover, when we push it. Don't forget that moving one regiment is a lot easier than moving an entire division. But, fine, figure on a three-day march—if you insist, make it four days. By seventeenth-century standards, that's *blitzkrieg*, Gretchen."

Lightning war. It was a German phrase, so Gretchen understood the literal meaning. And unlike most people of her time, she'd read enough up-time history to understand the reference.

"I will give you all that. I will also allow that you can probably seize Kraków. But... Jeffrey, if you take Kraków—*Kraków;* it's still officially Poland's capital, you know—you will surely bring down one of the Commonwealth's major armies on your head. A coalition of the great magnates, at least, if not the royal army. You can't possibly withstand that! Not once spring comes. So you will just have to retreat back to Silesia. What is the point of it all?"

Jeff now grinned, to her surprise. *What was her idiot husband doing, grinning like that? Had he gone mad?*

"On our own, no. But the Hangman won't be fighting on our own. To begin with, we'll have the forces you've assembled here in Lower Silesia along with us. That adds another—what? Two thousand men?"

"You most certainly will not!" she said. Her voice was a bit shrill. "I am the Lady Protector of *Silesia,* my beloved but idiot husband. I am *not* the conqueror—conqueress, whatever—of Lesser Poland!"

His grin seemed fixed in place. Apparently, he *had* gone mad. "You won't have to worry about protecting Lower Silesia. When the time comes—it's all been planned out already—Heinrich Schmidt will bring about half the SoTF's National Guard into Silesia. Those are good troops. Not as good as the Hangman, but they're as good as any provincial army in the USE. Plenty good enough to shield Lower Silesia, given that the Poles and Lithuanians will be preoccupied with Lesser Poland."

Utterly, completely mad. "*So what?*" Her voice was now definitely shrill. "Add all my forces to yours—we're still talking about less than four thousand men. Even great magnates on their own can assemble an army twice that size."

"Three times, we figure. We're expecting somewhere between twelve and fifteen thousand men coming against us. In the spring, of course; they won't be able to move that many men in the winter."

She stared at him. Kraków was a fortified city, true—but the fortifications dated back to medieval times. It was not protected by seventeenth-century *trace italienne* star forts designed to withstand artillery.

Jeff's grin now became a smile, and a rather gentle one. "Relax, hon. I'm not suicidal. We won't be on our own. Morris Roth will join us, with his army. Which has the ridiculous title—brace yourself; Wallenstein came up with it—of the Grand Army of the Sunrise."

She kept staring at him. Her mind was now fluttering around. Morris Roth—he was a *jeweler*. Also the hero of the Battle of the Bridge, yes, but... *Grand Army of the Sunrise?*

"How many men does he have?" she demanded.

"A little over four thousand. The infantry hasn't been tested yet, but the cavalry is very solid. His army is also well-armed and we've—the Hangman, I mean—got the new H&K rifle, the .406 caliber Model C. We've got mortars, too, good ones, which the Commonwealth troops won't be very familiar with. We'll be a lot better armed than they are, we figure."

Gretchen broke off her stare. For a moment, she looked out of the window. She had finally realized that this scheme was not something her idiot husband had cooked up on his own. Emperor Gustav Adolf had to have been part of the planning—it might even be his plan to begin with.

Her mind had stopped fluttering and was now working as well as it usually did. The logic was coming into focus. Keep Torstensson and his two divisions pinning the Polish king's army in the north, around Poznań. Move half of the SoTF National Guard into Silesia, to anchor it. They weren't needed any longer to defend the Oberpfalz against Bavaria. Then form an alliance with the Bohemians to drive a spear into Lesser Poland. Take *and hold* Kraków. The Bohemians would get the corridor they needed to expand into Ruthenia and—

"Have you talked with the Galicians yet? If you don't have them with you serving as the official face of the occupation, taking Kraków will stir up all of Poland. You'll be stirring things up even with them, because foreigners are involved."

Jeff shook his head. "Not yet. But Rebecca's flying out there as soon as Red tells us they've got an airfield at Lviv. We're pretty sure they'll go in with us. They'd be crazy not to, since otherwise they'd have to face a magnate army on their own. We're not sure how many men they could bring, but we figure it'd be at least two thousand. We'll probably—no, almost certainly—still be outnumbered, but not by that much. And like I said, we'll be a lot better armed."

And a lot less well-organized, she thought. Talk about a polyglot army! USE regulars, Vogtland guerrillas, Silesian amateurs, Slovene cavalrymen—professionals and veterans, yes; but there weren't a lot of them—joined to a Czech army of good cavalry but inexperienced infantry commanded by a jeweler whose only combat experience was the very circumscribed engagement on the Stone Bridge in Prague—and for the final touch, a ragtag force of Galician rebels. True, many of them would be former hussars and some of them would be Cossacks. Fierce fighters and probably just as fiercely undisciplined.

"You're going to need me," she said.

"Sure are," said Jeff. "Wearing that famous armor of yours. I can't wait to see you in it."

She ignored that and looked down at her son. Larry was asleep again. He looked like a cherub.

She was *not* bringing a cherub into a theater of war.

"I will have to take Larry back to Dresden, so he can be cared for there," she said.

"Yeah, that's what I figured," said Jeff. "But look at it this way. We already have a good governess for Wilhelm and Joe, and it won't be hard to find a reliable wet nurse."

Idiot husband. "I will still need to do it quickly. A week or two, not two months or more. Which means—"

She looked at him accusingly. "I will need to *fly* again."

Chapter 14

"Damn, that's a beautiful plane, if I say so myself." Looking up at the Kelly Wasp flying three thousand feet above them, Bob Kelly—the plane's designer as well as the owner of the firm that had made it—was smiling widely.

Standing next to him, also looking up, was one of Kelly Aviation's employees, Keenan Murphy. Keenan was the company's chief mechanic but he also handled whatever other jobs his boss came up with up—short of janitorial work, anyway, where he drew the line. Bob Kelly ran his company in what could charitably be called a haphazard manner and some critics might call a slapdash one. His chief up-time rival in the aircraft designing and manufacturing business, Hal Smith, once characterized Kelly's management philosophy as chaos theory.

Keenan was smiling also, but he wasn't smiling widely and there was some strain to the smile.

Keenan was worried. The test pilot who was flying the Wasp on its maiden flight was Lannie Yost. The two men had known each other since the first grade and had become good friends over the years. And like all of Lannie's friends—not to mention family—Keenan was known to say, "Yeah, Lannie likes to knock 'em down."

As the years passed, though—it had gotten worse since the Ring of Fire—Keenan had eventually been forced to admit (to himself only) that his friend was an alcoholic. Not just a heavy drinker, but an outright alky. A juicer; a boozer; a lush. Keenan wouldn't have gone so far as to call Lannie a wino, but that was just because Lannie didn't like wine. His tastes ran to bourbon and beer.

Lannie always knocked down a couple of drinks before a test flight. Keenan hadn't worried about it in the past because the crowd he ran with were all pretty heavy drinkers—including him. West Virginia working class culture didn't run toward touchy-feely psychology, so no one he knew spent a lot of time fretting over the mental problems discussed in the *Diagnostic and Statistical Manual of Mental Disorders*. None of them had ever heard of the book, in fact.

But Lannie's drinking had gotten heavier and heavier. Keenan was pretty sure that was the pattern for alcoholics. He knew that this morning Lannie had knocked down three drinks instead of his usual two—and they hadn't been two beers, either. He'd started with two shots of bourbon—no, two swigs of bourbon from a pint flask. Could have been three shots. With a beer chaser.

You wouldn't have known it from the way Lannie swaggered out to the plane and climbed into the cockpit, though. He hadn't staggered; hadn't shown any physical signs of inebriation. In times past, Keenan had been reassured by his friend's steadiness even when drinking. He hadn't hesitated to let Lannie drive him home after a night of carousing, before the Ring of Fire. Why should he? Lannie had only gotten into one car accident in his life and that had been a fender bender where the other driver was at fault.

Keenan had been chewing on the problem all morning. Finally, he decided he had to say something.

"Hey, boss, maybe we should cut the flight short this time."

"Why?" Kelly asked, without taking his eyes off the plane. The Wasp was now some distance to the west, starting to make a turn to come back toward the airfield. Kelly had told Yost not to fly too far off, and the pilot was following his instructions. Well... Maybe he was stretching them some. But you couldn't really expect test pilots to be slavishly obedient. That was just not the nature of the breed.

"Well. Lannie might be a little tipsy this morning."

Kelly puffed out his lips. He was well aware of Lannie's drinking habits, but he'd always chosen to overlook them. Yeah, sure, the guy drank a lot of liquor. But he still functioned okay, didn't he?

Keenan wouldn't let it go. "He had more than he usually does, Bob. I'm a little concerned."

Kelly sighed. "Look, let's not worry about it now. I'll talk to Lannie after he lands. For one thing, I don't want to distract him with a radio call."

Keenan didn't—quite—roll his eyes. The Wasp was

designed to be a fighter plane, which meant radio communication was considered an integral part of its activity. If a pilot couldn't handle the "distraction" of a radio call while he was flying, what was he doing piloting the plane in the first place?

He started to say something but Kelly held out his hand in a shushing gesture. "Not now, Keenan. He's approaching his first dive and I need to concentrate."

Keenan looked back up at the plane. In truth, it *was* a beautiful aircraft. Bob Kelly had designed it after the British de Havilland Mosquito of World War II fame. Like the Mosquito, it was made almost entirely of wood. It was a shoulder-wing monoplane with two engines mounted on the wings. Below the pilot's cockpit, mounted atop the fuselage, was a somewhat bulbous nose that in the original British plane would have a clear window and a bombardier's seat. In Kelly's smaller version, that nose had a machine gun mounted in it. The gunner would ride next to the pilot in a tandem seat arrangement and operate the weapon from that position. But, if the gun jammed, he could squeeze himself down into the nose to fix whatever the problem might be.

The big problem Kelly had faced was crude and simple. The de Havilland Mosquito had been powered by 1200 horsepower engines—that was 1200 *per* engine—which gave the Mosquito a top speed of around four hundred miles per hour. The engines Kelly had been able to obtain had a tenth that much power. Together, the two engines gave him less than 250 horsepower. Because of the size of the aircraft, that had required very light construction and a large wing area. Even then, the Wasp's top speed was only about one hundred miles per hour and its cruising speed was around eighty miles per hour.

Yes, it was a beautiful plane. But it wasn't the sturdiest plane you could imagine, either. That was why Bob had cautioned Lannie not to try any really fancy acrobatics until they had a better sense of how well the plane performed. This was a test flight, so they had the machine gun and its ammunition on board but not the gunner himself. Instead, they'd strapped one hundred and sixty pounds of sandbags in the gunner's seat to provide the needed weight.

Above, Lannie started his first dive. It was fairly shallow and he didn't push the plane's theoretical limits.

"See?" Bob said. "He's taking it easy, just like I told him."

Seeing that the worried expression was still on his mechanic's face, Bob shook his head. "Look, Keenan, I know Lannie's a borderline alcoholic."

Borderline, my ass. But Keenan didn't say it out loud.

"I read up about it," Kelly continued. "There's different kinds of alcoholics, Gammas and Betas. Your Gammas are the falling-down drunks. Betas are different. They drink too much, and they can eventually kill themselves from it—cirrhosis of the liver, heart disease, whatever—but they're what's called 'high functioning.' In fact, this kind of alcoholic actually performs better when they've had a drink or two. Psychologists call it 'maintenance drinking.' It's why guys like Babe Ruth and Mickey Mantle could knock down a couple of shots and still hit home runs like nobody's business."

Keenan was skeptical, but he didn't know enough

about alcoholism to be able to argue the matter. Especially with his boss. All he knew was that Lannie was drinking more and more as time went on and maybe he was a "high functioning drunk" but dammit he was still a drunk.

Thousands of feet above them, Lannie Yost had pulled out of his dive and was about to do another.

"Damn, this is one fine plane!" he exclaimed. "Bob, you done yourself proud."

Kelly's understanding of alcoholism wasn't wildly incorrect, but it was skewed. There were such people as high-functioning alcoholics and they did engage in maintenance drinking—and, indeed, their physical performance did actually improve after one or two drinks, which was not true of people who weren't alcoholics.

But that just spoke to their physical performance and reflexes. Yes, a great baseball player who was a high functioning alcoholic and had had a couple of drinks before going out to the plate could hit a home run. Just like a test pilot accustomed to flying aircraft still kept his physical skills after a couple of drinks.

What he started losing, though, was his *judgment*. His reflexes and coordination might still have withstood the effects of the alcohol, but his mind hadn't. He was, to use the vernacular, pickled.

Up until now, the Wasp had performed splendidly. Bob Kelly was indeed a good aircraft designer. But he'd gotten the performance of his new airplane partly by cutting corners.

Lannie was exuberant, now. His next dive was steep

and he wasn't going pull up until the last minute. This was a *war*plane, no? You don't pamper a fighting aircraft.

Down he went. Down and down.

On the ground below, Keenan hissed. Bob's jaws tightened. "Damnation," he muttered through tight lips.

Lannie broke off the dive and starting pulling up. But he was now putting more g-force on the wings than they could handle. A wire support on the frame pulled loose, screw and all. That threw six times as much weight on the other wire and it broke loose as well.

The Wasp's right wing started coming apart. The flaps on that side ripped loose. The crippled wing itself stayed attached to the fuselage but it was no longer functioning as a wing. It was just flapping aimlessly as the plane began plunging toward the ground.

The wing no longer provided any lift, but because it stayed attached to the fuselage it did provide drag—and even in a dive the Wasp hadn't been traveling all that fast. As it headed for the inevitable crash landing, the plane never achieved terminal velocity.

Never came close, really. It was probably not doing more than sixty miles per hour on impact.

A crash at sixty miles per hour is plenty good enough to kill someone, of course. But alcoholics have a patron saint of their own, a Dubliner by the name of Matt Talbot, and apparently he was on the job that day. Instead of smacking into the ground, Lannie's plane struck an oak tree.

No small oak, either. This was an old, mature, really *big* tree.

A *Quercus robur*, to be precise, a type of white oak. It had a circumference of thirty feet, stood eighty feel tall and had a crown about the same diameter. It had been alive more than four centuries before the Ring of Fire.

The aircraft never made it to the ground. It was pretty much torn to shreds as it passed through the branches, of course, as lightly constructed as it was. Pieces of the plane's wings that were too big for birds to use for their nests stayed in the canopy for the rest of the tree's lifespan.

Lannie Yost didn't make it to the ground, either. He and his seat finally came to a stop in a branch fork about fifteen feet up. He was still in one piece, although you couldn't exactly say he was intact. He had four broken bones and a lot of lacerations.

It took a while to get him out of the tree. They had to call in the Grantville Fire Department for help.

West Virginia firemen—and the down-timers on the crew weren't any different—do not have what you'd call a delicate sense of humor. So by the time they finally got Lannie out of the tree, he'd been subjected to a lot of ribaldry, quite of bit of which focused on his drinking habits. *Hey, Lannie, most guys don't wrap a plane around a tree when they go on a bender*, was a fair specimen of the jokes.

Bob's wife Kay was furious, needless to say. Fury came naturally to the woman.

That goddam drunk Yost cost us a fortune! It's not just the cost of replacing the materials, either. We've got penalties in the contract if we don't deliver on schedule.

Bob's view was less stringent. *We can salvage the engines, which are what's really expensive, and those so-called penalties have a lot of loopholes in them—thanks to you, since you negotiated them. It specifically exempts any time lost due to accidents during testing.*

That hadn't slowed Kay down at all. Not many things did.

Still! What's important is that we get back on schedule!

No, Kay. What's important is that Lannie didn't get killed.

Whether they got hit by penalties or not, the fact remained that Kelly Aviation wasn't going to be able to deliver the Wasp on schedule to the forces guarding Linz. It would be up to Hal Smith and his company to get the planes they had under contract to the front lines in time to meet the Ottoman onslaught that would resume in the spring.

Kay was irate about that, too.

That bastard'll get all the next contracts. You watch!

Bob's view was less pessimistic. *Relax, darling. He hasn't got that much capacity.*

He will if this goes on! And why haven't you fired Yost yet?

Kelly didn't fire Lannie, although at Kay's insistence he did make him sign a last chance agreement. So, Lannie started attending AA meetings. By now, as big as the population of Grantville had become since the Ring of Fire, there were at least a half dozen AA groups in the town. Down-timers joined readily, when their pastors cracked the whip—which seventeenth-century pastors were not shy about doing.

Lannie's first relapse came in less than two weeks. But Bob had been reading up on alcoholism some more, so he dug in his heels when Kay demanded that he fire Yost as the last chance agreement stipulated.

Relapses are inevitable. All the studies say so. They're just part of the treatment. The way I figure it, Lannie hasn't forfeited his job under the last chance agreement as long as he keeps attending the meetings.

There was a reason almost everyone in Grantville liked Bob Kelly, even his competitor Hal Smith. Almost no one liked his wife, though.

Chapter 15

Breslau (Wrocław), capital of Lower Silesia

In the end, they decided to take the children with them. Pawel would ride behind Christin; Tekla would ride in front of Jozef. Basically, it was the same seating arrangement—perhaps saddle arrangement would be a better term—that Jozef had adopted when he first encountered Pawel and Tekla and rescued them from their destroyed village. Except that now Jozef had Christin to assume half the burden instead of his carrying both children on one saddle.

He wasn't any happier at the arrangement, though. He'd have much rather left Pawel and his sister in the relative comfort and safety of Breslau. Christin had found a good family who were willing to take the children in until their adoptive parents could return.

Whenever that might be. Possibly never. Jozef and Christin were going to be riding into harm's way, after all. Leaving aside whatever perils and challenges they would face in Poznań, first they had to get there—across more than one hundred miles of open country in December. So far, the winter had been comparatively mild, but as far as Jozef was concerned the operative term in that phrase was *so far*. It would take them at least a week to get to Poznań. In a week, the weather could take all sorts of unfortunate turns.

To make things worse, while the territory they'd be passing through couldn't exactly be called "war torn," it had certainly been chewed by the war. The sites of two of the Third Division's major battles, Świebodzin and Zielona Góra, were only seventy-five miles west of where they'd be passing. Świebodzin had been the site of the atrocities committed by some units of the Third Division which had sent Mike Stearns into such a rage that he'd had two dozen of the guilty soldiers executed. Zielona Góra had only been taken after the Third Division effectively destroyed the whole town.

Depopulated it, too. Not by killing its inhabitants but simply by forcing them to flee, just as the residents of Świebodzin had fled in terror.

Similar events had transpired throughout that part of Poland, and almost all the inhabitants had fled to the east— that is to say, into the territory that Jozef and Christin and two young children would now be passing through. More than a year had gone by, but the area would still be unsettled—"unsettled" being the euphemism used by government officials to refer to areas which were either lawless or where law had been only partially restored.

But the decision hadn't been made by the adults involved. The decision had been made by the two children, who'd raised such an unholy ruckus at the prospect of being separated from Jozef and Christin that they finally capitulated and agreed to take Pawel and Tekla with them.

"Look at it this way," Christin had said. "If nothing else, they'll make our cover story sound better. Who'd suspect a man and a woman with two young children in tow to be nefarious characters?"

Unfortunately for his peace of mind, she'd said that as they were loading up their horses for the journey. Jozef had only to turn his head fifteen degrees to see the very lethal-looking and very up-time-looking rifle that Christin had insisted on bringing with her. It was nestled in a saddle holster that she'd had specially made for the weapon by one of the town's leatherworkers.

A Ruger Mini-14, she called it. In the Poland of the year 1636, she might as well have called it a Buck Rogers ray gun. The minute any down-timer got a good look at it they'd know something was badly amiss. Christin was either an American in disguise or—if her German was good enough to pass, which it might be—someone who had way more money than could be explained. An up-time weapon like that would have cost a fortune.

But she insisted on bringing it.

"Relax, will you?" she'd said, adding the indignity of patting him on the cheek. "Whenever we get to a town, I'll put it away in the baggage. It's only three feet long and doesn't weigh more than maybe six pounds. It's easy enough to hide."

"What if someone out in the country spots it?"

"'Someone out in the country.' Give me a break. Who are we most likely to run into 'out in the country' besides a pack of robbers? Wannabe robbers, it'd be better to say. I'm a good shot with that thing and I've got thirty-round magazines."

American women could be unnerving sometimes, for all that they so often seemed like delicate creatures compared to their down-time counterparts. Jozef had then fallen back on the chancy tactic of arguing on ordnance grounds.

"Seems like an awfully small caliber."

"Yup," she said, nodding. "It's a .223—otherwise known as a 5.56 millimeter. But it's got a muzzle velocity right around one thousand meters a second. I don't care how big a highwayman is—hell, I don't care if he's a hussar in full armor—the bastard's going down. If the first shot doesn't do it, I can fire three rounds a second."

Again, she gave him that disrespectful pat on the cheek—which wasn't improved by her next words: "My husband taught me how to shoot."

It was a bright, clear day when they rode out of Breslau, heading north. Cold, yes, but it was the sort of cold that was bracing rather than bitter.

The children were in a delighted mood. "This is going to be so much fun!" Pawel predicted, with all the enthusiasm of a six-year-old boy setting off on what he regarded as an adventure.

His sister didn't say anything. Tekla didn't know her exact age or even her birthday, but she was somewhere around four years old. Her eyes were big as she gazed at everything around her. She was warm and comfortable, riding just in front of her adoptive father and nestled inside his big furry coat. The world was a wondrous place. She paid no attention at all to her brother's chatter.

*Brno, capital of the Margraviate of Moravia
Kingdom of Bohemia*

To Morris Roth, it just looked like chaos. But he was sitting on a horse next to Franz von Mercy, and the general in overall command of the army seemed satisfied.

Well enough, at any rate. He wasn't exactly what you'd call happy.

Why can't you keep your men in order, Nottheffer?

Von Mercy had the sort of voice that Morris thought would be quite handy in the noise of a battlefield. Being not more than six feet away from him, though, it got a little hard on the ears.

Von Mercy must have sensed Roth's unease and confusion. "It's going well, General Roth, I assure you." Waving his hand at the column of men marching past them, he added: "The start of a march always looks like this, especially with an army made up of elements that aren't familiar with each other."

March. From what Morris could remember of his days in the U.S. Army, what was happening here on the outskirts of Brno was hardly what he'd have called a "march." It reminded him more of demolition derby, using horses and wagons instead of cars.

But he allowed that his memory might be playing tricks on him. Almost all of his experience with marching had come during basic training, in the tightly circumscribed and highly disciplined environment of Fort Ord, the big army base near Monterey, California.

Big at the time, anyway. He'd learned long afterward that the army had closed most of Fort Ord in the mid-90s. That had produced the sort of reaction someone often gets when they discover that a place remembered vividly but not fondly no longer exists. An odd combination of *good riddance to bad rubbish* and nostalgia.

Morris tried to remember if he'd marched anywhere once he got to Vietnam. Not that he could recall. So maybe his memories of the well-ordered manner in which the up-time U.S army went from Point A to Point B was so much hogwash. Maybe things had been just as chaotic as this seemed to be.

If he recalled correctly, the up-time military would have referred to this as an "evolution." If so, apparently they were still in the age of Homo erectus.

Where did you learn the difference between right and left, Betzinger? Hanging upside down in a cave with bats?

What Morris did remember clearly and vividly was his surprise at hearing von Mercy and his other top officers project that it would take the Grand Army of the Sunrise—God, what a silly title!—ten days to reach Ostrava. And that was assuming good weather.

Ten days? To go just a little over one hundred miles?

Assuming you only marched for eight hours each day, that was an average speed of less than a mile and a half per hour. An old lady using a walker could move that fast!

Well . . . not for eight hours, no. And certainly not if she also had to carry a backpack weighing sixty pounds or more.

Still. It had seemed kind of ridiculous to him.

Now, watching the "evolution" happening before his eyes, Morris was beginning to wonder if von Mercy hadn't been wildly optimistic.

Assuming the Grand Army of the Sunrise could make it to Ostrava on schedule, and assuming the Silesians could live up to their end of the deal, they'd then have to march to Bytom. That was another seventy miles. Almost two weeks, all told, even assuming the weather didn't turn sour and they had to wait in Ostrava for it to clear up.

What worried him even more was what would happen when—if, rather; whether it happened or not mostly depended on the Silesians—they launched the attack on Kraków.

Kraków was sixty miles from Bytom. When von Mercy first explained the plan to Morris, after he'd talked to the Silesians over the radio, Morris had thought the notion of launching an assault on Kraków from Bytom seemed quite reasonable.

Sixty miles. In *blitzkrieg* days, they could get there in a few hours.

Abstractly, Morris had known that *blitzkrieg* was three centuries away. But his reptilian hindbrain still thought in twentieth-century terms when it came to warfare. Only now, watching the sluggish way a seventeenth-century army actually moved, did it finally register on him that the "assault" on Kraków was going to require at least two days and probably three—maybe even four—before the Grand Army of the Sunrise even got to Kraków.

God, what a silly title. It'd have been better to call it

the Grand Army of Perpetual Dawn, as slowly as the sun comes up in Here-and-Now Military Time.

Three or four days to get from Bytom to Kraków—possibly five. Even the most sluggish garrison in the world could come alert in that period of time and get their defenses ready.

But von Mercy and his officers didn't seem very concerned about that. Hopefully, they understood something that Morris didn't.

Which ... they might. As he'd told Wallenstein time and time again, Morris was *not*—not not not—a general, whatever title they gave him. So maybe Wallenstein also understood something he didn't.

It was possible. The man who was now king of Bohemia did have an impressive military record, which suggested he was canny and knowledgeable about such things.

On the other hand, he'd also insisted on calling Morris' army the Grand Army of the Sunrise, which indicated he was a loon.

"I assure you, General Roth, it's going quite well," von Mercy repeated.

But all Morris could think of was the line by Groucho Marx: *Who are you gonna believe, me or your own eyes?*

Breslau (Wrocław), capital of Lower Silesia

The departure of the diplomatic mission to Vienna was a more elaborate affair than Jozef and Christin's leave-taking. For one thing, there were a lot more people involved.

Riding in the carriage were Lukasz Opalinski, the supposed ambassador; Noelle Stull, the supposed wife; Denise Beasley, the supposed concubine; and Jakub Zaborowsky, the supposed chief adviser to the supposed ambassador.

Although he was assigned to the carriage, Jakub didn't plan to ride in it very often until they had almost reached Vienna. No fool, he. Riding on a horse would be a lot less bone-rattling than riding in a carriage on the roads they'd be traveling.

Neither Lukasz nor the two women were at all happy at the arrangement, since all of them were familiar with what the seventeenth century called "roads." But, unlike Jakub, it had been decided that they needed to maintain the pretense throughout the entire journey. It was possible—not likely, but possible—that the Ottomans would have spies watching them before they got very far.

The carriage would also have two men driving it. As rough as the roads would be in places, the teamsters would need to spell each other.

Riding in the escort was a detachment of Slovene cavalry, twelve men in all. They were commanded by one of Lovrenc Bravnicar's lieutenants, a fellow by the name of Cvetko Horvat.

But the main reason the mission didn't set out at the same time as Jozef and Christin left for Poznań was the carriage itself. Here, problems had emerged.

First, there was no suitable carriage anywhere in the city. Few carriages existed at all, because most inhabitants of the city very sensibly chose to ride in litters carried by two horses rather than having their teeth rattled by hard wheels passing over harder cobblestones. Just as with *blitzkrieg,* "shock absorbers" and "suspension systems" lived mostly in the imagination.

Of the few carriages that did exist, none of them had been designed for long journeys over country roads, nor were they big enough for the purpose they would be used for.

So, back to the drawing board. A large and sturdy wagon would have to be used. Such vehicles did exist in Breslau—quite a few of them, if you included the farms in the surrounding countryside. The problem with them, however, was that they had clearly been designed for the purpose of hauling foodstuffs and other such lowly items.

What sort of "ambassadorial mission" to the Ottoman court would arrive in Vienna riding a farm wagon? At best, they'd be met with coarse jokes about cabbages and sent packing by the city's guards.

So, the vehicle had to be...not disguised, exactly, since there was really no way to disguise such a crude and simple vehicle. But it did have to be dressed up and decorated. A cabin had to be constructed and fixed to the wagon bed. Then, suitably painted. Then, suitably furnished.

And, last but not least, the cabin's design had to be much more intricate than it appeared to be, because four people were going to have to be smuggled out in it. So, cabinet makers had to be employed as well as carpenters.

The final delay—this cost them a full day, because the girl's mother had already left the city and was not there to squelch her—was caused by Denise.

Up until the last stretch before their departure, Denise

had been disgruntled by her assigned role in the mission. Concubine. Courtesan. Mistress. Pick whatever fancy name you wanted, you were still talking about a *whore*.

But Denise was not given to pouting for all that long. She'd been making silk purses out of sow's ears since she was old enough to wheedle, which she learned to do as soon as she could talk. So, a few days before the mission was to set out, she charged all over Breslau looking for a seamstress who had the skills (and background, which was trickier to find) to design and make Denise some suitable garments for a Polish nobleman's concubine.

Her "whore outfits," she called them cheerily.

She got them made, too. Just not quite in time.

They might have forced her to leave without the costumes, but Lukasz intervened on her behalf. "It's not a bad idea, actually. She's right that it will make her disguise more credible."

Jakub Zaborowsky, on the other hand, knew Lukasz was misreading the situation. Jakub had more experience dealing with Muslims than Lukasz did. Not from encounters with Ottoman Turks, of which he'd had few, but from encounters with Crimean Tatars, of which he'd had a fair number.

Yes, the Ottomans wouldn't be surprised that a Polish nobleman brought a beautiful concubine with him on such a mission. But they'd be astonished—and immediately suspicious—if he allowed any other men to *see* her. As a wife, Noelle would be able to move about on occasion so long as she was suitably clothed and veiled. But a concubine would not.

Without realizing what she was doing, Denise had consigned herself to rigid sequestration for the entire journey; what some Muslims (and Hindus, he'd heard) called purdah.

But he said nothing. First, because the net effect would be exactly what Lukasz foresaw: Her costume would indeed make her guise very believable. But it would do so upside down, you might say—or inside out. Denise would have to be kept completely out of sight so that their hosts would *think* that a beautiful young woman was inside the carriage. And if by chance (or by foul design by some enterprising young lad) she was actually viewed, her appearance would add credibility and luster to the charade.

Mostly, though, he said nothing because Jakub was an Orthodox Christian and none too devout about it. It was going to be a rough trip, especially when he had to ride inside the carriage. He had no objection at all to being pleasantly distracted along the way by Denise's appearance.

He'd have to keep her from realizing it, though. The girl was fierce.

Ottoman siege lines southeast of Linz
About three miles from the confluence of the
Danube and Traun rivers

Murad began the withdrawal after the third snowfall. As with the first two, not much snow fell. But those had melted within a short time and this one looked to be staying for the winter. He'd only kept his men in the siege lines this long because he judged that if he retreated to Vienna too soon the army's morale would suffer.

It was a slow and careful withdrawal, since he had to keep his troops in position to repel any sortie the enemy might attempt.

By now, the sultan knew that the commander of the forces opposing him was the king of Sweden, Gustav Adolf—or Gustavus Adolphus, as he was sometimes called.

The kâfir king also claimed to be an emperor, but Murad paid no attention to that absurd pretension. There were only two real emperors in the world, himself and the ruler of the Mughal Empire in India. (The Chinese might also have a real emperor, from the rumors, but he had too little information to know one way or the other.)

Gustav Adolf's imperial royal claims might be specious, but Murad did not underestimate his military ability. By all accounts, including those of the sultan's own spies and agents, the Swedish king was the best general among the Europeans. Only a fool would behave carelessly by withdrawing an army from such a man. True, the Ottoman army was bigger than the forces Gustav Adolf commanded; much bigger. But a big army trying to withdraw from a siege is an ungainly and clumsy beast.

It took four days, but eventually it was done. Within two weeks—perhaps only a week, if all went well and the weather didn't turn bad—the army would be safely back in Vienna.

Breslau (Wrocław), capital of Lower Silesia

The polyglot force that had no name beyond "Ulrik's army" set out from Breslau two days after the mission to Vienna left the city.

This evolution was even more chaotic than the one in Brno had been. Australopithecine, at best. But its commander didn't share Morris Roth's anxieties. The Danish prince was a calm-headed and imperturbable man, as he'd demonstrated during the Baltic War when he led the attack on Simpson's fearsome ironclads.

Perhaps more importantly, the officer he'd come to trust and look to for advice was even calmer and more imperturbable than he. The Dungeon Master, his men called him. Ulrik had looked up the reference. Would a good Dungeon Master allow his players to miss an engagement?

It didn't seem likely. Colonel Jeff Higgins would see to it they got to Bytom in time.

Vienna, official capital of Austria-Hungary
Now under Ottoman occupation

"I'm telling you," Judy insisted. "This time it's for real. They said the rescue mission was *underway*."

"'Underway' could mean anything," countered Minnie. "They're probably just trying to maintain our morale. The mission is 'underway' because they're still planning."

"You're too much the skeptic," said Cecilia Renata. "I think that comes from only being able to see the world through one eye."

"That helps, yes. I'm not subject to optical illusions so much. But I'm a skeptic mostly because my first memory in life was of the wife of the farmer I was bound out to because I was an orphan assuring me the food was going to taste good and there would be plenty of it. The first claim shaded the truth and the second one eclipsed it altogether."

"Enough," said Leopold. "We need a new game."

Judy decided to leave off the dispute over the message. What would be, would be. They'd know sooner or later.

"I've been thinking about it," she said, looking around the cellars. There wasn't much to see, beyond the few yards around their circle. They only had one candle lit. Most of the cellar they were in was in darkness.

"And you came up with . . . ?"

"I did an inventory of our candles. We've still got a ton of them—plenty to burn half a dozen at a time instead of the one or two we usually do."

"And this is needed because . . . ?"

"Hopscotch." She explained the game. It didn't take long.

"I'm against it," Leopold said immediately. "The last time you came up with one of these overly energetic American games—'Hide and Seek,' wasn't it?—when I was It and trying to find people I almost fell into the hole."

He pointed toward the entrance to one of the adjoining cellars. You could barely see it because of the poor lighting, but any one of them could have found it if they'd been blindfolded. By now, they knew these cellars very, very, very, very well.

"The one in there."

"Which shall not be named," Cecilia Renata proclaimed immediately.

"The shit hole," said Minnie. "I've got to say I'm with Leopold on this one, Judy. Hopscotch, in a dark cellar—five, six candles, it doesn't matter; it'll still be dark—you're just asking for trouble. Especially in the vicinity of plumbing—ha ha ha—left over from the Dark Ages."

Rome, Italy

"And you are certain this comes from the Sublime Porte?" asked Cardinal Borja.

"Certain? That is too strong a term, Your Eminence. We are dealing with intermediaries here. But I can think of no one else who would be interested in such an outcome. Not *this* interested, at least."

The agent extended his hand, in a gesture that combined presentation with a certain amount of caution. So might a servant present a dish of food to his master whose taste he wasn't sure would please the finicky fellow.

He wasn't all that cautious, however. Borja had employed the agent on several occasions, so he'd come to know him rather well. The cardinal was not a man with highly discriminate tastes, especially when it involved his own political ambitions.

The cardinal gazed out the window of his palazzo, his lips pursed. After a few seconds, he said musingly, "We have nothing to lose, after all, if the attempt fails. Even if Tuscany suspects us, what could they do?"

The agent wanted the commission, because he was short of funds and had creditors who were . . . vigorous. But he'd learned that playing the devil's advocate was usually the most effective tactic at this point.

"The payment they offer is not great, Your Eminence. You could almost say, disrespectfully low."

Borja shook his head. "That does not particularly concern me. What's important is that we will have opened a liaison that may prove fruitful in the future—and they will owe us a favor, not we them."

Now he sat up straight. The agent recognized the motion. The cardinal had traits which made him a difficult employer. But indecision was not one of them.

"Set it underway," Borja commanded. "Use an intermediary yourself, however."

The agent kept from smiling. He'd had no intention of doing otherwise, since he was no fool. Assassinations failed more often than they succeeded, in his experience. And the repercussions could be severe.

He didn't expect they would be this time, it was true. The target was in no position to launch a counterattack, even if he survived. Still, why take chances?

"It shall be done as you command, Your Eminence."

Part Four

January 1637

The ancient tree groans and the giant is loose;
All are terrified on the roads to hell

"The Seeress's Prophecy," from *The Poetic Edda*

Chapter 16

Poznań
Poznań Voivodeship
Polish–Lithuanian Commonwealth

Getting to Poznań proved to be harder than getting into the besieged city. They had to take shelter from the season's first storm for three days—in a village so small they had to share a cottage with its owners. A cottage that was barely more than a hut to begin with.

The owners themselves were delighted at their good fortune. The payment they received from Jozef was more money than they'd see in a year; in currency, at least.

Most people, when they heard the word "siege," thought of a city completely surrounded by enemy troops, with all entry and exit barred. In many sieges, though, there was a part of the city that was not being invested at all by the enemy or, if it was, not by very many soldiers.

In the case of the siege of Poznań, the USE was no

longer trying to seize the city, although for public consumption they kept referring to it as a "siege." Torstensson and his two divisions were really there to keep the main Polish army fixed in the north. That was partly so that Gustav Adolf could concentrate on fighting the Turks. Partly also—this was a more recent development—it was because he was beginning to think that the USE might be able to gut the PLC's underbelly. Between seizing Lower Silesia, and supporting the Bohemians and the Galicians . . .

It was a gamble, of course, but one that he thought had good odds. "Worth a try," as his up-time allies would say. But in order for the revolt brewing in southern Poland to have any chance of success, the USE had to keep most of the PLC's armed forces in the north. For the moment, at least, the rebels weren't strong enough to face those forces if they were assembled into one army.

So, orders had been sent to Torstensson to shorten the siege lines and make them as strong as possible. By the time that was done, no more than two-thirds of the city's circumference was really being invested any longer. The USE Army was just squatting down for the winter, strengthening and improving its fortifications and keeping its soldiers warm, well fed and healthy. Those fortifications were now designed more to fend off a Polish sortie than to serve as a base to assault the city.

Torstensson did send out cavalry units to intercept any large supply trains that the Poles tried to get into the city—and he had the airplanes to spot them long before they got near to Poznań. But he didn't bother with any supply attempts that weren't too ambitious. As long as it avoided enemy patrols, which rarely went out after nightfall, it was possible for a small party to make its way to one of the city's entrances. And in the case of Jozef and Christin, they had an extra advantage: Gretchen had sent word to Torstensson over the radio that they were coming, and the general of the USE troops besieging Poznań had passed that on to the officers in charge of the troops guarding the northern gate.

That gate was so lightly guarded to begin with that it was possible Jozef and Christin could have slipped past them anyway. But they had no need to make the effort. The evening before they planned to enter the city, they got in touch with Torstensson again and code signals were established. Early on the morning of the following day, before the sun had even risen, they made their way to the entrance.

They did encounter one of the USE cavalry patrols, but there was no difficulty getting past them.

"The grasshopper has no food."

"It should have prepared for the winter."

"Who comes up with this stuff?" Christin demanded quietly, once the patrol was out of sight.

"A student of the classics, I assume."

"'The Ant and the Grasshopper' is a classic? It's a kid's story."

"A very, very old one. That makes it a classic."

"No, it just makes it very, very old. Like my great-aunt Ava. She's very, very old—was, anyway; I haven't seen her since the Ring of Fire—but if anybody thought she was a classic it's news to me."

❖ ❖ ❖

Once at the city gate, of course, they had to persuade the Polish guards to let them in.

But that proved to be no great task, either. For a start, just as Christin had foreseen, the presence of the two children served to allay suspicions. Would evildoers bring children along on a mission to commit evil? It didn't seem very likely.

In addition, Jozef had the three necessary attributes for the task.

A goodly-sized bribe.

An indefinable air of szlachta arrogance.

A loud voice.

"Open the gates, you stupid bastards! Or I'll have my uncle skin you alive!"

One of the soldiers tried to take a stand.

"The grand hetman's dead, you dolt!"

"Then I'll have his ghost skin you alive! Open the fucking gates!"

At that point, the sergeant in charge intervened. It is unlikely that he was intimidated by the threat of Koniecpolski's ghost. He was a devout man whose priest had once explained to him that the common belief in ghosts was a sin, being as how it called into question the divinely proclaimed fates of eternal salvation or eternal damnation.

But the priest hadn't said anything about bribes, one way or the other, and the most devout commoner in Poland was also going to be practical. If his wife found out he'd spurned a good bribe, he'd never hear the end of it.

"Let them in," he commanded. "And that'll be enough from you, Mateusz, or you'll forfeit your share."

Two soldiers standing not far from Mateusz indicated their support of the sergeant's position, one by growling and the other by raising his musket. He didn't exactly aim it at Mateusz, but the barrel was in the vicinity. Mateusz was suitably cowed and the business could proceed.

Once they were through the gates and far enough from the guards not to be overheard, Christin said: "Now what? I'm warning you, Jozef, if you don't find us a place to sleep soon with a half-decent bed—that means no bugs, most of all—I'm not going to be happy with you."

"Fear not. That was my very thought." He reined in his horse and looked around. The street they were in was not all that wide and the buildings on either side were crowded together. To make things worse, at least half of the space available was taken up with jury-rigged dwellings and ramshackle vendors' shops. The street now had the functional width of an alley. By now, the sun had come up so there was plenty of light, but Jozef couldn't see anything beyond the street itself. He headed toward an intersection ten yards further on. Christin followed, with their pack horses trailing behind her.

Their progress was slow, because even this early in the day the street was jammed with people. Jammed with carts, too, most of them drawn by hand. Between the soldiers sheltered in the city and the civilian population that had remained, Poznań reminded Jozef of a bee hive.

By the time Christin forced her horse through the mob and got to the intersection, Jozef had a pleased expression on his face. "I was disoriented at first, because I've never used that gate before. But now, look."

Christin followed his pointing finger and saw a big structure that seemed to rise above the city.

"That's the royal castle," he said. "They built it on top of Castle Mountain—it's really just a hill—so it's easy to find if you can get into an open area. Now all I need . . ."

He rose in his stirrups and swiveled his head, looking. The motion woke Tekla, sitting in front of him, but only for a few seconds. Not finding what he was looking for, Jozef made his horse turn further around to give him a wider range of vision. Almost immediately, he had his finger pointed again. "Yes, there it is. Those are the spires of the famous cathedral, the Archcathedral Basilica of St. Peter and St. Paul."

Christin had never heard of it. Seeing the expression on her face, Jozef smiled. "Well, it's famous to us Poles, anyway. It's the oldest cathedral in Poland. Goes back . . . I can't remember when it was started. More than half a millennium."

If Christin had been a tourist who hadn't spent almost two weeks traveling on horseback in winter, with two no-longer-delighted young children complaining most of the way, she might have been interested.

Maybe. On her bucket list of *things I'd like to see before I die*—which she'd left up-time, anyway—cathedrals had ranked pretty low. Below Universal Studios; way below the Daytona 500. And then they started with Notre Dame in Paris, not a cathedral she'd never heard of in a city she'd never heard of either, before the Ring of Fire.

"Bed," she said.

"I haven't forgotten. The thing is, if you can find both

the royal castle and the cathedral, you're immediately oriented. The royal castle is on the western side of the city, right next to the wall, and the cathedral is to the northeast, on Ostrów Tumski. That means 'cathedral island.'" He frowned. "It's outside the walls so the damn Swedes probably hold it now."

She'd thought she'd recognized the word for island, "ostrów." Someday, if she decided to stick around with Jozef and he reciprocated the desire, she'd have to learn Polish, not just a few words and phrases in the language.

That day was not today, however. "Bed," she repeated.

He smiled. "Not long, now that I know where I am."

Jozef proved true to his word. True enough, anyway, that Christin didn't complain at any point. Or issue any threats or warnings. Less than fifteen minutes after he set off from the intersection, they were pulling up before an inn that looked . . .

Pretty good, actually. Better than Christin had expected.

It turned out that Jozef was known by the proprietor, a man named Niestor. No surname was given, but he might not have had one. Many commoners in Poland still followed the medieval custom of using patronymics only.

Niestor's wife and son were there as well. Her name was Helzbieta and his was not provided. Clearly, they too were familiar with Jozef.

Jozef waved Christin forward. By then, the two children were awake and she had them by the hand.

"This is my new wife, Cristina." That was the closest

they'd been able to come to Christin in German. "I met her in Nürnberg."

With a smile, he added: "They're her children. She was a widow. But I'm going to adopt them."

Niestor and his wife and son stared at Jozef; then, at Christin; then, down at Pawel and Tekla; then, back at Jozef. You could have hung a sign around their necks that read: *Dumbfounded*.

Very familiar with Jozef, obviously. If Christin weren't so tired, she would have laughed.

The tavern was as full of customers as you'd expect, in a city with this population density, but Jozef was able to get them a small room. It cost him a lot, but they had a sizeable purse.

The room was not actually a guest room but one of the proprietor's own. The four children who inhabited it were summarily ousted. They didn't even complain. Clearly, well-trained offspring of a tavern-keeping family.

The bed was softer than Christin would have preferred, but she was used to that by now. All down-time beds were soft and squishy, by her standards. The important things were that the room was warm enough and there were no bugs. Of course, she was using their own bedding, taken from one of their packs. Only a dimwit would use the bedding provided by an inn. You might as well get a tattoo that read *Free food* in Bugese.

She was asleep within two minutes of lying down. Pawel and Tekla, nestled on either side of her, had fallen asleep within two seconds.

✦ ✦ ✦

The next morning, Jozef set out to find the radio operator who'd sent the message warning him that Grand Hetman Koniecpolski had been murdered. That was Czesław Kaczka—or, at least, that was who Jozef thought was most likely to have sent it.

It might not have been, though. The last Jozef had known, Koniecpolski had had four radio operators all told. That might have changed, since his information was quite dated by now. But assuming the Grand Hetman had still had just the four, and assuming none of the personnel had changed, Jozef could eliminate one of them immediately.

Lucas Wojciechowski, that was. A sniveling, slovenly toad of a man whom Jozef wouldn't trust any farther than he could throw the fat swine. The only reason his uncle had given Wojciechowski the prestigious position of radio operator had been the man's family connections and the fact that, admittedly, he was capable with technical matters.

If Jozef approached him, only two things would happen: Wojciechowski would know nothing and he'd immediately rush to the authorities to report that Jozef Wojtowicz was back in town and asking suspicious questions. With his hand outstretched for a bribe.

The first of those outcomes mattered to Jozef more than the second. He wasn't planning to keep his presence in Poznań a secret anyway. What was there to be secretive about? Between his bastard origin and the nature of his work, few people knew of his connection to Koniecpolski in the first place. And those few who did know wouldn't think it suspicious that he'd returned to Poznań to pay his respects to his uncle's memory. Jozef was planning to do that in any event, once he found out where the grand hetman was buried.

That left Caspar Kowalczyk and Janko Nowak as the other two possibilities.

Nowak was unlikely, though. Jozef didn't distrust him, it was just that the man was . . . odd. The Americans had a term for a mental condition that, when it had been explained to Jozef during his stay in Grantville, immediately made him think of Janko Nowak. "Asperger's syndrome," they called it.

Jozef didn't know if Nowak had that condition or not. He had a wide streak of skepticism about American theories, especially when they involved what they called "psychology"—another theoretical concept he was skeptical of. Why couldn't a man just be what he was? Why look any deeper than the sturdy term "odd fellow?"

Whether Nowak's mind could best be described with one syllable or five, there was no chance he would have become suspicious of a man's death due to what appeared to be natural causes. His thinking just didn't work that way.

So. Kaczka or Kowalczyk? Which one had sent him the radio message?

It would be a bit risky to seek them out where they worked—whose location Jozef probably didn't know anyway. The radio operations were likely to have been moved since he was last in Poznań. He could find out, easily enough, but that would add another layer of risk. A thin layer, granted, but all such layers were to be avoided.

There was no reason to take the risk when he knew for

sure where he could find all three of the men at one time or another—that depended on what shift they worked—almost every day of the week.

He reached the entrance—down a flight of stairs to an outside cellar door—and went into Felix's Tavern.

Czesław Kaczka and Caspar Kowalczyk were both there. As it turned out, Kowalczyk was the one who'd actually sent the message.

"We knew something was wrong right away," Caspar explained, over a mug of beer. He jerked his head in the direction of the man sitting to his left. "Me and Czesław talked about it—"

"Right here," said Kaczka, rapping the table surface with his knuckles. "Right in these very seats."

"—the day after the grand hetman died. We both agreed it couldn't have been what the lying chirurgeon claimed to be spoiled food. You know what your uncle was like. That man could have eaten the most rotten food in the world and all it would have done was give him the shits. Tough, he was."

That analysis probably wouldn't have been accepted by up-time doctors, but they thought too much. It made perfect sense to Jozef. To describe Stanisław Koniecpolski as "tough" was like describing gristle as "chewy."

"Lots of men are suspicious," said Kowalczyk. "There was almost an outright revolt among some of the hussars. Would have been, I think, if they'd been able to figure out who was responsible."

Which ones? wondered Jozef. He'd have to look into that later.

"How about the two of you?" he asked. "Are you ready to revolt?"

Caspar and Czesław looked at each other. Then Caspar shrugged. "Sure, but against who, Jozef? I know the grand hetman was poisoned, but I don't know who did it."

"Yes you do—and you know it."

"Name him," challenged Kaczka.

"It's not a 'him,' it's a 'them,'" said Jozef. "You both know just as well as I do that a cabal of grand magnates must have ordered it done. They wouldn't have done it themselves, of course, but men like that know men who know where to find assassins—and they certainly have enough money to pay for it."

Kowalczyk frowned. "That was my suspicion also—still is. But what I can't figure out is why they would do it. The grand hetman was a law-abiding man. He posed no threat to them."

Kaczka was always the quicker-thinking of the two men. He slapped the table—not in anger, but in the way a man emphasizes an idea that has just come to him. "No, that's it, Caspar. They would have wanted the grand hetman killed because he *was* law-abiding—and they plan not to be. That's why they needed to get him out of the way."

Again, Kaczka and Kowalczyk exchanged glances. Then, looked at Jozef.

"This is leading up to something," said Kowalczyk. "Come out with it, Jozef."

He made a quick decision. He hadn't intended to go any further this first day than collect information. But his instincts—say better, his extensive experience as spy and secret agent—led him to believe that the two other men at the table were ready for what he had to propose.

"Have you ever heard of the Galician Democratic Assembly?"

"No," said Caspar.

Czesław nodded. "They're the rebels in Lviv, aren't they? Someone told me they declared themselves a konfederacja recently. But that's all I know, and I wasn't sure if it was true anyway." He shrugged. "You know how wild rumors spread. And Galicia's far away."

In for a penny, in for a pound, as the up-timers would say. The saying didn't make any sense, but the spirit of it was clear. Once again, Jozef made a note to himself to find out why Americans compared a coin to a unit of weight. Because a penny was such a light coin? Maybe Christin would know.

"Galicia's far away, but Kraków isn't," he said.

Caspar and Czesław both frowned at him. "It's not close, either."

"Must be . . ." Caspar waved his hand in a vague gesture. "What? Five hundred miles?"

He used a Polish term for the distance, but Jozef automatically translated that into the distance measurement used in the USE, as best he could. By now, he was more accustomed to the up-timers' rigorous system than he was to the archaic and imprecise Polish way of calculating such things.

"More like three hundred miles," he said.

"What's a—?"

"A mile is how they measure big distances in the USE,

Caspar. I use it because it's more accurate than the way we do it."

Again, the two men frowned in unison. "And how do you know—"

"It's time for the two of you to hear my story. A lot's happened since I saw you last."

It took him quite a while before he was done. Long enough that he was starting to worry that his companions had drunk enough beer to get fuzzy-headed.

In fact, Caspar and Czesław were pretty fuzzy-headed by then. On the other hand, liquor often lent courage—and once a man made a pronouncement, he was loath to retract it even after he sobered up. (Women, in Jozef's experience, were more astute about such things.)

"Here's to the revolution," Caspar proclaimed, raising his freshly filled mug of beer. Fortunately, the tavern was noisy and he didn't say it in a loud voice. So if anyone noticed the three men clanging their mugs together, they would have simply taken it for everyday good cheer.

The mug-clanking was followed by the traditional swigs. Then Caspar set his mug down on the table with a thump and said: "There's someone you need to meet. As it happens, he should be here any time, since his shift is almost over."

"That's stupid, calling it a 'shift,'" said Czesław. "He's still a prisoner, you know."

"A technicality, that's all. How long has he been here? More than a year, isn't it?"

"He'll have a guard. Probably two," cautioned Kowalczyk.

"And so what? If it's Androsz and Woitek or Zygmunt and Malosz, they drink by themselves." Czesław took another slug of beer. Then, shrugged. "If it's Kuźmin and his brother, that'd be a problem. But we'll just have to wait until tomorrow."

The guards who accompanied the mysterious prisoner into the tavern turned out to be the harmless pair of Zygmunt and Malosz, who, just as Caspar had predicted, went off to sit by themselves at a table in a corner. The table was much too far away, in the din of the tavern, for the guards to hear anything being said at Jozef's table unless everyone started shouting.

Before the prisoner had even taken his seat, Jozef knew he was an up-timer. He couldn't have explained why he knew that, exactly. But he was very perceptive about such things, as you'd expect a spy to be, and unlike most down-timers he'd spent a lot of time around Americans.

He waited until the man sat down before saying: "You're an up-timer." It was a statement, not a question.

The man stared at him. The expression on his face combined defensiveness with belligerence.

"What's it to you?" he demanded. "And who the hell are you, anyway?"

The up-timer was a young man. Jozef estimated that he was in his mid-twenties, although you had to be careful about judging age with Americans. Most people who met Christin thought she was five to ten years younger than she actually was.

"Think of me as a friend," he said. "A friend in need, yes—but I think you need some friends also."

The up-timer looked quickly at Caspar and Nowak. "What's this about? And I repeat—who is this guy, anyway?"

Jozef began to explain.

By the time he finished, the young American still had a combined expression on his face, but the combination had changed. There was doubt and suspicion in his face— but there was also hope.

"My wife gave birth, just a short while after I got captured," he said. "His name's Mark, like mine. Not Mark, Jr., just Mark. My wife told me in her first letter she did that because she thought I was dead. He'd be a year old by now. I've never laid eyes on him, not once. Don't even have a picture of him. If Stephanie tried to include one in any of the letters she sent me—and there were only three that got through, the last one almost three months ago—the damn Poles swiped it."

Caspar looked offended, although it was obviously a pose. "Us? You accuse *us* of being thieves? You should rather look to those dirty Germans squatting in their trenches outside the city walls. The letters have to go through them first, you know, before they come to us. One of the dirty pigs probably stole the letter to burn it, giving him a little heat while he shivers out there."

That was wishful thinking, for the most part. By now, almost fourteen months after the siege of Poznań had begun, the USE troops had fairly good quarters. Very good ones, by siege standards. The trenches were now just defensive positions. No one actually slept in them. Few of them even slept in tents, anymore. Jozef knew that

General Torstensson had had wood-walled bunkers made for his soldiers, with solid roofs. Say what you would about the damn Swedes, they knew how to wage war.

The up-timer, whose name was Mark Ellis—Mark Johnson Ellis, to be exact—ignored Caspar's badinage. The hope in his face was fading, and the suspicion swelling stronger.

"How do I know any of what you're saying is true?" he demanded. "How do these guys"—he jerked his head, indicating the two Polish radio operators at the table— "know either, for that matter? You could be . . . I don't know. Somebody's spy. A provocateur."

Kowalczyk started to object but Jozef interrupted him. "No, Caspar, it's a fair question. Which I can answer—but not until tomorrow. We meet the same time here? Yes?"

The two radio operators and the American looked back and forth at each other. Then, Ellis shrugged. "Yeah, sure, as long as the damn Poles don't decide to mess around with my schedule—which they do, from time to time."

"Stop whining," jeered Caspar. "The last time that happened was . . . what? Four months ago?"

"Still." Ellis looked a bit sullen.

Jozef finished his mug and rose to his feet. "Tomorrow, then. There is someone you need to meet."

Chapter 17

Bytom
Upper Silesia
Now under Bohemian control

By the time the motley army got to Bytom, Gretchen was feeling profoundly disoriented. Prince Ulrik of Denmark, the future consort of the USE's future empress Katrina, was officially in command. In that respect, it was "Ulrik's army." Politically speaking, on the other hand, there was no question in anyone's mind—including Ulrik's—that she was the central figure involved.

That was partly because of her longstanding reputation as one of the leaders of the revolutionary movement, partly because she was also—yes, it was incongruous, as she'd be the first to say—the Chancellor of Saxony and Lady Protector of Silesia. But perhaps most of all, in this enterprise, it was because of something that Gretchen herself considered ridiculous. Somehow, some way—did people have no common sense at all?—she'd become this political movement's version of Joan of Arc.

That was especially true of the German population of Silesia, which dominated the bigger towns and cities in the area. But the Poles in the countryside had become infected also. Why? So far as she could tell it was because her (admittedly vigorous) decrees supporting the rights of the Polish farmers against the overbearing German town councils and guilds had spread her reputation widely. This was still an era when religious and quasi-religious notions usually influenced people more than nascent nationalist sentiment or ethnic identity.

She recognized the phenomenon. It was the same dynamic that led so many Germans to think of Mike Stearns as the "Prince of Germany," and never mind that he was born across an ocean in another universe in a nation that didn't even exist in the one they lived in. Abstractly, she could even appreciate the political value that her newly acquired persona imparted to the revolutionary cause.

It was still ridiculous. She'd even been forced to wear her armor again! All the leaders of the expedition had been united on that issue.

At least they hadn't made her wear the helmet. In fact, they'd all agreed that it was essential she *not* wear it so that her face and—most of all—her apparently now famous long blonde hair was visible to everyone who witnessed the army's passage.

But that was not what she found disorienting. Truth be told—although she'd deny it vehemently—Gretchen was temperamentally very well suited to the role of a militant and semi-mythological champion.

No, what disoriented her was that people could say the

army was Ulrik's and the great cause was hers, but no one had any doubt at all who was really running the show.

The man they called the Dungeon Master.

Otherwise known as her husband.

Who *was* this man? She felt she barely knew him any longer. What had happened to the shy, awkward and self-effacing young man she'd met on a battlefield near Badenburg less than six years earlier? Barely more than a boy, he'd been then. But that had also been what drew her to him so powerfully. She'd had enough—more than enough; she despised the breed—of loud and domineering males. Brutes, by and large, and some of them were outright monsters.

Jeff had been none of those things. Hesitant in his manner, yes; but he'd also been more decisive than any man she'd ever met. She knew it was his gentleness and his caring nature that had led him to propose marriage to her the evening of the day they met, not lust or possessiveness.

Where was that man now? Had he gone away?

She'd known for years that her husband didn't lack courage, physical as well as moral. If there'd been any doubt of that—and she didn't think she'd ever had any—Jeff had settled the question during the siege of Amsterdam when he'd led an attack by a small boat armed only with a spar torpedo against a Spanish warship. She knew he'd proven it again on several battlefields since then.

But what she was seeing now wasn't courage, although a reputation for courage was obviously a prerequisite. What she'd been seeing since the army left Breslau was a young man—Jeff was only twenty-five, two years younger than she—who seemed to have the poise and self-confidence of Frederick Barbarossa, the legendary Holy Roman Emperor of the Middle Ages.

There was nothing flamboyant about that poise; not at all. If there was an opposite word for flamboyant—Gretchen wasn't sure; unassuming, maybe?—Jeff would personify it, just as much when he commanded an army as when he tended one of their children.

But this lack of presumption had nothing in common with diffidence or timidity. He issued orders almost instantly and with great certainty. That kept his subordinates relaxed and confident. She had no trouble understanding how valuable that would be on a battlefield.

Battlefields which, she now realized—for the first time, really—that her husband had passed through and emerged from, each time with added strength and stature. The Hangman Regiment which formed the core of the Silesian army had absolute confidence in him. So did Eric Krenz's men, who now considered themselves Hangmen as well—yes, that was the term they invariably used to identify themselves.

Bravnicar and his professional cavalrymen had needed more than a few days to come to the same assessment. It was taking the Vogtlanders and the new Silesian recruits a bit longer, but that was only because they had less experience.

By the time they reached Bytom, it was Gretchen who was feeling unsure of herself, hesitant, tentative. She hated it, but she felt herself fumbling as well. How was she to handle this?

✤ ✤ ✤

Jeff took charge of billeting the army, for which both Ulrik and Gretchen were thankful. Neither of them had much of an idea how to go about finding food and organizing shelter for almost three thousand men in a town that had a population less than a third that size.

Quite a bit less, these days. Two years earlier, Bytom had been ravaged by disease and half the population had either died or fled. The one positive aspect of that was that many of the homes in the town were vacant, so it was not necessary to expropriate anyone.

Jeff did require families to crowd into one room to allow the rest of the space in their homes to be billets for his soldiers—who were packed in more tightly than the civilians they displaced. But he also managed to calm their fears while doing so. Civilians forced to have a lot of soldiers living with them are understandably nervous. But the Hangman Regiment had a tradition, when it came to such matters, and they had no trouble imparting it to the rest of the army.

Gretchen helped, too. At Jeff's urging, she moved about every day, making herself visible to the population. Usually on horseback; that damned armor was heavy. But she'd also walk about a fair amount, since she was sturdy enough to manage that. She wasn't going to run any foot races, of course, but neither was anyone else. There was no room for it, anyway, unless you went out into the countryside.

Which no one was inclined to do, even before the first storm of winter struck less than two days after they arrived. There wouldn't have been room outside the city, anyway, unless you were prepared to travel a fair distance.

Not more than half of the army had been able to find billets in Bytom itself. It was really not a very big town. The other half had to camp outside.

Jeff handled that problem just as easily and smoothly as any others he took up. For a start, he set up a rotation system so that all of the soldiers were able to spend at least one or two nights in the relative warmth and comfort of the town's houses. The rotation was not perfectly fair, but soldiers didn't expect perfection; certainly not if they were veterans, and the newcomers looked to the veterans for guidance.

Jeff had also organized quite a good supply train for the expedition, so no one went hungry—not even the town's civilians. He'd put Krenz in charge of that. "Trust Eric to make sure there's enough food. There'll be some wine and schnapps, too," he'd told Gretchen, smiling. "That man does like his creature comforts."

In the course of the march from Breslau, Gretchen had come to a better understanding of the little saws that Jeff had told her about.

An army marches on its belly. Amateurs study tactics; professionals study logistics. He had a number of them.

She also now understood why neither he nor Krenz nor Bravnicar—the veteran officers of that polyglot army—were very worried about the final assault on Kraków. Gretchen had been disquieted when she realized that they expected it would take at least three days, probably four and possibly five, to make the march from Bytom to Kraków. By that time, she'd wondered, surely the Polish garrison would be alert and ready to defend the city.

When she'd raised that with Jeff in private, he'd reassured her that she was overly anxious.

"First off, that garrison's probably not Polish. Not mostly, anyway. Kraków's been out of the line of fire for years now. The PLC government's had more pressing places to put their better troops. The men guarding Kraków will be . . . well, not the dregs of the earth. But they certainly won't be what you'd call an elite unit.

"Secondly, they have no aircraft; no planes, no airships. That means they have to use cavalry to do reconnaissance and tell them what's headed their way. Either that or get a warning from the local residents. Third, it's winter and whatever cavalry they have is going to be reluctant to go out on patrol and will almost certainly shirk their duty when they do go out. See point one about substandard troops in the garrison. The cavalry won't be any different from the foot soldiers, so far as that goes."

"But what about—?"

He held up his hand to cut her off. "A warning brought by patriotic local residents? Fourth, it's winter and sensible peasants are going to be even less willing to venture out in the cold than Kraków's cavalry. Most of the time, the reason local residents bring warnings to cities about to be besieged is because they've been driven out of their homes or terrified into running because the approaching invaders have been committing atrocities."

For just a moment, Jeff's face had seemed twenty years older and fifty degrees colder. "That will not happen with this army. Not when the Hangmen are here. Finally, we *will* have our cavalry out on patrol ahead of the rest of the army and they *won't* be shirking their duty. So if an unlikely Polish cavalry patrol does show up—or a handful of fleeing civilians, who'll be on foot—Bravnicar and his men will deal with them."

He shrugged. "Nothing's guaranteed, not in life and even less in war. But I figure the odds are working way over in our favor."

She had a brief image of a mob of odds—they looked like squirrels, oddly enough—racing over to pile up on one side of a scale. She had to shake her head to get rid of it. "All right, I see that. But . . ."

That was the moment when it finally came into focus for her. All the while, she realized, she'd been thinking of Jeff as the eighteen-year-old boy she'd fallen in love with.

But he wasn't eighteen any longer, just as she was no longer the young woman she'd been then. Already tough and brave—she knew that for sure—but still unsure of herself in so many ways. Since . . .

The early work to create and build the Committees of Correspondence, culminating in Operation Kristallnacht. The Croat raid on the high school, which she'd played a leading role in driving off. The siege of Amsterdam. The siege of Dresden. She'd grown so much since the Battle of the Crapper outside of Badenburg. Not just grown—*expanded*. Why should not the same be true of her husband?

"You've expanded," she said, taking his head in her hands and bringing it down so she could kiss him. "I hadn't realized how much."

After she broke off the kiss and he straightened up, Jeff glanced down at his midriff. Looking a bit aggrieved, he said: "Hey, I think I've lost some weight."

The first elements of Morris Roth's Grand Army of the Sunrise showed up three days after Ulrik's army arrived in Bytom.

"My apologies for being delayed," General von Mercy said to the prince and Jeff, after getting off his horse. They had waited for him a short distance from the town. Looking around at the countryside, von Mercy added: "Judging by the snowfall, the storm was worse—quite a bit worse—on the route we took."

That wasn't surprising. The Bohemian army had had a shorter distance to march—Bytom was only sixty-five miles from Ostrava, whereas the Silesian forces had come almost twice that far. But the Silesians had an easy march down a well-established trade route in comparatively flat country. Von Mercy's forces had come across the Sudetes Mountains.

"No matter," said Prince Ulrik. "In some ways, it's an advantage since"—he spread his hands apologetically— "the town is so crowded there are no billets left and your men will have to camp in the open."

Von Mercy smiled. "Which, after a few days, would lead to grumbling and complaint. But as it is, we won't be staying here very long."

He cocked an eye at Colonel Higgins. Not Ulrik, which was perhaps undiplomatic, but von Mercy understood quite well who was really commanding the Silesian army. "How soon?" he asked.

"As soon as the Air Force arrives."

Higgins turned to his left and pointed into the distance at something too far away for von Mercy to make it out clearly. It looked like an open field with a few newly built huts off to one side. "There's the airfield. We just finished it last night. Eddie Junker should be arriving by midafternoon."

He lowered his hand. "It's about as primitive an airfield as you could ask for, but it should do the trick."

Do the trick. Von Mercy groped at the meaning. He was in the process of learning Amideutsch, and was finding the experience to be contradictory. The language—German dialect, call it whatever you wanted— was quite easy to learn in some respects. He appreciated the practically nonexistent declensions and simplified conjugations. But it was difficult in others. The mix of Low German words among the base Middle German was random and the horde of American loanwords posed a challenge, especially the slang.

The young American officer must have sensed his uncertainty. "It's good enough for the job at hand," he explained.

"Ah." Von Mercy nodded. "So we will have superb reconnaissance throughout the assault."

"Best you could ask for." Higgins held up a cautioning finger. "As long as the weather's fair. The planes we have can't handle bad weather or bad visibility. 'Flying by instruments' amounts to the pilot wetting his finger and sticking it out of the window."

The meaning of the last sentence was also unclear to von Mercy, but he thought he grasped the gist of it.

"In any event," Higgins continued, "we think it would be best if we only used the airplane on the last day. If we have it buzzing over Kraków for several days, that might alert the garrison that something's up."

Buzzing. Something's up. But, again, von Mercy thought he grasped the essence.

"That makes sense," he said. "But I ask again: How soon will we begin the march on Kraków?"

Higgins exchanged a glance with the prince. With a slight nod of his head, Ulrik indicated he should answer the question.

"You'll need to rest your troops," said Higgins. "For how long?"

"A day should be sufficient." Von Mercy looked around again. "Staying here longer than that, in these primitive conditions, will grow tiring quickly. Best we get to Kraków as soon as possible."

"Day after tomorrow, then. Bright and early."

Bright and early. Was it impossible for Americans to speak plainly?

Gretchen was in a very passionate mood that night, so the army's commander got less rest than most of his soldiers. He did not complain, however.

The next morning, he rose before she did to brew them some tea. When he came back into their bedroom he was carrying two cups. They had a separate room, unlike almost anyone else in Bytom. Gretchen had insisted on that, not in order to exalt her status but because she had foreseen the events of the night before. More precisely, she'd planned them herself.

He handed her one of the cups. "I'd better get out there and see how everything's coming along."

It was still dark outside. "That's not true. You have good subordinate officers. They can handle things for a while yet. Take off your clothes and get back into bed."

He smiled, set his cup down, and began carrying out the Lady Protector's commands. "Yes, dear," he said.

Chapter 18

Žilina
Royal Hungary
Austrian-Hungarian Empire

With a disgusted look on her face, Denise turned away from her examination of the disabled wagon and looked to the north, following the line of the Kysuca River whose right bank they'd followed to get here. Then she looked to the south, where the Kysuca flowed into the larger Váh River. The town of Žilina was somewhere nearby, across the Váh, but she couldn't see it from where she was standing.

Finally, she looked across the Kysuca at the only prominent structure anywhere in sight. It was a castle, built in the Renaissance style but with roots that were obviously much older, She could see the medieval foundations that were still in place.

"Well, this sucks," she pronounced to no one is particular. Then, pointing at the castle, she asked: "Does anybody know who owns that pile of pretension? Sorry, I meant to say 'palace.' Or is 'castle' the proper protocol here in—where are we again?"

Lukasz smiled. Denise irritated a lot of people with her teenager's *I don't give a damn what you think* attitude, but he didn't mind. Sometimes, when the target of the attitude was someone who deserved it, he found her quite entertaining.

Noelle didn't smile, because she knew from long experience that would just encourage Denise. But she'd been in some hairy situations with the girl and thought very highly of her. All things considered.

"We're still in Royal Hungary," she said. "The part that Austria kept, I mean. The Bohemian part"—she pointed at the Váh River—"starts on the other side of this river. In this stretch, anyway. The border runs further east once you go south a ways."

Nobody challenged her. That would have been rather stupid, since she'd been part of the negotiations between Austria and Bohemia that had produced the division of Royal Hungary.

"So that castle—palace, whatever—is Austrian, right?"

"No, it's Hungarian. Austria and Hungary are politically united mostly because they have the same king. They're not the same country."

Denise frowned. "So what's your official position here? Countess of Homonna or Mrs. Drugeth, aka wife of the Austrian emperor's best buddy?"

"I am not 'Mrs. Drugeth' and you know it, Denise." The custom of wives taking the surname of their husband was not followed in central Europe—or in most of

Europe, for that matter. In this historical era, that was a British custom.

"As to the question itself, I'm not sure. It's quite possible—even likely—that whichever nobleman owns that castle—yes, that's the right term in this neck of the woods—isn't in residence. He and his family might have packed up and gone to Linz in order to get Emperor Ferdinand's assurance that they won't be fed to the Bohemian maw."

"Only way to find out is to ask," said Lukasz. "So now the question becomes, where can we get a boat? Luckily the river hasn't frozen over yet."

Getting the boat took two and a half days, but most of that time was spent loading everything onto the boat after they made an agreement with the owner that he would transport them down the Váh to the town of Trenčín. There, he assured them, they would find a wainwright with the skills and materials to repair the broken axle on their wagon.

They wouldn't find him in Žilina, he explained, because he and his family had all moved to Trenčín—as had quite a few other of Žilina's inhabitants. Why? Here the bargeman went on a long peroration on the subject of Bohemian vices as compared to Hungarian virtues, and concluded with a not-so-veiled criticism of the feckless new emperor who had handed over Hungary's ancient sacred soil to the aforementioned wretched Bohemians.

"The old emperor, Ferdinand II—there was a stout fellow!—never would have agreed to such a thing," he concluded. The expression on his face could have been used by an artist for a painting titled *Lugubrious Man*.

Denise thought it was pretty funny, especially when Noelle made the mistake of trying to reason with the man.

"But that doesn't make any sense," she said. "Žilina is on the west bank of the Váh, which is clearly established as the border. Trenčín is supposed to remain in Austria-Hungary even though it's on the other side of the river. If they were really that worried about it, they should have stayed here."

"Exactly what I told them!" exclaimed the barge owner, looking more lugubrious than ever. He pointed to the east, where the central tower of Budatín Castle was still visible. "It's their fault. Those cowardly Suňogs!"

Here he went on another peroration, this one on the decrepit state of the Suňogs family who had owned Budatín Castle since their ancestor Gašpar Suňogs—there was a stout fellow!—had bought it almost two hundred years earlier. Instead of remaining in the castle to fend off the schemes of the dastardly Wallenstein—Denise thought he might veer off here into another tirade on the subject of Bohemians and their vices, but he managed to stay on topic—the wretched Suňogs—all of them! every last one!—had fled to Linz to cower under the supposed shelter provided by the new emperor—the same one who lost Vienna to the stinking Turks.

Indignation was now added to lugubriosity. Denise thought Artemisia Gentileschi, the great artist who'd painted Denise's own (definitely not lugubrious nor indignant) portrait on the nose cone of Eddie's airplane, would have had a field day with this guy.

Country Bumpkin, Beset by Woes.

Eventually he wound down. Noelle left off her attempts to reason with the man, for which Denise was thankful. A little rural lamentation was okay, but it wore out its welcome pretty quickly.

Fortunately, the barge was big enough to carry all their belongings except the horses. Those would have to be taken in tether by the Slovene cavalrymen. Also fortunately, whoever designed the wagon had shrewdly made the big cabin where the passengers rode detachable from the frame, so it could be hauled separately.

Unfortunately, Noelle and Lukasz got paranoid about what Noelle called "operational security" so Denise was forced to ride in the cabin on board the barge instead of riding a horse alongside the river. Apparently no self-respecting Polish nobleman would let his beautiful young leman ride a horse under these conditions. Never mind that if the delicate twit couldn't even ride a horse she wasn't likely to handle her official function all that well either.

But Denise's reasoned logic—*I'm too fragile to ride a horse but not too fragile to have that pile of bone and muscle*—here she pointed an accusing finger at Lukasz—*ride me?*—failed in its purpose. Into the cabin aboard the barge she was required to go.

Granted, the cabin was both more comfortable than a saddle, and a slow-moving barge on a placid river kept her a lot warmer than she'd have been on horseback.

"As long as the river doesn't freeze over and strand us out here," she warned Noelle. She looked out the window of the cabin at the very cold-looking river. "Which could happen any moment, you know."

"Denise, a river this wide is not going to freeze over before we get to Trenčín, even if the temperature drops like a stone."

"We're in the Little Ice Age, remember?"

"It's the *Little* Ice Age, not the Instant Ice Age. You're just grouchy because you don't like the barge owner's singing."

"Sure don't. Are we there yet?"

Aboard a barge on the Váh River
Between Žilina and Trenčín

It took four days to get from Žilina to Trenčín. Even though, as Denise complained bitterly, it was only fifty miles or so.

"Jesus H. Christ. How does a barge move this slowly? Because the stupid barge guy keeps pulling over and stopping."

"He's letting the people on horseback catch up with us. Remember them? Our friends and companions?"

Denise knew that perfectly well. She was just in a bad mood.

Which was made even worse when Noelle leaned over and patted her under the chin. "Now, dear—cheer up. If Artemisia Gentileschi were here she could do another great portrait of you. Only we couldn't call it *Steady Girl*, we'd have to call it . . . Help me out here. *Gloomy Gamin? Bummed Out Babe?* How about *Melancholy Maiden?*"

"I am not a maiden!"

"Well, that's true. Back to the drawing board. I know!

Artemisia could call it *Discontented and Downhearted, Though Only Eighteen*."

"Nineteen!"

Trenčín
Royal Hungary
Austrian-Hungarian Empire

The barge owner proved to be correct on at least one count. There was indeed a wainwright in Trenčín who had the skills and materials to repair the broken axle. And the sons and apprentices to do the work.

The problem now became what the prospective customer lacked, which was a suitable form of payment.

Noelle—Lukasz, officially, but everyone soon dispensed with that formality—began by dickering with the wainwright, based on the assumption they'd be dealing in Austrian currency. Since they were, after all, in Austria.

"That money can't be trusted anymore," said the wainwright, shaking his head. "It's probably adulterated. If the old emperor was still on the throne, I'd take it. But with this new one ... Who gave part of Austria to the dirty Bohemians and let the stinking Turks take Vienna?"

He gave the coins in Noelle's hand a look of great disdain. "I don't think so. For all I know, a month from now that money won't be good for anything except skipping it off the water for amusement. Very slight amusement which ends very rapidly. No. I need payment in something I can trust."

Noelle instantly decided that offering Bohemian currency was inadvisable. So she offered USE dollars.

"That stuff is paper," sneered the wainwright. "No, I want *money*. Real money. Gold or silver."

They had silver other than the reichsthalers, although not gold, but Noelle was reluctant to part with it. They didn't know yet who they might have to bribe once they got to Vienna, and the likelihood that Ottoman officials would accept payment in Austrian, Bohemian or USE currency seemed . . .

Low.

But, in the end, she had to relent. The only alternative, which was raised by the wainwright's wife, was that she pay them with the large and obviously expensive earrings she was wearing.

That, she refused to do. First, because they were a wedding gift from Janos. Secondly, because they didn't know yet who they might have to bribe once they got to Vienna, and the likelihood that Ottoman officials would accept payment in fine jewelry was . . .

High.

Long before the dickering was completed, Denise was back in the cabin, which was more comfortable and warmer. Well, not as cold. The cabin had been unloaded from the barge and was now sitting on the dock. Happily, the dock at Trenčín had a functional if crude hoist which they'd been able to use for the purpose of unloading the cabin. At Žilina, they'd had to load the cabin onto the deck of the barge by hand, which had not been a lot of fun.

For other people. Denise hadn't participated because she'd suddenly realized that maintaining her cover identity as a Polish nobleman's squeeze precluded her being able to do manual labor in public. There might be Turkish spies watching them. Not likely, but who knew for sure? Best not to take chances.

Lukasz joined her not long afterward. She wasn't entirely pleased at his presence. On the positive side, she'd have someone to talk to. On the negative side, she was holding a bit of a grudge against the hussar because in some indefinable way she figured he was partly to blame for the fact that she had to pose as his slut.

Denise was not stupid; far from it. She knew perfectly well that blaming Lukasz for the situation was illogical. But she had a teenager's conviction that a girl should never let logic get in the way of a good grudge.

They talked about the weather. On the one hand, Denise thought that was kind of pointless since the forecast ran from "cold and miserable" to "freezing cold and really miserable." On the other hand, the topic suited her mood, which ran from "grumpy" to "sullen."

Eventually, Noelle struck a bargain with the wainwright and fruitful labor began. Say this much about the region's inhabitants—they all seemed to be on the morose side, but they weren't incompetent. The bargeman had gotten them down here intact, and the wainwright got the wagon fixed in a reasonable amount of time.

Unfortunately, "a reasonable amount of time," given that they didn't start until midafternoon, meant that the ambassadorial mission had to stay over in Trenčín for two nights. Most of the party—all of the cavalrymen escorting them, the teamsters and Jakub—camped out in the town square. They tried to wrangle space in the Rathaus but the town council stoutly refused unless they paid in silver, which Noelle stoutly refused to do.

Then, when they started setting up their camp in the square, Trenčín's officials began making noises about payment. But at that point the escort started getting surly and the town council (wisely) decided that having a dozen really surly cavalrymen in town wasn't worth what they were asking for. They were Slovenians, to make things worse. Everybody knew that folk was barely civilized and prone to violent outbursts.

Lukasz, Noelle and Denise, however, had to rent a room in one of the town's taverns. They were charged what Noelle considered an outrageous price, but at least the tavern keeper was willing to accept Austrian reichsthalers.

The worst of it was that the three of them had to share a bed. Lukasz stoutly offered to sleep on the floor, but Noelle nixed that idea.

"You never know. There might be Turkish spies about. If they spot the supposed head of the mission sleeping by himself on the floor, our whole cover is blown."

"How would they see into this room?" Denise demanded. She pointed a finger at the room's only window, which was small and covered with a curtain. "Even if something—like what? a brisk wind in *here*? Which I don't think has seen a waft of fresh air in years—blew the curtains aside, so what? I'll bet you dollars for donuts that glass is so lousy you couldn't see through it anyway."

She marched over and drew the curtain aside. "See?"

The window panes were, indeed, suitable for letting light in but that was about it.

"I don't care," said Noelle. "I'm not taking any chances."

And that was that. Noelle didn't look like it, but Denise had been with her in a lot of hairy situations and knew the woman well. She had a steel spine.

So, they slept in the bed, all three of them. Gallantly, Lukasz took the worst spot, crowded up against the wall. Denise hoped Noelle would accept the middle spot, but, as she feared, Ms. Superagent insisted that if Polish spies spotted the arrangement they'd know something was amiss. What sort of arrogant, self-centered Polish high nobleman would sleep next to his wife instead of his concubine?

It's not fair!

But she made the complaint only to herself. Denise couldn't stand people who whined at every little thing. Having to crowd into a bed between a hussar who'd been perfectly courteous to her and a woman whom she admired and respected was hardly the worst thing that had ever happened to her. And being only nineteen, she was sure and certain that lots of worse stuff—way worse— was bound to happen to her in the future. She wasn't the carefree, happy-go-lucky numbskull she'd been at the age of eighteen.

Still, it sucked. Lukasz snored. So did Eddie, but Eddie's snore wasn't too bad. Sometimes it was almost cute. The hussar snored exactly the way you'd expect a hussar to snore.

But eventually morning arrived, and before the sun

had risen very far they were back on track. Their teeth rattling as the wagon made its way down a road that was possibly the worst excuse for a "road" that Denise had ever seen.

Her mood fluctuated between "dolorous" and "aggrieved." This was supposed to have been an *adventure*.

"Are we there yet?" she whined.

Chapter 19

Mark Ellis stared at the woman who'd just sat down across the table from him. His jaw was sagging. Jozef, who'd brought her there, smiled a little at the sight of the man ogling Christin as he took his own seat. If Ellis were a down-timer, Jozef would assume he was just ogling a beautiful woman, too rude or too stupid to realize that the man with her might take offense. Or that *she* might—which, with Christin, could get ugly. Once Jozef had met her, he'd had no trouble figuring out where Denise Beasley got her ability to become instantly belligerent—what Americans called "going to Defcon 1"—if she thought a man was behaving improperly toward her. Whether that was genetic or a mother's example remained unclear. Jozef suspected it was both.

But there was no danger of such a ruckus on this

occasion. Christin's reaction to Ellis' bug-eyed stare was a soft chuckle.

"Surprised to see me, Mark?"

Ellis squeezed his eyes shut for a moment. When he reopened them, they had resumed their normal circumference and protuberance.

"Holy shit," he said. "Is that *you*, Christin?"

"Do I look like a ghost?"

"Uh . . . no. But what are you *doing* here?"

She jabbed a thumb at Jozef. "The short answer is that I'm with him. The long answer gets pretty long, and Jozef can probably explain it better than I can."

Ellis now transferred his stare to Jozef. "You're with . . . ? Oh." He closed his mouth and swallowed a bit. "I was sorry about Buster, Christin. I didn't know him real well—or you, for that matter—but he always seemed like a decent guy to me, regardless of—ah—"

She chuckled again. "Regardless of his reputation? He wasn't a bully, Mark. That was the second thing I noticed about him. I liked that. Here was a guy who could beat the crap out of just about anybody but he never felt any need to prove it. You left him and his alone, and he'd do the same for you."

Now curious, Jozef asked: "What was the *first* thing you noticed about him?"

"He was really exciting." She gave Jozef a sly, sidelong look. "That was the first thing I noticed about you, too. The truth is, when it comes to men, I'm an adrenaline junkie."

Caspar now spoke. "Mark, who is this woman? Is she . . . ?"

"Yeah, she's an up-timer. Christin George. She's the widow of Buster Beasley. He got killed during the Dreeson Incident—although not before he took down a whole bunch of guys himself."

Caspar and Czesław now spent a few seconds staring at her.

"How *well* did you know her?" Czesław asked abruptly.

"Not real well. She and Buster were ten years older than me, and I'd already graduated from high school before their daughter Denise started, so there was no connection that way, either. But Grantville is—well, was, it's not any longer—a small town where you know almost everybody."

The underlying import of the question finally registered on him, and he shook his head. "It doesn't matter how well I knew her, Czesław. She's who she says she is—which means Jozef's story has got to be true. I can't see any other way to explain why she'd be with him. And why would she be lying?"

He placed his head in his hands and looked down at the table. Caspar started to say something but Czesław placed a restraining hand on his forearm. As was true of Jozef himself, Czesław understood that Ellis was considering something and he wanted to hear what it was.

After perhaps ten seconds, Mark raised his head and gave Jozef a very direct look that bordered on belligerence. "I want out of here," he said. "And I'm saying it in front of these guys"—here a little jerk of the head indicated the two Polish radio operators—"because I think they want to get out of here too."

Jozef looked at Czesław and Caspar. "Is he right?"

Caspar nodded immediately. "Yes. Czesław and I have

been talking about it. Neither of us has family here in Poznań and we don't like the way things are looking for us."

"Our guess is that sooner or later whoever murdered the grand hetman is likely to go after us," added Czesław.

"Why?" asked Christin. She wasn't challenging the statement, just indicating her curiosity. "Why would they suspect you of anything—and what could you do anyway? You're just radio operators."

Jozef answered the question before either of the two men to whom it had been addressed could speak.

"That's exactly why they *would* be targeted. Whatever Czesław and Caspar might or might not do—and they are well known to be my uncle's men—they were the two people in the world who could spread an accusation all over Poland. Anywhere in the continent." His chuckle was dry and had no humor in it at all. "I'd say they need to get out of Poznań as soon as they can. Which brings us back to you, Mark Ellis, because unless I miss my guess you have a plan for how to do it."

"I wouldn't call it a 'plan,'" said Ellis. "It's just an idea. The big problem with escaping Poznań isn't the guards at the gates, so much—some of those guys would sell their mother for a big enough bribe."

Czesław's chuckle had no more humor in it than Jozef's. "He's right about that. I can name four—no, five—guards I know would do it."

"More like a dozen," chimed in Caspar. He nodded at the American engineer. "But what he's going to tell you is that once you get out of whichever gate you choose, you'll then have a horde of hussars chasing after you. Even worse, you'll have some Cossacks in the mix."

"Exactly," said Ellis. "And whatever else you want to say about the smelly bastards, Cossacks can ride like nobody's business. You wouldn't get two miles before they brought you down."

"That depends," said Jozef. He now looked at Caspar and Czesław. "What's your best guess? How many angry Koniecpolski partisans are there in the city? Hussars, I'm talking about. And by 'angry' I mean ones who are willing to break out of Poznań and ride right over anyone who gets in their way."

Caspar and Czesław glanced at each other. "Maybe a hundred, hundred and twenty," said Caspar.

"More than that," said Czesław. "But not a lot more. A hundred and fifty, I'd say."

Jozef nodded. "And how many hussars would really press the pursuit?"

Again, the two radio operators exchanged a glance. "Not a lot more. Two hundred. Three hundred, maybe? Most of the Polish troops in Poznań thought highly of the grand hetman, and we're not by any means the only ones here who think he was murdered. But . . ."

He shrugged. "You know how most people are—and hussars aren't much different. As long as they're not directly affected, they'll look the other way."

"But they also won't move heaven and earth to capture other soldiers who broke out of the city. Not for long, anyway."

"Well . . ." Another exchange of glances took place. Jozef was beginning to wonder if these two fellows were joined at the hip, at least mentally speaking.

"Well . . ." That was Czesław, echoing Caspar's

hesitation. "Here's the thing, Jozef. It depends where they think we're going. The one thing almost all hussars are agreed upon"—he gave Christin an apologetic glance—"is that the USE is a nation of—never mind that. A nation that can't be trusted, let's put it that way.

"So if they think we're defecting to Torstensson, they'll get really pissed. A lot of them will keep a pursuit going, right up to the USE's lines—and those will be miles away because the only gate we've got a chance of escaping from is the north gate. That's about where the Swedes ended their fortifications, but it's also where we have a lot of troops gathered."

"Which means there's no way we could escape except by heading east once we got out of the gate," said Caspar. "And then if you wanted to defect to the USE you'd have to ride halfway around the city. And far out from it, too, or you'd get caught by a sortie."

Czesław shook his head. "It doesn't matter, anyway." He used a quick motion of thumb and forefinger to indicate himself and his partner. "We won't agree to it. Neither of us will defect to the damn Germans."

He gave Christin a little nod. "Meaning no offense."

She grinned in response. "No problem. I'm not German, remember?"

From the somewhat sour expression on Czesław's face, it was obvious that he considered that a pretty flimsy distinction. *No, you're not German—you're one of those damned Americans who gave the Germans what they needed to overrun a good part of Poland.*

But he left it unsaid.

Jozef was now looking at Mark Ellis. "In case you're

wondering, I'm with them. Part of my agreement with Richter—that's Gretchen Richter, yes, *that* Gretchen Richter—when she let me out of prison—"

"You were imprisoned?" That came from Caspar.

Jozef shook his head. "It's a long story which I can tell you some other time. The short version is that I was exposed as the grand hetman's spy, they arrested me, and then they let me go after my uncle was murdered because I told them I wasn't going to support the king or the Sejm. But I also wasn't going to go over to the USE. That was the deal we made—me and my friend Lukasz both. That's Lukasz Opalinski, by the way. You know him, I'm sure."

"Yes," said Caspar. Czesław nodded.

"What we are doing instead is giving our support to the revolutionaries gathered around Lukasz's brother Krzysztof and some other people."

"The ones in Galicia? The ones who declared themselves a konfederacja?"

"Yes, them."

He looked back at Ellis. "So you have to understand that. If we break out of here with you, we're not taking you back to the USE Army. We'd be taking you to Galicia. After that . . ." He shrugged. "If you can work out a way to get back home, we won't stop you. But keep in mind that Galicia is a long way from the USE."

"What is it?" asked Ellis. "About five hundred miles, thereabouts?"

"Not that far. You'd only have to get to Breslau, since the USE now controls Lower Silesia. Say . . . four hundred miles. Maybe a bit less."

"Might as well be the moon," said Ellis. Then, with a

shrug: "It's still better than being trapped here. Okay, here's my idea. It's not really a plan. If we take the APC, we can travel faster than cavalry can pursue us."

"Not really," said Christin. "Over open country, those coal trucks can't do better than ten, maybe fifteen miles an hour. The roads aren't much better—and don't argue with me; I had the joy of traveling on them to get here. A horse can travel faster than that."

"Yes, but not for very long," said Jozef. "Especially not if it's carrying a hussar in his armor. You might have to fend them off for a while, but after a short time the cavalry would start falling away. And what's a better mount to fend off cavalry than an armored coal truck with gunports?" His eyes narrowed. "Assuming we can find hussars who aren't so narrow-minded they don't know how to fire a gun."

Czesław grinned. "No hussar is *that* narrow-minded, Jozef."

His partner was less sanguine on the matter. "You might be surprised. What about Andruss Kozłowski—or Mieczysław Kaczmarek?"

Czesław scowled at him. "Excuse me. I should have been more precise. No hussar who would go with us in the first place would be that narrow-minded."

Caspar nodded judiciously. "That, I will accept. But, Jozef, that still leaves a problem. I've seen that APC. As big as it is, there can't possibly be enough room in it for all the hussars who'll come with us to fit inside. Especially since at least two of the ones I can think of who'll want to join us have families they won't be willing to leave behind."

"How big are the families?" Christin asked.

Caspar though about it for a moment. "Fiedor and his

wife have . . . three children. I think. Hriniec's wife died two years ago and he's only got one son, who's about five years old. But there's something wrong with the boy. His mind is . . . Well, he thinks slowly. And he looks funny."

The radio operator stretched his eyes with his fingers. "Like this."

"He's got Down syndrome," Christin said immediately. "But what's his disposition like? That's really what matters."

"Oh, he's a nice boy," said Czesław. "Quite cheerful almost all of the time and not disobedient."

"In other words, he won't be a problem." Christin nodded and turned toward Jozef. "We can fit the families inside the APC. Four kids and one mother to look after them shouldn't be a problem."

"Yes, but what about the hussars themselves?" asked Caspar. "If they can't keep up with the APC, won't the pursuers fall on them?"

Jozef had been thinking ahead and had already come to a conclusion on that matter. "I don't really think it's that big a problem, especially if we break out of the city early in the morning. This has been a long siege and Torstensson's troops haven't pressed any attacks on the city for quite a while. At least, that was the situation when I was here last. Has anything changed?"

Caspar and Czesław both shook their heads. Seeing that, Jozef displayed a derisive, lopsided smile.

"Right. So, that early in the morning—we're talking just before daybreak—how many hussars are likely to be alert and awake? And without hangovers?"

Caspar and Czesław both smiled at that. Their smiles were as lopsided as Jozef's own.

"Three, maybe?" That came from Czesław.

"That's what I figured," said Jozef. "By the time a pursuit gets organized and underway, we'll have a good head start. By the time they catch up—and it won't be soon—their horses will be tired. More tired than ours because we won't have been pushing them as much. And a lot of them will have fallen by the wayside. So then we pick a good spot for an ambush, we have one pitched battle with the APC as an anchor, and I think that will be all we need."

"Sounds good to me," said Mark. "Although I admit this isn't something I specialize in."

Czesław transferred the lopsided smile to him. "Who does? Unless my knowledge is a lot worse than I think it is, this will be the first pursuit of an armored motor vehicle by cavalry in Polish history."

"Anybody's history," said Jozef. "That's another advantage we'll have. It's not as if the commanders of the garrison will have a contingency plan to deal with it."

"What's a contingency plan?" asked Caspar.

"It's what your mother did every time she made hot soup for you," said Christin, "in case you spilled some in your lap. She knew how to handle it right away. Trust me on this one."

"Ah. A mother's foresight. Contingency plan." The lopsided grin came back. "No, I'm quite certain the garrison commanders will not have one for this."

"Okay, then." Jozef planted his hands on the table, preparing to rise.

But Mark had one last issue to raise.

"What about Tarnowski?" he asked. "What do we do about him?"

"Who is Tarnowski?"

"Walenty Tarnowski," Czesław provided. "He's the mechanical genius from the university in Kraków who figured out how the APC worked. He's been trying to get the authorities to approve his plan to build one of our own, but so far they've turned him down."

"'Turned him down,'" said Caspar. "More like ridiculed him for a daydreaming dolt and told him to stop pestering them."

Jozef looked at Ellis. "What's your opinion?"

"Let me talk to him. I think I might be able to persuade him to join us."

"That's a real risk," said Jozef. "What if he runs to the authorities?"

"That's . . . not like Walenty," said Mark.

"Ha! That's one way to put it." Caspar turned to Jozef. "Tarnowski is one of those fellows who thinks he's much smarter than anyone around him."

"Which he probably is," added Czesław.

Caspar nodded. "You're probably right. But the point is that he's not likely to betray us to people he considers imbeciles. Even if he refuses our offer."

"That's what I think, too," said Ellis. "But it doesn't matter, because unless we can get Walenty to go along we won't have the APC to begin with. He's the only one who can start the engine."

Jozef squinted at him. "You're an American. Surely you know how to—what do you call it?—hotrod the engine? Something like that."

"Hotwire," said Christin. "If he doesn't know how to do it, I do. Buster taught me the trick."

Jozef looked at her. "You?"

It was a day for lopsided, derisive smiles, it seemed. Christin now bestowed one on him. "Don't look so surprised. I told you I'm an adrenaline junkie when it comes to men. Buster used to take me on joyrides when we were dating."

"And 'joyrides' are . . . ?"

"Not what you're thinking. Boy, have you got a dirty mind."

Mark interrupted. "Doesn't matter," he repeated. "I know how to hotwire a car too. But it won't do a bit of good because Walenty takes the battery out every night and keeps it in his room."

"He distrusts you that much?"

"He doesn't distrust *me* at all. He says hussars are all a pack of thieves and they'd steal the battery just to sell it so they could keep getting drunk."

Jozef rose. "All right. See what you can do. In the meantime, I will start talking to some of the hussars I know best. We meet again—here—in . . . one week?"

Nods all around.

"We're off, then." Jozef extended a hand to help Christin to her feet, which she didn't need at all but made no objection to using. Like her daughter, Christin's feminist attitudes were idiosyncratic.

Once they got out of the noisy tavern, they linked arms.

"I still want to know what a 'joyride' is," said Jozef.

"No, you don't. You want to figure out one that suits *you*."

"Well . . . "

Chapter 20

Kraków, official capital of Poland
Actual capital of Lesser Poland

Gretchen wasn't normally all that interested in the technical aspects of warfare, however keenly she might pay attention to their practical results. But despite that usual indifference, this time she found herself engrossed in what was happening.

Why? The simplest explanation might be that this time it was her husband overseeing the technical aspects, and she was always interested in her husband. As was usually the case with simple explanations, Gretchen was partial to them.

"What are they doing, and why are they doing it?" she asked, looking at the crew handling the three-and-a-half-inch mortar. More precisely, since the mortar itself had been set off to the side, the crew was handling a heavy wooden platform about eight feet long by four feet wide with some holes drilled in it—one in the center and one in each corner.

The same crew had spent the day before digging up and leveling the ground upon which the platform now rested. That had been hard work—so hard that Jeff had worried that his whole plan might have to be scrapped. The same prolonged cold spell that had frozen over the Vistula and made it possible for their army to get quickly into position outside of Kraków had also frozen the ground. Digging into it, which would have been easy at most times of the year, had been just this side of impossible.

But, they'd managed. The one thing that had made it doable was that the terrain the scouts found to set up the mortar battery was already very flat and level. It had been more a matter of scraping soil and filling in some low places than what people normally thought of as "digging."

She and Jeff were standing in the center of the battery's position, just far enough back that they weren't getting in the way of anyone who was actually working. Looking in either direction, Gretchen could see half a dozen such level spaces on either side of her. In all of those positions, the mortar crews were now checking to make sure that the wooden platforms were indeed level, and doing whatever was needed to make them so.

"I'll start with why they're doing it," Jeff said. "There's one big problem with my plan."

He paused for a moment, thinking of how to best explain himself. While he did so, Gretchen found herself a bit amused by her husband's unthinking use of the term "my plan." Officially—this would certainly be how the historical accounts would report the matter—the plan was Prince Ulrik's. He being, of course, the commander of the entire army that had marched here from Silesia. But in the real world, Jeff had been the one to develop the plan, with the help of his immediate subordinates and the leaders of the Bohemian forces who had arrived two days earlier, just a few hours after the Silesian army took its positions. Ulrik's contribution—Morris Roth's also—was just to observe and let the real military professionals go about their work without interference. Gretchen had been there and done the same.

"The problem," Jeff continued, "is that everything has to unfold pretty quickly. Essentially, we're laying a trap for the city's garrison. We'll start with the half dozen mortars that we'll move into position during the night, not more than three hundred yards from the gate we'll be seizing." He pointed to the east. "You can't see it from here—or any part of the city except the castle on Wawel Hill down by the river—because of that rise in front of us. We need that rise to hide"—here he swept his hand around—"this much bigger battery of mortars. We're about five hundred yards from the gate here."

Gretchen visualized what he was describing. It seemed simple enough, but . . . "Can you reach the gates from here with these mortars?"

"Oh, yeah. We're well within range. If we were using black powder propellant, we wouldn't be. But we've got enough nitrocellulose donuts for about one thousand rounds, and those are quite capable of firing the bombs that far. Although, I'd like to use as few of them as possible. It's hard to get replacements for them—especially out here, this far into Poland—and it's even harder to get the RDX we use for the bombs themselves."

She decided to forego asking any questions about the way the mortars worked and the logistics involved. She could find that out from Eric Krenz later, if she felt it necessary.

"All right," she said. "So why is speed essential?" She smiled. "Other than the fact you're always going on and on about the central, metaphysical—almost sublime—nature of speed in warfare."

"Smart ass. The reason it's important is because we want to get into Kraków quickly. And the reason *that's* important is mostly political, not military. Which is your bailiwick so you can cut it out with the jokes about lowbrow soldiers. We want to do as little damage to the city as possible because we're going to want to billet all our troops in it for the duration of the winter—"

"That's a military issue."

"*And* we don't want the city's population to be furious with us." He cleared his throat. "Seeing as how you and Krzysztof and Red—God knows who else and I don't want to know—have settled on the grandiose scheme of turning the Galician Democratic Assembly into the Lesser Poland Democratic Assembly. With Kraków as the capital."

"Actually, the scheme is a lot more grandiose than that. What Opalinski and Zaborowsky and Sybolt and those around them—I'm just what you might call a consultant—really want is to take over the whole Commonwealth. But in order to do that they have to seem like a serious alternative to King Władysław and they can't do that if they've just got Galicia. That's why they want Kraków."

"Politics, like I said. To get back to the point, we've got to lure the garrison—a goodly part of it, anyway—to make a sortie. The way we do that is by positioning a small battery where they can see it along with what looks like a small infantry force, not too far from the gate. Then we start lofting mortar bombs into the city. We'll walk them back toward the gate as we get the proper range. We think the mortars will come as a complete surprise to them. They have been used in the war against Poland, but that was in the north. Whatever accounts have made their way down here aren't likely to be very accurate and they're certainly not going to be long on the details."

Gretchen could see the logic. "So they'll be frightened but seem to be dealing with only a small force, so . . ."

"They'll come charging out to destroy them. Or at least drive them off. And that's when we hit them with a double whammy." He stretched his hands out in both directions, indicating the line of a dozen mortars. "We start with a barrage that lands right on top of them. That kind of mortar fire hitting men out in the open is devastating—*if* it's on target."

"I can see that." She'd heard the plan laid out in the conference, but having it explained again, here where she could see everything, was bringing it into focus. "And the second part of the 'whammy,' as you call it?"

Now Jeff pointed to the north. "There's a good-sized woods up there—more in the way of a little forest. General von Mercy has been moving his cavalry into position, where they can't be seen by the garrison. Once the barrage starts, he and his cavalrymen will charge the gate. It's pretty clear and level ground once you get out in the open. That'll take a while, getting out from those trees, but the first elements of the cavalry should reach the gate within four or five minutes. We'll stop firing when they're three hundred yards out. They can cover that final distance in less than a minute. We figure they'll be able to seize and hold the gate easily. At which point we start moving the rest of the army in."

He waved his hand behind him. "They'll be positioned around here. Even the infantry can cross a mile within fifteen minutes, at a fast march. Twenty, at the outside. We don't think the garrison in there is anywhere nearly good enough to get themselves reorganized in time to set up a defensive line inside the city. Especially because most of the cavalry will be rushing in to seize the huge square in the middle of the city. They'll be at some risk because cavalry always is when it's operating inside the confines of a city. But they only have to hold the square for half an hour, which we're pretty sure they can manage given that we expect the garrison not to have been able to reorganize itself in that short a period of time."

"Why is half an hour—"

"Because by then—even sooner, I think; Kraków's a pretty small city—we can have at least one battalion of the Hangman Regiment reach the square also. With the rifles they have now, they *won't* be at great risk, especially because they can fort up inside the town hall and the Cloth Hall. If the cavalry's coming under bad fire because they're in the open, we can pull them out of the square at that point. But I don't think it'll come to that. Once we hold the central square and the two big buildings in the middle of it with both infantry and cavalry, we'll control the whole city. Even a top-flight garrison would surrender at that point."

"I still don't see why you're so concerned about speed."

"I'm concerned because once the sortie comes out of the gate we've got to start hitting them with mortar fire right away. Or they'll overrun the small force we set up to bait them. And the problem there is that"—he nodded at the nearest mortar—"these things are not what you'd call precision weapons. It takes time to get them ranged in, and that's time we won't have. So we're going to range them in today by firing"—he turned around and pointed in the opposite direction—"thataway, until each mortar has the right elevation set. Then we swivel the mortars back around facing the city, on a platform that's level enough and with spikes to keep the mortars from shifting. Come tomorrow morning, we'll still have some adjustments to make, but they should be pretty minor ones."

"Won't the garrison hear you firing?" She now realized that issue hadn't been brought up in the planning stage. Not that she could recall, anyway.

"Oh, sure. But they won't be able to see us." He looked up at the sky. "And Eddie should start buzzing the city any time now. We figure that between having an airplane doing something that seems just weird to them and hearing a lot of cannon fire but not knowing where it's happening and why it's happening, by next morning that garrison is going to be edgy as hell."

"But what if they don't sortie? It seems to me that sends your whole plan up in smoke."

Jeff shrugged. "I'm wedded to you, sweetheart, not the plan. If they don't sortie, then what happens is that we continue the mortar bombardment until we've driven off any troops except the relatively small number who've been sheltered in the barbican. By then, the whole regiment will be in position and we'll seize the gate with a frontal assault. After that, the garrison will probably surrender pretty quickly."

A droning sound came from somewhere above. Looking up and around, Gretchen spotted the plane. "And there's Eddie."

"Right on schedule. There's more than one reason we call that plane the *Steady Girl*."

Gretchen turned her head, looking to the southwest. "I wonder how Denise is doing."

"Once she gets to Vienna, she'll do fine. From the stories I've heard, I'd take that girl in a tight spot over most anyone else. Not counting you, of course. But until they get there..."

She made a face. "Yes, I know Denise. Nobody can be—what's that expression you use?"

"Pain in the ass."

"Yes, that one. Better than Denise can."

On the road to Pressburg
A few miles north of Trnava

"Are we there yet?"

Noelle tightened her jaws. "Denise, if you ask that one more time, I swear I'll strangle you. Well, no, you'd probably beat the tar out of me. I'd ask Lukasz to do it."

"I would accept," said the big hussar. He flexed his hands, laced his fingers together, and cracked his knuckles. "Gladly."

"I'm not afraid of you, tough guy."

"I know you're not. You're not really afraid of many things. I'm amazed you've survived this long. Some things, Denise, are true whether you fear them or not. One of those things is that I can throttle you regardless of your state of mind. I am twice your size and even proportionate to the difference in weight, I am much stronger than you. I am stronger than most men I know, no matter how big they are."

"Yeah, sure. I know that. Just as long as you understand you don't scare me. It's the principle of the thing." She looked out of the window of the cabin-atop-a-wagon which was laughably titled a "carriage." The right front wheel heaved up again and they were all tossed about. Again.

"Blasted potholes," Noelle groused.

"Potholes, my sweet little teenage ass. This stupid road has cauldron-holes. Are we—?"

Denise gave the other two occupants of the cabin a sweet little teenage smile. "—having fun yet?"

Chapter 21

Kraków, official capital of Poland
Actual capital of Lesser Poland

"We'll wait until it has passed over the city and is clearly heading to the southeast," said General Franz von Mercy, watching the aircraft that was flying over Kraków at an altitude he guessed to be perhaps half a mile. That was a very rough guess, as you'd expect coming from a man who'd had little experience with the American flying machines. He'd never been up in one himself, and hoped he never would. Von Mercy wasn't exactly afraid of heights, but they did make him queasy.

"That will distract the garrison and have them looking the other way when we begin the charge. We'll start the charge when the airplane has gone a mile or so beyond the city limits. Give the signal then, Captain."

His adjutant, Captain Reitz Aechler, pursed his lips. Belatedly, von Mercy realized he'd given the order to a man who had no experience at all with aircraft. He'd

313

never seen one until the day before yesterday. His ability to gauge distances would be tentative.

So was von Mercy's, but he probably had a better chance of getting it right. "Give it another minute," he elaborated. "These machines move very quickly."

Aechler nodded and turned in his saddle. "Ready for my command!" he shouted to the small group of trumpeters sitting on their horses some twenty yards away. Unlike von Mercy and Aechler himself, the trumpeters were still within the line of trees. Von Mercy hadn't wanted any more men than necessary to come out into the open until they began the charge. That meant him and one adjutant. He figured that even if an unusually keen-eyed and alert sentry on the walls of Kraków spotted them at this distance—it was at least half a mile—he wouldn't call an alarm. At most, he might call them to the attention of his sergeant. But that delay would be all they needed. Once the charge started they'd be spotted quickly.

Von Mercy could easily see the royal castle on Wawel Hill, as well as the Basilica of St. Mary. However, what his attention was concentrated on was the tower in the center of the city that rose up from the town hall. Adjacent to that town hall was the Cloth Hall, which sat in the middle of Kraków's famous *Rynek Główny*, the main square which was one of the largest in Europe.

That was their destination, once they got through the gate and into the city. The main square was at the very center of Kraków, not just in terms of crude geography but because well-built streets went out from it to every part of the city. If all went as planned, the garrison would be dispersed and still further disorganized, which would allow von Mercy to strike anywhere.

Jeff didn't wait until Eddie's plane was past the city walls. As soon as the *Steady Girl* crossed the city's walls on the northwest side, he gave the order.

"Tell the forward battery to start firing."

The order was passed by radio immediately. Mike Stearns had been known to complain about the slowness with which down-time officers adopted radio techniques instead of the tried-and-true method of sending couriers to transmit orders. But that was not a problem in the Hangman Regiment. The Hangman's radio chief before he got killed in the Bavarian campaign had been Jimmy Andersen, one of Jeff's close friends. Between his instruction and his example, the Hangmen had been quick to adapt to radio.

Within seconds, the six mortars stationed forward began firing. And, once again, Colonel Higgins had the unpleasant experience captured in the old dictum *no battle plan survives contact with the enemy.*

To add a bitter irony, in this instance the problem wasn't caused by the enemy but his own mortar crews.

The jerks were too accurate, right out of the gate! The very first salvo landed directly on the barbican of the gate they were aiming at. That was just blind luck. But then, to compound the problem, the mortar crews—who were in direct line of sight and could see how accurate their fire had been—kept it up. No doubt congratulating each other on their extraordinary skill.

Jeff waved over one of his remaining radio operators.

He'd send orders—stiff ones—telling the mortar crews to start moving their fire away from the barbican, toward the center of the city. How were the cavalry supposed to seize the gate if their own damn army was shelling them?

Then, to his astonishment, the medieval construction started coming apart under the bombardment. How in hell was *that* happening? The bombs the mortars were throwing were just not that powerful; they were designed as anti-personnel weapons, not bunker-busters.

But coming down they were. Watching, Jeff realized what must be happening. Kraków's walls were quite impressive to the eye—two miles long, with no fewer than thirty-nine towers and eight gates. The main gate was known as the *Brama Floriańska*, but that was quite a distance from the gate where Jeff intended to breach the walls.

However imposing they might appear to be, the walls had been erected in the thirteenth century. That was before cannons started being used in this part of Europe. Cannons were first developed in China in the twelfth century and spread westward over the course of the next hundred years, transmitted by the Arabs. Their first use in Europe was in the Iberian Peninsula. No one knew exactly when they started coming into use in eastern Europe.

But whenever it was, the walls of Kraków had never been designed to withstand cannon fire. Even so, they should have held up under mortar fire. But Jeff had picked this gate precisely because it was not used as often as most others. What he hadn't considered was that as the decades and then the centuries passed, it received only occasional maintenance—which was usually improvised and makeshift, to boot. The barbican had probably never been rebuilt, simply braced and shored up whenever it became too dilapidated. But the best that could be said for it was that it was ramshackle. If two or more bombs hit simultaneously on the same structure, that could set up shock waves that could rip or jolt the structure enough to start what amounted to a masonry avalanche.

However it had happened, the fact was that it had. Under the impact of the high explosive bombs, the barbican was coming apart and pulling down the adjacent walls with it. But "coming apart" didn't mean the stones they were made of disintegrated. No, as the barbican and walls collapsed the stones just started piling up.

An incongruous thought passed through Jeff's mind as he watched his plan of battle collapse like the walls of Kraków.

O, that this too too solid flesh would melt
Thaw and resolve itself into a dew!

He wished stones would do the same. Fat chance of that happening. The barbican came down completely, crushing the gates. How do you charge and open gates when the blasted things no longer exist? All there was now in that part of the walls was a pile of rubble.

On the bright side, part of the rubble fell into the moat that surrounded the city. That moat, which had been constructed at the same time as the walls, was still a formidable obstacle in places. But elsewhere it had suffered the inevitable decline that the fortifications of a city that had rarely been attacked were prone to. Originally—and it still was in places—the moat had been more than fifty feet wide and twenty to twenty-five feet deep.

Elsewhere . . . not so much. One of the other reasons Jeff and von Mercy had picked this gate to assault was because the moat here was no more than twenty feet across and seemed to be fairly shallow. Both of them were confident that it wouldn't take long for the combat engineers to fill a length of the moat with fascines and lay an already prepared corduroy road across it.

That task would now be easier. But then what?

A change of plans was needed. *Now.*

"This is why I get paid the big bucks," Jeff muttered. He turned to one of the three radio operators standing just behind him. "Tell the rear battery to adjust their elevation. We need them to fire into the city itself—and tell them to err on the side of 'too far in' rather than 'too close to the walls.'"

As the radio operator started transmitting, it occurred to Jeff that he probably shouldn't have used a hoity-toity verb like "err." Hopefully the radio operator knew what it meant and if the man at the receiving end didn't, he could explain it to them.

But he had more pressing issues to worry about. Von Mercy's cavalry would be arriving soon and they'd have absolutely nothing to do except mill around. Men on horseback were ill-suited to storming over a wall that had been turned into a pile of stones. And good luck getting the snooty bastards to get off their horses and use their own legs.

He turned to the second operator. "Tell Eddie Junker we need him to provide us with reconnaissance.

Specifically, I need to know if the garrison is still defending the gate—what's left of the gate—or if they've retreated into the city."

If the garrison had fled already, his life just got a lot easier. If they hadn't . . .

The first rounds fired by the rear battery started passing overhead. Jeff waited a few seconds until they started landing and he could hear the explosions.

"And tell Eddie we also need him to let us know where the bombs are landing. And—never mind." He'd been about to add the caution that Eddie needed to stay high enough or far enough out not to get in the way of the incoming bombs, but that was just twitchiness on his part. Eddie Junker was not a fool.

Now he turned to the third and last radio operator. "Order the Hangman Regiment—the whole regiment; make sure that's understood—to come forward. *On the double.* We're going to need them to get us over the wall, thanks to that bastard Murphy. No, skip that last clause."

Now what? he wondered. *Oh, yeah. Von Mercy.* He'd also had three couriers standing by, as a second string to his bow. He now summoned one of them to his side.

Pointing in the direction where the cavalry would be coming from, he ordered: "Go meet von Mercy and explain what's happened. Tell him to get close but then wait for my instructions." After the courier galloped off, it occurred to Jeff that his authority over Bohemian cavalry amounted to zilch. He'd just have to hope that von Mercy would have enough sense in the middle of a battle to let protocol take a rest. He seemed like a sensible fellow.

The forward battery was still firing at the barbican and the gate—or rather, the piles of rocks and shattered wooden planks that had once been a barbican and a gate.

That was just a waste of ammunition now, and he wanted to save as many of the RDX warheads as he could. He was sure they'd need them come the spring, since the general strategic plan—

He barked a sarcastic laugh. At the moment, so-called "plans" were a subject of scorn and ridicule, as far as he was concerned.

The radio operator who'd gotten in contact with the airplane pilot came up to him. "He wants to talk to you, sir."

Jeff took the mike. "What is it, Eddie?"

"*It would help if you explained what you're planning to do.*"

Quickly, Jeff sketched his new plan. Which came down to:

Blow the hell out of everything in this vicinity of the city with the mortars, and too bad for the civilians who got caught in the fire. They had to drive the garrison away from the walls here.

Storm the walls—pile of rubble—with the infantry. As soon as they could clear a way in for them, the cavalry could do the rest.

"*Gotcha.*" Eddie's American slang had gotten impeccable. One of the side effects of being Denise's squeeze. "*I can tell you already that the garrison isn't trying to hold what's left of the gate. So far as I can see, none of them are within fifty yards of the walls anymore. Out.*"

That was good news. Jeff handed the mike back to the operator. As he did so, he wondered if Eddie had gotten his radio training from Jimmy Andersen, who'd always been a stickler. Most people would have said "over and out" to indicate they'd ended their transmission, but that was not actually proper protocol since what it really meant was "I'm done talking and it's your turn except I'm hanging up."

For one of the many, many times since his friend's death, Jeff felt a pang of anguish. The worst of it—what he knew he'd never get over no matter how long he lived—was the sheer happenstance of the death. A bullet from nowhere, fired by a man who couldn't see Jimmy and had no idea he was there, had taken his life. It was as if God had chosen Jimmy Andersen to be a personal illustration of chaos theory.

But there was no time for this. Another courier had brought his horse up, knowing what had to come next—as did Jeff himself. He'd have to lead the infantry charge personally, under these chaotic and mixed-up circumstances.

In and of itself, that didn't bother him. What *did* annoy him was that he'd have to do it on horseback, just to make himself visible to the troops. Which, of course, also meant being visible to the enemy. Still worse was that he'd have to ride a damn horse without being able to concentrate on his horsemanship—which was mediocre to begin with. He was more likely to break his neck falling off the beast than he was to get hit by enemy fire.

Nothing for it, though. He clambered aboard his mount.

Then, made sure his sword was loose in its scabbard. He'd have to wave the thing around, too, which always made him feel stupid. But his men would expect him to do it. For some incomprehensible reason buried in the ancient and near-mindless reptilian brainstem, that seemed to make a difference to people under fire.

Jeff thought he could already hear the thrumming sound made by two thousand cavalrymen in a canter, but he wasn't sure. The mortar fire was like a thunderstorm up close. The bombs were raining down onto Poland's most prestigious city, which had been there for centuries. It was also the site of the Commonwealth's world-famous (Europe-famous, anyway) center of scholarship and learning, Jagiellonian University.

"If Melissa Mailey finds out about this, I'm dead meat," he muttered. "The fuss she raised when Harry Lefferts burned down one lousy thatch-roofed theater!"

Chapter 22

Kraków, official capital of Poland
Actual capital of Lesser Poland

While Jeff waited for the Hangman Regiment to come up, he got on the radio and gave the forward battery firm— you might almost say blistering—instructions to quit entertaining themselves blowing up an already demolished barbican and start firing further into the city.

Eric Krenz arrived right after he finished the transmission. He'd gotten there that quickly only by riding a horse, which Eric detested even more than Jeff did. But Krenz was a veteran and understood the unpleasant realities of life for someone who got to put the prestigious monicker "Major" in front of his name. Seeing the somewhat pickled expression on his friend's face, Jeff didn't doubt at all that at this very moment Eric was cursing himself—again—for having been stupid enough to accept an officer's commission.

But he didn't say anything once he pulled up beside Jeff. A bit of a wonder, that—Krenz was usually quick to lament his woes, volubly and out loud. To Jeff, at least. He didn't piss and moan in front of his troops.

Instead, the major's first words upon gazing at the now collapsed barbican were: "What the hell happened?" He looked around, feigning puzzlement. "Did Admiral Simpson somehow bring his ironclads across fields and meadows in order to bring down the walls with his ten-inch rifles?"

"Very funny. What happened, Eric, is that apparently this stupid barbican was on the verge of collapsing anyway. It didn't take more than a few minutes before the mortars brought it down."

"That's absurd."

"Yes, it is. Sadly, it's also true."

Jeff had never known anyone who could simultaneously crab and complain and think quickly at the same time. Krenz had immediately come to the right conclusion. "No help for it, then. We'll have to do a mass frontal assault right into the teeth of enemy fire."

"Well, there's the good news. According to Junker"—he pointed at the airplane which was passing over Kraków again—"the soldiers guarding the gate have already fled. If we move fast enough, we could get over the wall without suffering too many casualties."

There were bound to be some casualties, even if they encountered no enemy fire at all. Some of the men racing to clamber over a collapsed wall would stumble or trip or just lose their footing. The same would happen to men racing over a corduroy road laid atop a jury-rigged "bridge" made of rubble and fascines.

That was one of the dark secrets of war, rarely

mentioned in the history books. Jeff could still remember how surprised he'd been when he discovered, as a teenager who read a lot of military history, that a sizeable percentage of "deaths in combat" were due to accidents. That was not really surprising, when you thought about it. Men in a battle would take risks they'd never do in peacetime—and it didn't help any that most of the men taking the risks were still too young to have a good gauge of risk in the first place.

Krenz rose in his stirrups, trying to get a better view of the moat. Then, looked to the side and over his shoulder. Back there, hidden in the trees, would be the combat engineers and their fascines.

"You want to order them up now, then?" he asked. "If there's no enemy to fire on them, they can get a head start."

Jeff hesitated. He'd been considering the same thing himself. The sticky problem was that . . .

"I'll lead the charge," Eric said. His lips twisted into something between a whimsical smile and a snarl, an expression that Jeff didn't think anyone but Krenz could manage to pull off.

That had been the sticky problem, however. If the combat engineers saw one of the regiment's top officers leading the way, they'd be a lot more willing to press the matter forcefully, with a minimum of dithering.

Jeff glanced at his friend's hip. "You're going to do it with that to wave around? And what did you do with your sword, anyway?"

"Oh, I sold it long ago. Got a good price for it, too—enough to buy this fancy quirt and still have plenty left over for beer."

He reached down and drew the quirt from his belt, where it had been attached by a simple loop on the handle. Then, raised it and gazed upon it admiringly.

It was a fine quirt, true enough. It had a longer handle than most, and the forked lashes at the tips were comparatively short. The main purpose of it was clearly to brandish about, not to drive livestock.

"So light," he said. "Best of all, if—more like when—I fall off the horse I can't stab myself like I'd surely do if I was using a stupid sword."

Jeff had considered that option himself. Unfortunately, as the commanding officer of the regiment . . . There were limits to protocol that even the DM couldn't cross.

"All right," he said. "Have at it."

Giving credit where credit was due, Krenz did a fine job of leading the combat engineers up to the moat. Calling it a "charge" was mangling the term. Men rolling big bundles of sticks and brushwood tied up into crude cylinders—which was all fascines were, never mind the fancy Latin—could hardly be said to "charge." Still, they were crossing a level plain with not much in the way of obstacles. The plain was so devoid of vegetation, in fact, that Jeff wondered if the garrison had kept it so in order to provide a good field of fire. That didn't seem to match the general decrepitude of the fortifications, though.

They had about three hundred yards to cross, which a man walking could have done in three minutes. It took the engineers at least ten minutes to do the same. Happily, Eddie's intelligence proved to be accurate. No one fired on them.

Once they reached the moat, they began filling it with the fascines wherever the rubble hadn't already done the job. By the time they were finished, the engineers bringing up the pre-made corduroy road had arrived. They'd brought the road on a wagon, of course. The thing was much too heavy for men to carry and while it could theoretically have been rolled, there wasn't much chance of doing it without mishaps.

That took no time at all to lay across the support provided by rubble and fascines. The end result was undoubtedly the most wretched road within fifty miles— probably anywhere in Poland—but it would do the job.

And by then the Hangman Regiment was more than halfway across the field. With Jeff leading the way riding his horse and looking suitably martial. He even waved his sword a few times.

For a wonder, Murphy was slacking off. The leading companies got all the way over the rubble and into the city itself before they came under any kind of enemy fire—and that was pretty skimpy. A few snipers, nothing more than that. To make things even better, the snipers didn't seem to be armed with anything other than muzzle-loading muskets, judging from their inaccuracy and rate of fire.

Or they could just be lousy shots. Either way, they were soon driven off by the regiment's counterfire. Jeff's men were armed with breech-loading rifles that were far more accurate than whatever Kraków's defenders had.

Jeff didn't pay much attention to the sniper duel, though. A quick study of the collapsed barbican showed that it was just as badly ruined as it had looked from the outside. It would take at least two hours to clear a path wide enough for cavalry to come through, and he didn't want to lose that much time. In any event, there wasn't enough room for more than a company of one hundred men to work on clearing away the rubble. Any more would just start getting in the way.

So...

He turned to Eric, who had also dismounted. "Take the Nineteenth Battalion to the closest gate, which is . . . "

He thought for a moment, bringing up the map of the city in his mind. He had it well enough memorized not to have to haul it out of his saddlebag. "That way," he said, pointing to the northwest.

"How far away is it?" asked Eric.

"It shouldn't take you more than ten minutes to get there." Kraków in this day and age wasn't a big city—about one mile north to south and half that distance east to west. Jeff didn't know exactly how far away the nearest gate was, but it couldn't be more than three hundred yards. Of course, that was the distance as the proverbial crow flew. The battalion would have to make its way through the city's convoluted streets, which would take some time, especially if they faced opposition from the city's defenders.

Krenz smiled. "Don't need a horse for that." He handed the reins to the nearest courier and trotted off, shouting orders as he went. It would take him at least ten minutes before he got the battalion organized. Men were still swarming over the collapsed walls and they'd have to be reorganized into coherent units.

Jeff had to do the same with the 20th Battalion, working with its commanding officer, Major Casper Havemann. The major was new to the job, having recently been promoted to replace the former commander, who'd himself been promoted to serve as one of the regimental commanders for the new divisions being trained by Thorsten Engler. But Jeff let Havemann do most of that work while he concentrated on other matters. The man didn't have much experience yet commanding a battalion, but he had plenty of experience getting troops in order.

First, Jeff called the rear battery and ordered them to come into the city. Then, he called the forward battery and gave them firm—you might almost say blistering— orders to fire at their longest range for another five minutes and then *cease and desist* and come into the city. He was going to be leading the 20th Battalion right into the center of Kraków and the last thing he needed was for his men to be dodging their own mortar fire.

Finally, he called Eddie. "Okay, Eddie. Go get Krzysztof." He forgot to add "over." Jimmy would have chided him for the lapse.

"Will do. But I'll have to refuel first—and I'll be running low on fuel again by the time I get back. Over."

"Understood. As long as you get back before sundown, we'll be okay. Out."

He turned to another of his couriers. As antique as the custom of using couriers might be when it came to communication, the fellows made dandy gofers. "See to it, Lieutenant Vieck."

They'd already planned for this in advance. It was

politically imperative that before the day was over, a notable Polish figure was present as the official leader of the forces that had captured Kraków. Thankfully, they'd have several hundred Polish soldiers from the Silesian units to surround him with. It would still be obvious to anyone who came near that most of their forces were German and Czech. But by the time word could spread through the countryside—much less reach Warsaw—they should be able to fuzz things up enough not to trigger off an outburst of Polish national resentment.

It helped that they'd brought with them a large number of the newly designed flag of the soon-to-be-proclaimed Democratic Assembly of Lesser Poland. It was similar to the national flag, in that it had a broad red stripe beneath a broad white one. The existing flag had at its center the combined Polish and Lithuanian coats of arms surmounted by a gold crown. The flag of the Democratic Assembly kept the coats of arms but eliminated the crown and placed them inside a gold eight-pointed star. The star was quite prominent, large enough to make it easy to distinguish from the existing flag in the middle of a battlefield.

By the end of the day tomorrow, Jeff intended to have the flags flying from every one of the thirty-nine towers and eight barbicans on the walls of Kraków. He'd have to have a pole erected on the rubble of the barbican they had passed through, of course.

A thought occurred to him. Since he still had a few minutes before the 20th Battalion would be ready to begin the charge toward the central square, he summoned one of the radio operators. The radio squad doubled as the regiment's tech unit. "Who's the regimental photographer, Corporal Ollinger?"

The corporal's chest swelled. "I'm the regimental photographer, sir."

"Have your camera ready, then. We'll use it tomorrow."

What a splendid picture that would make! They could have half a dozen men raising the flag atop the rubble of the barbican, duplicating the U.S. Marines raising the flag at Iwo Jima. Of course, there'd have to be one change, since they couldn't very well use USE troops in their feldgrau uniforms. But they'd planned for that, also—not the flag-raising bit, but seeing to it that the Polish militia organized in Breslau by Lukasz Opalinski had their own distinctive uniforms. They were rather flashy, too, albeit not in hussar league. No ostrich plumes, no leopard skins.

"Colonel Higgins." Jeff turned and saw that von Mercy had arrived. He must have dismounted and clambered over the rubble.

"General von Mercy."

"What is the plan now?"

Jeff pointed toward the 19th Battalion, which Eric Krenz had gotten into formation and was starting to file down the street leading to the nearest barbican. "They'll take the next gate to the northwest and open it for you. Meanwhile, I'll take the Twentieth Battalion into the city's center. If all goes well, we should have the town hall and the Cloth Hall seized by the time your cavalry arrives."

"Good," said von Mercy, nodding his head. "That should eliminate the problem of coming under sniper fire once we get into the square. Reduce it, at least."

He turned to go; then, paused and looked back. "My compliments, Colonel Higgins. It's always a pleasure to serve with an officer who doesn't get flustered when his plans come unglued. Which they almost always do."

Off he went. Jeff allowed himself a few seconds—maybe half a dozen—to bask in the praise of a veteran cavalry officer. A general, no less.

But it was time, now. He was leaving one company behind to keep working on clearing away the rubble that blocked the gate. With the other three companies and the artillery unit attached to the battalion, he thought he'd have enough to take the two buildings in Kraków's central square. If worse came to worst, they'd just wait until the rear battery came up and started bombarding the buildings.

Hopefully it wouldn't come to that. Raising a flag over the rubble of a barbican would make a dandy propaganda image. Raising a flag over the rubble of Poland's most famous town hall would not, unless you were Attila the Hun.

One of the couriers brought up his horse. Jeff waved him off.

This was a charge down city streets, damnation. He did *not* have to ride a horse. There were limits.

He would have to wave the sword, though. Dutifully, he drew it from the scabbard, held it on high, and began striding down the street that led—hopefully—to the central square.

"Follow me!"

It was stupid protocol, but... The sound of hundreds of men marching right behind him demonstrated once again that there was a reason for military customs. Better stupid than dead.

"War sucks," Jeff muttered.

Chapter 23

Kraków, official capital of Poland
Actual capital of Lesser Poland

"I feel utterly useless," Ulrik grumbled. He squinted against the rising sun, as he studied the walls of Kraków half a mile distant. "It is ridiculous to say I am in command of this army."

Morris Roth, who was officially in command of the Bohemian forces participating in the assault, was more philosophical about the matter. Or perhaps he simply had the advantage of an additional three decades of life. He was in his mid-fifties; the young Danish prince, only twenty-six years of age.

"It doesn't matter, Prince," he said, trying not to sound like he was soothing a grumpy child. "Both you and I are just here for the historical record."

But Ulrik was in no mood to be soothed. "No, not both of us. You are the one who assembled the Grand Army of the Sunrise, armed it, provided it with its officers. Me? I am just, as the up-timers would say, along for the ride. I haven't done anything but nod sagely and agree to whatever Colonel Higgins proposes."

"So? Jeff's advice has been quite good, as near as I can determine."

"It's excellent advice, actually. Which just makes me wallow in uselessness."

From their vantage point on horseback atop a slight rise, Morris and Ulrik had a good view of von Mercy's cavalry force milling outside the gate that was northwest of the one which had collapsed. They were engaged in a caracole, riding in half-circles close to the barbican and discharging their pistols at the defenders. Who, for their part, were firing back with muskets that seemed to be no more accurate than the cavalrymen's pistols.

So far, Morris had seen only one cavalryman fall off his horse; whether because he was hit by a musket ball or just lost his seating couldn't be told at this distance. It was just as likely to be either one. Unlike Jeff, who'd read about it in a book, Morris had learned of the prevalence of mishaps in war from his own personal experience. One in seven American soldiers who died in Vietnam were killed in accidents, usually involving vehicles. And what Morris had learned since he arrived in the seventeenth century was that riding horses was just about as dangerous as driving cars. True, you weren't going as fast—but you had no protection and a lot farther to fall.

If the pistol shots were having any effect on the soldiers defending the barbican, Morris couldn't see it. Of course, at half a mile he wasn't likely to.

"Doesn't this seem like a waste of effort, Morris?"

asked Ulrik, still watching the Bohemians at their caracole. "And a rather dangerous one at that. I wouldn't have thought a general as experienced as von Mercy would choose this tactic. On a battlefield, it might be worth doing. But against men sheltered behind fortifications?"

Morris didn't answer. He'd been wondering the same thing himself.

Which was the reason that von Mercy was a real general and they were essentially just playing a role. The general who had been born in Lorraine, served in both the Austrian and Bavarian armies and now commanded Bohemian cavalry knew perfectly well that a caracole was a silly tactic to use if what you were trying to do was seize fortifications yourself. But it wasn't really all that dangerous, because at his orders the cavalrymen were staying at least fifty yards away from the walls. Given the quality of firearms in the possession of Kraków's defenders, that meant they could only be hit by a very lucky shot.

The reason he'd ordered the caracole, however, was that having two thousand cavalrymen seeming to threaten a barbican was a splendid way of distracting the relatively small number of defenders while *someone else* did the actual seizing.

Coming around another corner, Eric Krenz immediately saw the barbican, which was now less than fifty yards away. The silent curses he'd bestowed on the crooked street they'd been charging down—using the term "charging" very loosely; because of the narrow confines it had been more like a brisk walk—turned instantly into celebration. That same crooked and curving nature of the street which had slowed them down also meant that they hadn't been spotted yet.

From the din of gunfire he knew they'd had the additional benefit of von Mercy conducting the diversion Eric had asked for. Thankfully, von Mercy was one of those rather few down-time commanders who'd taken to radio quickly and easily.

He saw no reason to dilly-dally. *"Charge!"* he shouted, racing forward while waving his quirt in a manner that would have intimidated a few draft horses and not one bull in creation.

"Sergeant Kozłowski!" shouted the sentry who'd been stationed to watch the city side of the barbican. He'd been given the assignment because he was the youngest and least experienced soldier in the unit.

There seemed to be *thousands* of enemy soldiers rushing toward him. All of them wearing that monotonous gray uniform that rumor said they would, if they were from the United States of Europe. They might even be from the now famous—notorious, in Polish circles—Third Division.

"Sergeant Kozłowski!"

Kozłowski hadn't survived two decades of war by being an improvident fool. The use of a white flag to signal surrender had been common practice in Europe since the Middle Ages. He'd quietly made sure he had two stashed away on a shelf in the barbican once the rumors of an enemy advance had become more solid than the mist of which such rumors were usually made.

By the time he got a white flag draped outside one of the narrow gun slits—archers' slits, originally—the USE sappers had already blown the gate off its hinges and he could hear them storming into the barbican itself.

"Quickly, Jerzy, quickly!" the sergeant said to the young sentry. Pointing to the closed door that led down to the base of the structure, he added: "Open it! But keep to the side!"

Jerzy was frightened half out of his wits, but only half. He still had enough self-control to swing the door inward while keeping out of sight of anyone who might be charging up the stairs.

The second white flag, like the one Sergeant Kozłowski had already spilled out of the gun slit, was really just a linen bed sheet—and grimy enough that it was only "white" by courtesy. There being no place to hang it in the narrow confines of the barbican's staircase, he just draped it over the stairs themselves.

Then, followed Jerzy into a corner of the guard chamber where they'd be spotted as soon as anyone entered—it would most likely be fatal to try hiding anywhere—but weren't within sight of soldiers charging up the stairs. Those were likely to shoot first and figure out whether they'd needed to afterward. And not caring a lot either way.

"Raise your hands," he told Jerzy, doing the same himself. Spotting one of the other sergeants sticking his head into the chamber, shouted: "We're surrendering! Just do it!"

The sergeant disappeared. That was Nicolai, who came from somewhere east of Warsaw. A good fellow, not given to stupid nonsense. There was no way they could fend off what was coming at them. He'd see to it the rest of the unit guarding the barbican would behave sensibly. Like Kozłowski himself, Nicolai had volunteered to join the garrison because it was sleepy duty, and quite a bit safer than farming. No one had attacked Kraków in a long time.

The first man who came into the chamber was younger than Kozłowski would have expected, given the insignia on his gray uniform. If the sergeant remembered what he'd heard correctly—and assuming the rumors themselves were true—the gold oak leaves on the man's shoulders indicated he was a major. And the insignia on his cap confirmed that he was an officer in the USE Army. It was a simplified version of the crossed bars on a red field.

The officer glanced at him and Jerzy, just long enough to be satisfied they posed no danger. Then, looked at the open doorway that led up to the top level of the barbican.

"Am I going to have to kill anybody?" he asked in German with a pronounced Saxon dialect. His tone of voice was quite pleasant, which made the words that much more menacing. So might a butcher inquire if his customer wanted the ham whole or sliced.

Kozłowski knew German well enough to respond in the same language. Cluster of dialects, it might be better to say. He'd learned his version from Silesians. "No, sir! Everyone is surrendering."

He turned his head slightly and shouted in the same language: "Captain Gomółka! Your presence is required!" The captain knew enough German to understand the summons.

The seconds went by, with Kozłowski getting more worried with each one. Surrendering in the middle of a battle was always a tense undertaking. He'd had to do it twice before in his military career. On one of those occasions he'd come very close to being summarily executed by his captors. Next to him, he could sense young Jerzy trembling, followed by the unmistakable smell of urine.

"Haw! Look at that!" jeered one of the USE troops.

"Shut up, Baurer," said the young major. His tone now was not pleasant in the least. "He's just a kid."

Kozłowski would have sighed in relief, except he was too intent on remaining expressionless. A man as young as this major who was both calm and given to kindness was not the sort who'd kill someone unless he had to— which he certainly didn't here and now.

Finally, someone came down the stairs. It was Nicolai, though, not the captain.

"This is the unit's senior sergeant, Nicolai Korczak," Kozłowski explained. To Nicolai, he hissed in Polish: "Where's Gomółka?"

"In the toilet, drinking vodka and probably shitting his pants," was the answer.

Useless as always. Kozłowski cleared his throat and switched back to German. "Ah, the commanding officer is, ah, indisposed." He wasn't sure he was pronouncing "indisposed" properly, but from the immediate grin that appeared on the major's face he'd apparently come close.

"As officers so often are," said the major. "Where is the best place to keep the lot of you in captivity?"

"Ah... Well. Upstairs, I suppose. That's where we mostly spend our time when we're on duty."

"Upstairs it is, then." The officer waved one of his men forward. Not the one who'd ridiculed Jerzy. "Go up there and take their surrender, Sergeant Seiler. Take three men with you. Collect all their weapons—everything including whatever knives you find—and bring them down here. The weapons, I mean. We can leave the prisoners up there for the time being."

His expression grew darker. The distant sound of gunfire was swelling quickly. Somewhere in the city, a battle had started. "I have to go. Baurer, find Lieutenant Unger and tell him I'm leaving his platoon in charge of the barbican and the prisoners. The rest of us will head for the market square."

The soldier started down the stairs. The major turned back to Kozłowski. "As long as you give us no trouble, no harm will come to you."

And off he went. Finally, Kozłowski breathed the sigh of relief he'd been holding in.

By the time the 20th Battalion reached the central square, the Polish garrison had had time to regroup. They had snipers positioned in many of the windows of the Cloth Hall, and had what looked like almost a full regiment—call it eight hundred men—assembled in formation in the square itself. They had artillery, too: three cannons lined up in front of the infantry. Four-pounders, they looked like. If the officers in charge were competent, they'd have them loaded with canister.

Jeff did a quick estimate of the distances involved. The

square as a whole was almost the size of ten football fields, but the distance from the place where his battalion had debouched out of the street they'd been following to the assembled enemy force wasn't more than a hundred and fifty yards.

He and his men could cross that, certainly, even in the face of canister fire. But they'd suffer terrible casualties. There would be no cover at all.

"Screw that," he said. He now glanced around at the nearby buildings fronting on the square. Most of them were three stories tall and had two windows on each floor. The windows were wide enough for two riflemen.

"Skirmishing fire, that's the ticket." Quickly, he issued his orders and squads began racing off. To the rear, not into the square. They'd be able to break into the buildings from the back side, drive out the residents and take positions in the windows. All told, he'd have about fifty men able to fire at one time. That was far fewer than the soldiers who'd be firing back, but his men had breech-loading rifles which were accurate within several hundred yards and could fire ten to twelve rounds a minute. Even the main Polish army in the north didn't have guns that good, and he was sure the garrison down here in Kraków was even less well armed.

The H&K rifles would foul after a short while, since they were firing black powder. But while they were being cleaned and readied for use again, other men could have taken a place in the windows. He was sending three full companies into those buildings. They could maintain a continuous fire for at least an hour.

Jeff doubted very much if men standing in formation

out in the open would hold up for long under that kind of fire. And the cannon wouldn't do them much good, even after they got them realigned to fire on the buildings. His men could take shelter when the enemy artillery cut loose, and four-pounders would take forever to reduce those buildings.

Speaking of artillery...

"Where the hell are our mortars?" he demanded. He waved at one of his couriers. "Go find them and tell them to get a move on. I want them *here*, dammit." They couldn't possibly be far enough away to require radio communication.

The Polish troops in the square were starting to fire. Those were just nervous shots by individual soldiers, but it wouldn't be long before the garrison's officers ordered the cannon to open fire. At this distance, canister would wreak havoc on any men who'd come out into the square.

"Pull back!" he shouted. *"Now!"*

Within half a minute, the Polish artillery started firing, but by then Jeff had all of his men back into the street they'd come down and out of sight. The canister didn't do anything more than chew holes in the adjoining buildings. Small holes. The kind you could still see in the up-time world he'd come from, pockmarking the walls of French villages which had the misfortune to be caught between German troops and the Allied invaders following D-Day. Jeff had seen photographs of them.

A minute or so later, he could hear the sound of his own troops beginning to fire from the windows in the buildings fronting the square. Within another minute, the fire had become continuous.

That had to be a slaughter out there. The Polish troops in the square were completely exposed and while the snipers in the Cloth Hall had shelter that wouldn't do them much good if they tried to shoot anything. To do that, they'd have to get into their windows, and the USE's snipers would have them completely outclassed.

For a moment, he considered going into one of the buildings so he could see the action himself. But he stifled the urge. He had good company commanders and he needed to stay here where he had his radio operators.

Two minutes later, the first mortar crews arrived.

"About time," he growled. Not loudly, though, because he knew he was being unfair. Even 3.5-inch mortars were hard to move when you had to carry them by hand. Each one weighed close to two hundred pounds, although they could be broken down into three parts: tube, bipod and base plate. The ammunition wasn't what you'd call lightweight, either.

The first two mortar crews set up in the nearest intersection to the square, well out of sight of the Polish troops in the city center.

"Indirect fire, that's the ticket," Jeff murmured. More loudly, so the crews could hear him: "Set your range for two hundred yards and we'll go from there."

One of the radio operators came up. "Sir, Captain Foerster wants to talk to you."

Jeff took the receiver. "What is it, Steffan?" Once again, he forget to say "over."

"They've broken, Colonel. All of them are trying to get into the Cloth Hall. They abandoned the cannons, too. Over."

"All right. Stay where you are for the moment. Provide us with suppressing fire." He didn't add *while I figure out what to do next,* since that would be unseemly. The DM *always* knew what came next.

He did remember to say "Out," though.

In the event, Jeff didn't have to figure out anything. Less than thirty seconds later, gunfire started erupting from somewhere catty-corner in the square. Eric must have arrived with elements of the 19th Battalion, which meant they'd captured the other barbican and and—

Sure enough. He peeked around the corner and saw Bohemian cavalrymen pouring into the square. Within less than a minute, they'd started a caracole, firing at the Cloth Hall.

Fortunately, the first mortar bombs landed far away from them. The crews had misjudged the range by at least a hundred yards and they were landing too far to the south.

He'd have to put a stop to their fire, though. So long as von Mercy kept his men in the square, they would be at risk of being hit by friendly fire. He'd let the caracole go on for a while. As a straight-up tactic, it was pretty useless. But by now, Jeff's guess was that the garrison was on the verge of surrendering anyway. Having the square filled with cavalrymen blasting away at the Cloth Hall was bound to have a discouraging effect on the enemy's morale.

Sure enough. After another minute or so had gone by, the first white flags started spilling out of the windows in the Cloth Hall.

"So Kraków is ours and fairly won!" he announced loudly. It was a catchy phrase. He saw no reason to explain that he'd swiped it from William Tecumseh Sherman.

The DM was a fount of catchy phrases. Everyone knew that.

Chapter 24

Poznań
Poznań Voivodeship
Polish–Lithuanian Commonwealth

By now, after hours of negotiations spread out over several weeks, Jozef had come to recognize Walenty Tarnowski's little tics—"tells," to use the American idiom. The young man might be a brilliant mechanical engineer, but he'd make a terrible poker player.

"All right," Walenty said, rubbing his jaw. That mannerism indicated that he'd come to a decision and the vigorous way he was doing it suggesting it was a big decision. Jozef hoped so. Tarnowski didn't dither, exactly. He just insisted on taking days to ponder every issue they'd taken up. Negotiating with him was like being in a version of *Hamlet* where the prince of Denmark's inability to make up his mind was not so much due to indecision as it was to the need to decide slooooooooowly.

Thankfully, it was now at an end, as the next words made clear. "All right," he said, "we'll do it. But!"

He held up a cautioning finger. "I want your assurance that you will do everything in your power to see to it that Jagiellonian University creates a department of advanced mechanics—with full accreditation, mind—and that I am put in charge of it."

Jozef nodded, trying his best to make the gesture sage rather than irritated. "Yes, we've already agreed to that." *About a dozen times. At least.*

Tarnowski had started by trying to get Jozef to guarantee such a department would be created and Tarnowski put in charge of it, but Jozef had flatly refused. "I don't have that authority," he'd told him. "And you must know it yourself. What I can guarantee is that I will push strenuously for it and my opinion carries considerable weight with the people who will decide."

Tarnowski's expression had been skeptical. "Meaning no offense, Jozef, but I doubt if any member of the university's faculty has even heard of you."

"I'm quite sure they haven't," Jozef had said, smiling wolfishly. "So what? They won't be able to resist the decision if the new secular authorities make it, which they will be very inclined toward anyway. Our cause will be outnumbered for quite some time. We need to gain a technological advantage and retain it."

Again, he smiled wolfishly. (So he hoped, at least—but he was an accomplished smiler, as you'd expect of a spy.) "And how better to do that than creating a center for advanced mechanics in our new capital—and in Poland's premier university, to boot."

Now, Tarnowski got that mulish expression on his face that he did so well. "I will raise again the issue of who should be the driver—"

"*No*," said Jozef. He was echoed by Mark Ellis. Christin's contribution was to roll her eyes—but the violation of diplomacy went unnoticed by its target because Tarnowski wasn't looking at her.

"No," Jozef repeated.

"Walenty, be reasonable," said Mark. "You have no experience with either driving a motor vehicle or using a manual transmission. And this will be no time to learn on the job."

Tarnowski started to say something, but Ellis rode over him. "And please don't tell us again how you've driven the truck on occasion. That was inside the city's very constrained limits, and you never got it out of the low gears. Whereas we'll be driving at the highest speed we can manage, much of it off-road. I'll do the driving, thank you. As you know, I have quite a bit of experience driving multi-axle trucks."

Tarnowski glowered at him. For the first months of his captivity, Mark had pretended he knew nothing about automotive matters, being a civil engineer. *Merely a civil engineer*, he'd put it, playing into Walenty's existing prejudices. Only after their relationship grew close had Mark explained to the Pole that in point of fact he knew a great deal about cars and trucks. His father had owned a garage in which he'd worked off and on since he was twelve years old. He'd also spent three summers driving a three-axle flatbed while putting himself through Fairmont State University.

But the Polish engineer didn't pursue the matter any further. He just said: "How soon?"

It was all Jozef could do not to rub his hands. Finally! They'd be dealing with operational matters now. On such subjects, Tarnowski was an asset rather than a pain in the ass.

Eric Krenz would never know it—and Gretchen saw no reason to tell him, since the man tended to get swell-headed enough all on his own—but his actions on the morning they seized the barbican paved the way for the decision made over the succeeding weeks by a large portion of Kraków's garrison to switch sides and join the growing army of the Democratic Assembly.

Kozłowski was key to the process. The sergeant was well known and liked in the garrison, and his word carried quite a bit of weight, even among the officers. And he'd have all winter to spread the tale in the taverns of an officer who was simultaneously capable, good-humored and kind. Unlike so many of the bastards.

But Eric didn't know any of that. All he knew was that his commanding officer, Colonel Higgins, released him temporarily from the Hangman Regiment to concentrate on recruiting and training a unit from the surrendered garrison.

"But I don't speak Polish!" Eric protested.

"So? Learn. Give me a break, Eric. One third of Kraków's garrison is German, and of the rest, plenty of them come from all over Europe. You can get by in German well enough, while you learn to speak Polish."

At that point Jeff swelled out his chest. "I've been learning Polish myself."

"Ha! You, an American? Learning another language? You people are as bad at that as I am at riding a horse."

"Not really. You've got to make allowances, Eric. Our nation had a population of two hundred and eighty-some-odd million people. For most of us our borders were hundreds—even thousands—of miles away, and the people on the other side of one of those borders spoke English anyway." He shrugged. "People don't usually learn something until and unless they need to"—here he bestowed a look of stern reproof on Major Krenz—"as you of all people should know. Since the Ring of Fire, most of us Americans have been pretty good at picking up other languages."

Seeing his friend's highly skeptical—you might almost say, derisive—expression, Jeff smiled. "Well, not bad at it, anyway." The expression didn't flicker. "Not too bad. Better'n you can ride a horse, that's for sure."

Military training camp
Just outside Magdeburg
United States of Europe

Thorsten Engler was startled at who he saw coming into his office. Initially, until he knew who it was, he was startled that his receptionist had given him no warning. Given who his visitor was, however, the lack of warning was not surprising. Very few if any receptionists in the world are inclined to tell their monarch that he'd have to cool his heels while she went to see if the commanding officer had time to see him.

He rose immediately to his feet. "Your Majesty. I wasn't expecting you."

"*Papa!*" Gustav Adolf's daughter Kristina jumped to her feet, raced over and gave the emperor a hug. Given that she was a smallish girl and he was a large man, the end result was a bit comical.

The princess' governess, Thorsten's wife Caroline, rose to her feet and curtsied. She'd gotten quite good at that. She used the form of the curtsy that was standard in the seventeenth century, being just an outward bending of one knee while sweeping the other foot behind her. It was very similar to a male's bow, from which it had derived, and had none of the elaborate flourish of the later Victorian era, where the woman also held her skirt out as well.

Which would have a neat trick, since Caroline was wearing pants. Doing so was considered questionable for a woman, but the habit had been catching on since the up-timers arrived.

"Your Majesty," she repeated. "To what do we owe the pleasure?"

"Papa wanted to see me!" Kristina provided.

That explanation of the emperor's presence was . . . dubious. First, because he'd had no way of knowing that his daughter was in Thorsten's office, given that Caroline and Kristina's visit had been impromptu. Secondly, because while Gustav Adolf was a doting father he wasn't a particularly attentive one. As was the custom of the day, especially among society's upper crust, fussing over children was considered unnecessary—even a bit absurd. That was what governesses and servants were for.

The emperor was not unkind, however. So his response was to beam down at his daughter and say: "I most certainly did."

Gently, he pried her loose. "But I also have business with Colonel Engler."

Kristina had not expected her father to actually dote on her, so she returned readily to her chair.

Gustav Adolf now bestowed an equal beam of approval on Thorsten. "Brigadier Engler, I should say."

Thorsten felt that hollow feeling in the stomach that invariably accompanies the realization that no good deed goes unpunished.

Pescia, Grand Duchy of Tuscany
Italy

"I believe we're done, then," said Fakhr-al-Din. "At least for the moment."

Mike Stearns smiled a bit ruefully. "More than a 'moment,' Your Highness. There is a great deal that will have to be done before we can make our landing in Beirut."

He didn't have to glance around to see if there were any servants present. By now, two months after he'd arrived in Tuscany, he'd persuaded Fakhr-al-Din that having servants in the room when discussing critical affairs of state was a bad idea. He'd worn him down, at least. Mike was pretty sure the emir thought he was a bit obsessive over the matter.

"You will be leaving, then? We will miss your company, Michael." That sounded actually sincere, and Mike thought it probably was. On a purely personal level, he and the emir had gotten along quite well, and the same had been true of his wife Khasikiya once she lowered her guard. (Lowered it up to a point. She always kept her veil on in his presence.) "How soon?"

Mike shrugged. "Hard to say. I will send a radio signal to my—ah, to the people I need to—asking them to send an airship to Italy."

The emir looked somewhat alarmed. "Not here, surely? Not to Pescia."

Mike smiled reassuringly. "Oh, no. That would be a bad diplomatic mistake—not to mention a potential security risk. Those things are very hard to conceal, to put it mildly. No, I will instruct them to send the airship to Venice."

Fakhr-al-Din frowned. "That's quite a distance."

"Not so bad. A little less than two hundred miles, I estimate."

"In the middle of winter."

Mike shrugged. "Once I get over the Apennines, that shouldn't be a problem."

In point of fact, he had no intention of going all the way to Venice. Before he made this trip, he'd gone over the plans for his extraction at some length with Estuban Miro, who doubled as the new chief of intelligence for the USE as well as being one of the continent's largest airship operators. As soon as he got the word from Michael, Miro would make plans to send one of his newer hydrogen airships to be on call at Venice. That might take a few days—even a few weeks—depending on where his various airships were. But once Mike heard from Miro that the airship was waiting in Venice, Mike would leave Pescia and they'd make arrangements as he went for the airship to pick him up somewhere in the countryside.

It would have been simpler just to leave from Venice, since a two-hundred-mile trip on horseback really wasn't that much of a chore. Mike could easily make it in two weeks and be waiting for the airship when it arrived. The problem was that they'd gone to some lengths to disguise the fact that he'd stayed in Italy after Rebecca left, and if he went to Venice there was just too much chance he'd be spotted.

People would certainly spot the airship landing in the Tuscan countryside, of course. But they wouldn't know to whom the vessel was giving transport.

All in all, this had been a very productive trip, but Mike was looking forward to getting back to Linz and seeing his wife again.

Assuming she wasn't off gallivanting about somewhere. The woman had become a veritable globetrotter. But even if she was, sooner or later she'd come back home.

Kraków, official capital of Poland
Actual capital of Lesser Poland

"But . . . *can* you find room for all your troops in Kazimierz?" asked Gretchen.

"No, we can't," replied Morris Roth. He made a face. "Well . . . we *could,* but we'd have to take over the whole city, including the Polish neighborhoods. That would be likely to open a can of worms we'd all prefer to leave sealed."

Gretchen matched his grimace with one of her own. "True. But how will the Jewish residents react? Most of your troops are gentile."

"Yes, but six hundred of them are Jews from Prague—and we'll make sure to mix the Jewish troops up with the rest of them, so that every family that has soldiers billeted in their house will have at least one—usually more—Jews they can go to when they have grievances."

He didn't say *if* they had grievances. Grievances were bound to arise when civilians had thousands of troops sharing their homes. But as long as they could avoid the most severe transgressions—rape and murder, especially—they could get by all right. Happily, Morris' reputation as the "Prince of the Jews" had spread to Kraków, so Kazimierz's very large Jewish population was already inclined in his favor.

Gretchen moved to a window in the town hall's tower that faced to the south. The window was closed, it being a particularly cold January day, but the glass was clear enough that she could see Kazimierz in the distance. Morris came to join her.

Although most people considered it a district of Kraków, Kazimierz had been legally an independent city since the fourteenth century. It lay on an island south of Kraków formed by a branch of the Vistula River. The Jewish quarter was formed by a wall separating it from the rest of Kazimierz, and was known as the Oppidum Judaeorum.

From the corner of her eye, Gretchen could see the

sour expression on her companion's face. Morris Roth was what up-timers called a "Reform" Jew, a variant of Judaism that so far as Gretchen could determine was extremely cosmopolitan and relaxed in its religious views. She knew how much Morris detested the still-standing wall that delimited Prague's Jewish quarter from the rest of the city. What made him detest such walls all the more was that, often enough, they were there at the insistence of the Jews themselves, not because gentiles forced the walls upon them. That had been true here in Kazimierz, and it was still the more conservative elements in Prague's Jewish community that insisted on keeping the walls up there.

"It looks awfully small," Gretchen commented.

"It is—and the population density in the Oppidum Judaeorum is worse than it is in the rest of Kazimierz." Morris shrugged. "But as long as we keep the Bohemian forces out of Kraków proper, we can deflect at least some of the chauvinist propaganda that will soon be spewing out of Warsaw. It's worth avoiding that—minimizing it, at least—to have most of the Grand Army camping outside the city walls. I'll set up a rotation, of course, so everyone gets some time in the relative comfort of Kazimierz.

"Speaking of which," he said, seamlessly changing the subject, "it would help—a lot—if the Galicians sent us some of their forces. Right now, we're relying on Krzysztof and the two Galicians who came with him and the none-too-numerous Polish militiamen from Breslau to be our fig leaf. Very skimpy fig leaf."

"It's not a perfect world, Morris," Gretchen said mildly.

"You're telling this to a Jew?"

Military training camp
Just outside Magdeburg
United States of Europe

"So that's the sum of it," concluded Gustav Adolf. He straightened up from his perusal of the map Thorsten had dredged up and spread across the table in his desk. The map showed all of the USE and its immediate environs. "Oh, my aching back," complained the emperor, rubbing his spine with a fist. "I'm not as limber as I used to be."

A bit desperately, Thorsten tried to find some feature in the emperor's sweeping plans for troop transfers that he could object to. Sadly . . .

It all made quite a bit of sense, actually. At least, if you accepted Gustav Adolf's basic premise, which was that he could spare enough troops from the war against the Ottomans to seize some Polish territory and—hopefully; this was more complicated and uncertain—overthrow the existing regime of the PLC and replace it with a more congenial one. If nothing else, he was bound and determined to abase that branch of his own Vasa family that had caused the rulers of Sweden so much aggravation since the benighted Poles elected Sigismund III Vasa the king of the Polish–Lithuanian Commonwealth in 1587.

"If I understand you correctly, Your Majesty, you don't intend to seize outright any more Polish territory than you've—we've—already taken in Silesia and west of Poznań."

"Lower Silesia." Gustav Adolf waved a big and meaty

hand in a gesture of largesse. "Upper Silesia can remain in Wallenstein's hands—or the Galicians, if they can squeeze it out of him. All of the territories I will take have a mostly German population anyway. They'd be more comfortable within the USE than under the rule of the Polish–Lithuanian Commonwealth."

That was stretching it a bit. No one had ever taken a census in those regions, but Thorsten wouldn't be at all surprised if the result showed that the majority of the population of northwestern Poland and Lower Silesia was actually Polish, not German. What was true was that the cities and most of the bigger towns were predominantly German.

Thorsten wasn't really too concerned about that, however. They were still in an era where national identities were not as predominant as they would become in the world his wife and the other up-timers had come from. So long as their religious freedom and social customs weren't interfered with, most of the Polish inhabitants of the area would accept USE rule. A fair number would actually welcome it. The branch of the Vasa dynasty that ruled Poland had developed a reputation for being feckless at best, and the Sejm's reputation was not much better. And no one outside the szlachta had any use for the PLC's great magnates.

"I will see to it that Gretchen Richter's rulings—ha! You may as well call them ukazes—in Lower Silesia are adopted elsewhere as well. The ones granting Poles equal rights with Germans, which includes official equality of the two languages and no religious prohibitions or penalties on the Catholics." He made a little moue of distaste. Gustav Adolf's views had been ameliorated to a degree under the influence of his up-timer allies and supporters, but he still had the usual seventeenth-century ruler's dislike of religious freedom—or religious chaos, as he viewed it.

Thorsten used his finger to trace routes on the map. "So, you will begin by moving Horn's troops from Swabia to reinforce Torstensson at Poznań. That's what, Your Majesty? About fifteen thousand men?"

"More like twelve thousand. I'll leave a brigade in Swabia just in case Bernhard gets ambitious. Three thousand men won't be enough to defeat him, of course, but they'll be enough to serve us as—what's that handy up-time term?—tripwire, I believe. In any event, I don't think there's much likelihood that Bernhard would take the risk of seriously annoying us."

"Certainly not now, with that capricious new king on the throne in France," said Thorsten. He found himself nodding in agreement, to his dismay. There had to be *something* wrong with the emperor's machinations.

"I'll leave Brahe and his forces in the Province of the Main," Gustav Adolf added. "That new French king really is quite unpredictable."

"And you want to move most of SoTF's National Guard to Poznań as well."

"Yes—although we'll leave two regiments in Bavaria. Just in case—unlikely case, granted—that Duke Albrecht gets rambunctious."

Thorsten had been doing the arithmetic as they talked. "Add those to Torstensson's two divisions, the Saxon forces under von Arnim—that's another ten thousand, yes?"

Gustav Adolf waggled his hand. "Not any more. Von Arnim's suffered a lot of attrition. Today, I doubt he has much more than seven thousand men."

That wasn't surprising. Von Arnim's forces had been pure mercenaries, who'd signed on in the expectation that they'd be enjoying what amounted to garrison duty. Instead, they'd found themselves shipped off to siege lines at Poznań. In *winter*.

Thorsten leaned over the map again. "What about the troops Oxenstierna assembled at Berlin?"

"They're mostly under Swedish colors. I want to keep them away from the Polish front, because, well . . ." Again, he waved his hand, in a gesture indicating as little as possible.

Thorsten had no trouble filling in the blanks, though. *Because in this day and age there are no troops as hated in Poland as Swedish troops. Leave aside the existing history, which was bad enough. By now, every literate person in Poland—certainly every member of the szlachta—has heard enough of the future history brought by the Americans to have learned of the Deluge.*

The "Deluge" was the name that would be—would have been—given to one of the worst disasters in Polish history. In 1655, less than twenty years in the future, Swedish armies would invade Poland after Russian troops had already done so. Over the course of the next twelve years, Poland would suffer worse devastation than it suffered in the up-timers' World War II. An estimated one-third of the population would die, and Warsaw would be destroyed along with almost two hundred other cities and towns.

"And you'll send them to help defend Linz?"

"Yes," said the emperor, smiling genially. "Given that I'm diverting so many forces against that bastard Władysław"—that came with genuine venom—"it behooves me to bolster our forces facing the Ottomans as well. That will add around fifteen thousand men to the lines at Linz."

He held up an admonishing finger. "And I'm going to *insist* that King Christian send most of those twenty thousand troops he's got lolling about in Copenhagen down to Linz as well. He's slacked off long enough."

Thorsten felt as if a noose was being slowly tightened around his neck. "Which leaves . . ."

"Lower Silesia! Which is now completely undefended, seeing as how that firebrand Richter chose to take all her troops to seize Kraków. Ha! I'll say this much. She's a bold woman."

The emperor's implied criticism of Richter had as much sincerity as the proverbial crocodile's tears.

Thorsten considered, and then rejected, raising the fact that the original plan had been to send units of the SoTF's National Guard to defend Lower Silesia. Clearly, that idea had been plowed under by Gustav Adolf's swelling ambitions toward Poland.

"Which leaves you!" the emperor boomed cheerfully. "I have it on good authority—that would be my own judgment, which is the best authority of all—that you've done a good enough job of recruiting and training our three new divisions—"

"Your Majesty, we don't even have *one* division recruited yet."

"Don't quibble with me. You've set up the needed structure to continue the work under someone else. One of your many talents is that you have an eye for good subordinates. Don't deny it!"

Thorsten didn't because . . . well, he couldn't. That *was* one of his talents.

"So!" continued Gustav Adolf. "I hereby promote you to brigadier and order you to select the best of the two brigades you've already trained—"

Started to train, Thorsten thought glumly, but he didn't say it out loud. That would be pointless, given the emperor's current ebullience.

"—and take it to Breslau. Where better to complete their training?"

For the first time since the session had started, Caroline spoke up. "Your Majesty, Thorsten still hasn't fully recovered from his injuries."

Yet again, Gustav Adolf waved his hand. Dismissively, this time. "He's recovered well enough. I doubt very much if he'll be looking at any combat for at least six months. Ha! Not with Richter stirring things up the way she is in Kraków. Besides, I want you to go with him."

Now, Kristina spoke up. "Papa! If Caroline's going, then I want to go too!"

The emperor's genial smile was now bestowed on his daughter. "Why, yes. I think that's a splendid idea. Get the people of Lower Silesia accustomed to their future empress. As Americans would say, the cherry on top of the cake."

Part III

Part Five

February 1637

The sun turns black, earth sinks into the sea,
The bright stars vanish from the sky

"The Seeress's Prophecy," *The Poetic Edda*

Chapter 25

Linz, provisional capital of Austria-Hungary

"I'm a traitor," pronounced Melissa Mailey. Slowly, she lowered herself onto one of the armchairs in the apartment she and James Nichols shared in the provisional royal palace in Linz.

So-called "palace," it might be better to say. The edifice had once been Linz's town hall, which Emperor Ferdinand III had sequestered for royal use as soon as he arrived in Linz. He'd now had experience with up-time plumbing. The town hall had had no such plumbing, but it could be installed readily enough—and more easily than it could in the official royal palace in Linz. That was a large castle that dated back to medieval times, although it had been renovated and expanded a few decades earlier during the reign of Emperor Rudolf II.

The castle had become the government center, but the royal family resided in the former town hall, which had now been renamed the "imperial palace." Normally, commoners such as Melissa and James would not have been quartered there. But since James doubled as the doctor for Austria-Hungary's royal family as well as Gustav Adolf, and Melissa had become a close companion—a term she herself detested, under the circumstances—of Empress Mariana, they had been given some chambers in the palace.

"I know it in the marrow of my now creaking bones," Melissa continued, after coming to rest in the chair. "Traitor, turncoat, renegade, betrayer, quisling—you name it and the term could be branded on my forehead like they branded the 'A' on that adulteress in What's-his-name's *The Scarlet Letter*."

"It was written by Nathaniel Hawthorne and the letter A was actually just sewn onto her dress. She wasn't branded with it."

Melissa glared at him. "And since when did you become a connoisseur of American literature? Mister I'm-just-a-ruffian-from-Chicago's-ghetto and never mind the MD after my name."

James smiled. "What do you think? They made me read it in high school. God, I hated that book. Probably why I remember it so well." He studied her for a moment and then said: "Why don't you just face it, Melissa? You like the woman, that's all."

"She's a fucking *empress*, James. Got serfs and everything. Well, sorta-serfs."

"She was born into that station; she didn't choose it."

"So what? You think she *wouldn't* have chosen it, if given the option of being an empress or a peasant?" Melissa grimaced. "She'd have probably done better to have chosen the other way, though. Her life would have been a lot harder but it might have lasted longer. I looked her up in the records. Did you know she died in childbirth at the age of forty?"

The grimace got darker. "And then her husband's second wife also died in childbirth—at the age of *seventeen*. Seventeen, James! I swear, getting pregnant if you're in the upper crust almost amounts to a death sentence, in this benighted century."

"Pretty much all centuries up until the nineteen thirties," James agreed. "I hate to admit it, but that was often the fault of doctors—which rich women could afford and poor ones couldn't. Human childbirth is inherently more dangerous than it is for other mammals"—he reached up and rapped a forefinger on his skull—"because our heads are so big. But at least a poor woman's midwife wasn't likely to compound the problem, which doctors usually did."

"You forgot to mention that all doctors in this day and age—that didn't change until the twentieth century either—were male, and all the women who died were not."

James smiled again. "Come on, Melissa. You're not in a bad mood today because of rampant male chauvinism— which, I'll admit, does ramp around a lot in the seventeenth century."

"'Ramp' is not a verb."

"Ever the schoolmarm. To get back to the subject, what's really bugging you is that you've made Mariana probably the most popular empress in Austrian history." He clucked his tongue. "And that comes right on the heels of your buddy Mary Simpson making Mariana's sister-in-law Maria Anna—what is it with the Habsburgs fixation on names, anyway?—the most popular queen in the history of the dynasty. The 'Wheelbarrow Queen,' they call her. That's because—"

"Mrs. Admiral Simpson is *not* my buddy!" Melissa interjected. Then, sourly: "And I know why they call her the 'Wheelbarrow Queen,' thank you. As if one good deed makes up for centuries of royal exploitation and oppression of millions of commoners."

James rose from the couch and headed for the tiny kitchen. "I'm making tea. You want some? It's real tea, by the way. I got it yesterday. If you ask me what it cost, I'll invoke the Fifth Amendment."

"Yes. Thank you. I don't need to ask you what it cost because thanks to our coddling of their imperial majesties we're rolling in dough. Like I said: traitor, turncoat, renegade, betrayer, quisling—and now we can add overpaid lackey to the list. For God's sake, James! All I'm doing is shepherding a damn empress who doesn't know squat about medicine to visit wounded and sick soldiers. For this she gets showered with praise and I get showered with silver? It's disgusting."

Having started the water heating, James came back into the room. "Boy, you really are in a bad mood. Melissa, the reason you're doing all that is because it helps the war effort—which it does; don't deny it—and whatever gripes you have with Austria-Hungary's royalty aren't a tenth of what you'd have if we lived under Sultan Murad's rule."

He resumed his seat on the couch. "Of course, your complaints would be short-lived, since the standard

Ottoman remedy for displeasing the authorities is to have you garroted and tossed into the Sea of Marmara."

Melissa went back to glaring at him.

Gustav Adolf climbed out of the *Magdeburg*'s gondola. Then, stretched. He'd crammed himself into the armored turret and stayed there for at least five minutes, giving it a careful inspection despite the fact that it had been designed for a woman about half his size.

"Fortunately, I do not suffer from—what's your American term for it? Clusterphobia?"

"Claustrophobia," said Julie Sims. "'Phobia' means 'fear of,' and I don't know exactly what the 'claustro' part of it translates into English, but the whole word means 'fear of tight places.' 'Clusterphobia' would be fear of clusters. I guess."

Done with his stretching, the emperor of the USE looked down on her. His gaze combined respect, curiosity, and some genuine concern.

"Can you do it, Julie? You know what you will most likely be facing."

Julie shrugged. "Yeah, sure. Unless the Ottomans have suddenly lost their usual skill at war, the sultan will be having all his airships refitted for the sole and single purpose of killing me." She grinned. "I wonder if 'Juliephobia' is a valid medical term. It'd be nifty it if was."

The grin went away. "To answer your question, though—yes, I can do it. Yes, I know the risk. But it's nothing that my husband hasn't faced already a dozen times on a battlefield. I can't very well natter at him for getting a swelled head if I'm not willing to walk in his shoes."

"If that is all that concerns you, I can issue an imperial decree forbidding all officers in my service from bragging to their wives." He shook his head, with a doleful expression. "I probably couldn't enforce it, though."

Julie's grin came back. "No kidding."

The two of them climbed down the scaffolding that provided access to the gondola and began walking away from the enormous airship. The *Magdeburg* had flown in that morning from its hangar on the large lake in Bavaria known as the Chiemsee, about a hundred miles to the west. After Murad withdrew his forces to Vienna, it had become safe to station the huge airship there. Given the weather in winter, the *Magdeburg* was far better protected by its hangar on the Chiemsee than it would be just tethered to a mast in Linz.

The weather was mild today, at least by February standards, just as the meteorologists had predicted it would be. There were times when Gustav Adolf thought that was the greatest of all the American skills—to be able to foretell the weather in advance, if only by a day or two. Their predictions were sometimes wrong, given what the up-timers themselves complained were their limited resources. But they were certainly more reliable than such traditional measures as gauging the ache in a joint.

"How soon do you expect the Turks to resume the siege?" Julie asked.

"Hard to say, with certainty. But given Murad's proven boldness, I expect him to be willing to take more risks than another sultan might. A cautious commander wouldn't order his troops out of good billets into the hardships of trenches and camps until he was sure winter had passed. Which, in this part of Europe, wouldn't be until late April."

"*That* far into spring?"

The emperor smiled. "We are in the Little Ice Age, as you up-timers tell us continually. Even now, snowfalls aren't common in April, but they have been known to happen, especially in the first half of the month. Given Murad's temperament, though..."

Gustav Adolf stroked his beard for a moment. "He will come at us again in the middle of March. I'm quite sure of it."

He stopped, placed a hand on Julie's shoulder, and squeezed it gently. Over the years, since their initially rocky introduction, the emperor and the young American woman had developed a peculiar relationship. There was something paternal about it, although the difference in age was too slight and the difference in status was too great for that to be a very accurate term. Julie Sims—as he still thought of her; Julie Mackay, as she insisted she now was—sometimes reminded Gustav Adolf of a distant cousin with whom he'd become personally close. That provided an ease between them, which had allowed genuine affection to develop despite the fact that Julie was one of the very few people who never hesitated to criticize the emperor to his face.

Despite the fact? Perhaps because of it, he sometimes thought.

"I will repeat, Julie. You do not have to take this risk. You are not a soldier in my service, you know."

She started to shrug again but left off the gesture. Shrugging with that meaty hand on her shoulder was easier said than done. Julie was athletic but she wasn't a weightlifter. "No, technically I'm on the books as a 'military contractor.' But it doesn't matter. At bottom, what I really am is a patriot. The United States of Europe isn't perfect—not by a long shot—but it's way better than any alternative."

His hand on her shoulder came down, to be replaced by her hand tucked into his elbow.

They resumed walking toward the city. "And as emperors go, you're not perfect, either"—she grinned up at him—"not by a long shot. But I figure you're way better than any alternative."

He really was very fond of the girl. Although, in the darkest recesses of his soul, he sometimes envied the sultan's way with garrotes.

"She is still agitated over the issue?" Rebecca asked.

James nodded. "'Fraid so. You know Melissa. That woman can fret over anything that calls her radical credentials into question."

"Ha!" Smiling, Rebecca shook her head. "Perhaps we should make her the secretary of state. That way she—not me!—could listen to the complaints about her made by a few dozen dukes and royal councilors. Who have no doubt at all concerning her radical credentials."

James handed her a teacup and resumed his seat. "Seriously? Do you really get complaints like that?"

Rebecca took a sip of her tea. It was quite hot still, but she liked it that way. Michael had once joked, after seeing one of the many anti-Semitic woodcuts depicting her as a devil, that the only evidence supporting the accusation was that Rebecca did indeed seem impervious to heat.

On the other hand, she also liked to sleep in the nude—for which she'd never once heard her husband make fun of her.

"Oh, yes." She set the cup down on the small side table next to her chair. "Fairly often, in fact. James, I do not think you nor Melissa herself understand the way she is viewed across Europe. Her public status, you might call it. Her age and her reputation for scholarship—never forget that an American high school teacher, in terms of real learning, is easily a match for most university professors in this day— place her outside of the usual conceptions of radicals and malcontents. Those are generally viewed as being crude and lowly folk, which no one thinks is true of Melissa. So, over time, she has developed a somewhat...call it a mystical aura about her. A combination of the Delphic Oracle, Cassandra, and any one of the Greek furies—or a Norse seeress, in the Scandinavian countries."

"You can't be serious. *Melissa*? Just yesterday she predicted snow. As usual—she's practically a human barometer in reverse—it turned out to be the clearest and warmest day we've had all week."

Rebecca smiled and took another sip of tea. "James, which part of 'mystical aura' did you not understand? Her participation—it would be more accurate to say 'partnership'—with Mariana in tending to wounded soldiers is viewed nowhere as Melissa's submission to royalty. Quite the opposite, in fact. Apparently, she can even bend empresses to her will. Remember, this comes not so very long after she forced Cardinal Richelieu to agree to terms settling the war with the Ostend League very much against France's favor."

James rolled his eyes. "That wasn't because of her, that was because Torstensson crushed the French army at Ahrensbök."

"As I am sure Melissa would be the first to say as well. It does not matter, James." She set down the cup, which was now half-empty. "I have had no fewer than three ruling princes inform me that under no circumstances will Melissa Mailey be allowed into their presence."

"You're kidding."

"When have you ever known me to joke about matters of state?"

"You're kidding, right?"

Chapter 26

Wiśniowiecki town house
Warsaw, Poland

Prince Jeremi Wiśniowiecki beckoned the servant with a wave of his hand, without bothering to look at the man. The gesture was both imperious and impatient. The first, because of his status; the second, because of his nature. In point of fact, this particular servant was always attentive to his duty and was there almost instantly. But it did him no good because Wiśniowiecki didn't distinguish between his servants, any more than he would distinguish between different plates in his vast collection of dinnerware. He didn't know which servant was which, and didn't care because he was always impatient with all of them.

The prince would have been a great deal less uncaring if he'd known that this particular servant was very alert because he was keenly listening to the conversation, just as he had with every one of Wiśniowiecki's discussions with any of the men now visiting him.

"More wine for everyone," he commanded, gesturing to the men sitting with him at the table. It was a large dining table, although it was being used at the moment for a meeting rather than a meal.

"So what does that leave to be decided?" he asked his companions. "Now that we've all agreed that we must retake Kraków before we can do anything else."

"It's not a matter of 'must,'" said Prince Stanisław Lubomirski. "Those idiots in Kraków have just given us a great opportunity." He drained what was left in his wine glass, set it down and issued a harsh little laugh. "Quite without realizing it, of course. But what can you expect from peasants?"

Mikołaj Potocki, who was sitting directly opposite Lubomirski, was tempted to point out that the official leader of the so-called "Democratic Assembly," Krzysztof Opalinski, was hardly what anyone in his right mind would call a "peasant." In terms of social status, if not wealth, the Opalinski family was more highly regarded in the Commonwealth than was Lubomirski's own.

But he said nothing. He and Lubomirski had disliked each other since the Battle of Chocim in 1621, in which both men had participated in the struggle against the Turks. The PLC's commander, Grand Lithuanian Hetman Jan Karol Chodkiewicz, died in the middle of the battle and was succeeded in command by Lubomirski. Potocki had disagreed with Lubomirski's subsequent orders, but then-Prince Władysław (now the king of Poland, Władysław IV) had also been at the battle and had favored Lubomirski.

Their mutual dislike had continued unchanged ever

since. Potocki disliked Lubomirski because the man was a jackass; Lubomirski disliked Potocki for exactly the same reason—Lubomirski was a jackass.

Given their current situation, however, Potocki was doing his best to avoid having any open clashes with him.

He glanced at Prince Władysław Zasławski, saw that the youngster was watching him, and gave a little nod. As they'd discussed in advance; Zasławski now spoke up. Up until now, he'd kept silent at the meeting, as befitted a man still only twenty years of age.

"That leaves the matter of which of us will be in command of the army—armies—we send to Kraków."

Potocki immediately followed that by saying: "I propose that Janusz be given the position."

The voivode of Kiev, Janusz Łohojski, gazed at him from under lowered brows. The look combined appreciation with suspicion—but the suspicion was merely latent. Łohojski was a suspicious man by nature. Of course, that trait was shared by almost all of the Polish–Lithuanian Commonwealth's great magnates. A magnate who *wasn't* suspicious of his fellows usually saw a decline in his family's fortunes before too long.

"You are sure of this, Mikołaj?" he asked. "You are the more obvious choice. The word is that the king plans to make you a Field Crown Hetman soon."

Potocki nodded. "Yes, I've heard the rumor and I suspect it may well be true. But that's all the more reason for you to command our armies in this present endeavor. If I get made Field Crown Hetman, the king may well assign me to some other duty—and I could hardly refuse."

As he'd instructed him to do in advance, Prince

Zasławski now said: "Perhaps . . ." The pause was done splendidly; a young man hesitant to give advice to his elders. "Perhaps we could suggest to the king that our campaign be given official approval."

Lubomirski threw up his hands. "Augh—*no*. Not that, above all else!" But it wasn't said harshly, and Lubomirski gave his fellow if considerably junior prince a look that combined appreciation for the youngster's spirit with the sagacity of age. "You still need to learn this, Władysław— and learn it in the marrow of your bones. You *never* want to ask the king—the Sejm, neither—for their approval for something you intend to do. Let that become a precedent, and 'asking' will become something expected of you."

"He's quite right," said Wiśniowiecki, picking up the now full glass of wine that his servant had provided him just a few seconds after he'd demanded it. The same servant was now standing attentively a short distance away, as he had been before; staring at a distant wall and apparently oblivious to the conversation taking place at the table.

After taking a drink, Wiśniowiecki lowered the glass but didn't place it back on the table. "No, we should continue as we have all along." Again, he issued a harsh little laugh. "It's not as if that whoremonger is going to be paying much attention anyway!"

He used the glass to point at the voivode of Kiev. "By all means, let us have Janusz Łohojski as our bold commander."

The servant was not quite oblivious to the conversation, but he was no longer paying a great deal of attention because it had veered off into a discussion of the latest gossip concerning the king's latest favored woman. Leaving aside the salacious details, the subject was fairly boring. And it was of no use at all to the servant in his current effort to improve his fortunes.

Instead, he was spending most of his time wondering how his cousin Janek was faring. He should have reached Poznań by now. Several days ago, in fact, unless he'd encountered difficulties.

Poznań
Poznań Voivodeship
Polish–Lithuanian Commonwealth

Janek had encountered no difficulties beyond minor ones in his journey to Poznań, as it happened. But he was now ruefully remembering a wise old saw his grandmother had favored: *Beware of what you wish for.*

He'd wished to find persons in Poznań who would be willing to pay him and his cousin Andrzej Kucharski for the information Andrzej had discovered thanks to his position as a personal servant for Prince Jeremi Wiśniowiecki.

He had found them. What he hadn't considered in advance was that the type of people who would be willing to pay for such information were likely to be scary people.

Very scary people. Especially one of them.

"How do we know he's telling the truth?" demanded Wojtek Burzyński. He gave the small man sitting on a stool in the corner of the room a glance that was not quite hostile but came very close. The fellow seemed to shrink a little more under the scrutiny—and he was already doing a pretty fair imitation of a mouse in a room full of cats.

Jozef Wojtowicz considered yawning, but decided that would be a little extravagant. "We *don't* know whether he's telling the truth—but here's what I do know, Wojtek, from long experience. In my trade, you never know whether someone is telling you the truth or not; at least, not from the inside out."

"And what does *that* mean?" Burzyński's tone was surly, but that wasn't unusual. He was a surly man more often than not. "'Inside out.'"

"It means you never know what's going on in another person's mind, as you can usually assume you know when dealing with friends and family. What you have to do instead is match what you're being told against whatever else you know."

He wasn't going to give Burzyński any time to think up a response. Of the hussars gathered in the room, Burzyński was not only the least intelligent and the least pleasant, but also the least important. He was szlachta, as all of them were, but not from a prominent or important family.

Jozef leaned forward on his own stool and swept his gaze across the other six men gathered in the room. "So let's ask ourselves what those other things are, that we know. The first thing we know is that everything he says matches what we already think is true. The second thing we know is that the conspirators he named—I'm referring to Prince Jeremi Wiśniowiecki and 'Bearpaw' Potocki— make perfect sense. We'd already included them in our own list of possible suspects."

Again, he swept the room with his gaze. "Does anyone disagree with me so far?"

"No," said Mieczysław Czarny. "What you say makes sense. But I'd still like more."

Jozef nodded. "That brings us to the third thing we know—or I do, at any rate." He now gave the man named Janek his own not-quite-hostile scrutiny. "That's this—if it turns out he's lying to us, I'll track him down and kill him."

He said that in a calm, level down of voice. There was neither heat nor direct menace in it. He would have used exactly the same tone of voice to announce that if he spilled some beer from an overfilled mug he'd just wipe it up.

Janek seemed to shrivel up even more. He hadn't lifted his own gaze from what seemed to be a fixation on the floor for at least five minutes.

Burzyński now had a scowl on his face, but that didn't mean much of anything. He often had a scowl on his face. Jozef thought that was because he found the world a confusing place and reacted by being belligerent.

"How do you know that you'd be able to find him?" he demanded. "It's not that easy—"

"Wojtek, enough," interrupted Mieczysław Czarny. Burzyński instantly fell silent. Czarny was a hussar who came from a *very* prominent szlachta family. More importantly, he was a natural leader in a dominant mold— what up-timers called an "alpha male."

Jozef had always found the term rather amusing. He understood what the Americans meant by it. What he also understood was that, if need be, a man like himself could eat an alpha male for breakfast—to use another American idiom.

But alpha males had their uses, so he let Czarny close the deal—using still another up-timer expression.

"I have confidence in Jozef," Mieczysław announced. "I always knew"—he glanced at one of the men standing against the opposite wall—"so did Leszek over there— that Wojtowicz was one of Koniecpolski's top spies. Does anyone here think the grand hetman would have made him such if he didn't trust his loyalty and judgment?"

It was Czarny's turn to sweep the room with a hard gaze. "Anyone?"

The question was answered with silence. Czarny grunted, leaned back—in a large and comfortable chair, in his case, which Jozef had offered him the moment he came into the room—and planted his hands on his knees. "It is settled then. We will join Jozef in his plan to take the APC, break out of Poznań, and fight with the konfederacja in Kraków."

As the hussars began filing out of the room, Jozef gave Janek another meaningful glance. *Not you, little man. You stay here. We still have things to talk about.*

Once he and Janek were alone, Jozef rose from his stool, went into the suite's tiny kitchen—more like a pantry, since there were no means to cook anything—and came back out with a bottle of wine and a cup.

One cup, which he filled for himself.

"Do not think I was boasting," he said, in that same tone of voice. Calm, level—as certain as the tides. "I will not only find you, I will find that cousin of yours. It won't be hard. The only way he could have passed on to you the information you've given us was if he was a personal servant of either Wiśniowiecki or Potocki. I know you came here from Warsaw—that wasn't hard to find out; not for a man like me—and that means your cousin is almost certainly one of the prince's servants. Potocki has no residence in the capital."

Without taking his eyes off the little man, Jozef drank from his cup. "But I have no ill will. Quite the contrary—so long as you and your cousin continue to serve as my spy in the prince's camp, you will be in my good graces. You will also be the recipient of more of my money."

He took another drink of wine, and then smiled. "You will find me quite a generous paymaster, too."

Finally, Janek lifted his eyes. "How will we stay in touch?"

Jozef's smile widened. Happily, Gretchen Richter had had several of the devices to spare.

"It is time for you to learn about a wondrous American invention. It is called a 'radio.'"

After Janek left, Christin came out of the bedroom. "You heard all of it?"

"Oh, yeah," she said, heading into the kitchen. She came out with a cup for herself. "I have good hearing and that hole you drilled in the wall works just fine."

She sat down next to him and held out her cup. As he filled it with the wine bottle, she said: "I didn't understand all that much of it, though. My Polish still isn't good for anything except buying food and asking for directions. As long as they're both simple. Loaf of bread or where is a tavern, I can handle. Fried trout with potatoes and carrots or directions to anything more than two blocks away, not so much."

She drained about a third of the cup. "There was one thing that was really clear, though."

"And that was?"

She smiled. "You're a pretty scary son of a bitch. Good thing for you I've always been partial to bad boys. That's why you wanted me to listen, isn't it? Even though you knew I wouldn't understand most of it."

He frowned. Jozef was discovering that having a woman as smart as himself was disconcerting as well as exhilarating. There were times he pined for his paramours of old. A bit younger than him and a lot dumber.

Not often, though. "You think I wanted you to learn I was 'scary'?"

"No, of course not. I already knew that and you already knew I did. No, you wanted me to listen in because you're hoping I'll get interested enough in what you do to want to become your partner. Mister and Missus—using the term loosely—Superspy."

"Well . . ."

"Go ahead. Deny it."

Exhilarating. "I can't. You're right. Which brings up something I've been thinking about. There's something you could do—if you're willing—that I think would enhance our prospects."

"Explain."

By the time he was done, Christin had finished her cup of wine and was starting on another.

"Let me get this straight," she said. "You want me to wear a suit of armor. Just like a hussar."

"Not quite. We'll have to have one made for you specially, and it doesn't need to be as heavy. You also don't need a helmet. In fact, we don't want you to wear one. The whole point of this is for people to see your face and recognize you as a woman. Just like they do with Gretchen."

"Gretchen has long blonde hair. She's famous for it." Christin reached back and gave her own hair a little flip. "My hair's dark—it's almost black. That's because my ancestry's mostly Lebanese. And it's nowhere near as long as hers. Doesn't reach much past my shoulders."

"That's irrelevant," said Jozef, shaking his head. "Legends always have lots of variants. All we need is a beautiful, fearless woman in armor."

She grinned at him. "That's one of the things I really like about you. Most men would think I was flattered by being called 'beautiful.' You know better."

"Oh, yes. 'Fearless' is what makes you strut about."

"All right, I'll do it. But there are three conditions. First, I get a sword. Not as big as one of those hussar choppers, but still a real sword. I've always wanted a sword." She used a hand to wave off objections. "Don't worry, I'm not crazy. I don't plan to actually use it if it comes to fighting. For that, I've got my Ruger."

"Not a problem. What else?"

"A lance. I want a lance."

"Not a problem—as long as you're willing to fly a banner from it that's Polish." He made his own dismissive hand gesture. "Polishy, at least."

"I'm okay with a red-and-white banner. Just not with the coat of arms."

"Agreed. What else."

"I really really really *really* want hussar wings."

Jozef didn't have to spend more than a moment thinking about it. The wings were usually attached to saddles, not backs, so weight shouldn't be a problem.

"Agreed."

She drained her cup and set it down. "I remember how cool I thought it was when Buster gave me my first leather jacket. This is even cooler."

Exhilarating. Definitely exhilarating.

Disconcerting too, granted. But Jozef was willing to trade the one for the other.

Chapter 27

Pressburg, capital of Royal Hungary

Lukasz lowered the pair of binoculars he'd been given by Gretchen Richter before they departed Breslau and handed them to Jakub Zaborowsky. "So far as I can tell, our informants were correct. It looks as though Pressburg is still in Austrian hands."

As he raised the binoculars to his eyes, Jakub smiled thinly. "Best you don't say that to anyone in Pressburg—or anyone in these regions. You'll get a half-hour lecture on the manifold and crucial distinctions between stalwart Hungarians and feckless Austrians."

Opalinski chuckled. "And here I thought we Poles were the world's fussiest distinction-makers."

"Compared to Hungarians? We're rank amateurs." Zaborowsky scanned the city on the left bank of the Danube for a couple of minutes. Then, lowered the binoculars. "You're right, I think. At this distance, I can't make out the insignia on those red swallow-tailed banners, but the color and the very fact that they're banners is enough."

"That's what I thought also. The Ottomans use tughs instead. And I've never seen one colored red." The *tugh* was a horsetail standard which the Ottomans derived from the Mongols.

"Let me see," said Denise insistently.

There was no reason to argue with the girl—and if he refused, an argument was certain—so Jakub handed the binoculars to her.

"We'll have to go around the city," he said, musingly. "There's no way a Hungarian garrison would let us pass through to the Ottoman lines. The question is . . ."

"Where are the Ottoman lines?" Lukasz finished for him.

"They're over there," said Denise. Without removing the binoculars from her eyes, she pointed to the confluence of the Danube and the Morava rivers. That was at a distance Lukasz estimated to be eight miles away. The only reason they could see the confluence at all was because they were standing on a hillside north of the city. But at that distance, all Lukasz himself could see was the confluence itself.

Denise had better vision than he did, though. The girl's eyesight was better than that of most people.

Still, they couldn't afford any mistakes at this juncture of their expedition. "Are you sure?" he asked.

Denise sniffed. "Of course I'm sure. I wouldn't have said it if I wasn't." She handed him the binoculars. "See for yourself, O mighty hussar."

He looked through the binoculars at the confluence. It seemed . . .

"Yes, she's right. I can make out fieldworks."

"They might not be Ottoman," cautioned Jakub.

Lukasz lowered the eyeglasses and shook his head. "That's not likely." He used the binoculars as a rough wand to point to the much closer fieldworks just west of Pressburg. "Why would the Austrians—excuse me, Hungarians—put fieldworks that far out to fend off an attack, when they've got these? They can't afford to take chances like that; not when the main Austrian-Hungarian forces are more than one hundred and fifty miles away."

"I'm not arguing the point," Jakub said mildly. "Just raising it."

"You'd damn well better not argue it," interjected Denise. "Maybe all the mighty but myopic hussar can see are fieldworks, but I saw one of those horsetaily things. What do you call them? Tugs?" She used her hands to indicate a cylindrical shape. "Like Chinese lanterns, sorta, except they're round instead of a square and the walls aren't paper but cords of some kind. Horsetails, I guess."

She dropped her hands. "They remind me of something hippies would use."

Lukasz wondered why big-hipped American women would want a horsetail banner, but he didn't bother to ask. Up-timers had a multitude of weird customs. However idiosyncratic, Denise had provided a good description of the most common style of tugh used by the Ottomans.

He didn't even think of questioning her again. Denise was honest to a fault, in addition to being prickly when she was challenged. If she said the Ottoman standard was there and that was its design, he'd take her word for it.

"Good enough," he said. "Now all we have to figure

out is how we get from here to there hauling this great ungainly so-called carriage of ours." He gave the countryside a study that was dubious and wary. "Not going to be easy, that."

It wasn't. They required almost two days to get there and at least twice the eight-mile distance Lukasz had estimated in terms of crow's-flight miles. But, finally, they got the carriage onto the narrow road that paralleled the Danube's left bank and from there reached the Ottoman fieldworks.

Those were quite impressive, due mostly to the fact that the Turks had seized Devin Castle, which dated back for centuries. The castle had been erected on a cliff overlooking the confluence of the Danube and the Morava.

It was pretty spectacular, especially the small watchtower perched on a rock spire that was separated from the main castle.

"Boy, that looks awfully shaky," Denise commented, peering up at the tower from inside the carriage. She'd moved the heavy curtains aside with a finger to see outside.

Noelle, sitting across from her, had done the same. "Well, that tower's been there since at least the thirteenth century, so it can't be all that flimsy."

"Really? How do you know that?"

"I heard about it from people while we were still in Breslau," Noelle explained. "That tower is quite famous in the area. They call it the 'Maiden Tower,' on account of there being legends that it was used to imprison girls from noble families who got enamored of the wrong man. Some of them leapt to their death in despair, if you believe the legends."

Denise curled her lip. "You wouldn't ever catch me doing something that stupid. Getting hung up on the wrong guy, maybe. But jumping to my death over him? Not hardly."

She let the curtain drop back into place. "Of course, with me it'd be a moot point anyway, seeing as how I'm not a maiden."

"Stop bragging, Denise."

The girl's lip curled still further. "Just 'cause *you* took forever to get your cherry popped. I did it when I was still—"

"I said, stop bragging."

As Lukasz had expected, the Ottoman officials charged with keeping an eye on these outlying Austrian-Hungarian forces were indeed officious. And Ottoman standards of "officiousness" started with accusations of malevolent wrongdoing and only slowly eased themselves into mere suspicion. The process could be sped by bribes, of course, which Lukasz readily provided. He'd been given a large purse for that purpose by Gretchen Richter. For a woman who insisted she was a mere agitator for the low folk, she had coffers that most noblewomen would have greatly envied. That was one of the advantages of being a troublemaking malcontent who sported the title of "Lady Protector" and was in the good graces (using the term loosely) of Europe's most powerful ruler.

So, after three days of sometimes nerve-wracking but

mostly tedious dickering with Ottoman officialdom, they were allowed to proceed on to Vienna. Still better, they were given permission to hire water transport, so they made the last stretch of their journey aboard a barge on the Danube.

Beç, formerly known as Vienna
Capital of the new Ottoman province (eyalet) of Austria

"It doesn't look as badly damaged as I would have thought," said Noelle, again peering out of the carriage through a narrow opening in the curtains she'd created with her forefinger.

"They might have rebuilt stuff," suggested Denise. "They've had Vienna for six months already."

Lukasz shook his head. "But for most of that time Murad had his army camped outside Linz. He wouldn't have left more men here than he needed to, and given that most of the population had already fled that would have been a skeleton garrison. Even if he'd told them to start rebuilding, they wouldn't have gotten very far."

He moved the curtain on his side of the carriage, and looked out. "No, I think it just never got damaged all that much. This was a city taken by surprise, not one that saw days of fighting inside its walls."

He let the curtain slide back into place. "Whatever the explanation, it's good news for us."

"Why's that?" asked Denise. She was simply curious, not challenging.

"Because a little damaged and mostly unpopulated city

has plenty of billets for the occupying troops. That means there'll be some room for our mission to be given lodgings without us having to trip over Turkish soldiers every hour of the day and night. Leaving aside the headaches that would involve, it'll make our mission a lot easier. Well, easier, at any rate. Maybe not a lot. That depends on what quarters they give us."

"If they give us any at all," said Denise. "I'm skeptical about that, myself. Maybe they'll just give us the heave-ho right off."

Noelle frowned. "Why'd you agree to come, then?"

"Nothing ventured, nothing gained. And I really want to get Minnie out of here."

"They'll provide us with quarters," Lukasz said, confidently. "It won't be what you'd call a welcome, exactly. But Ottoman prestige is involved. Being hospitable to diplomatic envoys, no matter where they come from, emphasizes how mighty they are. It's not an act, either. They *are* mighty."

Denise nodded. "Okay, that makes sense. Would a lion begrudge a kitty-cat somewhere to sleep in his presence?"

Lukasz smiled. "A lion would, actually. That kitty-cat would make a nice snack. I take it you're not familiar with the creatures."

"Outside a zoo? Hell, no. Do I look crazy? And how would you know about them, anyway?"

"I've hunted them, of course."

The girl rolled her eyes. "I keep forgetting. Seventeenth fricking century, Denise."

A unit of sipahis guided them to the royal palace,

and served them as an escort at the same time. Of course, everyone involved understood perfectly well that, under the circumstances, "escort" was synonymous with "guards." But the officer in charge was perfectly courteous to them throughout.

Once they pulled up in front of the Hofburg—or whatever the sultan was calling the former Habsburg palace these days—Lukasz clambered out of the carriage. He made sure to open the door wide enough so that some of the escorting sipahis could get a glimpse of Noelle and, especially, Denise. For her part, the young woman was dressed in what she called her "premier prostie" outfit, which consisted of a minimum of clothing and most of that gauze. She did, however, wear a veil.

After Lukasz closed the carriage door, she leaned back in her seat.

"You should be ashamed of yourself," said Noelle. "You didn't need to be *that* flamboyant about it."

"Yeah, I know," Denise said cheerfully. "You think the Prick-Teaser League would let me join?"

"It'd have to be as an honorary member. Like the Nazis made the Japanese 'honorary Aryans.' On account of you've never to the best of my knowledge teased any pricks at all."

"Not one," Denise agreed. "Most of them I told to take a hike and the few I didn't had no complaint afterward. Of course, that's all behind me now that I've got Eddie."

She looked down at the gauze contraption that humorists would have called "clothing." The apparel displayed her midriff, along with the tattoo that Noelle thought must have scandalized two-thirds of the heavenly host when they found out about it. The image was that of a seductress wearing clothes that were fuller than the ones she had on but made up for it by being so tight they looked as if they'd been painted on. The caption above the image read *You can land here* and the one below *If you don't crash.*

"Eddie's going to love this outfit. I didn't have a chance to show it to him before we left Breslau."

Before Denise finished the sentence Noelle had her hands over her ears. "I can't hear you," she said, in a singsong voice. "La la la la—"

Lukasz came back into the carriage, and Noelle broke off her little ditty. "All right," he said. "Jakub's gone into the palace to start negotiating with the Turk officials. For today, of course, he'll just be haggling over our lodgings. That'll probably take hours."

But it didn't. Jakub was back in twenty minutes. Lukasz climbed out of the carriage again, closing the door behind him.

On each opposite bench in the carriage, Noelle and Denise slid over immediately so they could listen to the two men outside. Both opened their respective curtains to get a view, as well. Not much of a view, though, since they were using a finger to hold the curtains aside just enough to see through.

The first thing Denise noticed was that Jakub had a peculiar expression on his face—a heavy frown that she'd swear was holding back a grin.

"You won't believe this," he said.

Chapter 28

Beç, formerly known as Vienna
Capital of the new Ottoman province (eyalet) of Austria

It didn't take more than two minutes for the carriage to get around a portion of the palace grounds so they could look at their assigned quarters.

"That's it, all right," said Noelle. "Fits the description to a T." She let the curtain slide back into place.

Denise still had her curtain open a bit. "Wow. Talk about *luck*. This is like winning the lottery."

"Not really. It just proves how far down the pecking order we are in the Ottoman scheme of things."

Lukasz had been peering over Denise's shoulder, with an intent look on his face.

"Wait here," he said. Commanded, rather. He flung open the carriage door and practically leapt out of it. Then, charged toward the doorway leading into the detached section of the palace. Apparently, he was so agitated he forgot to close the door and provide his women with their needed privacy.

Hastily, Noelle reached out, seized the door handle, and drew the door shut. She caught a glimpse of one of the sipahis staring at her.

Well, no. Staring past her. Once the door was closed, Noelle turned her head and saw that Denise was resuming her seat on the padded bench on her side of the carriage. The girl would have been quite visible—spectacularly visible—to the sipahi.

She was looking smug. "This Mata Hari stuff is fun," she said.

Noelle resumed her own seat and shook her hand. "You do know that Mata Hari came to a bad end, right? Executed by a firing squad for espionage."

Denise's smile didn't fade in the least. "That's not a *bad* end, Noelle. A bad end is dying of old age in a rest home after you've lost all your marbles and your family never visits you on account of you don't remember any of them anyway. Getting shot by a firing squad is way better. Of course, you want to postpone it as long as you can. How old was she when they shot her?"

"Mata Hari? I'm not sure, exactly. Somewhere around forty."

"Oh, hell." Denise flipped her hand as if she were batting away a fly. "That's so far in the future it's not worth worrying about."

Outside, they heard a sudden commotion. Peering through the curtains again, they saw that Lukasz had emerged from the palace annex and was gesticulating almost wildly. He was half-shouting, too. They couldn't make out any of the words, since they were Polish and being rattled off to Zaborowsky like machine-gun fire.

For his part, Zaborowsky had his head hunched down and his hands spread in a pleading gesture. He appeared to be almost groveling—which was utterly unlike the man.

Lukasz broke off his harangue and charged toward the main palace. Zaborowsky trailed after him.

"What's he doing?" asked Denise.

Noelle had her lips pursed. "I imagine he's going to protest to the Turks about the cruddy quarters we got assigned."

"*What*? Is he crazy? We couldn't have asked for a better place to stay." Now agitated, Denise jabbed her finger in the direction of the annex. "That's where Minnie is!"

Noelle still had her lips pursed. "Yes, I know—but we can't be seen to know that. If we were what we claimed to be, this is exactly what Lukasz would be doing. Raising bloody hell."

She leaned back and took a deep breath. "He's a lot smarter than he looks, you know. I just hope . . . "

Denise slumped back in her own seat. "Oh, hell. What if he pisses the Turks off so much they just order us out of here altogether?"

"That's the risk he's taking, yes." Noelle ran fingers through her hair, which she'd been letting grow ever since they decided to send her along on the mission. She preferred it rather short, but the style had been too exotic-looking—for a down-timer, not an American. By up-time standards, she'd had the haircut you'd expect from a female government official.

"I think it's a pretty safe gamble, though. From everything I've heard from Janos, Ottoman officials have rhinoceros hides when it comes to the protests of people they consider beneath them. Which is just about everybody except the sultan and their own superiors. They're quite competent, he says, as a rule. But they're hardly what we Americans would call receptive. If you told them the customer was always right, they'd think you were a moron."

"Well, sure. You *would* be a moron. I've worked in retail—as little as I could. A lot of the times, the customer is a jerk."

She slumped still further in her seat. "I just hope he doesn't screw it all up."

Eventually, Lukasz came back. When he stuck his head through the curtains he had a ferocious scowl on his face—which instantly transformed into a grin once he couldn't be seen by anyone outside the carriage.

"In like Flynn," he said.

"Where and when did you see *those* movies?"

"Wojtowicz told me about them. One of his favorite actors."

"Yeah, he would be." Denise rolled her eyes. "God forbid he should be a fan of somebody classy like Sean Connery playing James Bond."

Noelle was getting impatient with the badinage. "So what's the situation? Are we staying in the annex?"

"Yes, indeed. It was made clear to me in no uncertain terms that we could consider ourselves privileged to get *any* quarters connected to the royal palace. The imperial palace, now."

"I really, really want out of this damn carriage," said Denise.

"Please. A bit of patience. Propriety must be maintained. You have to stay out of sight."

"Now there's a lost cause . . ." muttered Noelle.

But she didn't argue the point, despite her own great desire to get out of the carriage. After weeks inside the thing, she thought she might have developed a permanent case of claustrophobia.

It didn't take more than a couple of minutes, though. All they had to do was bring the carriage alongside the now open door to the palace annex, so Noelle and Denise could quickly pass from the one to the other.

Needless to say, the sipahis were watching keenly while pretending not to be. Denise stumbled getting out of the carriage—oh, sure; the girl was normally as agile as a gymnast—and gave everyone a quick look at her legs. Which, for good reason, were prominently displayed in the nose art on Eddie Junker's airplane.

Noelle was simultaneously annoyed and approving. Annoyed, because Denise took such obvious glee in shenanigans like this; approving, because in terms of their mission her antics were perfectly designed to lay any suspicions to rest. *Mata Hari, eat your heart out*.

Once they were inside the annex, they looked around.

"What a dump," said Denise. "Are those saddles, for Chrissake?" She used her chin to point to a wall on which dozens of saddles were suspended. Old, used saddles—and they hadn't been fancy ones even in their prime.

The whole place was like that, as far as she could see in the dim lighting provided by a few windows, all of which had glass too cloudy to see through. On this ground floor, anyway. But she had no great hopes the two floors above would be much better. It was clear that the annex had been used entirely for storage for quite some time.

But she didn't dwell on the matter. They'd come here for a reason, after all.

Denise was the one who found the stairs leading up to the tower that had been described over the radio. She started up without asking anyone's permission, practically racing.

Noelle hurried after her, followed by Lukasz. Behind them, she could hear Jakub positioning their Slovene escort to impede any Ottoman who tried to get into the annex—without, of course, starting an open clash with them.

"Denise, slow down," she hissed.

The girl ignored her. By the time Noelle reached the level where the door was supposed to be, Denise was already scratching at the stone walls.

"Cut it out," she said. "You'll just break your fingernails. Let me do it."

Denise peered at her. "And how will you not break your own nails?"

Noelle started whistling. Softly, but it was the sort of whistle that carried well.

Yankee Doodle, which segued into *When the Saints Go Marching In.* Denise started to chime in, but broke off—wisely—after a few seconds. Denise had her own quite impressive whistle, but it was the sort to summon dogs, not carry a tune.

Suddenly, a crack appeared in the stone wall. Until it did, neither woman would have had any idea that a door existed at all. It was no wonder the people in the cellars had never been detected by the city's conquerors.

The crack widened. Widened.

A whisper came through. "Who's there?"

"That's Judy!" said Denise, excitedly—but she didn't lose her good sense and training. She'd still spoken in a whisper.

"Denise?"

"Yeah, it's me. Noelle's here too."

The door swung open further, and now they could see Judy Wendell's face. Which suddenly burst into tears.

"Oh, thank God you're here," she said, stumbling out of the narrow passageway into the tower. Noelle eased the girl down to the floor, cradling her.

Denise, meanwhile, pressed herself into the passageway and went down those stairs. A few seconds later, she emerged into a room of some sort. She couldn't see it very well because the only lighting was provided by three candles in the hands of—

The two royals barely registered on her at all. Two seconds later, she had Minnie enfolded in her arms. Her friend barely had time to drop the candle onto the floor.

Neither said anything, for a while. Denise could hear exchanges between Noelle and Judy and the two Habsburgs, followed after a while by Lukasz's voice. Later, she'd marvel that the big hussar had managed to squeeze his way down that tight passageway, but for now her only thoughts were of Minnie.

Eventually, Minnie said: "I knew you'd come for me. Took your time about it, though."

"Give me a break. Nobody told me you were even alive until not long ago."

She could feel Minnie's head nodding on her shoulder. "Well, sure. Good tradecraft. You didn't need to know, at first."

"Jesus. Still a Goody Two-shoes, I see."

There was a moment of silence. Then Minnie said: "Well . . . not so much. I think I'm pregnant. Not sure yet."

"You *slut*."

"Hey, I learned it all from you."

"Did not!"

"Did too. I was an innocent orphan. Missing an eye, on top of that."

They fell silent again, for a while. Then Denise said: "Not to worry. We'll deal with it."

"I wasn't worried, I was just telling you. I like him. A lot."

Again, they fell silent. Their embrace hadn't lessened at all.

"I'm really glad to see you, Minnie," Denise said eventually. "But I gotta tell you . . . You really stink."

"You try living in a cellar for months."

"I'm not criticizing. I'm just saying."

They were interrupted then, by Noelle. "Come on, girls. We've got to get moving."

Finally, Denise and Minnie separated. "Get moving where?" asked Denise. "We can't leave this soon—the Ottomans are bound to smell a rat."

"Who needs to smell a rat when they can smell *us*?" That came from Judy Wendell, who stepped forward out of the gloom. "God, I need to take a bath for, like, hours.

Hours and hours. Now that we can finally get some water we don't have to ration."

"Yes!" hissed Minnie. "There's a well not far away. But we never dared get water from it."

Fortunately, there were several buckets in the annex. Before long, the cavalrymen were trooping back and forth from the annex to the nearby well. At one point an Ottoman official came out to inquire about their profligacy with the sultan's well water, but he retreated hastily when Lukasz and Jakub began berating him for the foul and filthy nature of the quarters they'd been given.

Rather than trying to bring heated water down the narrow staircase in the tower that led to the cellars, it was decided that once night fell it would be safe enough for the people hiding in the cellars to come out, one at a time, and use the tub on the annex's ground floor that Jakub had found. The tub was moved into one of the smallest rooms on that floor, which had apparently been a walk-in pantry at one time. Jakub would stand guard, to fend off any curious Ottoman in the unlikely event one of them came into the annex.

The two Habsburgs went first, Cecilia Renata and then Leopold. Rank hath its privileges. Then it was Judy Wendell's turn.

When she arrived at the newly created bath room, however, Jakub had her wait a bit. "We've got fresh water coming, but it isn't hot enough yet. There's a stool inside you can sit on."

Twenty minutes later, he knocked on the door. "Come in," she said.

He had a bucket in his hand, which he emptied into the tub. "This won't take long," he said, and left.

To Judy, it seemed to take forever. But Jakub probably didn't spend more than a few minutes filling the tub, one bucket at a time. It was a lot of work.

Finally, it was full. Judy stood up. "Praise be—and my fervent thanks. Will you marry me?"

"I'm thinking about it."

Startled, she looked at him. "I was *joking*."

"Yes, I know. I'm still thinking about it. Now, enjoy your bath. If you need anything, I'll be just outside."

A moment later, he was gone, with Judy now staring at the closed door.

Chapter 29

Pescia, Grand Duchy of Tuscany
Italy

Mike Stearns wasn't sure what had caused him to wake up, at first. He was not what people meant by a heavy sleeper, but he'd never been fidgety in the middle of the night, either.

Christ, I'm getting old, was the first coherent thought that filtered into his mind. Mike had recently turned forty, an age which he'd always considered one of life's inexorable benchmarks.

Up to thirty: *I'm still young!*

After thirty: *Still on the young side.*

After forty: *Stop kidding yourself, buddy. Middle age has arrived.*

Fine. Early middle age. The key word is still "middle."

But then he heard a faint noise that he realized was an actual noise produced by something other than himself. Not something in a dream.

Produced by *someone* else.

Someone here. In his bedroom.

Someone *near*.

He flung aside the blankets and threw himself onto the floor, in as close to a roll as he could manage—which was an actual roll, in fact. Mike had always been athletic and he was still in pretty good physical condition.

The roll didn't go more than a foot, though, before his torso slammed into something.

Someone's legs. That someone issued a little grunt and collapsed onto Mike, his knees digging into his ribs.

Mike heaved himself up, which lifted the someone and sprawled him across the bed. Then, now on his feet, turned and seized the someone by the scruff of his neck.

Details were emerging. Dawn had arrived and enough light was coming through the window curtains for him to see.

Male. On the young side. Nobody I know.

That's a knife in his hand. Not a Bowie, no—but it wasn't designed to spread butter, either.

All of that passed through his mind in a second or two. The man squawked again, louder.

Have to put a stop to that until I know what's happening.

Mike's reflexes might have slowed some over the years, but he'd lost little if any of his strength—and he'd been a very strong man since he was a teenager. He lifted the man's torso off the bed, dragged him a couple of feet to the left, and slammed his head against one of the bedposts. Then repeated it; once, twice.

The man was no longer conscious and the knife was no

longer in his hand. He might have a broken skull, too, but Mike wasn't concerned about that at the moment, nor about the blood that was starting to soak the bed sheets.

There was very little likelihood anyone would have come into Fakhr-al-Din's villa in order to murder Mike Stearns. He was almost certain he'd just been an incidental target. A stranger—large; male—that the assailants wanted to get out of the way while they attended to their actual target.

Mike bent over, opened the lid of his trunk, and came out with a revolver in one hand and a small box in the other. It was the same Smith & Wesson Model 28 Highway Patrolman .357 Magnum that he'd used to kill a man on the day of the Ring of Fire. That was still the only time he'd ever killed a man with it—or with any other weapon he'd wielded personally. Mike had gone straight from civilian to major general.

The revolver was still in its clip holster. He slid it out. He had nothing to attach the holster to, since all he was wearing was a T-shirt and a pair of sweatpants, so he just tossed it on the bed. Then, opened the box, shook out a handful of bullets and stuffed them into one of his pockets.

For a moment, he considered putting on his shoes, but decided against it. There might be very little time at his disposal, and bare feet would be quieter anyway.

Carefully, he opened the door to his room and peered out into the corridor.

It was empty. He was on the top floor of the three-story villa. Fakhr-al-Din and Khasikiya slept in a room one floor down and all the way across the building. The emir's guards slept in rooms on the bottom floor, except that one of them was always stationed on guard outside the emir's chambers.

Quickly, making almost no sound in his bare feet, he moved down the corridor to the staircase. There he paused, listening. He heard nothing until—

Something between a shout and a scream exploded from below, followed by a hoarse grunt. Then, another grunt; then, the faint sound of what sounded like a body falling. That was followed by the much louder sounds of a door being broken in.

Still trying to be as quiet as possible—which was only possible at all because he was barefoot—Mike raced down the stairs. Once he neared the floor below he sprang over the last two risers, twisting his body as he went, and landed facing the direction from which the noises had come. If he'd misjudged and there was a man in the corridor in the other direction, he was in a world of hurt.

But he didn't think there would be, because whatever men were available to the attackers would mostly likely be breaking into the emir's quarters.

He'd guessed right. The corpse of the guard was slumped against the wall to the left of the doorway. One man was in the doorway passing through, and Mike thought he could see at least one other in front of him. It took him a split second to steady himself before he brought up the revolver in both hands, cocked the hammer, and fired.

One shot only. Mike was partial to revolvers for several reasons, one of which he'd readily allow was silly romanticism on his part—he'd sweet-talked his father into taking him to see the Clint Eastwood movie *Dirty Harry* when he was barely six years old. But among the other reasons was the fact that a man armed with an automatic pistol was prone to blasting away indiscriminately. That could be done with a revolver, but the weapon didn't favor it.

His aim was good, too. The bullet struck the target in the middle of his back, slightly below the shoulder blades. At this range—the man wasn't more than thirty feet away—the high-powered bullet would have punched right through his torso and destroyed his heart in the process. He fell forward into the room beyond.

In the course of falling forward, the man he'd just killed stumbled into the man in front of him. Between the impact and the sound of the gunshot—a .357 Magnum fired inside a corridor was *loud*; Mike's own ears were ringing—that man turned around.

Spun around—except the weight of his falling comrade knocked him off balance and he just barely kept his footing. He also had a very startled expression on his face.

Mike cocked the pistol, took aim and fired again. And, again, his aim was good. Good enough, anyway. He'd been aiming for the man's heart and struck him four or five inches higher. But that wound was even deadlier, because Mike hit him in the so-called "sniper's triangle." The assassin's aorta was severed and blood came gushing out of his mouth. He fell instantly, as if a string holding him up had been cut.

Mike raced forward. He could hear shouting and screaming in the rooms beyond. One of the shouting voices he recognized as Fakhr-al-Din's. The screams sounded like they were coming from Khasikiya.

When he reached the door, he faced the problem that the entry was blocked by the corpses of the two men he'd killed. He couldn't see into the room itself because the entryway was a short corridor of its own—six feet long, roughly—which opened to the right into the emir's chambers.

Nothing for it. Doing his best to contain his revulsion, Mike got through the doorway by stepping on the corpses. It wouldn't have been so bad if he hadn't been barefooted. He could feel blood coating parts of his feet.

But it was over and done within a few seconds. He had his revolver held in front of him, expecting someone to come around the corner to investigate the gunshots.

There was no one, though. From the din coming from within—Khasikiya was still screaming, which he took to be a good sign given the situation—he suspected the remaining assailants had been too preoccupied to wonder about the gunshots.

He was about to find out. Once again, he sprang forward, half-twisting, and landed on his feet facing into the chambers with his revolver held in both hands.

For an instant, his mind couldn't quite process what his eyes were seeing. Then everything sorted itself out.

One man was lying off to the side, still alive but clutching his chest. Presumably he'd been stabbed by Fakhr-al-Din. The emir himself was on his back with a second man pulling a knife out of his stomach and getting ready to stab him again. Off to the right, Khasikiya was struggling with a third assailant. He had a knife in his hand also but so far as Mike could see the woman hadn't been badly hurt yet.

He didn't spend any time thinking about that, though. Fakhr-al-Din was about to be murdered. His wife would have to wait.

There was no time to cock the pistol. Mike just fired. And... almost missed. Luckily, the bullet grazed the arm that the assassin was using to hold the emir down, jerking him aside just enough for the stab to strike Fakhr-al-Din in the hip instead of his torso. The injury produced was gory but not deadly.

Now off-balance and half-sprawled across the emir, the assassin stared up at him. Mike didn't want to risk a head shot but he had no choice. If his aim was off on a body shot, he might hit Fakhr-al-Din instead of his assailant.

Settle down, dammit. He made himself cock the pistol and squeeze the trigger instead of jerking it.

And didn't miss, this time. The bullet struck the assassin in his left eye. He fell backward, the wall behind him splattered with blood and brains.

That left—

He turned to the right and saw that the man wrestling with the emir's wife was now just trying to fend her off so he could deal with Mike. For her part—bless the woman!—the plump and middle-aged Khasikiya was still shrieking—more with fury than fear—while she clawed at the assassin.

Mike couldn't remember how many bullets he'd fired. He thought he still had one left but he wasn't positive. He knew from things he'd been told by men with more experience than he had in a gunfight that you almost always fired more shots than you'd remember afterward. He might be empty.

He stepped forward two long paces and smashed the revolver's gunbutt into the man's forehead. *Hard.* He let go of Khasikiya and started to slump but Mike held him up by his blouse and struck him again.

Hard. He thought he heard the skull break. It might not have, but there was no doubt the assassin was unconscious.

One left. He turned again and looked at the assassin who'd been lying propped up against the far wall. His hands had now fallen away from his chest. There was enough light in the room for Mike to see that the assassin's eyes were open and he was staring at . . .

Nothing. He'd died from his wound, apparently.

Khasikiya was now cradling her husband, softly sobbing. Mike looked at the couple and decided they could wait for a bit. He needed to make sure there was no more danger.

He dug into the pocket of his sweatpants and started reloading. His memory had been right, as it turned out— he did have one round left. Normally, he only loaded his revolver with five bullets, leaving the chamber empty as a safety precaution. But under these circumstances he wanted a fully loaded weapon, so he filled the whole cylinder.

Then, left the room and hurried down to the ground floor, the revolver held out ahead of him.

But there was no danger left. The door in the entrance leading out to the street was half-open. It didn't look as if it had been smashed in, so Mike assumed someone had picked the lock. He'd tried to persuade Fakhr-al-Din that the lock on that door had been an antique—practically medieval—and that at the very least a crossbar should be installed, but the emir had shrugged the warning off.

Mike didn't spend any time fussing over the door, though. What was done, was done. Instead he hurried down another corridor to the chambers where the guards lived.

One guard—the one on duty—had been killed already in the assault. The other two...

Dead. Both of them. Their throats cut while they were sleeping, obviously.

Mike lowered the revolver and headed back up the stairs. By the time he got back to the emir's quarters, Fakhr-al-Din was conscious and even alert. Well, sort of alert. He looked ten times as weary as Mike felt. Khasikiya was still cradling him, but she'd stopped weeping.

"I should have listened to you, Michael," said the emir. He even managed a little smile. "But now, I am afraid, it is all too late." He winced. Looking down, Mike saw that Fakhr-al-Din had his hand tightly pressed against the wound in his abdomen.

"Men don't survive a wound like this," said the emir. His tone was calm and matter-of-fact. "Almost never."

His wife cried out an inchoate little protest. Fakhr-al-Din reached up and gently stroked her head.

"It's called peritonitis," said Mike. "Yes, it's deadly—but it doesn't have to be. Let me see... Wait here."

He hurried out of the room, realizing as he left that his last two words were fairly silly. *Wait here.* As if a man in his mid-sixties who'd been stabbed in the stomach and hip was likely to get up and go anywhere.

Once he got back into his room he checked the man he'd struck down first. He was still unconscious and there was no sign he'd be recovering soon. As savagely as Mike had slammed his head into the bedpost, he might never recover.

He'd deal with that later. For the moment, he had more pressing issues to deal with. He opened the trunk and drew out the radio.

"Don't fail me now, Estuban," he muttered.

After he finished the transmission, Mike had to spend a few minutes just sitting on the bed next to the still-unconscious assassin—would-be assassin—in order to settle his nerves and restore his normal breathing. In his days in the ring, Mike had never had much of a problem dealing with the after effects of adrenalin. But fighting a professional boxing match and killing several men in a gunfight were not the same thing.

At all. In the real world he was not Dirty Harry—and from the perspective of a forty-year-old man instead of a six-year-old boy he didn't think anyone was, except for maybe the members of elite commando units. Whether or not he'd develop full-blown PTSD from the events this morning remained to be seen. But he didn't have any doubt at all that he'd be waking up more than once in the future from nightmares.

When he returned to the emir's chambers, he saw that Khasikiya was pressing down on her husband's abdomen and hip with a folded-up bedsheet. That would prevent too much blood loss, which could potentially kill Fakhr-al-Din long before infection would. She'd always seemed like a quiet, reserved and very pampered person to Mike, but he'd clearly underestimated her.

"Okay," he said. "We might be able to still save your life, Emir. But the only way to do it is to take you to Linz."

Fakhr-al-Din's eyes widened. "*Linz*? Michael, that's halfway across Europe. And why go there?"

"It's somewhere around six hundred miles away," said Mike. "As for 'why,' it's because the world's best doctor is there along with one of the world's two or three finest pharmacies."

"But—"

"The airship I was planning to use is already in Venice—and luckily for us, it's already fueled. By now, it's off the ground and heading our way. Unless the weather turns sour—which it might, but it doesn't look bad at the moment—it'll probably get here by midafternoon. By the end of the day, for sure. We can leave tomorrow morning—you and Khasikiya can, at any rate. There probably won't be enough room—enough lift, rather—for me to come with you. You'll fly to Venice so the airship can refuel. You should get to Linz within a few days. You'll probably be quite ill by then, but at least you'll have a chance."

Fakhr-al-Din stared up at him. "You expect me to *fly*?"

"Be quiet, husband! For once, just do as you're told."

Bless the woman.

Part Six

March 1637

And they remember there the great events
And the ancient runes of the Mighty One

"The Seeress's Prophecy," *The Poetic Edda*

Chapter 30

Breslau (Wrocław), capital of Lower Silesia

"I'm staying up there," Kristina pronounced, pointing up to the tower rising from the city's impressive town hall. "As high as possible."

Riding to her left, Thorsten Engler looked up at the prospective residence in question. The expression on his face was dubious. "I don't think—"

Caroline Platzer interrupted him. She was riding on the other side of the princess. "Of course, dear. Whatever you want. You're the future empress, after all."

"That's right!" Kristina proclaimed. The expression on the ten-year-old girl's face was simultaneously proud and disgruntled. "Even though some people"—here she cast a sidelong glance at Thorsten—"often don't treat me like they're supposed to."

For his part, Thorsten was looking at Caroline, who was giving him a meaningful look. The gist of which he had no difficulty interpreting: *Butt out, amateur. If you tell Kristina she can't do something, you'll spend the rest of the day squabbling about it. Let her find out for herself and you'll have some peace and quiet.*

By the time they reached the town hall, a small crowd of notables had come out of the building and were gathered at the entrance to welcome them.

Kristina was pleased as well as excited. The girl's character had many sharp angles which were not well aligned with each other. One of those angles was that she cared deeply if people liked her. Another was that she considered herself better and smarter than most people—which was in fact true, at least as far as smarter went. Yet a third angle was that for all her egotism she wasn't mean-spirited and she took as much pride in her good conscience as she did in her intelligence. The conscience wasn't always engaged whereas the intelligence was—but you could always appeal to that conscience, and she would listen. Grudgingly, sometimes, but she'd still listen.

Over time—yes, it had taken a while—Thorsten had come to like and respect the princess, all things considered. His betrothed Caroline Platzer had come to love her deeply. Which was a good thing, given that by now Caroline was the closest thing Kristina had ever had to a real mother.

Once the formalities were over, Kristina insisted on going immediately to her future chambers in the tower. Up the stairs she raced, passing floor after floor. Not counting the uppermost spire, the tower was close to two hundred feet tall. By the time Thorsten and Caroline got there, they were both somewhat exhausted while Kristina had already had time to explore her new residence.

Sadly, the exploration left her displeased. The first thing she said when Thorsten and Caroline reached the top floor was:

"This is terrible! There's no toilet!"

Manfully, Thorsten refrained from uttering his immediate response: *I could have told you that two hundred feet down, you silly child. Of course there's no toilet this far up. The building dates back to the fourteenth century.*

Caroline put the matter more diplomatically: "Kristina, this isn't a modern palace like the one your father had built in Magdeburg. It's very old. They didn't have what you think of as 'toilets' back them. Just—"

"I know what they had," Kristina said crossly. "I'm not ignorant, you know. They had"—here she made a quick and exceedingly improper squatting motion—"stupid and disgusting holes in the floor."

She looked up at the two adults, now with a pleading expression. "Could we have one put in, maybe?"

Caroline, exhibiting the treachery of a true governess, elbowed Thorsten and let him explain the facts of life.

It's not practical, Your Highness. To have a toilet here you'd have to be able to pump water all the way up.

"There are steam engines! I've seen them!"

Yes, Your Highness. But there still aren't all that many steam-powered pumps—I don't believe there are any at all in Breslau—and there will be other problems as well. Think of the difficulty of getting waterproof pipes this far—

"They have those new pipes! The Americans can make them! They're called Pee Vee . . . something."

"*PVC. It stands for polyvinyl chloride and it's not easy to make. There hasn't been much of it made yet and none of it is very good so far. We'd have to use old-fashioned clay pipes and stacking those this high wouldn't be very—*"

"It's not fair! This has a great view!"

Kristina often found reality disrespectful, but she'd eventually accept that it existed. And she couldn't figure out any way to send reality to the headsman. So—in this instance it took perhaps fifteen minutes—she eventually agreed to look for quarters elsewhere in the town hall.

They found suitable rooms for her in what amounted—would amount—to a royal suite once the silly clerks and their stupid papers got summarily moved somewhere else. The view wasn't that good—they were only on the third floor—but there was a sort of primitive toilet that Thorsten assured her could be modernized fairly quickly. Best of all, the suite was near the stables, so the princess would be able to ride any time she wanted to, at least in daylight. Kristina was a genuinely superb equestrienne.

After she was settled in, Thorsten and Caroline went in search of quarters for themselves. They found them not far away and on the same floor. Once again, clerks and their papers had to be evicted. But Thorsten wasn't given to worrying over the plight of bureaucrats. If they objected to the travails of life, let them join the army and discover what real travails were like.

Caroline was more sympathetic, but not much—and that little was just the professional courtesy of a social worker. If the clerks were discomforted, let them see how well they liked dealing with troubled people instead of papers day after day after day and for lower pay.

"So now what?" she asked, once they finished unpacking.

"I believe the town council is preparing a feast for us. Well, for Kristina."

Caroline ran fingers through her hair. "Tonight? Damn, I was hoping to rest for a day or two. You know how excited the girl's going to be. She loves being feasted. She'll be bouncing all over."

"Look on the bright side. At least she's not a princess who's fussy over what she's fed."

"*Kristina?* I think the only thing she'd refuse to eat is horse meat—and that's just because she likes to ride the critters."

Florence, capital of the Duchy of Tuscany
Italy

Once he got back to Florence, it took Mike more than a week to finish all the business he needed to take care of before he could return to the USE. About half of that time was spent making sure Fakhr-al-Din's household would be taken care of until—whenever—the emir could return. That was not especially difficult, since Grand Duke Ferdinando was cooperative, but the affairs involved were somewhat complex and Mike had to remain out of sight while he handled them.

The other half of the time was due to a simple problem—it would take that long before Estuban Miro could get an airship to Florence. There still weren't very many of the new hydrogen airships and the distance from Venice to Florence was too great for a hot air ship given that there were no refueling stations available between the two cities. Push came to shove, Miro was running a business, not a charity for wayward adventurers. If it had been an emergency, he would have diverted one of the airships anyway. But Mike assured him there was no need for him to get back at once.

Mike considered taking a land route to Venice. The distance wasn't more than two hundred miles, across terrain that was not especially difficult and had good roads all the way. But he didn't spend much time considering the idea. The problem was that there was no way to get from Florence to Venice overland except by passing through the Papal States or the Duchy of Modena, which was allied with the Spanish Habsburgs. That was very unfriendly territory, to put it delicately. If Mike got stopped and arrested...

Best not to risk it. So, he'd just have to wait until an airship arrived.

The airship arrived early in the afternoon. It would have left Venice at daybreak in order to be sure it could make the round trip during the day. It was possible to fly an airship at night but doing so was riskier.

The airship came to earth in the same Boboli Gardens adjacent to the Palazzo Pitti where Rebecca had met with the grand duke and his wife, Vittoria della Rovere. The gardens were so big that Mike had little fear he could be recognized at whatever distance a spy could manage, but he was in disguise anyway, just to be on the safe side. The "disguise" didn't amount to much, just a voluminous cloak that would obscure his figure and a very wide-brimmed and floppy hat that would put his face in shadows.

What he hadn't expected, once he climbed into the gondola, was to find his wife waiting for him.

Rebecca had a strained expression on her face.

"Hey, hon, I wasn't expecting—"

"Michael, it's your mother."

Grantville, West Virginia County
Former capital of the State of Thuringia-Franconia

By the time Mike got to the house where his mother had lived most of her life—his father also, but he'd died many years ago—she was no longer conscious. His sister Rita was there, thankfully, and had gotten there while their mother was still awake. Very weak, but awake.

"She asked for you and I told her you were on your way," Rita said. "Then she smiled and fell asleep. She hasn't woken up since, and Kunigunda"—Rita nodded toward a youngish woman sitting in a chair in a corner of the bedroom—"she's the nurse—she was trained at the high school—she doesn't—" Rita stifled a little sob. "Kunigunda doesn't think Mom's going to wake up again. Not ever. I hope she's wrong, but . . ." Again, his sister stifled a sob. "She's been out for almost sixteen hours now, Mike."

Mike was stifling his own grief, as best he could. A part of his mind knew that his mother had lived longer than anyone—including herself—had thought she would. She'd been born Jean Lawler, in 1939 by up-time reckoning, and had married Jack Stearns in 1964, at the age of twenty-five. She'd given birth to Michael on January 12, 1966. His sister was quite a bit younger than Mike; she'd been born twelve years later, in 1978.

Their mother wasn't very old, by normal up-time standards—she was still in her sixties. But she'd been an invalid for more than a decade and had been unable to replace many of the medicines that had helped her before the Ring of Fire. Still, year after year had gone by. She'd never gotten any better, but she'd never seemed to get any worse, either.

There was a famous saying: *No one expects the Spanish Inquisition.* That wasn't actually true, as Mike had come to know since he'd arrived in the Inquisition's heyday. As a rule, people *did* expect the Inquisition, since by Spanish law they had to provide people with a month's notice they'd be coming.

But one thing he knew wasn't a myth. He'd discovered it on the day his father had died, and he was pretty sure he was about to learn it again.

No one expects the death of a parent.

For the next four hours, with Rebecca hovering nearby, Mike and his sister sat across from each other at their mother's bed. At any given time, one or the other would be holding her hand, and usually both.

The time came when Kunigunda gently moved Mike aside so she could monitor their mother's pulse. After perhaps twenty minutes, she said: "She's gone."

She never had woken up again. But at least Mike had been there when she passed.

He and Rita hugged each other for a while. Mike found himself wondering, as he had on the day his father died—he'd been there, and had gotten home while his father was still conscious—on the mystery that sometimes accompanied death. He'd seen plenty of death since the Ring of Fire, most of it due to violence and most of the rest due to clearly evident illness. There's no mystery when a man dies because his skull has been shattered by a cannon ball, and not much mystery when a child dies of typhus or dysentery. But both of his parents had died quietly, both while they were peacefully sleeping. One moment they were still part of the world; the next, they were gone.

What happened in that instant, exactly? He did not know and knew he never would. Not even when his own death arrived, whenever that might be.

Of course, in his case, it was likely there would be no mystery at all. *Here lies what's left of Mike Stearns. He shoulda ducked.*

That finally broke the spell. He had to stifle a laugh.

The funeral was held two days later. As they were walking away from the grave, Mike said to Rebecca: "You know, we'll have to cover the cost of that airship ride ourselves. I'm sure Estuban won't raise the issue, but we can't let something like that slide. Most people in the here and now wouldn't think of it as public corruption if officials and military officers used government transport for something like this, but we're trying to put a stop—"

"Michael, relax. I already took care of it," said Rebecca.

Michael looked at her. "That quickly? I thought our finances were pretty tight."

"They were. They are no longer. Two weeks ago, the publisher gave me the first royalty payment for my book."

"That soon? How much—"

She told him. He was silent for a while. Then he whistled and said: "Damn. I wish Mom was still here. She always told me to marry up."

Rebecca gave him a sideways look. "In that case, you blundered badly. You should have married Eva Katherine von Anhalt-Dessau instead of me."

"Harry Lefferts' new girlfriend? I've never even met the woman. Is her family *that* rich?"

His wife laughed softly. "It is irrelevant. Neither she nor Harry will ever have to worry about whether she has her family's approval or not. Dowry be damned. She wrote a book too, you know—*The Adventures of Captain Lefferts, as told to Eva Katherine von Anhalt-Dessau*. The publisher barely noticed me when he handed me my check, he was so morose about having refused to publish the book about Harry. Instead, Harry and Eva sold it to Ron Stone—he created a new publishing house in Hesse-Kassel, if you didn't know—and the book wound up filling his coffers instead."

Mike's laugh was a lot louder than hers had been. "I get a real kick out of that. Since the Ring of Fire, everything the Stone family touches turns into gold. Buncha hippies!"

Rebecca smiled. "So it would seem. I think the seventeenth century now has its own—what do you call it—runaway blockbuster bestseller? Something like that."

"You mean to tell me that a trashy tell-all scandal book is outselling my wife's brilliantly reasoned treatise on the proper conduct of government and state affairs?"

"Outselling it by what Harry would call a country mile."

"Well, thank God. The world is back to normal."

Chapter 31

Beç, formerly known as Vienna
Capital of the new Ottoman province (eyalet) of Austria

"I hope they don't get suspicious," Denise said, trying not to sound as nervous as she felt. After another couple of seconds, she removed her forefinger and let the curtain on her side of the carriage fall back into place. They were nearing the gates they'd be using to leave the city.

"They won't," said Lukasz confidently. He and Noelle were sitting on the padded bench on the opposite side of the carriage. He had his arms crossed over his chest and his eyes closed, as if he were meditating. Which . . . he probably was, in his own hussar sort of way. Like a martial artist, Denise thought, rather than a monk.

"We've only been here a few weeks," she said. "They might think it's strange we're leaving so soon."

He shrugged, still without uncrossing his arms or opening his eyes. "They're Ottomans and we're supposed to be the envoys from a distant, unimportant—and

432

probably soon-to-vanish—principality they'd never heard of until we arrived. That means they're full of sublime—and not unreasonable—arrogance, and we're presumably as scatterbrained as you'd expect such envoys to be. They don't care what we do. By the time we pass through the gates, no one except minor officials will even remember we were here."

"He's right," said Noelle, although she didn't sound as confident as Lukasz did. "I'm sure he's right."

"The longer we stayed, the greater became the risk someone would get suspicious," Lukasz added.

"Of what?" Denise's question was more curious than demanding.

Lukasz shrugged again. "It could be anything. 'Suspicious' and 'Ottoman official' are practically synonyms."

The carriage lurched, throwing Denise against Judy Wendell, who was sitting next to her.

"Sorry," she said.

Judy helped Denise sit back up and smiled. "S'okay. The streets of Vienna sucked even before the Turks came marching in. No harm done."

She used her hands to rub her bare shoulders. "I wish we had a heater in here, though. Damn, it's cold—and I gotta tell you, Denise, this outfit of yours really sucks when it comes to providing any insulation."

"Don't it, though? If it makes you feel any better, the one I'm wearing is just as sucky, warmth-wise."

Judy glanced at the apparel Denise was wearing and then glanced down at her own. Allowing for minor variations, they shared the common themes of being gauzy and scant. "Whore outfits, indeed," she muttered. "Denise, you oughta be ashamed of yourself."

"Yeah, people have been telling me that as far back as I can remember. Well, not my parents so much. Mom only gave me a hard time once in a while and Dad almost never did. Not even when I got this tattoo." Grinning, she slapped the image on her belly.

Judy gave the tattoo a look that fluctuated between disapproval and envy. She really did think the image was in poor taste—questionable, for sure. On the other hand, she'd always secretly wanted to get a flashy tattoo herself.

"Look on the bright side," Denise said. With the palm of her hand, she patted the cushion they were both sitting on, which covered the bare wood of the bench. "I betcha Minnie and the Habsburgers are plenty warm; wrapped up the way they are in blankets so they don't get jolted to death. Would you rather be down there with them?"

"God, no," said Judy.

A muffled voice came from beneath them. "I heard that," said Minnie. "You're both going to rot in eternal hell."

"Indeed you will," chimed in the voice of Archduke Leopold, which was equally muffled from having to pass through the bench and the cushion on top of it. "On one of the lower hells, which according to Dante are freezing cold. So you won't actually rot, you'll just wish you could."

Before they set out, the decision had been made that Judy could risk riding in the cabin of the carriage, instead of being crammed in with Cecilia Renata in one of the spaces beneath the benches—as long as she wore one of Denise's "whore outfits." Ottoman soldiers had caught glimpses of Denise, true. But she and Judy had similar physiques, were about the same size, and Denise had always been wearing a veil when she was spotted. Even if they were stopped and soldiers insisted on looking into the carriage, they'd simply discover that the Polish grandee had brought two concubines with him instead of one. That was hardly something they'd find surprising.

Minnie and Leopold were crammed together in one of the spaces, but they were accustomed to that. At least Cecilia Renata would have a bit of space in her hiding place beneath Lukasz and Noelle.

Once they got out of Ottoman territory, they'd be able to relax a bit, at which point the three people hidden under the benches could come out and ride in the carriage proper. At that point, Leopold could join Lukasz in riding on horseback along with Jakub and the Slovene cavalrymen, leaving the carriage to the five women.

But that wouldn't be possible for days. In the meantime . . .

"Are we there yet?" asked Minnie.

Poznań
Poznań Voivodeship
Polish–Lithuanian Commonwealth

Jozef traced his finger across the map, indicating the escape route he was proposing. "Through the north gate—that's the only one we can be sure the APC can pass through—and then we loop around the walls to the east. Once we reach this bridge"—he tapped his finger on a marker—"we can get over the Warta and we'll be on Ostrów Tumski. We'll pass across the island, staying south of the Basilica, until we reach this bridge"—again, he tapped his finger on a marker—"which will put us back on the mainland. Then we follow the Cybina River until we get to this new bridge the USE engineers built while they were still investing the whole city. That will allow us to cross over to the south bank of the Cybina, after which . . ."

He leaned back from the table and stood straight again. "From there we can choose any number of routes that will take us down to Kraków."

"Which is what?" asked one of the hussars gathered around the table. "Four hundred miles?"

"Not that far," replied Jozef, shaking his head. "More like three hundred."

"Still a long journey, especially given the pursuit we'll be facing." The hussar smiled thinly. "Excuse me. Facing away from, I should have said."

Another hussar spoke up. "I'm not very worried about the pursuit. I don't think they'll press it, once we get well out of the city. What I am worried about are those bridges, especially this one." He reached over and placed his finger on the marker indicating the bridge that would allow them to leave Ostrów Tumski. "I've been on that bridge. I wasn't concerned about it at the time, but I was just one of a party of four hussars. Even on horseback and wearing our armor, we didn't weigh nearly as much as that APC does."

He turned his head to look at Mark Ellis. "How much does it weigh?"

"Somewhere between five and seven tons."

Several of the hussars made a face.

"It'd be a lot more than that if it was loaded up with coal, of course," said Ellis. "But all we'll be carrying are people and their guns, and some equipment, food, water. Two barrels of fuel. Figure..." His eyes got a little unfocused as he quickly did the math involved. "Add another ton and a half. Two tons, at the most. No matter what, it'll be less than ten tons."

"Less than ten tons..." muttered the hussar who'd asked the question. "That's a *lot*, to cross that bridge."

"Not really," said Ellis. "Timber is stronger than people realize. I grant you that bridge is the least sturdy of them all, but I don't think we'll have trouble getting across. By the time the APC reaches the bridge we should have a good lead over any pursuit. So we'll have the time to stop, let everybody except the driver get out, and then drive slowly across. I'm not worried about it— and I'll be the driver, don't forget. If anybody goes into the water, it'll be me."

The seven hussars in the room stared at him for a moment. Then Mieczysław Czarny nodded and said: "That's good enough for me." A moment later, two of the others were nodding as well. Czarny commanded a lot of respect from his fellows, even if not outright obedience.

The hussar named Jarosz Grabarczyk leaned over and made a circular motion with his forefinger just above the island labeled Ostrów Tumski. "What if the Germans move their troops back?"

Torstensson's two divisions had held Ostrów Tumski since they began their siege of Poznań, more than a year ago. They'd only withdrawn their forces from the island a few weeks earlier.

"I don't think that's likely," said Jozef. "Why would they withdraw them just to move them back a short while later?"

He was tempted to add *I have it on good authority . . .* but that would be unwise. The hussars in the room detested the USE just as much as they did King Władysław and the Sejm. They knew that Jozef hadn't been able to reach Poznań without the connivance of some elements among the Germans, but they were willing to overlook that. If they realized just how closely he was coordinating his actions with those of their longstanding enemy, they'd feel otherwise.

Besides, it wouldn't be true anyway. He didn't understand what he did because he'd met privately with General Torstensson or anyone else in the USE government except Gretchen Richter and the people around her in Breslau. But he had no trouble following the logic of what they had to be thinking.

Let the Polish revolutionaries gut the Polish regime down south, while the USE troops in the north pinned down their shoulders. There might have been a time when Gustav Adolf had intended to conquer Poland outright, but Jozef was quite sure he'd given up any such ambition—if for no other reason than that he didn't want to add that many Catholics to his realm. No, he'd settle for ousting his despised Vasa cousin from the throne of the PLC and replacing him with a less hostile regime.

The truth was that the "siege" of Poznań was no longer a siege in anything but name. The "siege lines" and fortifications that Torstensson now had in place were designed to protect his own army, not invest Poznań. So long as he maintained that army where it was—if anything, his forces were being enlarged—he could force the Polish king to keep most of the royal army in the north.

Jozef doubted very much if Torstensson had withdrawn his forces from Ostrów Tumski for the specific purpose of providing Jozef with an escape route from the city. He probably didn't even know Jozef was in the area, much less that he was planning to break out of Poznań with a captured APC.

But the Swedish commander did have radios—lots of them, in fact—and when the time came Jozef would see to it through his contact with Gretchen that Torstensson knew what was about to happen. He might even help them with a sortie. Not likely, no. But he certainly wouldn't get in their way.

"We're all agreed, then?" he said, looking around the room.

When he got back to the rooms he shared with Christin, she was studying herself with a mirror.

Studying her cuirass, more precisely.

"I wish you heathens knew what a full-length mirror was," she complained, shifting the angle of the small mirror in her hand. That was her own possession; one of the many things she'd brought with her in her luggage.

"We are not heathens," Jozef protested. "We are Catholics. Adherents to the true faith."

"What's religion got to do with it? You don't have full-length mirrors. You don't have walk-in closets. The less said about the plumbing, the better. You're heathens."

She shifted the mirror's angle again. "How does it look?"

"On you? Better than on any hussar, that's for sure. The—ah—additions are especially noteworthy, even if they'd be insane in an actual battle." He pointed to the additions in question. "I'm not sure what to call them, though."

"Neither am I. Breast plates, I guess. Except no woman who ever lived had tits this pointed, not even the Wicked Witch of the West."

"Who was she?"

"Like I said. Heathens."

Linz, provisional capital of Austria-Hungary

"He'll live," said James Nichols, "but it was touch and go for a while. If I hadn't flown out by plane to meet the airship in Venice, I don't think he would have survived at all. Once I got him stabilized—that hospital the Venetians have been building is damn impressive, by the way; even has an operating room—we were able to fly him here where we have a bigger and better pharmacy. We might need it. Peritonitis is nasty stuff."

The doctor returned to the seat at his desk and sat down. "He's still awfully weak, Mike. I wouldn't visit him just yet."

Mike took a deep breath and let it out slowly. "That's okay. We don't have anything we really need to talk about until he recovers further. I just wanted to make sure he was on the mend. I'd hate to think we went to all that time and trouble just to have it go literally belly-up. Not to mention that I've come to like the guy."

"I'm glad to see you're not just a heartless, conniving political schemer."

"Well . . . I am, actually." Mike drew himself up a little. "But I'm not a damn heathen. I have finer sentiments. I went to concerts, you know, back when I lived in LA."

Nichols eyed him skeptically.

"Okay, rock concerts. But they were still concerts. Had screaming girls waving their arms around, the whole high-culture nine yards."

Chapter 32

Radom
Sandomierz Voivodeship
Poland

Prince Stanisław Lubomirski looked around the interior of the hall he and his fellow magnates had entered just a few seconds earlier.

"I hope you didn't pay much for this," he said disdainfully.

Prince Zasławski's young face got a bit flushed. "Well... Perhaps more than it's actually worth." Then, defensively: "But we needed something suitable as quickly as possible, and—"

"You did well, Władisław," said Mikołaj Potocki. "Very well. The location is splendid—sixty miles or so south of Warsaw, where we can readily assemble our forces; not more than one hundred and thirty miles north of Kraków. Once we're ready to launch our offensive, we can be there in a week."

He avoided mentioning the dilapidated state of the

castle in Radom that the young prince had recently acquired. Potocki had hopes that, over time, he could wean Zasławski from his attachment to Lubomirski.

Judging from Lubomirski's glare, he was making some progress in that endeavor. Not for the first time, Mikołaj wondered how a man as sullen and unpleasant as Lubomirski retained his status in the upper circles of the Polish–Lithuanian Commonwealth. His great wealth explained much of it, of course, but there were men in the PLC who were as wealthy as he was—two of whom were in this very room. Jeremi Wiśniowiecki lorded it over almost a quarter of a million people on his vast estates in Ruthenia, and the young prince whom Lubomirski had all but openly derided was the richest magnate of Volhynia.

Lubomirski certainly didn't have a distinguished military record. Nothing to compare to the now deceased Koniecpolski, of course, but that was true of everyone. Koniecpolski was—had been—one of the martial giants of Polish and Lithuanian history. But Lubomirski's record was mediocre compared to any of the PLC's major military figures. His assumption of command over the Commonwealth's forces at the Battle of Chocim after the death of Grand Hetman Chodkiewicz had produced nothing better than a stalemate.

Still, the man continued to be given posts and positions: Krajczy of the Crown, Secretary of the King, Voivode of Ruthenia, and there was no sign that would change in the future.

It was aggravating. But, life often was.

"Will there be room for all of us in this palace?" asked Wiśniowiecki. The expression on his face as he looked around wasn't much less derisory than Lubomirski's. "Not just for ourselves but for our aides and adjutants. This building has to double as our military headquarters as well as our lodgings."

Zasławski was getting a beleaguered look on his face. "There's no other good choice." He gave Potocki a thankful glance. "As Mikołaj says, the location is very good. As for the state of the castle"—he shrugged—"you have to take into account that Radom was swept by an epidemic less than fifteen years ago and half the city burned down five years later. That's the reason not only for the price of the castle but for obtaining billets throughout the city as quickly as we did."

"Enough of this," said Janusz Łohojski. The voivode of Kiev placed a hand on Zasławski's shoulder. "This will do fine, young man. Yes, the castle hardly deserves the name of 'palace,' but so what?"

His lip didn't quite curl up enough to be called a sneer, but it came close. "In a few weeks, these delicate fellows will have to cope with tents and fieldworks. They'll be wishing they were still sleeping here, don't think they won't."

Lubomirski started to bridle, but Prince Wiśniowiecki just laughed. "You've got the right of that! I haven't forgotten what the Smolensk campaign was like. But I don't think it will take us a year and a half to defeat that pack of mongrels we'll be facing in Kraków."

"Not likely!" said Potocki, laughing himself. The five magnates in the room who constituted the leadership of the army that would soon be marching on Kraków didn't share many sentiments. But on this subject, they were of one mind. By early summer, at the latest, Poland's official capital would be in their hands.

Theirs. Not the king's, not the Sejm's. Things would proceed from there accordingly.

Near Pressburg
Capital of Royal Hungary

They had to detour around Pressburg on the way back, also. They hadn't expected that, but in the few weeks since the rescue expedition had avoided the city on their way in to Vienna, Sultan Murad had apparently decided his troops were getting fat and lazy in their winter quarters and needed some exercise. So, he'd bolstered the Ottoman forces investing the city. It would be much too risky now to try to enter Pressburg or even to skirt it too closely.

"We'd already decided to head for Kraków anyway," said Lukasz. "We'll take the alternate route."

"*Which* alternate route?" asked Leopold. "You've mentioned at least three."

His tone of voice was a bit sullen. The "decision" to head for Kraków had been more in the way of a declaration by Lukasz than something mutually agreed upon after long and deliberate discussion. Leopold had argued for taking a route that would enable them to return to Austrian territory as quickly as possible.

Sadly for him, the Slovene cavalrymen who served as their escort viewed Lukasz as their commander, not an Austrian archduke who had no authority over them whatsoever. Still more sadly, and quite to his surprise, none of the people he'd expected to rally to his side did so.

Minnie didn't, because she wanted to stay with Denise and Denise was anxious to get back to Kraków so she could find out how her mother fared.

Cecilia Renata didn't, partly because she was feeling adventurous and had a pretty good idea of how cramped and tiresome her life would be in an overcrowded jury-rigged royal palace in Linz. But partly she was being influenced by Judy Wendell, who'd become the best friend she'd ever had in the course of their months-long stay in the cellars.

For her part, Judy was inclined to continue on to Kraków because for one of the few times in her life she'd gotten attracted to a man. For whatever reason—she didn't understand it that well herself—Jakub Zaborowsky had piqued her interest.

Denise found out about that from Minnie, who'd also become Judy's friend during their months in the cellars.

"She's pretty uncertain—and more than a little confused—about the whole thing," Minnie had told Denise the day before they got to the outskirts of Pressburg. "I told you she's still a virgin. She doesn't have our experience with the weaker sex."

Denise shook her head. "I still find it hard to believe about Judy. Not the part about Jakub—he's seems okay to me—but about her maidenly state."

"It is strange, as good-looking as she is."

"Screw looks. She's always seemed pretty levelheaded

to me. Being a virgin past the age of sixteen is . . ."
Again, she shook her head. "The only ones I know are
dimwits."

"You hang out with a bad crowd."

"That would mostly be *you*, Minnie."

"No, it's more than just me. Bad Influence Number
One was—is—your mother."

Denise chewed her lip. "Well . . . Yeah. Mom lost her
cherry even earlier than I did. Dad wasn't the first bad
boy ever caught her eye."

"She told you about it?"

"Sure. It's a mother's duty to educate her daughter and
raise her properly."

"You mom is really cool."

"Yeah. I just hope that Polish bad boy she's hanging
out with now hasn't gotten her killed yet."

Poznań
Poznań Voivodeship
Polish–Lithuanian Commonwealth

Not for the first time since she'd made the man's
acquaintance, Christin George had to restrain herself
from laughing at the expression on Walenty Tarnowski's
face. She was even more determined to avoid giggling.
Christin had learned while still a young girl that she
giggled at the proverbial drop of a hat—and she detested
doing so, because she thought it made her seem girlish.

The problem was that Walenty's expression almost
seemed permanently fixed on the man's face. The

emotions displayed therein were a combination of frustration, exasperation, humiliation and disgrace.

Frustration because he really wanted to accomplish something, but couldn't. Exasperation because he understood how to do it but didn't have the necessary tools or equipment. Humiliation because his failure was something he took personally instead of accepting it as an inevitable concomitant of the world he'd been born into. And disgrace because he was sure that his humiliation was the source of contempt from that same world.

Christin thought the frustration and exasperation were understandable; the humiliation was childish; and the sense of disgrace was downright idiotic. In point of fact, the people around Tarnowski were far more likely to be astonished and amazed by the man's intelligence and talent than they were to be derisive. If Christin herself had been told before the Ring of Fire that there were people in the seventeenth century—not many, no; but there were some—who were innately brilliant mechanical engineers she would have scoffed at the notion.

Walenty Tarnowski had proved to her otherwise, several times over. But the man himself didn't believe it. He took every setback as a personal failure.

The occasion for his disgruntlement this day was his inability to invent welding. Any kind of welding except forge welding, which had been around for millennia—but he didn't consider that real welding. Oxyacetylene, arc welding, mig welding, you name it and he couldn't do it, even though he understood how each could be done.

His inability to use oxyacetylene was particularly annoying to him. It was so *simple*. Blend two gases together—oxygen and acetylene, or any number of substitutes for acetylene—set them afire, apply the heat to the two pieces of metal you wanted to join, and it was done.

The problem was he couldn't get pure enough oxygen. He was certain—sourly, bitterly, angrily certain—that somewhere in the dark industrial bowels of the United States of Europe some unworthy fellow was employing one or another form of fractional distillation.

But him? In benighted and backward Poland? The best he'd be able to manage for some time was to use a throttling effect—the so-called Joule-Thomson effect, named after two scientific dilettantes in the pampered universe the up-timers came from—in order to cool air down enough to separate out the oxygen.

Eventually he could do it, certainly. But he didn't have *eventually*. He had just a few weeks before the breakout from Poznań.

Once she was sure she had her giggling-impulse throttled, Christin tried to console Tarnowski.

"Walenty, cheer up, will you?" She pointed to the two men atop the APC who were constructing the gun turrets. "The rivets they're using will work just fine."

"Rivets," Tarnowski muttered. The word practically dripped with contempt. "They've had rivets since ancient times."

Christin shrugged. "For this, they'll work fine. I don't think welding the armor plates together would be much better."

One of the workmen set down the bucket he'd used to haul up a heated rivet from the man working the furnace on the floor of the workshop. Then, reached in with a pair of tongs, lifted the rivet and inserted it through the drilled holes that lined up two of the iron plates. On the other side, a blacksmith pounded the tail of the rivet with a hammer until it was deformed enough to lock the two plates together.

Tarnowski turned and began walking away. "Yes, I know it will work. But it's not *elegant*."

Now Christin did laugh. She couldn't help it. "My husband was a welder, Walenty. Probably the best professional welder in Grantville. If he'd heard you call what he did 'elegant' he'd have thought you were crazy."

She stopped and turned around, looking back again at the APC. "Speaking of which, you do understand that cutting the top plates into crenellations and painting the turrets to look like medieval brick-and-mortar fortifications is purely insane."

Finally, that managed to elicit a smile from the man. A sour smile, true, but it was still a smile.

"The hussars insisted on it. If there's a distinction between 'hussar' and 'lunatic,' I have yet to discover it."

"They'll come in handy during the breakout, though."

"That's because it's a lunatic enterprise to begin with."

"You agreed to it."

"Yes, I know I did. That's because in this century there's no clear distinction between 'mechanical engineer' and 'lunatic' either."

She just couldn't help herself. She giggled.

✦ ✦ ✦

Before they left the warehouse where the APC was being prepared for the breakout, Christin donned the hooded cloak she always wore when she came there. She did so partly for the warmth it provided. Poznań had a more pleasant climate than most of Poland, especially in the number of sunny days it enjoyed. This far into March, the temperature during the day was usually five or ten degrees above freezing, but at night it could drop down almost to zero degrees Fahrenheit.

Mostly, though, she always wore the garment because it made her very hard to recognize. By now, the fact that Jozef Wojtowicz had brought with him a German woman he planned to marry—said he did, at any rate—was fairly common knowledge. But her visits to the warehouse would draw attention, if people realized how often she made them. And the explanation...

She's actually an American and she knows way more about machinery than any proper woman should. She's probably a witch.

Would be awkward.

"It's too bad Lukasz insisted you ride a horse and wear that silly armor," Walenty said, as they made their way toward their lodgings. "I'd be happier if you were driving the APC than Mark was."

She smiled. "Not too many up-timers would agree with you. Men, at any rate. They used to make fun of women drivers, you know."

"It's outrageous. Odious."

"The term you're looking for is 'male chauvinist.'"

Tarnowski waved his hand dismissively. "Not that. What's odious is that men so unthinking should have had such splendid technology. It's like—like—"

"The phrase you're looking for is 'putting lipstick on a pig.'"

"Precisely." After a moment, he asked: "How do you make lipstick?"

Chapter 33

Linz, provisional capital of Austria-Hungary

The summons came as a knock on the door, just as the sun was coming up.

Julie answered it, yawning. A young man was standing at the front door of the apartment that she and Alex and daughter Alexi lived in, which was on the building's ground floor. There was enough light for her to discern that he was wearing Austrian colors. That consisted simply of an ocher sash running diagonally from his right shoulder that featured the newly adopted coat of arms of the recently proclaimed Austrian-Hungarian Empire.

Emperor Ferdinand—the new one, the Third—had gotten the idea from one of Grantville's history books. He'd simplified the double-headed eagle he'd seen in the book, because the up-time version was the so-called "medium common coat of arms" adopted in 1867. Unfortunately, that particular coat of arms included the armorials of Galicia, Salzburg, Tyrol, Silesia, Transylvania,

Illyria and Bohemia in addition to the undisputedly Austrian provinces of Styria, Carinthia and Carniola. Given that Ferdinand III would have to wage war against every single one of his neighbors in order to enforce his claim to those territories, it seemed more prudent to just modify the coat of arms.

She recognized him as one of Gustav Adolf's couriers and knew immediately what his presence at her door this early in the morning had to mean.

"They're coming," she said.

"Yes, My La—ah . . . "

Julie was amused by the youngster's fumbling attempts to come up with the proper cognomen for a Swedish baroness who'd begun life as an American commoner and was married to a Scot nobleman who'd need to display the bar sinister if he made so bold as to adopt a coat of arms of his own.

"Mrs. Mackay will do just fine," she said. "But whatever you do, don't call me 'Ma'am.'" Julie was firmly of the opinion that "Ma'am" was a title reserved for women in their dotage.

She looked past him and saw that he'd brought an extra horse for her use.

Fat chance of that happening. Julie had been exceedingly disgruntled that she wouldn't be able to scramble properly, as she'd seen done in movies about the RAF during World War II. The approach of enemy airships just didn't require any such measures. So she'd insisted that she had to be provided with a motorcycle, which, after a few weeks, was delivered from Grantville.

She loved that motorcycle, although she had to be

careful with it on some of the city's streets. It was a dirt bike, of course. She'd been adamant on that point. Riding a motorcycle through a seventeenth-century city wasn't too different from motocross racing.

"Forget the horse," she said. "I'll get to the airfield long before you do."

She closed the door. By then, Alex had come out of their bedroom. He understood what was happening just as well as she did, and had a strained expression on his face.

"I'm coming with you," he pronounced.

"Okay—but you ride in back."

"Yes, certainly. I don't know how to operate that infernal machine. I'm a cavalryman."

She went into the bedroom and started dressing. "Take Alexi over to Grizelda. I'll pick you up there after I get something to eat."

As soon as he finished dressing, he left. Julie was done a minute later and went into the kitchen. She already had a lunch ready—she'd made sure she did for the past week—and took it with her to the shed in the alley where she kept the motorcycle.

Once she removed the padlock from the shed, she stuffed her lunch into the bike's saddlebag. It was just a cloth sack with a small loaf of bread and some cheese. She would have liked to include an apple as well, but one of the bitter realities of life in the seventeenth century was that the season for apples was autumn, not supermarket aisle.

She started up the bike and raced off. Still a little peeved that she wasn't able to scramble properly, she made up for it by doing a wheelie—which was probably a really stupid thing to do, but war was hell.

After a minute or so of enjoying her improvised scrambling, Julie turned around and went back to her apartment building. By the time she arrived, Alex was waiting for her. He climbed onto the bike, and off they went. She was driving fast, but she refrained from doing another wheelie. It wasn't that she didn't think she could, it was that she knew if she did Alex would retaliate by boasting about his horsemanship.

Linz was not a big city, geographically speaking, even though it now had a population density that would have rivaled any equivalent-sized portion of Tokyo. But this early in the morning the streets were not packed yet, and the bike made enough noise that by the time she passed by all the pedestrians and most of the horse-drawn vehicles had moved aside.

Not all, though, which kept the ride from getting boring. A couple of flustered pedestrians who had to jump aside yelled at her, but they were instantly shouted down by the others nearby. Most people in Linz understood perfectly well why Julie was racing through the streets. A fair number of them cried out her name in praise.

So, in five minutes she had passed through the city's western gates—which had already been opened for her—and was coming out onto the field where the *Magdeburg* was moored. She left the bike in the care of a courier, gave Alex a fierce but quick kiss, and raced up the wooden staircase that had been erected to provide access to the huge airship's gondola.

"Where's Dell, Konrad?" she asked the young officer who helped her clamber into the gondola.

"He's not here yet," replied Lieutenant Neydell.

"How much time do we have?" She started climbing into the gun turret, which was located in the upper portion of the gondola.

Captain van Buskirk turned away from his inspection of the instrument panel and said, "At least ten minutes before we have to lift off."

Julie stopped on the ladder. "*That* long?" In practice runs, she'd never gotten to the airship with more time to spare than five minutes—and sometimes by the proverbial skin of her teeth.

The captain smiled. "Once again, we discover the discrepancy between simulation and reality." He pointed at the narrow slit in the armor through which he'd have to guide the airship. "The Ottoman fleet is still several miles away, and they seemed to have stopped all forward progress."

Frowning, Julie finished climbing into the gun turret. Her Remington Model 700 was resting in its case, and the Karabine was positioned against the left wall. If they decided to use it, Dell would help her get it into position. If need be, she could do it herself, but it helped to have an assistant. The Karabine was heavy and awkward to handle.

She was hoping she'd be able to stick with the Remington, though. Julie was extremely confident in her marksmanship—with good reason—and was fairly sure that at any range the Ottomans needed to get within in order to have a chance at hitting her, she'd be able to strike them before they got there. They'd have their own gun turrets, of course, but they couldn't make the firing slits too narrow or they'd simply be useless.

Once she was settled in, she went back to pondering the problem.

Why had the Turks stopped coming?

It was perhaps as well for her peace of mind that she didn't know the answer, which was quite simple. The one and only purpose of the current Ottoman airship attack was to kill Julie. And since the *Magdeburg* hadn't detached from its mooring mast yet, what was the point of coming any closer? If the airships got over the city itself, there was the risk that they could be struck by groundfire. Over the winter, the Turks had observed the rockets test-fired by the Austrians on several occasions. The missiles were not at all accurate, but they could reach altitudes of between one and two thousand yards. Unless the Ottoman fleet stayed well clear of the rocket batteries, nothing would prevent the *Magdeburg* from staying at low altitudes. If the Ottomans wanted to kill the American woman, they'd have to come down and get her.

They might have to do that anyway. But they thought the *Magdeburg* would choose to come at them. So, they waited.

Three miles east of Linz

"The commander orders us to stop and hover," the radio operator said.

Moshe Mizrahi had been expecting the order. "Signal the other ships in the line."

The radio operator doubled as the airship's signal flagman. Within seconds, he was leaning out of the stern of the gondola and giving the signals to the other four airships in the *Chaldiran*'s line. Theirs was the second line in the assault. As before, the first line of five ships was commanded by Mustafa bin Ramazan, aboard the *Turnadağ*. Moshe could see the *Turnadağ*'s radio operator making the same flag signals. The action would be duplicated by the lead ships in all four lines involved in the attack.

Moshe found that an unsettling feature of today's mission. By now, Turkish artisans had made enough radios to equip every single one of the airships in the Gureba-i hava, as Sultan Murad's air force was called. The problem was that the radios were quite heavy—that was mostly due to the batteries—and in this mission weight was at a premium. In order for the Gureba-i hava's gunners to have a reasonable chance of killing the Jooli, they had to fire from within armored turrets. And given that the Jooli had already proven that she was quite capable of killing the crewmen, they also had to be protected with armor. The end result were gondolas so heavy they could only just be lifted off the ground.

So, only the lead ships had radios—which, to Moshe's consternation, they accommodated by reducing the armor protecting the crew. Among them, of course, being himself. Rather prominently himself, since he had to guide the airship and that required him to take a position in the front of the thinly armored gondola.

For the others, signal flags would do. Signal flags weighed very little.

"So now, we wait," he said, to no one in particular.

Airfield just west of Linz

"About time," Julie groused, when Dell Beckworth climbed into the turret.

"Gimme a break. I don't have a motorcycle."

"I offered to get you one. I've got a lot of clout with the emperor these days, you know." It didn't occur to her just how bizarre that sentence was. In her days as a small-town girl back up-time, the thought that she'd someday have a personal relationship with an actual *emperor* had never once crossed her mind. Emperors were people who only existed in history books and *Star Wars* movies.

"I don't *want* a motorcycle. I'm a gun nut with a proper sense of safety, not a lunatic."

"You're just jealous."

"That is sooooooo not true." He eased into his position to her left. "We gonna start with the Remington?"

"Hell, yes. I'm not a lunatic either."

He smiled. "C'mon, Julie. The Karabine doesn't kick *that* bad."

"Then why don't you volunteer to shoot it?"

"I'm not the world's best marksman."

"Mark*swoman*, dammit."

"I'm not that either."

✜ ✜ ✜

The *Magdeburg* cast loose from the mast and began rising.

North bank of the Danube
About a mile west of the village of Langenstein

Atop his observation tower, Sultan Murad watched the huge enemy airship begin its ascent. He turned to one of his aides and said, "Inform the troops that the battle has begun."

The aide hesitated. Understanding the reason, Murad shook his head. "No, we will not begin the assault today. If our ships succeed in their mission, they will need the rest of the day and much of the night to refit the gondolas for a bombing mission. But tell the men the battle has begun. It will lift their spirits."

It *might* lift their spirits, assuming the Jooli was destroyed today. But since he took Baghdad and Vienna, Murad IV was not very concerned with maintaining his army's morale. Following the greatest sultan in the Ottoman Empire's history, the men would absorb a few setbacks easily enough.

Three miles east of Linz

"Commander Mustafa bin Ramazan reports that the kâfir ship is coming," said the radio operator.

Moshe suppressed the impulse to snarl, *I am not blind.* All he said was "Signal the other ships in the line."

Then he had to suppress the impulse to rap the sheet of metal in front of him with his knuckles. He'd done that once or twice before, when the *Chaldiran* was on the ground in its hangar. Even then, the tinny sound had been depressing.

"Armor," they called it.

He tried to console himself with the fact that the armor protecting the gunner was quite a bit more substantial. Surely he would be the Jooli's target.

Surely.

Chapter 34

Four thousand feet above Linz
Provisional capital of Austria-Hungary

The airship *Preveza*, commanded by Abraham Zarfati, was in its usual position in the first of the four lines of attack. The command ships of each line flew on the far left, which in Zarfati's case meant his immediate superior was the commander of the *Turnadað*, Mustafa bin Rámazan. Abraham's own vessel was the next one over in the line.

Once the huge enemy airship reached the same altitude as the Ottoman fleet, it began moving toward them, at that same frightening speed Abraham remembered from the year before. Between that velocity and the sheer size of the thing, Abraham had to clench his jaws for a few seconds to keep himself under control.

In the attack ordered by Sultan Murad the year before, the front line of airships had been armed with nothing but smoke generators. For that reason, the *Magdeburg* had ignored them and attacked the second line of ships. But it was soon obvious that was not going to be the case today. The *Magdeburg* was heading directly toward them.

At least, so it appeared at the beginning. But after a short while, it became apparent that the *Magdeburg* was angling slightly. It was now headed for the fifth ship in the line, almost at the opposite end from the *Preveza*'s station.

Abraham started to sigh with relief, but restrained himself. True, there were no janissaries on the *Preveza*'s command deck who could have observed the little betrayal of fear. The only janissary aboard was the rifleman, and he was positioned in the gun turret below the command deck. Still, it was not a good idea to get in the habit of displaying any emotions while carrying out the duties of an officer in the Gureba-i hava.

As they had planned, Julie shifted to the first of the two gunports on the right side of the turret. The *Magdeburg*'s size meant that it could support a much larger turret than the ones on the enemy airships. From reports brought back by spies, the allied forces knew that the small Ottoman turrets only had a single gunport—a wide one which faced straight ahead. The *Magdeburg* had five: one in the very front and two on each side. That would allow Julie to shift her angle of fire and meant the *Magdeburg* didn't have to be flying directly at an Ottoman airship to pose a threat to it. It was their hope that this would prove to be a significant advantage, one that could offset the much greater number of the enemy's vessels.

They were about to find out. Two minutes earlier, the pilot of the *Magdeburg* had shifted course. The enormous airship was now headed directly for the fifth and last Ottoman airship in the first line. Which meant . . .

That within a few seconds, from the gunport where she was now stationed, Julie would have a clear shot at the gunport of the first or second ship in the line.

The second, as it turned out.

Abraham heard the distinctive cracking sound that he remembered well from the year before. The monster had fired.

But at what? He hadn't spotted a rifle barrel emerging from the gunport at the upper front of the enemy's gondola.

The commander of the *Preveza* hadn't spotted Julie's rifle because it was eight feet away from the forward gunport and only a few inches of the Remington's barrel protruded from the gunport she was using. He simply wasn't looking there.

The janissary who served as the *Preveza*'s gunner had spotted Julie's rifle, just before she fired, since he was looking directly at that gunport. But he wasn't seeing anything anymore.

Abraham was a bit surprised that his own gunner hadn't returned the fire. True, he didn't have a very good angle of fire at the forward gunport of the enemy ship, so it would have been a difficult shot.

Difficult, but not impossible. Abraham estimated the range as being somewhere between two hundred and two hundred and fifty kulaçs—a *kulaç* being roughly equivalent to the height of a tall man, about six feet. Between four and five hundred yards, if he used the enemy's measurements.

That range was at the edge of performance for the best of the sultan's rifles and marksmen, but it wasn't beyond it.

Perhaps the gunner had decided to save his ammunition for a better shot later. He was using special ammunition, which was expensive and in short supply.

In any event, it was none of Abraham's concern. His authority over the airship's crew did not extend to the janissary in the turret below. The janissaries had been quite insistent that they would not accept being subordinated to zimmis, the term applied to the empire's Jews and Christians.

Dell was stationed at the first of the two gunports on the starboard side, to Julie's left. Julie made a note to herself that they needed to come up with a suitable terminology for the things. "First of the two gunports on the starboard side" was at least eight syllables too long under battle conditions.

Because he was positioned at the port itself, rather than behind the railing in the center of the turret that Julie was using as an arm rest, Dell had a better and much wider view of the whole situation.

"The next ship's coming into line, Julie," he announced. "It should appear in your port any—"

"I see it. Thanks."

This was going to be a more difficult shot. The first airship had been almost completely level with the

Magdeburg. This one's altitude was at least thirty or forty yards below theirs. Julie's turret was above the main deck of their gondola; that of the Ottoman ships was below. From this angle, most of the enemy gondola was obscured by the gas bag. She could see the ship's gunport, but didn't have the clear and straight line of fire into the interior of the turret that she'd had with the first airship.

On the other hand, the range was a bit shorter. She estimated it at four hundred yards, thereabouts.

Difficult, but not impossible.

"This is why I get paid the big bucks," she murmured. The shot went off an instant later.

The third ship in the first line was named the *Krbava*, after the Ottoman victory over the kingdom of Croatia at the end of the fifteenth century. It was the third of the six airships commanded by a Jew, Isaac Capsali, a friend of Abraham's who had recently been promoted to command his own airship.

Again, Abraham heard the sharp *crack!* that was the distinctive sound of the Jooli's weapon. But, again, he could not see what effect it had, if any.

Aboard the *Krbava* itself, Isaac Capsali was apprised of the effect of the shot immediately. The unmistakable sounds of a bullet ricocheted about were accompanied by a piercing screech. Moments later, the janissary rifleman came swarming up the short ladder into the gondola proper. He was clutching his side above the hip with his left hand, blood oozing out from between his fingers.

"She's an *afreet*!" he shouted. "No human can shoot like that!"

It took a couple of minutes to calm the man down enough to inspect the wound. Once he was able to do so, Isaac assured the janissary that the injury, however bloody, was not life-threatening. He was able to bind it up and stop the bleeding within a short time.

Soon enough, he found himself wishing it had been a fatal injury, however. The janissary cursed him for a fool and insisted he had no chance of surviving such a demonic wound. He went on in that vein for some time. And he adamantly rejected any suggestion that he return to his post.

Eventually, Capsali was able to shut the man up and get him to go back down below. He couldn't command the hysterical fellow, of course, being a zimmi. But he did point out that regulations required the commander of an airship to write a report after each action, depicting in detail what had transpired. If the sultan discovered that a still-conscious and functioning gunner had refused to return to his post . . .

In the end, the janissary was more afraid of Sultan Murad IV than he was of a demon. A wise man, no; but not a complete idiot, either. Perhaps he bolstered his courage by telling himself the afreet was a mere female. That probably didn't bring much comfort, however. So might a man cast overboard assure himself that the fin cutting toward him surely belonged to a female shark.

For the first time since the battle began, a bullet struck the flank of the *Magdeburg*'s gun turret. It didn't hit near any of the gunports, but Dell went to investigate anyway.

"There's a good-sized dent here," he announced. "But it didn't penetrate the armor. That's the good news. The not-so-good news is that from the looks of the indentation I don't think it hit the armor head-on. If it had . . ."

Julie would have shrugged, except the rifle was back at her shoulder. "We always knew any armor light enough for an airship to use wouldn't stop a high-powered bullet fired straight on. Way it goes. I need you to start spotting again, Dell. I think that last airship in the line will be coming into view soon."

North bank of the Danube
About a mile west of the village of Langenstein

"So far, My Sultan," reported the radio operator, "the Jooli has killed one man and injured another. So far as we know, she herself remains unharmed."

"And the airships themselves?" asked Murad.

"Ours remain undamaged in any significant way. So far as can be determined, the same is true of the enemy craft."

The sultan nodded and went back to peering through the telescope atop the observation platform. By now, Murad thought he finally had a good grasp of the logic by which the airship battle he was observing was unfolding. It was like watching men wading through mud and trying to club each other with very light and heavily padded cudgels. On one hand, the airships themselves were slow for their size and ungainly. On the other hand, they could only be injured under extremely constrained conditions. Two people firing at a great remove through narrow firing slits, at least one of whom had to be pointing directly at their target for either of them to score a hit. All the advantage was on the side of the defense.

The problem that remained was that his airships had a very limited lifting capacity. So long as they were armored, the Jooli could do little damage. But the armor was so heavy that the airships could not lift any significant number of bombs. But if they removed the armor to enable the airships to carry out bombing missions, the Jooli would become deadly again.

The solution was obvious. So he thought, at least—and this was a good time to test it.

"Tell the second line to advance directly on the *Magdeburg*. Crowd it as closely as possible. Then tell the third line to bypass that battle and fly directly over the city."

He considered instructing the ships of the third line to climb high enough to be out of range of the Austrian rockets, but decided not to. He himself was skeptical of the effectiveness of the missiles, given their inaccuracy. Sooner or later, that would have to be tested, and he saw no reason not to do it now.

Four thousand feet above Linz
Provisional capital of Austria-Hungary

"Relay the order to the rest of the line," said Moshe Mizrahi, who commanded the second line of airships. The radio operator of the *Chaldiran* took up the flags and began signaling to the other four ships.

This done, the commander took a deep breath.

Crowd the enemy ship. He felt like a mouse ordered to take his fellow rodents to crowd a cat.

The cat was likely to object. And it—no, this one was a she—was much bigger than they were.

Chapter 35

Tom Simpson's voice came into the turret via the intercom that had been installed for the purpose. "Julie, they're up to something."

From her vantage point inside the railing, Julie didn't have a wide view of what was happening outside, but Dell was positioned right in the front gunport. He practically had his head sticking out of it.

Hearing Tom's statement, Dell drew back into the turret and said to Julie, "He's right." He moved his hands in such a way as to suggest a ball of dough being squeezed. "The whole next line is crowding in—I swear, a couple of 'em are practically touching—and they're moving directly at us."

Julie frowned. "Sounds like they plan to fire a barrage. Well, insofar as five rifles constitute a 'barrage.'"

The intercom had been designed to pick up any voice

in the turret, so Tom responded to her immediately. "I don't think so, Julie—or not entirely. I don't doubt they'll fire one or two barrages but what I think they're really doing is playing football."

"Huh?"

"Football. You know, old-fashioned up-time—"

"I know what football is, thank you." Her tone was a tad acerbic. "But you'll have to explain what you mean."

"What I mean is that I think Murad has ordered this line of ships to serve as blockers, holding us off or at least impeding us while the next line moves around and goes for the city. They might even be planning a bombing run. Or—what I think is more likely—Murad's testing us to see if the tactic will work."

"So what are we going to do?"

Julie didn't even think of what the *Magdeburg*'s captain thought they ought to do. The Dutch officers and crewmen who actually flew the ship had made clear from the beginning that they were there purely as technicians—the aerial equivalents of ship pilots. Any decisions involving military tactics were entirely the responsibility of the man who was the real commander of the *Magdeburg*.

That would be one Thomas Simpson, formerly an artillery officer in the USE Army but recently promoted to colonel and put in charge of the brand spanking new "USE Army Air Corps." That had occasioned a wrangle with the Air Force, but Gustav Adolf had come down firmly on the army's side—mostly because he had direct control of the army and wanted tight control over the *Magdeburg*.

Tom himself thought the whole thing was a little ridiculous. The "Army Air Corps" had exactly one aircraft—the *Magdeburg*—no other officers but himself, a handful of enlisted men—few of whom actually flew in the *Magdeburg*—and two military contractors, Julie Sims and Dell Beckworth, who so far did all of the combat stuff.

Granted, the promotion was nice. Already a full colonel at the age of twenty-eight and something of an apple in his emperor's eye, Tom had a bright career ahead of him, assuming he decided to stay in the military after the war. Also assuming the war actually ended—always a chancy proposition in the seventeenth century—and assuming he survived.

Tom's answer didn't come for perhaps fifteen seconds. The man was quite intelligent, but he deliberated on things before making a decision.

"We'll go straight at them—but you and Dell stay away from that front gunport. They'll all be firing at us and I don't want to risk you getting shot."

Julie frowned. "Then what's the point—"

"They want to play football, we'll teach them another American sport. The one called 'chicken.'"

Julie rolled her eyes. "Oh, swell."

"Are you serious, Tom?" asked Dell. Being technically a civilian, he saw no reason to waste time with long-winded military protocol. "What happens if we run into one of them?"

"I have no idea," was Tom's—absurdly cheerful—answer. "So far as I know, we have no records of what happens when two airships collide. But I do understand basic physics. There's a reason"—they could hear the clap made by a meaty hand slapping a meatier chest—"that football lineman are built like me instead of a ninety-eight pound weakling. And those ships coming at us are just a pack of ninety-eight-pound weaklings."

"Oh, swell," Julie repeated.

When he saw the *Magdeburg*'s maneuver, Moshe Mizrahi hissed softly through his teeth. This was exactly what he'd been afraid of.

But . . . He was considerably more afraid of the sultan's wrath. So he turned to the signal man and said, "Order the ships to tighten the formation. As tight as possible— even if the gasbags come in contact with each other."

That wasn't as risky as it sounded. At least, Moshe didn't think it was—although this was something no one had any experience with. Still, by their very nature the envelopes would provide a cushioning effect, and they were so big that the gondolas were in no risk of colliding.

As the five ships closed toward each other, however, one of them was lagging behind. That was the *Çýldýr*, commanded by Juwalji Hasan. The ship's engineer had started having trouble with the engine a few minutes earlier and the *Çýldýr* hadn't been able to keep up with the other ships in the line.

They hadn't lagged very far behind yet—no more than a hundred feet or so—but as the line compressed they were being squeezed out of the formation. Seeing what was happening, the commander ordered the engineer to slow still further. He could be faulted for that—Sultan Murad certainly would have, had he been present—but his actions were simply the result of deeply ingrained human instincts.

Within a short time, the *Çýldýr* was no longer part of the formation. A five-ship line had become a four-ship line with the fifth vessel flying behind them.

Juwalji Hasan could no longer see anything of the *Magdeburg* except the top swell of its enormous envelope, coming toward them like a mighty wave.

The captain and pilot of the *Magdeburg* couldn't see the *Çýldýr* at all.

"Fire!" Moshe shouted. The gunner of the *Chaldiran* fired his rifle. The sound was the cue, and an instant later the rest of the gunners fired.

Or rather, three of them did. Moshe wasn't positive— the shots had been very closely spaced—but he thought he'd only heard three.

He turned his head away from the pilot's slit in the gondola's forward armor. "What—"

"The *Çýldýr* failed to shoot," said the signal man, who had a view out of the rear of the gondola. "They've fallen completely behind."

"Juwalji Hasan better have a good explanation," Moshe said grimly.

"We're zimmis," the signal man said, jeeringly. "What does he care what we think?"

"Nothing—but he will care what the sultan thinks. Possibly for a very short time." He made a gesture with his hands at his neck which simulated a garrote being applied.

But Moshe had no time to worry about that now. As

he'd expected, the gunfire seemed to have accomplished nothing—and the *Magdeburg* was still coming right at them.

Mice do not play chicken with cats. That is simply a law of nature.

"Tell the ships to divide," he ordered the signal man. "*Now*. The *Sokhoista* with us, to the left. The *Raydaniya* and *Marj Dabiq*, to the right."

It seemed to take forever for the signals to be transmitted, but it wasn't more than half a minute before the four Ottoman ships began splitting the line.

Just in time. As the *Magdeburg* passed through the gap thus created, her envelope brushed against that of the *Sokhoista*.

That glancing near miss was enough to jolt everybody in the *Sokhoista* and send its gondola into a frightening back-and-forth lurch. But the people aboard the *Magdeburg* barely noticed.

They had a much bigger problem on their hands.

"Holy sh—*Dive! Dive! Dive!*" The thought went through Tom's mind that there was something ridiculous about using terminology he'd only encountered watching submarine movies. But it was all he could think of.

It didn't matter, anyway, because the *Magdeburg*'s Dutch pilot hadn't needed Tom to tell him that he needed to send the huge airship into as steep a descent as possible. He didn't even think of trying to fly above the Ottoman ship that was almost upon them, because that ship had already been at least fifty feet higher in altitude than the *Magdeburg* when they spotted her.

Tom braced himself as best he could. Through a slit, he could see that the enemy airship was trying to climb as rapidly as possible. Maybe—

It was a wishful thought. The Ottoman ship simply couldn't climb fast enough. It passed over the brow of the *Magdeburg*'s envelope, but couldn't avoid the tail. Within seconds, the two airships had collided.

The laws of physics are what they are. Mass matters— and sometimes it *really* matters. This was one of those times.

The impact stripped the *Çýldýr*'s gondola completely off its hull. For a few seconds, the gondola teetered atop the *Magdeburg* before it slipped off and plunged toward the ground almost a mile below.

For the same few seconds, Tom was hopeful that the *Magdeburg* hadn't suffered any catastrophic damage. But that was only because he couldn't see what had happened to the envelope.

The *Çýldýr*'s gondola had torn a great rent in the *Magdeburg*'s upper envelope and ruptured one of the gas cells. Had that been the only damage, the airship would have lost considerable lifting capacity but perhaps not so much as to cause it to crash.

And the people aboard the *Magdeburg* had one great piece of luck. The hydrogen spilling out of the gas bag had instantly mixed with the oxygen in the atmosphere and produced a hydrogen-oxygen mixture within the combustible range—which with hydrogen was huge: anywhere between four and seventy-five percent. All it took now was a flame—any high-heat source—to produce a conflagration. Once started, fire would have rapidly destroyed the airship.

Such an ignition source did exist: the oil-burning engine that drove the *Çýldýr*'s propellers. Except that seconds before the collision, the *Çýldýr*'s engineer had shut it down temporarily. He hadn't even been aware of the imminent collision, because he'd been completely engrossed with trying to fix the engine.

The flame was gone by the time the ships collided and the shell of the low-powered Ottoman engine wasn't hot enough to ignite the mixture. Given more time, it might have, but the gondola was only in the gas plume for a few seconds before its fall to earth took it away.

So there was no fire, no explosion. But the gondola had also damaged the control structures at the tail, badly enough that the crew had no way to avert the coming disaster. The *Magdeburg* was out of control. The best they could do now was dump the ballast to reduce the rate of fall to something that would hopefully be survivable.

Tom managed to refrain from shouting any further advice to the crew. The pilot knew better than he did what the *Magdeburg*'s limits were, and the one thing that was blindingly obvious is that they were going down. That was now a given. What they needed was to touch down as gently as possible.

Touch down. That was a euphemism for "controlled crash." Probably "not all-that-controlled crash" and possibly "completely uncontrolled crash."

There was nothing Tom could contribute here, so he clambered up the ladder into the gun turret.

"Is there anything you need—I mean, *really* need—to try to salvage?" he asked.

Dell looked longingly at the Karabine.

"Forget that," Julie said. She had the Remington in hand. "Just grab the .308 ammo, Dell. If the rest makes it, fine. If it doesn't, screw it."

Despite the tension of the moment, Tom almost laughed. *Gun nuts!* Not for the first time, he wondered if they suffered from an actual clinical disorder.

FAD, maybe. *Firearm Attachment Disorder.*

North bank of the Danube
About a mile west of the village of Langenstein

The sight was mesmerizing. Murad had barely noticed the gondola of one of his own airships plunging to the ground, taking the entire crew to their death. He'd given even less notice to the now unsteered envelope, which was drifting with the wind and would end up . . . wherever.

The huge kâfir airship wasn't plunging to the ground, but its descent was so steep that it reminded Murad of a stooping hawk—no, a stooping dragon. A gigantic monster, approaching the world as if it was its prey.

What would happen when it struck, as it was so clearly bound to do?

He didn't know—but he did know what his army had to do. No matter what happened, the *Magdeburg* would be out of action for weeks, at the very least.

He turned to the radio man. "Call the *Pelekanon*," he commanded. "Tell Semsi Ahmed to order the entire fleet back to base immediately. We need to start refitting the airships for a bombing mission."

He went back to watching the *Magdeburg*'s dive. The entire army would have to be prepared as well. Murad doubted if the airships could repeat the success they'd had at Vienna. But . . . they might. His army needed to be ready to launch a massive assault on Linz on a moment's notice.

They'd have enough time. The sultan estimated that it would take a least one full day, and more likely two, to refit the airship fleet. No one including himself had expected that they'd have such a splendid victory today.

The distant enemy airship came to ground. From his vantage point on the observation tower he could see that much, but he couldn't see what damage it had suffered.

Enough, hopefully, to kill the Jooli.

A pasture two miles west of Linz

Tom lowered Julie to the ground, then Dell, and then the two remaining Dutch crewmen. The rest of the crew including the captain, the pilot and the engineer had all jumped as soon as the gondola had touched ground— showing, to Tom's way of thinking, a disturbing lack of martial tradition. Of course, they weren't actually soldiers.

So, it would fall to him to be the last man off the ship.

Last *person*. If Julie heard him say "last man," he'd never hear the end of it.

✛ ✛ ✛

Once Tom was on the ground, he joined the others in moving a very respectful distance from the airship. No one *expected* the ship to explode, since it hadn't already—it had never once caught fire—but . . .

Who knew? He sometimes wondered if he knew anything anymore.

"Can it be salvaged?" Julie asked.

"Who knows?" said Tom.

The confluence of the Danube and the Traun
A few miles southeast of Linz

From his own vantage point several miles to the east, Emperor Gustav Adolf hadn't been able to see the final moments of the *Magdeburg*'s fall to earth. But he'd seen enough to realize that even if the great airship could be rebuilt, it wouldn't be available for weeks. Maybe months.

Maybe never, for that matter.

Murad wasn't going to give him more than a few days.

He turned to one of his couriers. He'd briefly considered trying to use one of the radios, but he was unsure if any of the radios he had on hand could reach the Baltic.

"Go immediately—quickly as you can—to the main radio station. Send a message in my name to Colonel Wood. Order him to bring the entire Air Force to Linz. Every plane that's available."

He paused for a moment. "Well, no. He can keep one of the Belles to provide reconnaissance for General

Torstensson. But I need the rest of the airplanes down here. *As soon as possible.* Make sure that's clear."

After the courier left, Gustav Adolf looked to the east instead of the west. He could see the nearest fieldworks of the huge Ottoman army that had resumed its siege of Linz.

Could airplanes that had never been designed to fight other aircraft be of any use against the Ottoman fleet that would soon be coming at them?

He had no idea. Just the surety that he'd find out before too long. He could remember feeling the same way on the eve of his first battle. He'd still been a teenager, then.

What he couldn't remember was what it had felt like to be a teenage king, on the eve of his first battle. Such were the blessings of age.

Part Seven

April 1637

She sees, coming up a second time,
Earth from the ocean, eternally green

"The Seeress's Prophecy," *The Poetic Edda*

Chapter 36

Kraków, official capital of Poland
Actual capital of Lesser Poland

"About time," Jeff muttered, looking down from his bedroom window in an upper floor of the Cloth Hall. "I was starting to wonder if they'd get here before the heat death of the universe."

Below him, the troops from the Galician Democratic Assembly were filing into the city's huge market square.

"Filing in," Jeff muttered. "What a laugh. Piling in with neither rhyme nor reason, what it is."

Next to him, his wife smiled. Jeff had the trained habits, by now, of a military officer. Disorder and confusion offended his tidy soul. She, on the other hand, had the trained habits of a political organizer. A state of disorder and confusion was her natural habitat. She moved through it like a fish through water.

Admittedly, the soldiers pouring into the square seemed distinctly short of training and discipline. Of orderly formations, there were essentially none. The closest she could see was what looked like a battalion-sized unit in the southwestern corner of the square that was making some attempt to come to order. Given that "making some attempt" seemed mostly to consist of officers on horseback yelling furiously at each other, she didn't think Jeff would find much comfort there.

But what was also evident to her was that the morale and fighting spirit of the Galician Assembly's forces seemed every bit as high as their decorum was low. They were all in for savage struggle when the army of the magnates that was nearing Kraków arrived. Savage struggles were won with fighting spirit and morale, not decorum.

"Relax, husband," she said. "You and Prince Ulrik will bring order to this chaos soon enough. My military expert tells me that it will be at least a week before the magnates are ready to launch an assault."

"Which military expert?" His tone was still peevish. "We got so many of those—in their own minds, anyway—that they're tripping over each other."

"I was thinking of the one I sleep with every night. Who murmured into my ear just a few hours ago that we still had plenty of time to engage in carnal relations—you put it less delicately—before we had to break off to crush the wicked magnates. You put that less delicately also."

"Did I say that? I don't remember."

She glanced up at him. "That's a truly sinful expression on your face. Smug self-satisfaction is the most charitable term I can think of. If you were a believer, you'd be on your knees praying for forgiveness."

Jeff's expression got smugger and more self-satisfied. And why not? He *wasn't* a believer. Not in a kind and benevolent deity, at any rate. He did believe in the woman standing next to him, on the other hand. Which, the way he looked at the universe, was plenty good enough.

Is "smugger" a word? he wondered.

In the square below, Lukasz Opalinski was wondering if he should add his voice to the shouting multitude.

He was tempted. Since he and the mission to rescue the people in the cellars had arrived in Kraków two days earlier, he'd gotten a good estimate—what the up-timers called "feel"—for the army assembled to confront the oncoming magnates.

His initial assessment had been quite positive. Colonel Higgins, the commanding officer of the USE's forces, was obviously competent. So was the military commander of the Bohemians, General von Mercy. Perhaps even more important was the quality of the political leadership that had gathered in Kraków. Gretchen Richter had already established her stature in his eyes, which sometimes bordered on awe. Prince Ulrik inspired a quiet confidence and so did Morris Roth.

From there...

Things went downhill. Over the course of the next day, Lukasz became familiar with the disparate elements that made up so much of the "army of liberation"—the Silesian militias, both German and Polish, and the volunteers who made up the infantry of the absurdly named "Grand Army of the Sunrise." A large percentage of those were Jewish, of all things. Any Pole was familiar with Jews, of course.

But that very familiarity made it hard for him to imagine Jews as soldiers. Theirs was simply not a culture with any martial traditions. Unless you went back to the Biblical era, but that was a very long time ago.

Still, the biggest problem he saw was political. As a military force, the alliance assembling in Kraków had quite a bit of promise. Higgins' overlarge regiment provided an iron core. They called themselves the "Hangmen," which Lukasz found a bit grotesque. But the steely confidence that lay beneath the word was obvious.

The Bohemian cavalry was quite different. They were professional soldiers with little if any of the strong political convictions of the Hangman Regiment. But they were definitely professionals at their trade and seemed to be good ones. Almost all of them were veterans.

The remaining forces were much shakier, but they were clearly not hopeless. If nothing else, the Silesian militiamen and the Jewish volunteers in the Bohemian infantry had a morale that was anxious but determined. The gentiles in the Bohemian infantry...not so much. But they could be whipped into shape—literally, if need be.

No, the real problem was political. With the exception of a few hundred Polish militiamen, it would be hard to make a clear distinction between the "army of liberation" and a foreign army of occupation. Germans and Czechs, everywhere you looked.

So far, they'd gotten away with it, by the shrewd way they'd always placed his brother Krzysztof in the foreground, and made sure to display the Polish militias from Silesia at every opportunity. But that wasn't enough; not nearly enough.

Happily, the army from Galicia had arrived yesterday, late in the afternoon. It was a small army: perhaps two thousand Poles, with another five hundred Cossacks, most of whom were also Polish. Still, provided his brother remained in the forefront, Lukasz thought it was enough to give the rebellion a fundamentally Polish rather than foreign "feel" to it.

And that was all they needed for the moment, in his estimation. If—this was a very big "if," of course—they could inflict a defeat on the oncoming magnates' army, the victory would be enough to rally a large number of Poles—Lithuanians, too, if not as many—to the revolutionary cause. The cause which he himself had come to champion since the murder of Grand Hetman Koniecpolski.

Alas, he'd been away too long. He'd forgotten—half-forgotten, at least—just how infuriating the Polish "feel" could be.

Why in the name of all that was holy did his fellow Poles have to be more devoted to their overweening self-importance than they were to the very God they claimed to be the source of that Polish greatness?

He'd spent the whole evening and a good portion of the night with the Galician army.

"Army." What a joke.

By dawn, his assessment of the situation was that the "army of liberation" might as well be called "the madhouse."

It was now two hours later. The Galicians had entered Poland's most prestigious city and taken their rightful place in Poland's most famous public square.

"The madhouse," indeed.

A shouted chant was started up by a small group of szlachta cavalrymen milling around nearby. The heart of it—the chant was only semi-coherent—seemed to be a celebration of the famous *liberum veto*, which Lukasz and his friend Jozef considered to be the quintessential essence of Polish idiocy.

His restraint finally broke. No, shattered.

"You fucking idiots—!"

Judy Wendell was lying on a bed looking out of the window of a bedroom on one of the upper floors of the Cloth Hall. In her case, not her own bedroom. The same night the rescue mission had arrived in Kraków, she'd made a decision she'd been pondering ever since they left Vienna.

Two days had gone by since then, and she'd tentatively decided that her decision had been the right one. Only tentatively, true, but Judy was not the sort of person who rushed to judgment. The fact that it had only taken her a day and half to reach the state of "tentatively the right thing to do" was impressive. She thought so, anyway—and she was not someone who got easily impressed.

"Dear God, he has a loud voice," she said, gazing down at the figure of Lukasz Opalinski. The hussar looked bigger than ever, sitting on his magnificent warhorse and bellowing angrily at the men around him. He wasn't waving his saber at them, but it was obvious even at this distance that he had to restrain himself from doing so.

"He's normally pretty soft-spoken," she said.

Jakub Zaborowsky levered himself up on an elbow so he could look into the square himself. His cheek came to rest against Judy's and his hand began a slow and gentle caress of her back.

Her thoroughly unclothed back. She shivered a little. That was pleasure, not fear, with excitement starting to come back to life as well. Judy had always suspected that sex was not what it was cracked up to be. Over the past forty-eight hours, she'd discovered she was wrong.

"I've been studying him for weeks now," said Jakub softly. "And I've come to a conclusion. The trick now is figuring out how to make it come to pass."

"What conclusion?" asked Judy. "Come what to pass?"

Still maintaining the caress, Jakub nodded toward Lukasz, down in the square. "If things go as I plan to have them go, you're looking at the future king of Poland."

Judy's eyes got wide. Then, wider still.

"You have got to be kidding. He's not related to the Vasa dynasty."

"Or any other royal dynasty," Jakub agreed. "Except distantly, at any rate. In some nations, that would be important, but not in Poland. Not all of my countrymen's customs are as idiotic as the *liberum veto*. We also have a tradition of electing our kings—and even after they are chosen, they are very far from the so-called 'absolute' rulers whom the French yearn for and the Russians worship."

He levered himself up a bit higher, so that he could put his arm around Judy. He was now caressing her shoulder instead of her back. "You can't be a commoner, of course, or a scruffy szlachta like myself. But the Opalinski family is as highly ranked as those of any magnate in the Commonwealth, without the drawback of being obscenely wealthy. They're admired by most of the nobility without being detested by most commoners. Any commoners, so far as I know."

Up-time, Judy had had little interest in politics. She'd just been a small-town high school girl from a moderately prosperous family. As the years had gone by since the Ring of Fire, however, she'd found herself learning politics from sheer necessity. She was now very wealthy, to begin with—a state of affairs that always made it hard to avoid politics. And she'd also become a close friend— probably the best friend, in fact—of an Austrian archduchess who belonged to Europe's most prominent and powerful royal dynasty.

So, she pondered the problem. "Why Lukasz, though? Why not his brother Krzysztof? He's the older brother, after all."

Jakub shook his head. "Primogeniture doesn't matter. What does matter is temperament—and Krzysztof's is all wrong. For a king, I mean. He's . . . how should I put it? I don't mean to sound disrespectful, because I like and admire Krzysztof. But he's . . . eccentric, let's say. Often, very impractical."

"You think other Poles would find him too . . . Is unmonarchy a word?"

"It is now, since you used it. And, yes, that is the problem. Lukasz, though . . . "

Jakub grimaced a little. "I don't entirely approve, but Lukasz has all the attributes of the ideal Polish king. He's fiercely courageous, and by all accounts ferocious in battle—always a trait Poles slobber over, especially the szlachta. He's straightforward and honest. He's intelligent but without that devious edge that makes people wary of his friend Jozef."

"And you, Jakub." Judy's brow creased, not in disapproval but simply as a way of expressing firm conviction. *Don't bullshit me, buddy.* "You've got some pretty sharp edges yourself—and you want to talk about devious? *You?* Who is even as we speak plotting to overturn not only the established order but the next establishment before it even gets started."

His grin had a sharp edge to it. "I will not deny any of that—but I am not proposing myself as a king. That would be truly absurd."

Judy had been thinking ahead. "You haven't raised this idea with Krzysztof and Red Sybolt, have you?"

"No. Not yet—although I will have to, before much longer."

Judy winced. "I don't know about Krzysztof, but Red will have conniptions. A shit fit, as we Americans would put it."

"Shit fit . . . " Jakub rolled the expression on his tongue for a moment. "That's rather nice, actually. But in this instance it's quite inadequate. Red will not have 'conniptions,' he will erupt with fury. At the very least, he'll accuse me of betraying our cause."

Judy gave him a sidelong look. "Well . . . aren't you? At least, in a way. I thought you believed in a democratic form of government yourself."

"I do. If I had my preference, the Polish–Lithuanian Commonwealth would eliminate the monarchy altogether and replace it with a republican structure. I'd prefer a parliamentary one, but I wouldn't object strongly to a presidential system."

"So why are you now in favor of replacing that Vasa bum on the throne with Lukasz?"

"The problem with the way Red looks at the PLC is that he fixates too much on the political issues. Those are certainly important, but they are not primary."

Up until now, Jakub's expression had been relaxed, pleasant—even cheerful. Now, his face hardened.

"The fundamental illness of the Commonwealth isn't political, it's social and economic. It's the damned *szlachta*." The word came out in a hiss. "Especially the great magnates. So long as they dominate Poland and Lithuania—not to mention the Ruthenian lands—so long as they even *exist*—they are a cancer in my nation's body. They are killing my country. They must be *excised*. Removed. Obliterated; not as people, of course, but as a class. Do that, and all the other issues become soluble. Without doing it, none are."

He let his arm fall away from her and sat up straight. "This is what Red Sybolt simply doesn't understand. I don't fault him for it. He comes from your country, one that never had a powerful hereditary aristocracy. So he thinks of the magnates as Polish equivalents to your American tyke— What's the word?"

"Tycoons. In our neck of the woods, we called them the coal barons."

"Yes, them. But they were simply powerful because of their wealth. Whatever social pretensions they might have had were just that—mere pretensions. In Poland—

Lithuania, too—that is not true. The szlachta *believe* in their special status. They cherish it. And that belief—that delusion—poisons everything."

He took a deep breath and let it out. "It won't be easy. It certainly won't be simple. But I am convinced it can be done. And I have come to believe that the best way to start, at least, is to use an elected and pretty decent king as the sword to start cutting down the aristocracy."

His face relaxed again. He even smiled. "That's what the Jagiellon dynasty did, you know? If they had stayed in power, Poland and Lithuania would have had the chance to evolve along democratic lines. You do understand that is what your Michael Stearns has been scheming and plotting for ever since the Ring of Fire, don't you? He must have decided very early on that striking directly for a democratic republic would be too risky, and certainly too bloody and destructive. I think he was right. I've read a great deal of your up-time history, Judy. We are still in the early seventeenth century, not the late eighteenth—certainly not the nineteenth."

In point of fact, Judy had never once considered what Mike Stearns might have been thinking in strategic terms. Now that Jakub raised it, though . . .

She shivered again. "You're a little scary, Jakub." Again, though, there was more pleasure and excitement in the shiver than fear.

He gazed at her for a few seconds. "Will you help me?" he asked abruptly.

A bit to her surprise—but only a bit, after the months she'd spent in the cellars—she found herself nodding.

"Yeah, I will. What do you want me to do, though?"

"I believe you have become close to the archduchess. Cecilia Renata."

"Yes, I have. So?"

"So, if we can get Lukasz elected king—we'll start with King of Lesser Poland, I think—there is nothing that would increase his political stature as greatly and as quickly as if he married the Habsburg archduchess of the Austrian-Hungarian Empire."

She stared at him. "You're kidding me, right?"

He said nothing. Just continued to gaze at her. Both of them were sitting up in the bed now. Both of them thoroughly unclothed.

She shivered again. "Come here," she said.

Sometime later, Judy levered herself up on an elbow and looked down at Jakub. "Okay, in for a penny, in for a pound."

He looked at her, frowning a little. "And that peculiar expression means . . . ?"

"I'll explain it later. I've been wary of men since I was twelve. First, because I was too good-looking."

"You're beautiful."

"I guess so. That's one of the things I like about Denise—neither one of us cares about that crap. But since the Ring of Fire, I've been wary for another reason."

"Which is . . . ?"

It was her turn to take a deep breath and let it out slowly. "That was one of the things that got me interested in you. Never once—not one time—have you asked me how well-off I am."

"You're an American," Jakub said. "I assumed you

were well-off. Most Americans are. But that didn't matter to me." A quick, rather savage grin came to his face. "If I cared much for money I'd hardly have dedicated my life to overthrowing a king, a Sejm and an entire class of scoundrels."

"No, you wouldn't. Okay. Like I said, in for a penny, in for a pound. I remember Ms. Mailey once telling us in a social studies class that one of the big problems any social movement has—especially the really radical ones—is raising funds."

He barked a little laugh. "To say the least! More than once in our travels, Red and I—Krzysztof too—had to share a single loaf of bread. That was our meal for the day."

She smiled down at him. The smile was full of nuance.

"Well, your lucky day just got luckier."

Chapter 37

"Talk about 'just in the nick of time,'" Julie muttered, as the strange airplane landed on Linz's airstrip. The aircraft came to a stop and then began taxiing toward the hangar near to which she and her husband were standing.

As the plane approached, the pilot steered it directly toward the hangar, bringing the front of the fuselage into view. The artwork on the nose cone was . . .

"Oh, gimme a break," Julie said. "Next time I see Denise, she's getting an earful."

Alex Mackay's expression was . . . judicious. As was usually the case when men contemplated a certain type of artwork while standing next to their wives.

He cleared his throat. "I believe that portrait of her—what did he call it? 'Steady Girl,' I think—was her betrothed's idea, not hers."

The curled-lip expression that adorned Julie's face

would have made a splendid portrait itself. "Right. Now you're going to tell me that Denise raised bloody hell about it, put down her foot and demanded that the not-quite-pornographic image be immediately removed. Being, as it was, an affront to herself and all of womankind."

"Well . . ."

"Right." Julie gave her husband a sideways look. "Fair warning, buster. You ever paint a portrait of me looking like that—"

"I'm a cavalryman, not a pilot!" Alex protested.

"So you'd have it painted on your horse's ass. What an improvement."

"I assure you, dearest—"

"Never mind," she said, waving his protest down. "Just like I said, 'fair warning.'"

The plane was now close; close enough that Julie could make out the features of the pilot, who was sitting in the upper of the plane's two cockpits.

"And speaking of a horse's ass," she said, "here's one of Grantville's finest."

Alex gave her a sideways look. "You know that pilot?"

"Unfortunately, yes. He's Dustin Acton. I went to high school with him. I was the head cheerleader and he was the head asshole. I knew he was in the Air Force but I didn't realize he'd become a pilot. Last I heard he was on the ground crew. Jesse Wood must have had an off day when he signed him up for flight school."

Alex's expression was now somewhere between amused and surprised. As a rule, Julie was charitable in her assessment of people. He'd rarely heard her express this caustic an opinion.

"Is he really that bad?"

"Yup. Even my ex-boyfriend Chip thought he was an egotistical jackass—and Chip was no slouch in the ego department himself, as you may recall."

"Yes, I remember him." But there was no heat in his voice. Alex's *contretemps*, as the French would call it, with Chip Jenkins had taken place years before. In any event, he'd come out ahead.

The plane came to a halt.

"I wonder who the bimbo on the nose cone is."

Alex squinted. "The caption just reads 'Lady Fair.'"

"Yeah, I can read it. That's probably because Dustin swaps out girlfriends like most men change shoes. This way he's got a reusable all-bimbo portrait."

"You really do dislike him."

Her voice rose. "The bastard pinched my ass once!"

Alex tried to imagine any man stupid enough to pinch Julie on the ass. His imagination failed.

"What happened?"

She shook her head. "Nothing. Well . . . nothing from me. I was still trying to decide which way to retaliate when Chip found out about it and beat me to the punch. Pretty much literally. I was half-pissed at him and half-pleased."

The pilot climbed out of the cockpit. "Hey, Julie!"

"Hey," she replied, her tone expressing as much enthusiasm as she'd express looking down at a sink full of cold, dirty dishwater. Which was still full of dirty dishes.

But she brightened up when the lower cockpit was slid aside and another man emerged. That cockpit had a peculiar design that only provided a narrow forward view, so she hadn't been able to make out his features until then.

"Ent!"

"Hi, Julie. Been a while."

"Sure has." She frowned, theatrically. "Last I knew, though, you were a pilot. What happened? Get demoted?"

Still smiling, he finished getting out of the cockpit and shook his head. "Nope. I'll go back to being a pilot once this is over. We've got a new—really new—weapons system here and Colonel Wood wanted me to do the combat trial so I could give him a full report."

He glanced at the plane's pilot, who was now entering the hangar. The glance did not seem to be an admiring one. "Ol' Dustbucket there is the pilot on this mission because he's the one who trained on this bizarro new plane. This time around, I'm the nose gunner."

By then, he'd reached them. Julie waved back and forth between the two men. "I don't think you two ever met. Not to speak to each other, anyway. Ent, this is my husband Alex Mackay. Alex, meet Enterprise Martin."

"But please don't call me 'Enterprise,'" he said, shaking Alex's hand. "I always go by 'Ent.'"

Julie was now looking at the plane. "It is pretty weird-looking. I've never seen a plane that's got the propeller on the rear end instead of the front end."

Ent turned his head. "It's called a 'pusher.' The big advantage to it is that you don't have a propeller you have to shoot around since it's behind you."

Alex frowned. "But I've seen—in more than one movie—where you had planes with propellers in front that were shooting at other planes."

"That's because they had what are called 'synchronization gears.' They were developed in World

War I, up-time. They timed the rounds fired by a machine gun so that the bullets always passed in between the spinning propellers."

"That seems awfully . . . "

Ent grinned. "Chancy? In our day and age, it's just not possible. Not so far, anyway. We have only two practical plane designs that will allow us to mount machine guns. One of them is to put the gun or guns somewhere far enough away from the propeller that it fires around it. Usually that's on the wings. Alternatively, if you have two engines you put them on the wings. That's the design Kelley Aviation is following. The other is to make a pusher, where the propeller is out of the way entirely."

"How well does it fly?" asked Alex.

Ent shrugged. "Well enough. It's not a fast plane—top speed is a hair below ninety miles per hour—and it's pretty ungainly. Being fair about it, that's not so much because it's a pusher as that it's got"—he pointed his finger at the cockpit he'd emerged from—"that big bulbous nose. That's where the machine gun and the gunner ride. We're slung a bit below the pilot's cockpit so he can see clearly."

"Do you really have a machine gun in there?" Julie asked. "A real one, I mean, not a mitrailleuse or a Gatling."

"No, this is a genu-*ine* machine gun," said Ent. "The first ever made in this universe. Come here, I'll show you how it works."

"Good thing Dell's not here," Alex muttered, as the three of them headed toward the aircraft. "We'd be lucky to get home before sundown."

"Before sunrise, you mean," muttered Julie.

Ent heard them, and chuckled. "You're talking about Dell Beckworth, right? This is based on one of his designs. Well, partly. Paul Santee had a lot of input too. Enough so that Dell got grouchy and broke off working with us on it. You know what gun nuts are like. Put two of them in the same room and within five minutes it's either Best Friends Forever or Family Feud. We got Family Feud."

When they reached the cockpit, Ent waved Julie forward. "Climb in. You can see it better that way."

At first, Julie didn't know what she was looking at. It was like no gun she'd ever seen.

"What the fu . . . frog?"

Ent laughed. "That was my reaction, too, the first time I saw it. Start with this, Julie—we made it out of two semiautomatic rifles. FN FALs, to be precise."

She nodded, knowing the weapon. She'd fired one herself, several times. The FAL stood for *Fusil Automatique Léger*, which was French for "light automatic rifle." The FN came from the manufacturer, a Belgian company named Fabrique Nationale.

It was a rugged weapon, and had been one of the two major NATO battle rifles of the Cold War era. More than ninety nations had adopted it. But the United States hadn't been one of them, so it wasn't as familiar to Americans as by rights it should have been.

Julie had once asked her uncle Frank why the US hadn't adopted it. His answer had been caustic and blunt. "Whaddaya think? If there's anybody in the world who suffers worse from Not Invented Here Syndrome than the U.S. military-industrial complex, I don't know who it is."

"It's a .308, if I remember right."

"Not quite, although you can load it with a .308 cartridge. But it's technically a 7.62 by 51 millimeter."

Julie nodded. "Same difference, pretty much. Nice straight trajectory." She was partial to that caliber. Her beloved Remington 700 was a .308.

Ent smiled. He wasn't as good a rifle shooter as Julie—who was?—but he'd been a deer hunter and he shared her appreciation of firearms. Of course, saying that someone in West Virginia appreciated firearms was like saying someone in Los Angeles appreciated cars.

"What's even better is that we actually have examples of tracer rounds in stock. I forget exactly what the bullet boys told me, but it's either one or two tracer rounds in each of the one hundred round belts that came along with that M-60 your uncle swiped from the army."

"Hey! He didn't *swipe* it," Julie protested. "Frank just figured that since they made him fight in that stupid war in Vietnam the least the army could do was let him take a souvenir home."

"Pretty damn big souvenir."

"My uncle's a pretty damn big improviser. How do you think he went from coal miner to army chief of staff, after the Ring of Fire?"

"Point. Getting back on topic, we've had to modify the copies a little bit, just to make sure that they burn hot enough and long enough. But that's a whole lot simpler than coming up with incendiary rounds from scratch."

Julie continued her examination of the strange-looking

weapon. "I'm guessing it must be the same thing with this machine gun, because you sure didn't build this out of downtime parts."

"Not hardly. Looks like hell, but it's a lot simpler and a lot more reliable than having to create a brand-new machine gun using local metals and technology." He leaned over the dual-barreled device. "Probably the most disorienting thing about it is that the guns are on their backs. And only six inches apart."

"Why the hell did you put them on their backs? Isn't the brass flying out of them right into the gunner's face going to be a problem?"

He leaned over further and pointed. "See that? We've fixed downsloping shunts over each ejection port. That'll keep the casings bouncing down, not flying up. And as far as putting the FALs on their backs, there's no reason not to in terms of accuracy and operation. But there's a *big* reason to do so when it comes to reloading."

She reconsidered the gaping—and very handy—magazine wells of the twinned weapons. "Okay, I see it now. In a cockpit, or any enclosed environment, it's going to be easiest to reload them from the top. Kind of like an old Bren gun."

She was sitting behind the weapon and leaned forward as much as she could. From that vantage point, she realized that it was neither as big nor as awkward as it seemed at first. The stocks of both weapons had been removed, reducing their overall length considerably. Held together rigidly in a welded brace made out of what looked like steel salvaged from an old car, all the pieces now made sense. Except for a black box that straddled the two weapons, both stabilizing them and encasing their respective trigger guards. She looked up at Ent and asked, "So is that where you keep the magic machine-gun power?"

He reached over her shoulder, and flipped down the access panel on the back of the box. Inside were mechanical guts that looked like the rear axle of a car had mated with a spring-driven clockwork.

She frowned. "Okay, so no magic. But we could either spend half an hour while I try to figure out what all these doohickies do, or you could give me the short version now."

"My pleasure." His tone bordered on that which a parent uses to brag about a child's report card. "You see the camshaft that runs between the trigger guards of the two guns?"

"You mean the thing that looks like a car axle?"

"Yes. That. Every time it makes a one-half revolution, the cam on one end of that shaft pushes down the trigger on that gun. In the next half-revolution, that cam releases that trigger, just as the cam on the other end of the shaft depresses the trigger of the other gun."

She nodded again. "So they're shooting in rapid sequence, one after the other."

"Right. Now in most machine guns like this, you have to turn the crank by hand to operate the camshaft. But that makes the gun unwieldy and really hard to aim accurately. So we found a way to turn the crankshaft just by pushing a button. Except we made it by pulling a trigger on account of shooters are cranky and set in their ways."

"That's because 'cranky and set in their ways' translates

into gunnerese as 'hits the target regularly.'" Her eyes grew as wide as her sudden smile. "I get it. That's what the coiled spring is for. When you push the button—pull the trigger—it releases the spring and the camshaft starts turning."

"Got it in one. We adapted the mechanism from the guts of a wheel lock, just made it bigger. And although you could re-crank it while you are in the cockpit, that spring has enough stored energy to fire off every round you can carry on the aircraft."

Julie spent another couple of minutes studying the weapon and handling its various components. It really wasn't hard to learn. She was quite sure she could fire the thing successfully herself, even in combat conditions.

"You done good, Ent," she pronounced.

Ottoman headquarters
Ennsegg Castle
Enns, Austria
Eight miles east of Linz

"And they are sure about this?" Sultan Murad demanded. His finger was planted on one feature of the sketch.

"Yes, My Sultan," said Süleyman, who commanded the irregular cavalry and scouts known as the akinji. "It is definitely placed at the rear of the machine, not the front."

Murad turned to look at the three chief artificers whom he'd summoned to the castle. "Can you explain to me the significance of having this . . . whirling thing, what do you call it?"

"Propeller, My Sultan."

He remembered the term now. His airships used propellers to move themselves—and now that he thought about it, many of them were facing to the rear as well.

"We are not certain, My Sultan," said one of the artificers, answering the first question. They all knew full well that not telling Murad the truth was far more dangerous than shading it in hopes that his temper would not be roused. Angering the sultan in that way would result in a beating, sometimes. Not telling him the truth—all of it, blurring not a thing—was likely to get you garroted.

One of the other artificers spoke up. "One possibility is that the kâfirs have succeeded in mounting a small cannon in the nose of the aircraft. They would then place the propeller at the rear so as not to impede the weapon."

That made sense. "And could such a cannon—it would have to be a very small one, yes?—do great damage to one of the airships? How accurate could it be?"

Before any of the artificers could answer that question, Murad added: "I see no way it could be aimed, other than to fly the vessel directly at one of our airships."

"We believe that to be true, yes, My Sultan. As to the possible damage . . ."

He looked to one of the other artificers.

He provided the conclusion. "It could, My Sultan. There is such a thing as what the unbelievers call an 'incendiary round.' We have not been able to make one ourselves yet, but we believe there are several ways it could be done. If the cannon could fire such a round—"

Murad provided the answer himself. "Then it could—might, at least—set the flying gas on fire."

"Yes, My Sultan."

Murad stroked his beard for half a minute or so, pondering the matter. Then he turned toward the commanders of his janissaries and sipahis. "Be ready to launch an assault tomorrow. We will need to test this new aircraft of the kâfirs before we begin any attack. But I want you ready in case we can defeat it."

"Yes, My Sultan." The four of them left the chamber.

Murad now turned to Semsi Ahmed, the commander of the Gureba-i hava. "We will modify the plan for tomorrow. Leave the janissary gunners in ten of the airships. Both of the forward lines. We will only use the rear two lines as bombers."

Semsi Ahmed hesitated, but only for a second. He knew as well as the artificers that the greatest danger when dealing with Murad IV was not to speak frankly to him. That had its risks, true—no sultan reacted well to disagreement—but if Murad discovered later that you had not told him something you should have . . .

"The gun turret armor has been removed from all of the ships, My Sultan."

"Yes, I know. But that simply means—"

He paused, wincing a little at a crashing sound. The whole meeting had been taking place against the background noise of the castle being rebuilt. The kâfirs had erected the stone structure centuries earlier and had let it become dilapidated with the passage of time. Since there was now at least the possibility that the siege of Linz would be protracted, Murad had ordered the castle to be repaired.

It made for a lot of noise, though, which could

sometimes be an impediment. He waited for a few seconds before resuming.

"The janissaries in the airships will take some risks, that's all." He shrugged. "Why should they not? The whole crews will be taking the same risks. I want those gunners in the first ten ships in case this new airplane can attack us. I want to know what will happen—especially, can we fight against it?"

"I understand, My Sultan. It will be done." And with that, he left.

Linz airfield
Linz, provisional capital of Austria-Hungary

Late that afternoon, Rebecca Abrabanel landed in Linz. There was only a small delegation to meet her, however, along with a carriage. She'd given the authorities very short notice that she'd be arriving.

By now, however, they'd gotten accustomed to that. The term "jet-setting diplomat" hadn't entered Amideutsch lexicon—yet, anyway—but Rebecca was getting a large portion of the European continent accustomed to the concept. She not only traveled frequently but also took full advantage of the mobility provided to her by having an aircraft specifically assigned to the secretary of state. One of King Fernando's diplomats had been heard to complain, "That pestiferous woman moves so quickly she's got both sides of a dispute in full agreement before either of them has had time to think about it. She *cheats*, I tell you."

"It looks like the hangar's already occupied, boss," said her pilot, Captain Laura Goss. She'd been promoted just a few weeks ago, at Rebecca's insistence. Colonel Wood had just been another victim of her diplomatic knife work.

Her opening argument: *How can I expect to be safe, being flown about by a mere lieutenant?*

The colonel's rebuttal: *Her rank has nothing to do with how well she flies.*

Her concluding argument: *Perhaps so. But we are not dealing here with how well she flies. We are dealing with my expectations of how well she flies. As it stands, I worry constantly. Once Laura—Lieutenant Goss—is a captain, I will be able to relax and concentrate on important matters of state.*

Jesse Wood had stared at her for a bit. Then: "You're cheating," he'd complained.

"It shouldn't matter, Laura," she said, as the plane taxied to a halt next to the hangar. "I don't expect to be here more than a day or so."

Goss nodded. "No partying, in other words. Sobriety is the order of the day."

Rebecca smiled and climbed out of the cockpit.

"Madame Secretary!" exclaimed the Austrian courtier who advanced to greet her. "What a surprise! Another surprise, I should say. Your husband just arrived yesterday evening."

Rebecca frowned. She and Michael tried as best they could to spend time with their children. "I thought he was back in Magdeburg. He was *supposed* to be."

"He was. But the emperor summoned him here yesterday morning. He's thinking the Ottomans may be planning an assault."

Rebecca turned her head to look at Laura Goss and held up a couple of fingers. Then, off she went.

"Two days or so. Got it," Laura said to herself, smiling. As she climbed out of the cockpit, she pondered over whether the extended time meant she could party this evening.

Laura enjoyed partying. As she liked to put it: "Yeah, getting plastered and having a good time is a dirty job, but I don't think it's fair that men should have to do all the heavy lifting."

Linz was a great town for partying, too. These days, anyway. Sieges had their bright side, as long as the supplies didn't get cut off.

Three drinks, that's it, she decided. *Well . . . maybe four, if the guy's cute enough.*

Chapter 38

Observation platform atop the royal castle
Linz, provisional capital of Austria-Hungary

Julie had a somewhat peculiar and certainly unique relationship with Gustav Adolf. So, the next morning she was able to wheedle herself and Alex onto the best observation platform in the city, the castle that overlooked the Danube. The foundations went back into medieval times and possibly even earlier. It was said there was once a Roman fort on the same location. The castle had been rebuilt twice: once by Emperor Frederick III, who made it his residence from 1489 to 1493; the second time in 1600, by Emperor Rudolph II.

Julie had gotten interested in the castle's history when she found out it had been successfully besieged and seized by rebellious peasants just a decade earlier in 1626. *Score one for the home team*, as far as she was concerned. She'd never been especially interested in politics and still wasn't, but insofar as she thought about it her opinions leaned heavily towards a *sans-culottes* view of things. If that struck anyone as being inconsistent with her friendship with Gustav II Adolf, Emperor of the United States of Europe, King of Sweden, and High King of the Union of Kalmar, that was their problem. She'd never heard the quip, but if she had she'd have been in full agreement with Ralph Waldo Emerson: *A foolish consistency is the hobgoblin of little minds.*

Shortly after Gustav Adolf arrived in Linz to take command of the city's defense, he'd realized that aerial combat was likely to become a significant feature of the siege. At that point he'd ordered an observation platform erected atop the castle. (More precisely, he'd requested Emperor Ferdinand's permission to do so.) Gustav Adolf was still more likely to be found several miles to the east, in the fortifications that had been erected at the confluence of the Danube and the Traun rivers. But on any day that an air battle seemed likely, he took a position atop the castle.

He was there today, and welcomed Julie to his side. She'd been at his side at the crossing of the Lech where his opponent Tilly had been killed, more than four years earlier. Indeed, her marksmanship had played a significant role in the battle. She'd also been at his side at the Alte Veste, where Gustav Adolf had defeated Wallenstein, the second of his two great imperial opponents. Julie had come close to killing Wallenstein herself at the Alte Veste, with a shot that Gustav Adolf had witnessed personally. To this day he was convinced that shot had a miraculous aspect to it. Perhaps an angel had accompanied the bullet. The argument against that theory, of course, was that the bullet hadn't quite killed Wallenstein. But God was known to move in mysterious ways, so who could really say? Wallenstein's survival had eventually enabled the USE to become allied with Bohemia, after all.

So he viewed Julie as something of a lucky charm, and was quite willing to have her join him on the observation deck.

"Are the Turks coming yet?" was the first thing Julie asked when she got up the steps to the platform. She remembered to add "Your Majesty," this time. She had a tendency to forget.

"I believe they are, yes. But here"—he handed his binoculars to her—"tell me what you think. Your eyesight is better than mine. Better than anyone's, probably."

Julie peered through the binoculars. After overcoming the disorientation that she always experienced when she first looked at something through binoculars, she was able to find what she was looking for quickly.

"Yes, they're coming, Your Majesty. Looks like they're in their usual formation: twenty ships in four lines. Well, I'm sure about the four lines. Not positive about the total number yet." After a couple of seconds she remembered to say "Your Majesty."

He chuckled. "Be at rest, Julie. You have fulfilled your quota of 'Your Majesties' at least until lunch."

She grinned and made to hand back the binoculars, but he shook his head. "No, you keep them. Even with these"—he tapped the sports glasses he was wearing—"my vision is not good at a distance. You can tell me what's happening better than I could see it for myself."

"Okay," she said. She was tempted to add: *You are the*

coolest emperor since Nebuchadnezzar, but didn't. First, because she was pretty sure that would fall into the category of *lèse-majesté*, which was French for "way too cheeky." Second, because she couldn't remember if Nebuchadnezzar had been one of the good guys in the Bible. She thought so, but...

Sunday school had not been her best academic subject. In fact, it had been all the way at the bottom except for biology, and the only reason biology ranked last was because they'd partnered her with Dustin Acton when it came time to dissect a frog and that's when the asshole had pinched her butt. She'd held a grudge against the whole science ever since. She didn't like frogs, either.

As the minutes passed, the Ottoman air fleet drew near. Julie looked through the binoculars again and announced: "Yeah, I was right. Twenty airships again. They must have found a replacement for the one that went down with the *Magdeburg*. Hey, what happened to that ship, anyway? I lost track of it after they hit us because... well, when you're going down and hoping against hope that the envelope doesn't catch fire, you tend to concentrate on what's right in front of you."

One of the emperor's adjutants provided the answer: "Nobody knows, actually. The ship—the envelope, yes?— was last seen heading toward the Alps."

"Hoo, boy," Julie muttered. "If it gets there... talk about no contest."

An unmistakable buzzing sound crossed her hearing threshold. She turned her head in that direction.

Sure enough. "It's coming. The *Vasa*."

❖ ❖ ❖

When Ent had told her what the new plane was called, she'd burst into laughter. "Hal Smith! Talk about a guy who never fails to play the political card! First, the Gustav; now, the Vasa. What's next, d'you think?"

"I'd say that was obvious," had been Ent's reply. "The Kristina."

Julie had shaken her head. "No, Gustav Adolf would put his foot down. You name a plane after Kristina and you won't believe the ruckus she'll make until her father lets her fly it. Ten years old be damned."

"You got a point there. I dunno. You probably couldn't name it after the queen because she's dead now and by all accounts I've heard the emperor wasn't that taken with her to begin with. Maybe after his father, Charles?"

Alex shook his head, then. "No, Hal's a lot cannier than that. He'll name it the Ulrik. You watch. That'll irritate Ulrik, because he dislikes being flattered. But on the other hand, he'll understand the political advantage and there's no prince in Europe who's cannier than he is. The emperor will understand it also. Kristina won't, but she'll be pleased anyway because she really likes her future husband so she'll forgive Hal for not naming it after her."

Julie had gotten a little dizzy trying to follow the political logic. After her head finally settled down, though, she spotted the hole in her husband's theory.

Ent had spotted it also. "But if Hal names the next one after Prince Ulrik, he'll have to name the one after it for Kristina. If he doesn't"—he'd whistled softly—"boy, you wanna talk about a princess raising hell."

"Yes, you're right," said Alex. "But he's being guided by the same reasoning followed by the thief in that ancient tale where he's sentenced to death but gets his execution postponed for a year if he can teach the king's horse to sing."

"I know that story!" Julie exclaimed. "I always thought it was clever. One of the other prisoners makes fun of him and the thief replies"—her voice got a little sing-songy—"a year is a long time and many things might happen. I might die. The king might die. The horse might die. And maybe the horse will sing after all."

"Exactly," said Alex. "It will take Hal Smith a year—well, half a year, at least—to design and build another plane. In that time, someone important might die in a way that makes them a martyr, like Hans Richter."

"Like who?" Ent asked, skeptically. "Aren't too many people lying around who are more important than Kristina. Not in her eyes, anyway—and she'd be the one making the fuss."

"For Pete's sake, Ent, we're in the middle of a war. I can think of lots of candidates. Mike Stearns could get killed in a battle. What's even more likely is that Gretchen Richter gets knocked off. She came within a hair of it less than a year ago."

"Why in the world would Gustav Adolf want—"

"I grant you, it'd seem a little weird. But ever since she took Silesia, Gretchen's been in the emperor's good graces. And if she gets killed, he'd win lots of brownie points with the CoCs if he told Hal to name a new plane after her. And there's no downside for him because, what the hell, the witch is dead."

"Okay, okay. But what happens when you run out of martyrs?"

She shrugged. "By then, Kristina might be old enough to fly the plane. I figure—given Kristina—that wouldn't take more than another couple of years."

Ent's eyes seemed to bulge. "At the age of twelve? Are you nuts?"

"What part of 'given Kristina' are you having the most trouble with?"

It didn't take long before the new airplane was visible to everyone on the observation deck, including the myopic emperor. And no more than a minute further before it was clear that the Vasa was headed directly for the approaching Ottoman fleet of airships. Whatever his flaws might be, clearly Dustin Acton didn't suffer from cowardice. It was like watching a very small knight in armor charging a pack of very large dragons.

Or . . .

Don Quixote charging a windmill. Julie had never read the book, but she'd heard about that episode in it by the time she was eight years old.

The closer the Vasa got, the more anxious she got.

"What the hell is he doing?" she said. "Climb, you—you—not smart person. Get above them where they can't see you and then attack from the rear."

Gustav Adolf was frowning at her. "You seem very concerned. Why?"

She pointed her finger at the plane, which was now close to the first line of airships. They'd started closing their formation as soon as the Vasa appeared. By now they were quite near each other, at least by airship values of "near." They reminded Julie of a line of musketeers getting ready to fire a volley.

Which, she realized, was exactly what they intended to do.

"He's going straight at them! Uh, Your Majesty." Protocol then got completely shredded. "Does the fucking idiot think Turks can't shoot? They've got to have their best marksmen in the entire Janissary Corps up there! And he's giving them a perfect target! Does that man always have to be a jackass?"

In point of fact, Dustin Acton did assume that Turks couldn't shoot. That wasn't a conscious assessment on his part. It was simply racial prejudice so deeply ingrained he wasn't even aware of it.

Acton had even less interest in politics than Julie did. But his parents had been vehement supporters of John Chandler Simpson's campaign against Mike Stearns back in 1632. Because they were teetotalers, neither had ever entered the Club 250, notorious during the campaign for being the lair of Grantville's most vociferous bigots. But they would have been quite comfortable there otherwise.

Dustin had absorbed that view of people since he was a toddler, and because he was a self-satisfied, unreflective man, he had never once in his life thought to question his family's attitudes.

To him, Turks were just targets.

Being fair to Acton, he'd been rushed through flight school because they needed someone to be ready to fly the new Vasa as soon as the first one became operational. Jesse Wood had been short of pilots because several had been injured or gotten sick, and even at the best of times there were never all that many pilots available. What was the point of training a lot of pilots when there were so few planes available for them? The USE in 1636 and its jury-rigged airplanes were a far cry from the USA in 1944, with fighters and bombers pouring out of the rapidly expanding aviation industry.

Plus, Jesse had been preoccupied with the problems the Air Force had encountered due to the winter conditions in northern Poland, which was where Gustav Adolf had insisted on deploying most of its aircraft.

And the truth was that Jesse was not really temperamentally suited to his job. The only reason he'd been made the head of the Air Force was because he was the only person in Grantville after the Ring of Fire who'd been an officer in the up-time Air Force.

He tended to think like a pilot, instead of a commander—and trainer—of pilots. And he tended to focus on the problem in front of him rather than thinking about next year's problems. As a result, he'd overlooked what you'd expect would have been one of the main things emphasized in military flight school.

Aerial combat techniques and methods.

Why bother? Until the Vasa came into being, aerial combat had been nonexistent. The best anyone could have managed was to carry a pistol in their cockpit and shoot at nearby planes with it—a technique that could be rivaled in futility only with hunting geese by throwing rocks at them.

So, as he headed into his first combat with other aircraft, Dustin Acton didn't know his ass from his elbow—and was not the sort of man who'd have contemplated the problem beforehand. Why should he? His ass was spectacular and his elbow was the finest the world had seen in decades.

Had Ent Martin been the pilot, he would have avoided the head-on approach Acton was taking. But as the gunner, he was so concentrated on his approaching target that he didn't think of the danger he might be in.

Not, at least, until they were close enough that he could see the firing slit in the gondola of the airship they were facing directly. But by then he had already started to fire, and all other thoughts were swept aside.

He couldn't have done anything, anyway. Another man was flying the plane.

Acton wasn't actually stupid. He had planned to approach the Ottoman airships from above, since that would give his gunner the best field of fire and the Vasa would be shielded from enemy fire by the envelopes of the enemy ships.

Alas, he hadn't considered the fact that the enemy airships were approaching from the east.

He hadn't considered that it was still early in the morning with the sun not all that far above the horizon.

And he'd forgotten to bring sunglasses.

The sun was blinding. For a short while, he tried shielding his eyes with one upheld hand, but that wasn't very practical. The Vasa was a somewhat awkward plane to fly and really needed both hands to do the job.

The solution was simple and obvious. He dropped

down in altitude until the big envelopes of the Ottoman airships were blocking the sun.

The other four riflemen in the first line of airships fired before Tufenkci Gülhan did, although his ship, the *Mohacs*, was the one directly in line with the kâfir aircraft. But they were forced to fire because the closer the enemy airplane got, the worse their firing angle became. He intended to wait until the last possible moment.

He couldn't believe his good fortune. The enemy was clear in his sights.

Then the kâfirs started firing and he was so startled he lost his aim for moment. He'd been expecting cannon fire—small, by the standards of cannons, but still cannons. Powerful, but not quick. Instead, what seemed like a storm of bullets slammed into the gondola above him. He heard the screams of wounded crewmen.

But he paid no attention. He had his aim back. He fired.

It was a powerful rifle. The Turk's bullet punched through the Vasa's fuselage as if it wasn't there, struck Ent's left forearm and sprayed the interior of his cockpit with blood. Then, smashing into the frame of his seat and ricocheting upward, the bullet punched into the cockpit above and still had enough force to pass through the pilot's seat and penetrate the back of Dustin Acton's right thigh. It came to rest against his femur.

There was no spray, but Acton's seat was instantly soaked with blood. He cried out in pain and shock and lost control of the plane. It swerved down and to the side.

That swerve killed Tufenkci Gülhan. Ent still had the machine gun's aiming mechanism in his right hand, along with the trigger. By instinctive reflex, he clutched it in response to the sudden swerve. The bullets shifted their trajectory and shredded the lower portion of the gondola where the rifleman had been positioned.

He would have died soon, in any event. Enough of the incendiary rounds had struck the airship to start one fire, then two, then three. Even if half of the crew hadn't already been killed by that first murderous volley, they still couldn't have put out the fires and brought the vessel down safely.

In less than a minute, the entire envelope was sheathed in flames and the *Mohacs* was plunging toward the Danube.

It took Julie a while to realize that the Vasa heading back to the airfield was in trouble. But when it got close enough that she could see it more clearly, it became obvious that it was barely under control. The pilot had to have been injured—which would explain why it was coming back so soon. She'd been surprised by that, but perhaps it had already run out of ammunition. She hadn't thought to ask Ent the day before how long the gun could be operated before the ammunition was gone.

"I'll be back!" she yelped. Then, raced for the staircase. Glancing over her shoulder, she saw that Alex was following her.

"Stay here!" she shouted. "You can't do anything!"

As she started down the stairs, a residue of irritation combined with her natural sense of humor. "You're a cavalryman, remember? There ain't no horse that can reach the sky!"

Once on the ground and out of the castle, she hopped on the motorcycle that she'd used to get her and her husband there.

Off she went. Happily for them, most of Linz's inhabitants were either soldiers at their posts or civilians taking shelter indoors. Anyone still on the street when Julie raced by would have felt like wheat before a scythe.

At the airfield, she found what she had expected. Medics had Dustin Acton on a stretcher and were loading him into a wagon. He looked to be unconscious.

Ent was sitting on the ground, propped against the hangar. A medic was attending to him also. His arm, it looked like.

He was conscious, though. When he saw Julie, he gave her a little nod.

"Is that gun still working?" she demanded.

He stared at her for a moment, as if his mind was trying to process the question. Then, his teeth clenched with pain, nodded again.

Julie looked around, a bit wildly. By now, there were dozens of people on the airfield.

"Is there anybody here—Laura!" She'd just spotted Laura Goss in the crowd.

Julie pointed at the Vasa, which had come to rest about twenty yards from the hangar. "Can you fly that thing?"

"Huh?"

"Dammit, do you know how to fly a Vasa?"

Goss stared at the plane for a moment. Then, shrugged. "How hard can it be?"

That was a question Julie wasn't going to go anywhere near. "Okay, then. Let's go."

"Huh?"

"You heard me! You're the pilot; I'm the gunner. How hard is that?"

For two seconds, Goss still looked confused and uncertain. Then, suddenly, she grinned.

Chapter 39

Linz airfield
Linz, provisional capital of Austria-Hungary

To Julie's displeasure (and to some degree, embarrassment) their takeoff was delayed by the ground crew. The problem was one that a shooter like Julie should have foreseen: What happens to the spent shells of a machine gun fired in an enclosed space?

Brass cartridges were still far too valuable to just toss them aside without a care. But given the haste with which Hal Smith and his people had had to design and build the Vasa, they'd cut a lot of corners along the way. One of those corners was as simple as possible. The spent cartridges expelled by the machine gun and shunted downward wound up in a metal bin—what amounted to a large, oblong tin can. (Except it was cheap iron, not tin.)

A fair number of the shells missed the can and wound up on the floor of gunner's cockpit. The seat was designed so that none of the shells came to rest against the gunner's feet, but other than that it was catch-as-catch-can.

Cartridges that have just been fired are *hot*. And when enough of them pile up in a small enclosed space like a cockpit, the cockpit gets hot. Not hot enough to kill the gunner outright, no—not even close. But certainly hot enough to make them uncomfortable.

Part of the reason Hal Smith had decided that crude design was good enough was itself simple. The plane could only carry a small amount of ammunition. Not "small" by deer hunter standards, of course, but certainly small by warplane values. This was not a B-17 Flying Fortress whose multiple machine guns could blast away on a mission that lasted for hours.

Given that they'd encountered their mishap very quickly, Acton and Martin returned to the airfield before Ent had used up more than a quarter of the ammunition on board. But since they had to clear out the spent cartridges anyway, the ground crew also saw to it that the machine gun was fully loaded again.

Following the philosophy *let the pros do it*, Julie and Laura waited by the plane while the ground crew did their work. Julie was a little amused to see that they filled up the fuel tanks as well. Looked at from one angle, that was pointless, since the Vasa would run out of ammunition long before it ran out of fuel. But Julie approved nonetheless. A ground crew that rigidly followed procedure was not a ground crew likely to screw up, either.

The wait had another benefit, which that it gave Julie and Laura time to talk over their plans and the tactics they would use. They would not have to improvise once they were in the air.

Julie was even more amused when she saw the method

used to retrieve the spent cartridges. She'd noticed when the plane had first arrived that there was a small hatch in the bottom of the fuselage, just before the nose. She hadn't thought much of it at the time, or what it was there for. Fish swim. Dogs bark. Airplanes have hatches. But now she saw its purpose.

The hatch was opened by the member of the ground crew who'd gone into the gunner's cockpit. Another member of the crew then slid a metal tub on a wheeled platform under the open hatch. A moment later, a small torrent of spent cartridges came out of the plane. Clearly, the ground crewman had emptied the container holding the spent shells.

Then—this was the amusing part—the crewman outside gave what looked like a large paintbrush to a hand sticking out through the hatch. A few seconds later, little piles of shells started coming out. A skill was being applied to aviation that had first been developed by so-called cave men. A cave woman, more likely.

Next to her, Laura laughed. "Will you look at that? It's like the French say: '*plus ça change, plus c'est la même chose.*'"

"What does it mean?"

"The more things change, the more it's the same thing. I learned it from a French guy."

Julie eyed her sideways. "And just where did you meet a Frenchman in West Virginia?"

"Where d'you think? A party at West Virginia University in Morgantown. He was an exchange student. I thought his accent was cute. He was even cuter."

"I thought you went to a community college."

"Yes, I did. A year and half at Pierpont Community and Technical College in Fairmont. But for parties I always went up to Morgantown. *Way* better parties. You could usually get free booze, too, if you were a girl."

Julie pursed her lips. "I think I'm sorry I asked."

Laura grinned. "Look at this way. Would you rather be flown into a dogfight by a virgin or a party girl?"

Ottoman siege lines southeast of Linz
About three miles from the confluence of the
Danube and Traun rivers

"Press the attack," Murad commanded, lowering his eyeglass. "I don't know why the kâfir craft has been gone so long, but it can't be good for them. And there's only one of them, anyway."

He'd paused the attack after the *Mohacs* went down, and was now regretting that he'd done so. Still, it might not cost him anything. He had far more aircraft than the Austrians and their allies did and if the worst the enemy could do was destroy one of his airships every half hour, he could afford such casualties.

"Press the attack," he repeated. Then, spent a minute or so just enjoying the breeze atop the observation platform. So far, it had been a pleasant spring.

A mile above the confluence of the Danube and the Traun

"They're definitely coming, Julie," said Laura. Her voice

was piped into the lower cockpit by a simple tube. As long as the two of them spoke loudly, they could hear each other. Of course, that would stop being true when the machine gun opened up.

"I can see them." The view from her cockpit was better than Julie had thought it would be, looking at it from the outside. The fact that the enemy fleet had resumed its advance on Linz was obvious, even with sunglasses on.

That same visibility would pose a danger—could pose, at least—once they started engaging the enemy. But Julie and Laura had no intention of repeating Acton's mistake. Julie thought she was probably the best rifle markswoman—marksman too—in the whole world. But there were sure to be others who were very good, eighty-five percent to her ninety-five percent, and a shot fired by Mr. Eighty-Five Percent could kill you just as dead as any she could fire.

"Climbing," Laura announced.

Ottoman siege lines southeast of Linz
About three miles from the confluence of the Danube
and Traun rivers

It didn't take long for Murad to understand what the kâfirs were doing. They were now far enough above his own ships that they couldn't be fired upon. Leaving aside the impossible ranges involved, the gunners aboard his fleet couldn't even see the enemy airplane because of the great envelopes overhanging their gondolas.

Nor did he have any difficulty understanding why the enemy had made no attempt to attack his ships yet. So far, they were just flying above the Ottoman lines. Within a minute, they would have passed across the fourth and last line.

At which point, they would turn around and come at his ships from the rear, with the sun in his gunners' eyes instead of theirs—which was probably irrelevant anyway. The design of the Ottoman ships had the gondolas very far forward. An aircraft attacking from above and behind would soon be shielded by the envelope.

What remained to be seen was the effectiveness of the kâfir gun. It was quite possible, using a small cannon, that a lucky shot would have spectacular results while most of the shots missed entirely or did little damage. That was often true even with the largest cannons.

A mile above the confluence of the Danube and the Traun

"Coming around," Laura announced.

"How's it flying?" asked Julie.

"Thing's a tub. At worst, it's like wrestling a pig. At best, it's like wrestling a piglet. But what really ticks me off is how goddam slow it is. I feel like getting out and pushing."

Julie smiled, but didn't say anything. From her standpoint, the slower the better, so long as the plane didn't stall. Even firing automatic rifles, it would be a lot easier to hit a target—even a big target like an airship envelope—going eighty miles an hour than a hundred and fifty.

"Coming up on the first one," Laura said.

❖ ❖ ❖

Observation platform atop the royal castle
Linz, provisional capital of Austria-Hungary

When the word arrived, Melissa Mailey got the Austrian queen she now spent half her days with to get them onto the observation platform on the royal castle. Gustav Adolf was already there when they arrived.

Melissa was certainly not on a first-name basis with the Emperor of the USE, King of Sweden etc. etc. etc., but she'd had enough dealings with him to address him directly.

"Your Majesty, the rumor is that our aircraft"—she scanned the sky, looking for it—"I mean the one that went up to fight the Ottomans, is being flown by two women."

"Flown by one woman, actually. The other woman—that would be the baroness Julie—is aboard to operate the weapon." He frowned. "If you came to complain that I put two women at risk, I did no such thing. The two of them chose to do this entirely on their own. Technically speaking, the pilot is guilty of insubordination and the gunner—she's a civilian—is grossly stretching the provisions of her contract."

He smiled, then. "Not that I think anyone is likely to press charges, given the circumstances."

Melissa smiled as well. "I assure you I didn't come to complain. I came so I'd have the best view to watch two women kick some royal ass."

It occurred to her that might be an unfortunate turn of phrase, spoken in the presence of emperor and a queen. "Of the sultan variety, I mean."

❖ ❖ ❖

A mile above the confluence of the Danube and the Traun

Julie started firing. It took a few seconds for her to get a feel for the peculiar weapon, since it was like no gun she'd ever fired before. But no more than a few. She was very familiar with many firearms, after all.

But a few seconds was long enough, even with as slow an aircraft as the Vasa, for them to pass over the airship before Julie could do any significant damage. She might not have done any damage at all, although she'd swear some of the rounds she'd fired had hit the envelope.

"Damn!"

"Take it easy," said Laura. "We're almost at the next line."

Eight of her rounds had indeed struck the envelope, but they came in too squarely. They punched deeply enough into the airbags that the incendiary rounds were wasted in an almost purely hydrogen mixture. The "trick," as it were, of shooting down airships with incendiary rounds was to rip the envelopes open so that you brought enough oxygen into the mix.

Ottoman siege lines southeast of Linz
About three miles from the confluence of the
Danube and Traun rivers

"Nothing," Murad murmured. "Nothing at all."

The kâfir craft was now coming up on the rear of the *Sapienza*.

A mile above the confluence of the Danube and the Traun

Julie had figured out what she'd done wrong. This time she fired far enough ahead that the bullets ripped gashes in the envelope and the gas bags beneath. She was using the rounds to mix the gases as well as ignite them.

Then it occurred to her she'd overlooked something.

"*Laura, pull—!*"

The gas plume ignited—just as the Vasa flew into it.

The airship started to burn.

Ottoman siege lines southeast of Linz
*About three miles from the confluence of the Danube
and Traun rivers*

"That's not a cannon!" Murad exclaimed. He turned and glared at the small cluster of artificers standing in a corner of the platform. "You told me they would use a small cannon!"

A mile above the confluence of the Danube and the Traun

Fortunately, the Vasa had flown fast enough that it suffered no damage beyond scorching parts of the fuselage—but only enough to discolor it, not to set it aflame.

"I guess that's what they call baptism by fire," said Laura. "Thank you for sharing, Julie. But how about next time we just share a bottle instead of a fucking inferno?"

"Sorry. Next one, stay off to the side a little." The machine gun couldn't be shifted as far to either side as it could be up and down, but she had at least a fifteen-degree angle available.

"Will do. But I don't have time for this line—"

That was obvious. They were already passing over it. There was only the front line of airships ahead of them.

"—so we'll go for the next."

Moshe Mizrahi was relieved to see the enemy warplane passing over his line without firing. As the commanding ship in the line, positioned on the left, the *Chaldiran* wouldn't have been the kâfir's target anyway. Passing near the center of the line it would have struck either the *Sokhoista* or the *Raydaniya*.

He looked back—and down. By now, it was obvious the *Sapienza* was doomed. The flames had spread rapidly across the envelope. The airship still had some buoyancy, but it would lose almost all of it within another half a minute.

He saw a crewman climb over the gondola's railing, and hesitate for a few seconds. Then a blast of flame scorched him and he made his decision. No death could be as bad as a burning one. He relinquished his hold on the rail. He was perhaps three thousand feet above the ground. At the speed he was falling, he would die in less than twenty seconds.

Moshe looked away. Then, looked to see where the enemy plane was headed.

It was about to attack the *Preveza*, Abraham Zarfati's ship. Moshe and Abraham had never gotten along very well, for reasons Moshe himself had never understood. Zarfati was just hostile to him. Not ferociously so, just ... unpleasant.

But it probably didn't matter any longer. Moshe wished the man well.

It wasn't long before he knew his wishes would not be granted.

Coming in alongside the enemy airship as well as above it made Julie's task more difficult. But by now she had a good feel for the machine gun.

She opened fire and within seconds she knew she'd slain a monster. By the time they passed over Linz, the giant creature was headed for a fiery death somewhere on the east bank of the Traun, at a guess.

She looked down and gauged her ammunition.

"Another run?" asked Laura.

It was tempting, but ...

"No, better not. This gun uses up ammunition like nobody's business—and we can't carry all that much to begin with."

"All right. Homeward bound it is. We done good, girlfriend."

Not long after Julie made her decision, Abraham Zarfati made his own.

He would not burn. Not that, whatever else. By now,

at least half of the giant envelope was engulfed in flames. The *Preveza* was doomed, and himself with it.

Do not think. Just do.

He went over the rail.

He did not pray for himself, as he fell. What would be the point? Whatever he had done, it was done. Whatever he had failed to do was done also. God would make His decision.

He did not pray for his family, because there were too many of them. His had been a good life, that way. A wife—still healthy—four children, three boys and a girl. A grandson and two granddaughters now, too.

There was not enough time.

He managed to shape his fall in such a way that he was looking up at the sky. Let that glory be his final sight.

He would pray for his sultan. Murad IV was a good sultan. Hard, but fair. If he demanded loyalty, he gave it also. So long as the sultan lived, he would see to it that Abraham Zarfati's family was cared for.

He could not remember the best prayer to use for this. He was a devout man, but had never been a studious one.

So he began reciting one he thought would suit this time and this place, and could only hope that God would think so as well.

"Have mercy upon him; pardon all his transgressions."

He needed to speak louder. The wind rushing by was almost deafening.

"Shelter his soul in the shadow of Thy wings."

He could not remember a time the sky had been so blue.

"Make known to him—"

Chapter 40

Ottoman siege lines southeast of Linz
About three miles from the confluence of the
Danube and Traun rivers

"Order them back," Murad commanded. He hadn't needed to use his eyeglass to follow the course of the battle. When huge airships are engulfed in flames and fall out of the sky, they could be seen by anyone within line of sight.

He tightened his jaws. Later, when he was alone in his quarters, he could afford to express his true feelings—rage, disappointment. Even some worry. But not here; not now.

"All of them, My Sultan?" asked one of his adjutants. A spike of fury passed down Murad's spine. Almost, he turned and struck the man down with his fist. *Who was he to question—*

But again, he restrained himself. The man's question was reasonable. Murad had considered himself the option of continuing the aerial assault, at least with the airships equipped to drop bombs on Linz. They could drop their bombs before the peculiar new kâfir aircraft returned, judging from the length of time it had taken it to return previously. And—there was still a great deal of uncertainty—perhaps they could get away before the fire-spitting aircraft returned. The enemy had withdrawn the first time after damaging only one airship. The second time, it had withdrawn after destroying two and possibly—no report had come in yet—damaging a third. Clearly there was some factor that was preventing it from remaining in combat for very long. Either they ran out of fuel quickly or—this was Murad's own guess— their bizarre rapid-firing rifle ran out of ammunition quickly.

Yes, it was tempting to give the order. Very tempting. But in the end, what would be the point? The airships needed to do extensive damage in order to clear the way for the assaulting troops. That required the fleet to spend time over the target, because each airship couldn't carry very many bombs. He would have to maintain a continuous bombardment for at least three hours, by his estimate. That would mean alternating the lines of airships. Two lines bombing—possibly not even that many—while the rest returned to refuel and reload.

Unless they managed to destroy the new kâfir aircraft, the Gureba-i hava would suffer horrendous casualties. And how were they to destroy the thing? Shoot at it with rifles on airship gondolas? That was feasible against other airships because they all moved slowly. This new winged aircraft...

No. He had better uses for his airships than sending them into a slaughterhouse. They would make excellent reconnaissance platforms, especially for his navy.

"Bring them all back," he repeated. "Tell all my aghas and chorbaji I want them to assemble in the headquarters tomorrow morning. We need to plan for a siege."

He had hoped to avoid that. Taking Linz by traditional siegecraft would be a slow process and would tie up most of his army, probably until well into next year. He had hoped he could repeat the same assault by overwhelming force that had enabled him to capture Vienna without a siege.

So be it. God's will was not always clear. It remained His will.

He headed for the staircase that led down to the ground, but stopped when he remembered something. He beckoned another of his officers.

"See to it that the families of the men killed today are taken care of—and do not stint the care. If I discover any officers are skimming the funds provided, they will die—and not quickly."

"Yes, My Sultan."

Observation platform atop the royal castle
Linz, provisional capital of Austria-Hungary

"I just want to make sure I understand exactly what happened, Your Majesty." Melissa pointed to the west, in the direction of the airfield. "The pilot and gunner who brought the plane—the Vasa type, it's called, right?—"

She didn't wait for an answer to that. "The two men who brought the plane here and did the first attack run—

is that the term for it? Never mind, we know what I'm talking about—were both injured and couldn't continue. Do I have it right so far?"

As was usually the case, Gustav Adolf found dealing with Melissa Mailey to be simultaneously aggravating and amusing. But he was willing to make allowances, partly because she was an American but mostly because she had done such a superb job of negotiating the treaty with France that ended the Ostend War. He was quite sure that Cardinal Richelieu had found the woman infuriating and never once been amused by her.

"Yes, that is correct. And before you ask, what the radio operator says"—he pointed down to the castle roof supporting the platform—"he's right there, you know, and my aides bring his messages immediately. What he says is that acting on their own initiative, the secretary of state's pilot and Baroness Julie Mackay commandeered the aircraft and carried out the mission—I believe that's the term the Air Force prefers—which destroyed two of the Ottoman airships and repelled the assault." He gazed at her quizzically. "Why do you ask?"

"Just want to make sure that if anybody asks me what happened, I don't misrepresent anything. And now, Your Majesty. I should really return to the hospital."

She turned to Queen Mariana. "Do you wish to come also, or would you prefer to remain here?"

"Oh, I think I will come with you. I don't see where there's anything further we can do here."

Off they went.

On their way down the staircase, Melissa started

vocalizing a tune, in the soft manner of someone singing to herself.

"I am not familiar with that melody," said Mariana. "Is it an American one?"

Melissa hadn't realized she was singing out loud. "Um...yes, it is. It's by a woman back up-time named Helen Reddy. The song is called 'I Am Woman.' It was very popular in its day."

Among women, anyway. Men, not so much.

"Since the deed was done by women," Melissa said, "I think it would be most suitable if the decoration were named after you."

"Me? What decoration?"

Melissa pursed her lips for a moment. This was not a subject she was very familiar with.

"It would be what we Americans would call a 'medal.' It's for meritorious deeds in combat. We had ones called the Bronze Star, the Silver Star..." She tried to remember others. "The Congressional Medal of Honor, of course, but that would be a little over the top here. Most people who got it died in the doing. Let's see...the Navy had the Navy Cross. What else...?"

A fact elbowed its way into her memory. "Ah, yes! One of Austria's future empresses—well, the future I came from—established a medal named after her. It was called the Military Order of Maria Theresa. So, there it is! The 'Military Order of Mariana.'"

She saw no reason to burden the queen with the inconsequential details. If she remembered correctly, the Military Order of Maria Theresa was reserved for military officers. That would rule Julie right out.

Mariana was looking doubtful. "I'm not sure Ferdinand will approve."

"I'm sure he will." *Especially after I get a bunch of wounded soldiers and nurses to start hollering for it.*

She muttered something, again without realizing it.

"What did you say?"

"Ah . . . nothing."

Oh, world of the Ring of Fire, you are sooooooooooooooooo never going to hear the end of this.

"I'm thinking a statue would be nice, too," she said.

Radio operators' room, the royal castle
Linz, provisional capital of Austria-Hungary

Rebecca frowned at the radio message the operator had just handed to her. Michael had returned to Magdeburg after his brief visit, to make arrangements for the children. Gustav Adolf wanted him back in Linz as soon as possible to resume command of the Third Division, now that the Ottomans had returned to their siege lines.

> DEAR BECKY STOP SORRY THERE IS A GLITCH IN MY TRANSPORT PLANS STOP WILL NOT ARRIVE LINZ UNTIL TOMORROW STOP OR NEXT DAY STOP CHILDREN ARE FINE STOP

By now, she would have thought her English vocabulary was complete. But it could be such an elusive language.

"What is a 'glitch'?" she asked nobody in particular.

❖ ❖ ❖

Magdeburg airfield
Magdeburg, capital of the United States of Europe

"You sure you won't reconsider?" Mike asked Eddie Junker. "I'm sure you could get me down to Linz in plenty of time to get up to Poznań soon enough for whatever Torstensson wants you there for."

Eddie shook his head. "You're thinking in terms of flight time only, General Stearns. In that respect, yes. You're right. The distance from Magdeburg to Linz is a little over three hundred miles. We could be there in less than three hours. The distance from Linz to Poznań is about the same, which would add another four hours or so."

Eddie glanced at the sun, which was now well above the horizon. "We are not too far past the spring equinox, so daylight is perhaps eleven and a half hours—but I estimate we have already lost three of those hours. That gives me almost no margin of error."

"The weather is supposed to be—"

"Good. Yes, I know. But the weather predictions are by no means perfectly reliable. If someone can figure out a way to put one of your up-time satellites in the sky, no doubt they would improve. But right now, they are nowhere nearly good enough for me to be willing to risk my life on them."

He held up his hand. "But that doesn't begin to plumb the depths of the problems involved."

Mike didn't actually clench his teeth, but he came

close. He knew when a refusal was looming. "Go on," he said.

"General Stearns—"

"Will you can the formalities, Eddie? You're not in the military and we're in private. 'Mike' will do fine."

Eddie smiled. "All right, Mike. The really big, intractable issue is fuel. This plane"—he nodded toward the *Steady Girl,* a few yards away on the tarmac—"can get about four hundred miles when it's fully fueled. But I don't ever fly it more than two hundred and fifty miles before refueling, because lots of things can vary that range and problems can always come up. Just to name a simple one, I have to navigate by eyesight and if we get bad enough visibility—fog, even low cloud cover—I'm wandering around lost, with my fuel running out while I'm trying to figure out where I am. There is no way I am going to be willing to fly even one three-hundred-mile leg in a day, much less two. Which means we're going to have to refuel three times before I can get to Poznań, which is where I'm supposed to be by the end of the day. That's according to *Lieutenant* General Torstensson."

Mike didn't miss the emphasis on "Lieutenant."

"I am well aware that Lennart outranks me, Eddie. So what? You're not under his command."

"True, but I try to get along with the fellow. A stance, by the way, which I was instructed to take by Francisco Nasi, who *is* my employer."

Eddie started counting off his fingers. "So. First we fly to Grantville and refuel there. That's a busy and efficient airport so it should take no more than an hour to refuel. We have now used up perhaps three and a half hours—

but it would be safer to assume four. Then"—he tugged his middle finger—"we fly to Linz, where you disembark, leaving me to the chaos that will be rampant in that airport—say better, glorified airfield—because in his wisdom the emperor ordered all but one of the functioning airplanes in the Air Force to come there. By now, I wouldn't be surprised if all the fuel has been used up and I have to wait for resupply to arrive. At the very best I will have used up all of today. Perhaps—but more likely not—I can get an early start on my flight to Poznań tomorrow morning."

Now he tugged his ring finger. "Except that when I arrive in Breslau to refuel, who knows what I will encounter? As I'm sure you know by now, the Lady Protector has taken all her forces and seized Kraków. I was told she plans to construct an airfield in Kraków as soon as possible, which means she probably cannibalized some of the equipment and fuel in Breslau."

"All right, all right. I understand your point. So what do you propose instead? You're the only plane available for the next several days. Maybe a week."

"You fly with me to Poznań today. Right now. It's only a two-and-a half-hour flight and Torstensson has the best equipped and efficient airfield in the world. You oversee the refueling while I find out why Torstensson summoned me there."

"And then . . . ?"

Eddie shrugged. "And then we proceed however best we can. I can't answer that until I find out why Torstensson wanted me there by this evening. But it's the only option you have, Mike, unless you want to wait here in Magdeburg until I return. Whenever that might be."

"Screw that," Mike said. "I've been to too many labor conventions not to know the basic rule about overcrowded elevators. Just get on it, no matter if it's headed up or down. You wait for an elevator going the right way that isn't already jammed full, you could starve to death. So, Poznań it is."

USE Army airfield
Just outside the main army base at Wartheburg
Poznań siege lines

Eddie got back from his meeting with General Torstensson less than two hours after they'd landed. By then, the *Steady Girl* had been refueled and was ready to go.

When Eddie came up to Mike, he had a strange expression on his face. Mike wasn't sure whether to call it *strained* or *dumbfounded.*

His stomach started sinking.

"You're not going to like this, Mike," said Eddie. "I mean, you're *really* not going to like this."

Chapter 41

Poznań
Poznań Voivodeship
Polish–Lithuanian Commonwealth

"You were right," said Mike. His hands were clenched so tightly on the plane seat's armrests that his knuckles were white. He was speaking through clenched teeth, too. "I don't like this. Not one damn bit."

Eddie Junker got a long suffering look on his face. More precisely, he got that sort of *faux* long-suffering look that was a kissing cousin to *schadenfreude,* the German expression for "pleasure in the misery of others."

"Stop smirking at me," Mike growled. "I'm scared to fly, okay? My sister's terrified of spiders. I know it's irrational."

"If it'll make you feel any better, this time around there might actually be some risk involved. Not a lot. But I'll probably wind up flying closer to the ground than is called for in the Official Safe Flying Instruction Compendium. 'Osfic,' we call it."

"You made that up."

"Well, yes, I did." Eddie gave Mike a glance that was now a bit exasperated as well as amused. "Mike, nobody made you come along on this mission, as I pointed out to you before we took off. Torstensson made that clear as well."

"Screw that. I told you—it's the elevator principle. I need to get to Linz as soon as possible and because of the emperor's order bringing all planes except one observation Belle down to Linz, you're the only ride available."

He hissed, for an instant, in response to a spot of turbulence. "And you have no idea where you're going to wind up before the day is over—much less tomorrow. Am I right?"

"Well . . . yes. My orders are to provide reconnaissance and—I love this part—'whatever else may be needed'—to the party about to flee Poznań. Torstensson refused to tell me who the party is or how he knows all this, but I'm guessing it's Jozef and Christin. I have no idea where we'll wind up and when. What I'm mostly worried about—will worry about—is where to get refueled. The only realistic options are Poznań, Breslau and"—here he grimaced—"whatever there is in Kraków. Which is probably a cow pasture to land on and a two-gallon can of fuel."

"What I figured. I'll stick with the elevator."

Eddie pointed to the radio. "In that case, General, I'd appreciate it if you'd handle the radio. I believe the mysterious party we're to provide reconnaissance for will be contacting us soon. I've already got the frequency set."

Mike frowned. "How do you know they have a radio?"

"General Torstensson told me they would. He's also the one who gave me the frequency to use."

"Fer Crissake, why the James Bond need-to-know run-around? Who else besides Jozef and Christin would have a radio in Poznań?"

"Presumably, the people who sent the message to Breslau that they suspected Koniecpolski had been assassinated."

Mike rolled his eyes. "Who are obviously connected to Jozef or why else would they have sent him the message?"

Eddie shrugged. "You're probably right. We'll find out soon en—"

The radio squawked. "*Anybody there? Anybody there? Over.*"

Mike brought the speaker to his mouth. "We're here. Who is this? Over?"

"*Jozef Wojtowicz, of course. Who else would it be on this frequency?*"

Mike rolled his eyes again. "What I said," he muttered. Into the speaker, he said: "Just checking. What do you want us to do? Over."

"*How close are you to Poznań? Over.*"

Eddie held up three fingers.

"About three miles away. Straight to the east. Over."

"*Good. In five minutes, fly straight across the city, north to south. As low as possible. Then check back. Over and out.*"

Mike replaced the speaker on its mount. "Why does he want that, do you think?"

"At a guess, he wants to draw everyone's attention to the south. The Air Force overflies the city regularly, but they usually stay at least half a mile high. There's not much chance the Poles have any effective antiaircraft guns yet, but why take the chance?"

Mike studied him for a moment. "You don't seem too worried about it."

"It's not that easy to hit something going more than a hundred miles an hour, especially when it's close. The one mistake you have to avoid is flying straight for more than a short time. That's how Hans Richter got killed."

Mike pointed at the mic. "'Straight across,'" he said.

Eddie smiled. "I'm sure that was just poetic license. We'll cross the north gate and we'll exit across the southern wall. That's straight enough for a poet like Jozef. What we do in between is our business."

Mike pursed his lips. "'My business,' is what you really mean."

"Well, yes."

"Why do I think I'm not going to like this?"

They were nearing the imposing north gate. Christin couldn't help but feel nervous. Mieczysław Czarny had assured her that by the time she reached the gate he and his handpicked team of hussars would have seized it.

Very confident, he'd sounded. But he wasn't the one who had her ass hanging out in the breeze, figuratively speaking, while she trotted down the street in full armor except for having no helmet so everybody and their great-uncle could see that she was a woman.

No, correct that. A woman in armor holding a great long lance with a big banner flying from it. Just in case anybody might have missed her at first glance.

She could count eight—no, nine—people within thirty feet who were gawking at her. Even the big APC rolling fifteen yards behind wasn't drawing as much attention.

What is it with you people? You never seen a woman before?

The problem was that by now the APC was a fairly familiar sight in Poznań, even though nobody had ever seen it decked out like this before. There were riflemen in all four turrets with their weapons ready and huge banners hanging on either side of the vehicle. At periodic intervals the banners had been cut away, exposing the gunports. If you looked closely you could see rifles protruding from them.

And just for good measure, Jozef had insisted on dyeing her horse blue.

"In case someone hasn't raised their eyes yet. A blue horse will catch their attention."

For the first time in years, she found herself thinking it was maybe too bad she'd never been attracted to choir boys who went on to become accountants.

First, a biker. Now, a master spy.

A deep sort of buzzing noise drew her attention. She looked up just in time to see an airplane flying over the north gate in her direction.

Jesus, he's flying low. It looked as if he'd barely cleared the gate.

The plane swept overhead too fast for her to get a good look at it, but she was sure it was Eddie in the *Steady Girl*. You wouldn't think it, looking at him, but beneath that placid-seeming exterior lurked a daredevil.

He'd done the trick, sure enough. Glancing around,

Christin saw that all the people who'd been gawking at her were now gawking up at the plane.

Which would be true as well, if Jozef and Czarny's scheme worked as planned, of the men guarding the north gate who hadn't already been won over to their side.

The gate was close now. She was about to find out if the plan worked.

Maybe her parents had been on to something, years ago, when they told her she was an idiot.

In the next few minutes, Mike made an interesting discovery. The hair-raising aerial acrobatics that Eddie Junker indulged himself in flying over Poznań—*thisaway, thataway, let's go back where we came from, oh, hey, why not do a couple of barrel rolls and a loop the loop while we're at it?*—didn't bother him at all. It was a lot of fun, actually, like riding a rollercoaster in an amusement park.

Go figure.

Mieczysław Czarny came from somewhere, leading his horse. "*Go! Go! Go!*" he shouted, waving Christin forward through the now open gate.

She spurred her horse into a gallop. Just in time, she remembered to lower the lance. Then, felt pretty stupid because the APC was taller than the lance. They'd measured the height of the gate to make sure the huge vehicle could pass through. Which it could, barely.

Behind her, she could hear the former coal truck's engine roaring. She winced when she heard Mark Ellis grinding the gears when he shifted. That sort of main-and-auxiliary transmission could be tricky to use if you weren't used to it. So Buster had told her once, anyway. She'd never driven one herself, although she preferred a stick shift in her own cars.

She'd gotten that from Buster, too. *Automatic transmissions are for sissies.*

Her parents had always driven automatic transmissions.

She passed out of the gate onto the bare strip of land beyond the walls. Then, turned her horse to the right and started circling the city following the wall, staying just out of rifle range—well, musket range. She slowed down to a canter. They had at least a mile to go before they'd be free and clear of the city.

One quarrel Christin hadn't had with her parents was that they hadn't objected when she'd wanted to learn to ride a horse. She'd gotten quite good at it by the time she was a teenager, even though the skill had no practical application in the West Virginia of the 1980s. She'd been pretty rusty by the time of the Ring of Fire, but riding horses was like riding bicycles or swimming—once you knew how to do it, you never forgot.

She glanced back and saw that the APC was still following her, although it had dropped back thirty or so yards. Following the vehicle, she could see hussars pouring out of the gate. There would be upwards of two hundred of them, according to Jozef. Their recruiting had gone better than they'd expected.

The loud sound of the APC's horn startled her. Glancing back again, she saw Walenty leaning out of the passenger's window and jabbing his finger at her. He seemed pretty frantic about it. Why—

She realized that he wasn't pointing at *her*.

Turning back around in the saddle, she saw a group of horsemen—hussars, judging from the armor and saddle wings—who were staring at her. They were maybe fifty yards off.

Oh, hell.

The one in the lead lowered his lance and spurred his horse toward her, the other four following him.

Hell's bells. Now what?

A few yards back she'd leapt her horse over a ditch. She hadn't thought much about it at the time—Christin's equestrian skills had returned within a year after the Ring of Fire—but now she looked back again and saw that the APC had almost come to a stop. It might or might not make it over the ditch without getting stuck.

She looked back at the oncoming hussars. Forty yards away.

The sound of gears grinding again drew her head back around. Mark had apparently decided he couldn't get across the ditch here and was heading north to a spot where the ditch wasn't as wide. Which meant—

You're on your own, girl.

She reined in her horse. The hussars were thirty yards away.

Trying not to get frantic, she threw away the lance and reached down to draw her rifle out of the saddle holster. Thankfully, she'd drawn the line at wearing gauntlets with the armor. For a second or two, her hand fumbled to get a good grip.

Twenty yards away.

She got the rifle out and brought it up—

To a shoulder that didn't exist any longer, being now

encased in whatever they called that stupid shoulder guard. Poltroon? No, that meant coward.

Her brain was fluttering like a bird. *Pauldron, that's it.*

Fifteen yards away. The lance was completely lowered, the blade coming right at her.

Concentrate!

She'd have to shoot from the hip. She swiveled the gun down into position.

Ten yards.

She hadn't even heard the plane coming. A shadow covered her as the *Steady Girl* passed so low over her head it stripped her cap off.

The hussar who'd been about to spear her raised the lance, apparently thinking he might be able to spear the plane. And, in fact, Eddie was flying so low that the tip of the lance *did* strike the fuselage. But that just sent it flying out of the hussar's hand and sailing at the man behind him.

Who managed to duck, but in so doing caused his horse to stumble and fall. That spilled him onto the ground and tangled up the three men behind him.

For a moment, at least. Christin had only one opponent. He was bringing his horse around and was drawing out his saber.

She wasn't used to firing from the hip, but the range wasn't more than five yards. How hard could it be?

You're terminated, fucker. She'd always loved that movie.

She wasn't sure how many shots she fired. Four? Five? *Maybe six?*

However many it was, the hussar was down. Down and out, clearly.

The one who'd spilled was also clearly down and out. Unconscious, badly injured—maybe dead.

One of the three hussars left was still trying to control his horse. The other two were staring at her.

For not more than a second, though. The APC might have to find a way around the ditch, but the hussars on her side were just as capable of jumping a ditch as she was. Hearing them coming, she had the sense to raise the rifle and take her finger off the trigger.

Three—four—five of them swept past her. Their lances took two of the hussars out of their saddles. The third tried to flee but another lance caught him in his armpit, lifted him right out of the saddle and sent him sprawling. Christin didn't think the lance tip had penetrated the armor, but it hardly made any difference. As hard as the man had landed, he was bound to have some broken bones, at the very least. Falling off a horse was no joke.

She was feeling a little lightheaded, now. Not knowing what else to do, she looked around to see what had happened to her cap. She really liked that cap. It had a feather in it and everything.

She was lightheaded enough that, again, she didn't hear the plane coming. This time, though, the *Steady Girl* passed overhead at a reasonable altitude.

More or less. Eddie was still not more than thirty feet off the ground.

Now there's a son-in-law worth keeping, she thought.

Mike leaned back in his seat. "Well, that was exciting," he said. Then, realized that he meant it.

Eddie started singing. Softly, but Mike could make out the words.

"Sent from down below,
Mother-in-law, mother-in-law."

Mike chuckled. "You'd better not let Christin or Denise hear you singing that."

"Who do you think taught me the song?"

Chapter 42

Breslau (Wrocław), capital of Lower Silesia

As Eddie had feared, Gretchen Richter had stripped most of the equipment and supplies from the Breslau airfield—you could hardly call it an "airport"—when she began her march on Kraków. She'd also taken most of the gasoline, but she'd left two full drums containing thirty gallons each. That would be more than enough to allow Eddie to refuel and resume his assistance to Jozef and the people fleeing Poznań.

It would have been much easier and quicker, of course, to operate out of Torstensson's military airfield in Wartheburg. But there were political considerations involved that made that impossible. Everyone involved wanted to keep the USE's support for the Polish revolutionaries as covert as possible.

The *Steady Girl* had made one landing at the USE airfield. That had been unavoidable given that Torstensson insisted on conferring in person with Eddie. But it was quite possible that one landing would have gone unnoticed. And even if it hadn't, plausible explanations could be advanced. The aircraft had developed mechanical problems, was getting short of fuel, whatever.

But if Eddie started operating regularly out of that airfield, the fig leaf would get shredded quickly. So, once he and Mike Stearns had done what they could to assist the initial breakout from Poznań, Eddie flew to Breslau to refuel. Kraków would have been much better from a political standpoint, obviously. But Kraków was too far away given the fuel they had left—and Eddie still didn't know what facilities or fuel would be available there anyway.

The unexpected problem they encountered when they landed at the Breslau airfield was that another airplane was already there and had drained one of the thirty-gallon drums and was about to start on the other.

An unexpected problem . . . and a very complicated one.

You'd think a husband would recognize his own wife's aircraft, but no. Mike didn't have Eddie's familiarity by now with just about every aircraft in existence. Mike could tell the difference, even at a distance, between a Belle and a Gustav and a Dauntless and a Dragonfly. But the insignia weren't clearly visible and the subtle differences between the military version of the Dragonfly and the modifications made for the needs of the State Department were too subtle for him to grasp.

When they passed over the airfield so that Eddie could get a sense of its condition, he realized immediately which plane was parked on the tarmac—grass field, rather—next to the hangar. But he didn't tell Mike right away because . . .

Why in the world would Rebecca Abrabanel be in Breslau now, of all times? Eddie could think of several possibilities, none of which boded well for tranquility and an orderly universe. For a wild, brief moment, he considered flying back to Poznań. He might have even done it except they didn't have enough fuel.

Nothing for it, then. He'd have to land.

Once they were down and taxiing toward the hangar, the insignia on the fuselage of the Dragonfly became easily readable.

UNITED STATES OF EUROPE

DEPARTMENT OF STATE

"Hey!" Mike exclaimed. "That's Becky's plane!"

It was even worse than Eddie had feared. He'd hoped to have at least an hour or so of peace and calm before they got into the city and found out what ill news Rebecca had brought with her.

But it was not to be. She'd just landed herself, as it turned out, and was still in the hangar talking to someone on the radio.

"Michael!"

"Becky!"

An embrace and kisses followed, needless to say. Eddie would have been charitable about it except he hadn't seen Denise for almost three months and had no idea what had happened to her.

That last worry got resolved, at least. Sort of.

Laura Goss was there. She gave Eddie a little wave of her hand and came over.

"Hey, Eddie."

He nodded. "Lieutenant Goss." Then, spotting the new insignia on her cap, corrected himself. "Captain Goss, rather. Congratulations."

Driven by impulse, not really expecting an answer, he asked: "I don't suppose you've heard anything about Denise?"

Laura's eyes got a little wider. "You didn't know? They all got out of Vienna okay and were headed toward Kraków. That was about a week and a half ago. Don't know what's happened to them since."

"*Kraków*? Why in the name of—" He broke off the incipient blasphemy. Despite Denise and her mother chipping away at it, Eddie still had most of his Lutheran habits left, if not all of his former religious beliefs. "Why would they go to Kraków, of all places? It's about to become a war zone!"

"Probably why they went. But don't ask me." Goss nodded toward Rebecca, who was now speaking intently to her husband, in a tone too low for Eddie to make out the words. "She might know. Of course, that doesn't mean she'd tell you. Just 'cause you're Denise's honey doesn't give you a need to know what's happened to her." She shrugged. "When it comes to callous unconcern for human sentiment, government officials are hard to tell apart from crocodiles."

"Need to know" be damned. Eddie headed toward Rebecca.

But before he could take more than two steps, she and Mike broke off their discussion and looked at him.

"Change of plans, Eddie," said Mike. "Turns out— Becky was just on the radio with Gretchen—there's plenty of fuel in Kraków. So we're all headed there—Becky will fly with us, since there's no reason to take two planes."

"Why don't you take the Dragonfly, then?" Eddie asked. "It's a two-engine plane and has more room and that way I can get back to what I'm supposed to be doing."

Rebecca shook her head. "That would be unwise. For the time being, at least, we need to keep a distance between the USE and the rebels in Kraków. Gretchen was quite insistent on that point."

Eddie all but threw up his hands in exasperation. He did lapse into blasphemy. "For Christ's sake! She's already there herself—and she's been prancing around in that silly armor of hers! How do you expect to keep that quiet?"

By the time he finished, though, he already knew the answer before Mike put it into words:

"Gretchen is in a category of her own, especially the way Polish revolutionaries look at the world. Nobody—that includes Gustav Adolf himself—doubts that she'd kick over the official traces in a minute if the needs of the struggle called for it. That's the way she'd put it, too: 'the needs of the struggle.' Yes, she holds the USE titles of Chancellor of Saxony and Lady Protector of Lower Silesia. Doesn't matter. Whereas if Becky and I land in Kraków in a plane that's got 'USE Department of State' plastered on the sides, that'll be a different story."

"And that is not all," Rebecca added. "There is no point not telling you since you will find out soon enough anyway. We will be leaving Michael in Kraków while you fly me and a passenger whose identity needs to be kept secret back here. Then Captain Goss will fly him and me to Prague while you can resume your help to the people coming south from Poznań."

The machinations of what people euphemistically called "high politics." Eddie felt like his head was spinning a little.

"So who's this mystery passenger? And why does he need to get to Prague so quickly and secretly?"

"It's Morris Roth," said Mike. "Wallenstein is dying."

Rebecca, whose expression had heretofore been serious and solemn, broke into a big smile. "Cheer up, Eddie. Gretchen told me that Denise just arrived in Kraków. Well, not exactly. She told me that the rescue expedition to Vienna just arrived. But I am sure that if anything had happened to Denise, she would have mentioned it."

"Oh. Well. Okay, then. Off to Kraków we go! I just have to refuel. You're sure there's plenty of fuel in Kraków, because"—here he gave Laura Goss a reproving look—"I'm sure she drained most of what was in those two drums."

"Stop crabbing, Eddie," said Laura. "I left you half of the second drum. Kraków's just a hundred and fifty miles away. You could get there on ten gallons and some fumes."

Before they could leave, however, a new complication arrived.

Princess Kristina, with Caroline Platzer in tow.

"I want to go! I want to go! Wherever it is. I love to fly! I'm going to become a pilot myself, you know. Papa promised me I could learn when I turned sixteen. But I'm sure he meant fourteen. Maybe even twelve."

Eddie kept busy with the refueling. Above his pay grade, this was. He could only imagine the diplomatic repercussions if the heir to the thrones of the USE, Sweden and the Union of Kalmar arrived in Kraków at this particular juncture.

Not to mention that the city was about to be put under siege.

"Well . . . Kristina, I am afraid—"

"You're just the secretary of state! You can't tell me what to do!"

Caroline Platzer intervened. "Kristina, stop it. She can in fact forbid you to go."

Kristina was a Vasa, bred and born. Even at the age of ten, she could lawyer like nobody's business.

"Only as the future empress! As the future queen of Sweden and the Union of Kalmar, she can't order me to do anything! And that's how I'd be going. Wherever we're going."

She pointed a stiff finger at the *Steady Girl*. "And don't try to tell me that's an official plane! With that painting on it? Ha!"

Laura Goss intervened. "Your Highness, with the secretary of state's permission, of course, I could give you some flying lessons. The Dragonfly has dual controls, you know. And it's a twin engine six-seater. Way better than that raggedy old thing Eddie's flying."

Under other circumstances, Eddie might have taken offense. Under these . . .

Bless you, Captain Goss.

"That's a splendid idea," said Caroline. "With the secretary of state's permission, of course."

Bless you, Caroline Platzer. Governess Excelsior.

"Well... I suppose there'd be no harm in that," said Rebecca. "I won't need the plane for a day or so."

Bless you, Rebecca Abrabanel. Diplomacy's Reigning Queen.

Kalisz, capital of Kalisz Voivodeship
Greater Poland

As they had planned, the people who'd broken out of Poznań stopped for the night in Kalisz, a town about sixty-five miles to the southeast. A distance that the APC could have traveled in an hour on up-time roads had taken a full day. That sixty-five miles was "as the crow flies." As the APC lumbered along, it had been at least half again as far, and the roads in the Polish countryside in the year 1637 resembled up-time highways about as much as the ox carts that used them resembled a sports car.

Kalisz was still a major center of trade, despite having declined somewhat in importance since its heyday in the Middle Ages. They'd be able to replenish whatever supplies they needed except fuel, and they had plenty of that.

Thirty hussars were immediately sent to seize the town's famous Jesuit college to keep the instructors and students locked up for the night. Partly that was to prevent any of them from escaping the town and bringing word to any pursuers. That was of minor concern, though. There had been no sign of pursuit for hours, and although they no longer had the advantage of Eddie Junker's aerial reconnaissance, before he left the area to refuel he'd told them the pursuers from Poznań had turned back already.

The likelihood that anyone escaping from the college would be able to find anyone worth reporting to, stumbling around in the middle of the night in the Polish countryside, was . . . minimal, to say the least.

No, the main reason they locked up all the residents of the college was that the Jesuits of Poland had made very clear that they were siding with Borja in the civil-war-in-all-but-name that was raging within the Catholic church. That also meant they were rabid partisans of King Władysław and bitter enemies of the USE. It wouldn't be long before they were bitter enemies of the revolutionaries in southern Poland as well.

The enmity of the Jesuits in Kalisz could be shrugged off easily enough. What couldn't be shrugged off was the certainty that if they observed which people in the town were *helping* the escapees, they would be sure to report that to the Polish authorities when they arrived tomorrow or the day after.

There were two such groups. Kalisz had a large Jewish population, among whom were some hidden agents for Morris Roth. More importantly, the town also had a sizeable settlement of Bohemian Brethren, pretty much all of whom had already decided to become allied with the Galician revolutionaries who had now seized Kraków.

While Jozef went about his master spy affairs, Christin climbed into the APC. She was exhausted. Although she knew how to ride a horse—quite well, in fact—she'd never in her life spent a whole day on horseback, and if she had she would have been wearing something sensible instead of hussar armor.

Before stripping off the armor, though, she went to see how the children were doing. Tekla and Pawel and the other four children had ridden in what amounted to a large, lidless wooden crate that had been fixed to the APC's floor and piled full of blankets and quilts to keep them from being too badly battered by the vehicle's lurchings. They had been tended to during the escape by the mother of three of them.

Everyone inside the APC looked just as exhausted as she felt. The soldiers who had been stationed at the gunports had been provided with some cushioning also, but for the most part they'd kept themselves from being slammed around by holding onto the handgrips provided. A day of that was at least as tiring as a day spent on a horse, even if they hadn't had to wear armor.

When Christin peered over the side of the Kiddie Krate, as she thought of it, six anxious little faces looked up at her. The mother of three of the children was slumped in a corner of the crate, either asleep or just too exhausted to open her eyes.

Pawel said: "Mama, Tekla's really scared." After a couple of seconds, he added: "I am too."

The other four children said nothing, but it was obvious they were just as frightened except the boy with Down syndrome. He seemed in fairly good spirits.

So . . . taking off the armor would have to wait. It would probably help bolster the kids' spirits.

Clambering into the Kiddie Krate while wearing armor was no fun at all. But eventually Christin squeezed herself

into a space the children made for her and—blessedly—
could lean back into the blankets. Her butt felt like it was
about to come off, if butts were built to do that.

"Okay, kids. There's nothing to be afraid of. Let me
tell you a story. Several stories."

Christin had told her daughter a lot of stories when
Denise had been a little girl. She still remembered most
of them quite well.

She didn't know if seventeenth-century Polish kids
were familiar with Aesop's Fables. If so, they might get a
little bored. But she was absolutely, one hundred percent,
dead sure they'd never heard the Uncle Remus stories.

"Okay, children. Let me tell you the story about a
rabbit—he was called Brer Rabbit—and the tar baby and
the briar patch."

Kraków, official capital of Poland
Actual capital of Lesser Poland

When the mysterious person who'd arrived in Eddie
Junker's plane came into the conference room that served
as the revolution's headquarters, his face couldn't be seen
because of the wide-brimmed floppy hat he was wearing.

Then he swept it off in a manner that was barely short
of flamboyant, and Jeff felt an enormous sense of relief.

So did Prince Ulrik.

So, after trying to resist it for a couple of seconds, did
Gretchen.

So did Morris Roth, until he saw that Rebecca had
entered the room behind Mike Stearns and was looking

right at him. He would never understand why, but he knew in that instant what she had come to tell him. Wallenstein was either dead or dying—and the weight that Morris had felt on his shoulders ever since the king of Bohemia had handed him the Anaconda Project just doubled.

Red Sybolt grinned. He and Mike went back a long ways and had generally gotten along, even if Mike sometimes found Red's *in-your-face* stance toward the UMWA's enemies reckless and a bit childish, and Red sometimes thought Mike suffered from the *can't-we-all-just-get-along?* heresy.

Lukasz Opalinski was simply curious. So this was the famous Prince of Germany?

"I am sure glad to see you," said Jeff. "Uh, General."

Stearns held up a cautioning hand. "I'm just here as an adviser. Actually, I'm not here at all."

Then he looked at the large table in the center of the room. "Is that a campaign map I see before me?" he asked, moving toward it.

Chapter 43

Kraków, official capital of Poland
Actual capital of Lesser Poland

The next day, the advance elements of the magnates' army began taking positions northwest of the city. By then, Eddie had returned from Prague and had done a reconnaissance flight over the oncoming enemy forces.

"And you're sure about the guns?" Mike asked him. He and Eddie were at the big table in the headquarters, every side of which was packed by people.

"Positive, Mike. There are nine of them. I can't swear I'm exactly right about their size, but they're at least culverins. Some of them might be forty-two-pounders."

"How did they get them so close already?" wondered von Mercy.

Lukasz Opalinski had a wry sort of smile on his face. "You're not accustomed to Polish warfare, I take it. You always have to remember that in Poland and Lithuania the great magnates have their own private armies. We know of at least five magnates who've contributed forces to this campaign—and while their estates will usually be concentrated in the Ruthenian lands they will have them all over the Commonwealth."

He leaned over the big map spread across the table and planted his finger on a spot south of Warsaw. "We knew they were assembling their forces at Radom. But there's no reason they couldn't also have been moving up their heavy artillery still closer to Kraków. At a guess . . ." He moved his finger southward. "Here. Somewhere in or around Kielce. That's no more than eighty miles away."

"It doesn't matter how they got them here," said Mike. "By Eddie's reckoning, they'll have those siege guns moving into position three days from now. Once they start firing, it won't take them long to bring down enough of the walls to launch an assault. Kraków's fortifications were never designed to withstand heavy artillery."

"What do you recommend we do, then?" asked Prince Ulrik. "They outnumber us. Not by enough to overcome the advantage we'd have of fighting behind fortifications, but if the fortifications are brought down . . ."

"Make a sortie as soon as they bring the guns up," said Mike immediately, "but before they've had time to build fortifications for them or siege works for the rest of their army. If we don't—ah, you don't—capture or destroy those guns, you can't hold Kraków."

Mike took off his hat and set it down on the table. Barely, he managed to restrain himself from wiping his brow with the back of his sleeve. Even though it was a chilly spring day, the fireplace in the chamber in the Cloth Hall they were using for a headquarters had a roaring fire going which was heating the room to an uncomfortable degree.

"I'd go farther than that, too," he added, "depending on how well the sortie looks to be going. I think there's a fair chance we could send that magnate army packing."

They'd been using Amideutsch as their lingua franca. Seeing the puzzled looks on the faces of von Mercy and his two adjutants, Mike realized their familiarity with the language didn't extend to all the American slang expressions which peppered it.

"'Send them packing' means rout them," he explained.

Von Mercy's expression changed from puzzlement to doubt. "General Stearns, even doing a sortie that soon in the siege is a gamble. Pushing it strongly enough to have any chance of defeating the enemy in the open field strikes me as very risky."

"It *is* risky," said Mike. "But I don't think it's as risky as being cautious. If we use what you might call a traditional strategy, we're bound to lose. If they didn't have those siege guns, we could probably stand them off, given that we—you'd—have the advantage of being behind fortifications and they don't outnumber you all that much. But they do have them, and it won't take them long to breach Kraków's medieval walls."

He picked his cap up and put it back on his head. For some obscure reason rooted in military tradition, wearing it made him feel more general-like. He'd put up with the sweat if it would help him persuade the other people standing around the table.

"There's another factor at work here, as well," he said. "A political one. You don't just need to defeat *this* army.

You have to be able to defeat the next army, and the one after that, and the one after that. There is no way the king and the Sejm will allow Lesser Poland to rebel successfully. If need be, they'll cede Poznań to Torstensson in order to free up the royal army. They can afford to lose Poznań permanently. They can't afford to do the same with Kraków."

Lukasz, who'd been stroking his beard, abruptly dropped his hand. "I agree with General Stearns. Even if we hold Kraków, it will be a long siege. What we need is a quick victory. If we drive off the magnates—not just hold them off but *drive* them off—then we'll start gaining adherents quickly. A long siege . . . "

He shrugged his shoulders. "That will not be enough, even if we hold out."

Gretchen spoke up, for the first time since the meeting began. "We did well enough at Amsterdam and Dresden," she pointed out. "I'm not disagreeing with what Mike is proposing. I haven't made up my mind about that. I'm just playing devil's advocate, for the moment. We had a long siege at Amsterdam that did us quite well, politically. And while the siege of Dresden didn't last long, our ability to hold the city is what forced the Swedes—ah, Oxenstierna and his counter-revolutionaries—to send Banér against us."

Prince Ulrik now spoke up. "The situation is different, I think. By holding Amsterdam, you produced an acceptable political settlement between Don Fernando and the Prince of Orange. But I think there is no chance of such a settlement here."

"There certainly isn't!" said Krzysztof Opalinski.

"No chance at all," chimed in Jakub Zaborowsky.

Ulrik nodded. "As for Dresden..." He gestured toward Mike. "Let us be honest. What made the decisive difference at Dresden was the intervention of General Stearns and his Third Division, not the uprising of Dresden itself."

"Although without the Saxon revolt, we couldn't have intervened at all," said Mike. "But I agree with your general point. There is no equivalent to the Third Division waiting in the wings to come to Kraków's rescue. We will have to make do with the forces we have at hand."

As always, General von Mercy found the idiosyncrasies of Amideutsch a bit maddening. *Waiting in the wings. Make do.* Why did Americans insist on such oblique language?

Still, he grasped the essence of what was being advanced. He was still skeptical of the wisdom of Stearns' proposal—which was quite in line with the boldness for which the man had become known since he donned his uniform. On the other hand...

Mentally, von Mercy shrugged. Stearns had so far been successful with his methods, after all. And, in any event, von Mercy was a professional soldier serving an employer, not a revolutionary. Wallenstein had never had any intention of holding Kraków, once his forces helped to take the city. He wanted the territory south of the Vistula. Even if they took Kraków, the casualties the magnates would suffer would make it difficult for them to interfere with Bohemia's goals.

Assuming those goals survived Wallenstein's

apparently imminent demise. Either way, von Mercy was fairly certain he could extract his own forces if the defense of Kraków began to crumble. There were advantages to having an army whose principal component was cavalry. They could usually get away if they lost a battle.

It would be tough in the infantry units Morris Roth had raised, of course. But those were not really von Mercy's men, when all was said and done.

Mike looked around the table, gauging the degree of skepticism in the various faces gathered there.

Still too much. "We do have a couple of advantages, you know."

"And these are . . . " That came from Ulrik, whom Mike gauged to be middling-skeptical. Of course, that was the Danish prince's default stance toward the world in general.

"The first is that, in a different way, our enemy's forces are just as disparate as our own. Except theirs is a matter of attitude, not skill. Yes, they're mostly professional soldiers and most of them will be veterans. But they serve five different paymasters. What is the likelihood that if one of those magnate armies gets hammered badly, the others will rush to their aid?"

Lukasz chuckled heavily. "About the same as one crocodile rushing to aid another."

"That's not quite fair," said von Mercy, with a smile. "A crocodile is likely to attack another one in distress. The armies of the magnates won't go *that* far. But you're right. Their instinct will be to look to their own."

The Bohemian commander crossed his arms over his

chest, and leaned back a little. "What you are proposing, I think, is that we adopt Tilly's tactic at Breitenfeld, where he focused his initial attack on the Saxons, figuring that he could rout them more easily than the Swedes. I would remind you, however, that Tilly lost that battle, *despite* his success in routing the Saxons."

Mike shrugged. "That's because Gustav Adolf stood his ground, used his artillery advantage—and seized Tilly's artillery, to boot. None of which factors will come into play here. First—I don't think you'll disagree with me, General von Mercy—the top commander of the magnates' army is not likely to be Gustav Adolf's match. Speaking of which, who is their top commander? Do we know yet?"

"No," replied von Mercy. "It has to be one of three men, however—Mikołaj Potocki, Prince Stanisław Lubomirski, or the voivode of Kiev, Janusz Łohojski. Neither of the other two princes, Wiśniowiecki and Zasławski, are old enough and have enough experience. Of the three, I gauge Potocki to be the most capable. But not even he is the equal on a battlefield for Gustav Adolf. You spoke of two advantages. What is the other one?"

"Our technology. We have two assets that the magnates not only don't have but won't be familiar with: Eddie Junker's Dauntless and the APC. What I propose to do is use them as the knives to carve out one of the five magnate armies and crush it. Then, use that victory to start routing the others. Once the five armies start separating from each other, all of them are lost."

"All right," said von Mercy. Then, remembering a quip in Amideutsch that was actually rather charming, he added, "But as always, the devil is in the details."

"Indeed so." Mike leaned over the map and placed his finger on a small tributary of the Vistula west of the city. "This river—the Rudawa—?"

"It's more what you Americans call a 'creek,'" said Krzysztof.

Mike shook his head. "The size of the stream itself doesn't matter. What are the banks like? Soggy? Solid? And if they're solid, is there a road running alongside it?"

Krzysztof and his brother glanced at each other.

Lukasz provided the answer. "If I remember correctly—I was only there once—the ground is not soft and there's . . . well, I wouldn't call it a 'road,' exactly. Not what you Americans mean by the term."

"How wide is it?"

Again, the Opalinski brothers glanced at each other. And, again, Lukasz provided the answer.

Such as it was. "I don't remember."

Mike studied the map for a moment. "All right. When is Eddie getting back from Prague?"

The answer to that question was provided by Denise Beasley, who was sitting in a chair next to Minnie against one of the chamber's walls. The two youngsters had parlayed their way into the meeting on the grounds that as Francisco Nasi's agents they needed to be kept up to date on what was happening. Lest—this had been Denise's contribution; she was always the more brazen of the two girls—Nasi decided he had better things to do with his airplane.

"Eddie told me he'd be back sometime today. Pretty soon, I think."

"And we have radio contact with him, right?"

Gretchen provided that answer. "Yes, we do. Why?"

"Tell him to follow the Rudawa on his way in. We need to know how wide that road is—and whether there are any major obstructions on it."

"Why?" asked Gretchen.

After Mike explained his plan, Denise immediately raised an objection.

"Hey! That's my mom you're talking about!"

Mike shook his head. "Not exactly." He turned to Gretchen again. "We also have radio contact with the APC, yes?"

Near Kępno
Poland

Christin could only hear Jozef's side of the radio conversation, but she heard enough to know that she was somehow involved. Her, and the kids.

"What's up?" she asked, once Jozef got off the radio.

"Change of plans," he said. "We'll go to Breslau first, instead of heading directly for Kraków. We'll let off all the children there, along with the women."

"Bullshit," was her immediate reply. "No way am I getting off in Breslau. My daughter's in Kraków, remember?"

"Not you," said Jozef, shaking his head.

"Well, okay then. So long as I'm staying with the APC, we're cool."

"Ah . . . not exactly."

Chapter 44

Airstrip south of the Vistula
Kraków, official capital of Poland
Actual capital of Lesser Poland

"This is really such a not-good idea," said Laura Goss, between tight lips. She didn't quite have her teeth clenched, and she managed to keep her hands from clutching the wheel. If she ever needed a light touch as a pilot, this was the day.

No, this was the *evening*.

"It was an even worse idea for you to come along, boss," she added.

Riding in the front passenger seat of the State Department's Dragonfly, Rebecca Abrabanel seemed quite composed. Of course, she always did. "Relax, Captain. You are doing quite well, I think."

She looked at the horizon. The sun had set several minutes ago and the ground below them was now only dimly visible. Still not quite dark, though, and ahead of them...

"Look," she said, pointing. "They've lit—are lighting—the landing lamps. You can see the runway clearly."

Laura refrained from snarling what she would have snarled to anyone else but Rebecca. *Those aren't 'landing lamps,' you dimwit! They're not 'lamps' at all. Lamps have volts and watts. These are the medieval—so, Stone Age—equivalent. Planes don't fly by instruments in the year 1637. They fly by fucking campfires.*

It was true that the fires provided Laura with a clearly marked landing strip. What they *didn't* do was actually light the strip itself and make it clearly visible. She could see where it was, in two dimensions—length and width—but she'd still have to gauge the third dimension using nothing better than twilight.

That third dimension being height. That was to say, the difference between landing a plane and crashing it.

She'd made exactly two night landings since she graduated from flight training. Both of them had been necessary because unexpected bad weather had forced her to detour before she could land—and neither landing was at the airfield she'd been headed toward.

Luckily, the Magdeburg airport had been in range on one occasion and the field at Grantville for the other. Those were the two airfields—the *only* airfields—which had a powerful enough source of electricity to use real spotlights to illuminate the landing strips. And even those two landings had been on the hairy side.

At least on those occasions she'd had the rationale of necessity. Today's—no, *tonight's*—exercise in daredevil folly was the result of so-called strategic planning on the part of the woman sitting next to her and her husband.

"We need to get a lot of supplies from Prague to Kraków," Rebecca had explained that morning, just after dawn. "And we need to get them there this evening."

Quickly, Laura had done the calculations. From Breslau to Prague and back was two hundred miles, thereabouts. Refuel in Breslau. Then, fly to Kraków, which was somewhere between one hundred and sixty and one hundred and seventy miles to the east.

"Piece of cake," she said. "We can be there by midafternoon."

Rebecca shook her head. "I am afraid not. Once we reach Prague we will need to take out the four rear seats—well, two of them, anyway—and load the plane up with the supplies."

Laura shrugged. "That can't take more than two hours. So, late afternoon. As long as it's daylight, we're fine."

Rebecca kept shaking her head. "I did not make myself clear. I did not say we had to get to Kraków *by* evening. I said we had to get them there *this* evening. That is to say, after sundown."

Then came the three words Laura was learning to detest:

"Matters of state. It is still imperative that no one be able to see us landing at Kraków. So it must happen in the evening."

Laura had been a bit mollified when she saw the supplies being loaded onto the Dragonfly. She'd never made the stuff herself, or even seen it made, but she knew what went into making the sort of low-grade napalm available in the here and now.

That also explained why they'd had to fly to Prague. Supplies of that nature weren't available at most cities serviced by an airfield. Not readily, at least. Given Wallenstein, he'd probably had the stuff already stockpiled. He wouldn't have been able to stockpile styrofoam as the thickening gel, true. This many years after the Ring of Fire, there was very little left of the styrofoam that Grantville had brought with it. Styrofoam made down-time was coming onto the market, but there wasn't much of it and so far as she knew none of it had made its way to Bohemia yet.

But it didn't matter for their purposes at the moment. Soap made a good enough substitute. And at least this way, if Laura died crashing the plane, she'd die for a better reason than *matters of state*.

In the event, the landing went smoothly. To her surprise, Laura found that the small bonfires that marked the perimeter of the landing strip did provide enough light for her to be able to gauge the height as they descended.

"Damn, I'm good," she murmured, as she started taxiing to what she would have called a "hangar" except it was obviously too small for an airplane to fit inside—any airplane, much less a Dragonfly. Except for the Jupiters being made in the Netherlands, the Dragonfly was the biggest fixed-wing aircraft in the world.

"So when are we leaving, boss? Just before the crack of dawn, I'm assuming, so we can get off without anyone seeing us." She wasn't worried about taking off in poor lighting. The nice thing about heading for the sky instead of coming down from it was that there was nothing up there to run into except an occasional bird. And they weren't much of a risk because the airplanes in this day and age were so slow that any competent bird could get out of the way before they got hit.

"No, we will be staying here indefinitely. I have decided to wait out the siege with Michael. If need be, we will both evacuate using the Dragonfly."

"So how do we keep out of sight? No way is this plane going to fit—"

She broke off, seeing men approaching with nets in their hands. Obviously, they were planning to drape the nets over the plane and then disguise it with tree branches.

"Oh, that is so cool. Just like in the movies."

Breslau (Wrocław), capital of Lower Silesia

By the time they got to Breslau, Jozef had been behind the wheel most of the way; long enough that he was confident he could drive the APC. He'd developed "the hang of it," to use the idiom favored by his instructor, Mark Ellis.

Never mind that in the course of bringing the huge vehicle to a stop in the central square he almost knocked down the pillory positioned there. The thing was a medieval relic, anyway. He was quite sure no one would have missed it. Criminals, not at all; law-abiding citizens . . . maybe a little.

After setting the parking brake, he turned to the man sitting next to him in the cab. That was Mark Ellis, who been coaching him on the ways and means of driving a big coal truck. "So, Mark, here you are. In Breslau, not Kraków—which is as close to your home as I can get you."

"And I thank you for that, believe me that I do. Now... what are the chances I can catch a plane ride back to the USE?"

Jozef got a crooked little grin on his face. "Unless I badly miss my guess, this *is* now part of the USE. Or will be pretty soon. I gauge the chances that Gustav Adolf will relinquish Lower Silesia to be the same as the snowball in hell referred to in one of your American quips. I just hope the Swedish bastard leaves it at that and doesn't gobble up still more Polish territory."

"You're probably right. But I need to get to Grantville."

"There's no way of knowing when a plane might be free—and if there'd be an empty seat on it, even if it were. What I recommend you do is wheedle your way into one of the merchant caravans that are now going back and forth to Dresden. Getting from there to Grantville should be easy."

"By seventeenth-century standards of 'easy,'" Ellis muttered. "We're not talking Greyhound bus here."

That idiom was not familiar to Jozef, but the meaning seemed clear enough. "Good luck," he said. He and Ellis climbed down from the cab.

"You left the keys in the ignition," Mark chided him.

"Yes, I know. And the chances that someone here will steal the APC for a joyride are..."

"Okay, okay. Snowball's chance in hell, I admit. Still, you shouldn't get in the habit of it."

By then, Christin had emerged from the interior of the APC, with Tekla and Pawel in tow. The other children had also come out, along with the mother of three of them.

Fiedor and Hriniec, the fathers of the four children, were gathered there also. They were just there to say farewell, since it had already been decided that the two hussars would be staying with the APC for the coming battle. There were no practical matters to discuss, since Jozef had already gotten lodgings at one of the city's taverns for Fiedor's wife and the children she was caring for.

But Jozef didn't pay much attention to them. He had his own family problem to deal with.

"They *insist*," Christin said. "They won't stay here with the other children. One or the other of us has to take care of them. I vote for you."

Jozef looked down at the two children he'd come to informally adopt, both of whom were now looking up at him imploringly.

"Tekla's scared, Papa," said Pawel. After a moment, he added: "I am, too."

"I'm going into a *battle*," protested Jozef.

"So am I," said Christin.

"Yes, but it's different." He pointed to the sky. "You'll be up there, where they can't shoot you."

Christin snorted derisively. "The hell they can't. It's called antiaircraft fire. 'Ack-ack,' if you're a Brit."

Jozef glowered at her. "Allow me to clarify. The chances that they will hit you are almost nonexistent. As you know perfectly well. Whereas I—" He pointed to the APC they were standing next to "—will be in that great fat target. Which will be on the *ground*."

Christin was not impressed. "You need to clarify that statement as well. That great fat *heavily armored* target, is what I'm sure you meant to say."

She spread her hands. "Look, Jozef, the best I can do is fly them to Kraków. I'm pretty sure, as small as they are, that both Pawel and Tekla can fit into the Dauntless' back seat. But then what? God only knows how long Eddie and I will be buzzing around up in the sky—or where we're going to land at any given point in time, given what the weather's like this time of year." She pointed at the two children, who were now looking at her anxiously. "Which means I'd have to leave them with somebody."

The children's response was predictable—and immediate. "*Noooooo*—!"

Jozef threw up his hands with exasperation. Then, reconciled himself to the inevitable. Pawel and Tekla had been so traumatized by the murder of their family and the destruction of their village by mercenaries that they had a completely irrational but understandable need to stay in close proximity to either Jozef or Christin. Or "Papa" and "Mama," as they now called them.

"Fine," he said. "But!" He leaned over and wagged his finger in front of the children's faces. "You do exactly as I say. Is that understood?"

Two little heads nodded with vigor. "Yes, Papa!" they said in unison.

The relief in their faces was almost too much to bear. Jozef looked away before he started tearing up.

Away—and then, at Christin. In some mysterious way, in some indefinable fashion, he knew that a decision had been made in that instant. Made by *him*, at least. He wasn't sure yet about Christin. But the wry little smile on her face seemed promising.

✤ ✤ ✤

After he and the two children climbed into the interior of the APC, Jozef took a moment to glare around at the dozen men gathered there.

"Tekla and Pawel are staying with us," he said. Pointing to the padded box in the middle of the interior, he added. "They'll be in there. During the battle also."

He was braced for an argument, but the soldiers just grinned.

"They're good luck for us," said one of them.

"Better than any charm," added another.

It didn't take more than an hour to refuel the APC. Tata, who was running the city in Gretchen's absence, was nothing if not well organized. The moment she discovered the APC had broken out of Poznań she'd gotten on the radio and made sure that a supply of diesel was airlifted from Dresden. There wasn't a big stockpile of the fuel in that city—most of it was either in Magdeburg or at the Wietze oil fields—but Dresden was closer. Tata didn't figure they would need that much, anyway. The coming battle at Kraków would either be won quickly or they'd have a lot worse problems than a shortage of diesel fuel.

How had she done it, when all military planes except the one Belle in Poznań were supposed to be in Linz? Jozef had no idea. Knowing Tata, she'd probably bullied the emperor into approving it.

He and Christin enjoyed a long and lingering kiss before he climbed into the cab and drove off. That kiss seemed to have a lot of promise in it as well.

"You seem quite taken by that woman," commented Walenty Tarnowski, tactless as always.

You have no idea, Jozef thought. But he didn't say it
out loud, of course.

Eddie flew into Breslau the next morning. Christin was
waiting for him, holding a small valise with the few
belongings she still had on her person.

To her surprise—and joy—Denise had come with him.

She hadn't seen her daughter in months. After she and
Denise finished hugging each other, Denise announced
that she was the plane's bombardier.

"Fat chance, honey," was Christin's response. "That's
my job. If you want to be part of the mission, that's fine.
But you ride in back and you get to pull the switch.
Levers, rather. I'll call the shots."

"That's not fair," complained Denise.

Christin smiled and shoved the valise into her
daughter's arms. "Oh, it gets worse. You have to hold this
thing in your lap until we land in Kraków."

"Hey!"

Christin held up her hands and wiggled her fingers.
"I've got to be unencumbered in case Eddie has a sudden
heart attack and I have to take the controls. I'm also the
co-pilot."

"Eddie's not gonna have a heart attack. For Chrissake,
he's only twenty-four years old. And how are you the
'copilot' when you've never flown a plane once in your life?"

"We have to rise to these challenges."

"Mom!"

Chapter 45

Kraków, official capital of Poland
Actual capital of Lesser Poland

"Hobelar," Jeff explained. "H-O-B-E-L-A-R."

"You made that up," Mike Stearns said accusingly. "I've never heard of a 'hobelar'—and I'm the major general here, remember? Not to mention that I've been reading up on military matters pretty much nonstop since Gustav Adolf made me a general."

Jeff grinned in a manner that had to be a gross violation of military protocol when bestowed upon a major general by a measly colonel.

"I don't doubt it, sir," said Jeff. "But here's what else I don't doubt is true: You misspent your youth in prizefighting. I misspent mine playing Dungeons and Dragons. *Advanced* Dungeons and Dragons—and I was always the Dungeon Master. I practically had the *Dungeon Master's Manual* memorized. It covers hobelars pretty early on; in the section on 'Hirelings,' if I remember right."

Mike shook his head. "So how is a 'hobelar' any different from a dragoon?"

"Well . . . it's admittedly a gray area. But dragoons are expected to be able to do some fighting on horseback, although they're not as skilled that way as cavalrymen are. They carry sabers, for instance. A hobelar, on the other hand, is a pure and simple infantryman—except he knows how to ride a horse, and how to handle a packhorse. Even then, his horse normally just walks or trots. Occasionally, he might break into a canter. A full-out charge—a gallop—only happens if he screws up and loses control of the horse."

Mike took off his hat and used the back of his sleeve to wipe the sweat off his brow. As usual, the headquarters were kept too hot for his comfort by a huge fire in the fireplace.

Thankfully, on this occasion the only people in the headquarters besides Jeff were a couple of soldiers standing guard at the entrance. They were low enough in the pecking order that Mike figured he could bend military protocol since he knew damn well Jeff didn't care.

"All right, I get it. The one and only point is to provide infantry with more mobility. But do we have enough horses for more than a handful of them?"

"We're in better shape than you might think," Jeff answered. "These don't need to be warhorses. Regular plain-vanilla draft horses will do well enough for the purpose."

"So how many of these hobblers—"

"*Hobelars*," Jeff said sternly. "Sir."

"—whatevers can we put together?"

"I figure we can turn all our mortar crews into hobelars."

Mike's interest immediately spiked. "*All* of them? What about the mortars themselves?"

"Them, too, sir. Each mortar weighs about two hundred pounds, no more than a big man."

"Ammunition?"

"Yes, sir. Not all of it, but at least half of what we've got. That'll be enough for three hundred rounds, thereabouts."

"That wouldn't leave us much if we get into an artillery duel with the siege guns," Mike pointed out.

Jeff shrugged. "We're planning to hit them right off. If that succeeds, there won't be an artillery duel because they won't have any heavy artillery left. If it doesn't—" He shrugged again. "Unless the enemy commanders are completely incompetent, there wouldn't be a long artillery duel anyway. By now, they have to have gotten word from the troops who fled the city about what our mortars are capable of. So they'll hold back when they come up and start to build siege works. Trenches, covered bunkers for their big guns, the whole nine yards. As you've kept pointing out, that's a fight we're bound to lose, sooner or later. If we had unlimited ammunition for the mortars..."

Mike waved his hand. "Yeah, and if cows could fly we'd have the world's most spectacular cavalry. You make do with what you've got. Okay, Jeff, we'll go with your plan. If nothing else—"

He broke off there. The jest he'd been about to make—*if nothing else, you'll have bragging rights with the D&D crowd*—would have been tasteless to the point of cruelty. Jeff Higgins had been part of a small D&D

group. Himself, Eddie Cantrell, Larry Wild and Jimmy Andersen—half of whom were now dead.

Some of what he'd been about to say must have seeped through, since Jeff's expression became a bit somber. "You haven't heard any news about Eddie lately, have you?"

Mike shook his head. "Nothing recent. He's still in the Caribbean, doing . . . whatever he's doing."

"Putting himself in harm's way," said Jeff. His face lightened up, then. "But what the hell, sir, so are you and so am I. Life is what it is."

Right bank of the Bialucha River
About two miles north of Kraków

"We'll keep the siege guns half a mile from the walls, for a start," said Janusz Łohojski. From the rise they were all standing on, perhaps a mile away, they could see the walls of Kraków as well as the tower of the town hall and the Cloth Hall. The voivode of Kiev pointed to another rise off to their right and about halfway between the city and where they were now standing. "There, I think."

Stanisław Lubomirski frowned. "Why so far away? The guns will reach into the city, certainly. But we want to bring down the walls. To do that we need to be within a quarter of a mile."

Łohojski started to scowl, but managed to keep the expression off his face. It was a given that all his fellow magnates except (hopefully) young Prince Zasławski would quarrel with him. Łohojski had known that from the moment he agreed to be the top commander of their assembled forces. Still, he found Lubomirski particularly annoying. The voivode of Ruthenia argued about everything, it seemed.

He managed not to snarl the answer. "Until I—we— have some experience with them ourselves, I think we need to be wary of the capabilities of the rebels' mortars— which are probably being employed by USE forces who are surreptitiously aiding the traitors."

"Mortars!" jibed Lubomirski. "The stupid things are as inaccurate as they are hard to move."

Łohojski would have agreed with him, if they were dealing with the sort of mortars they were accustomed to. But whether or not the astonishing rate of fire reported by the soldiers who had escaped the seizure of Kraków was accurate—Łohojski was skeptical, himself; defeated troops always exaggerated the capabilities of the enemy—the one thing that seemed clearly established was that they were firing explosive shells. If the reports on their rate of fire were even half-true, that could make them effective against exposed troops, which was not true of the traditional type of mortars he and his fellows were familiar with.

They were also, as Lubomirski said, heavy bastards. Łohojski had muscled them around himself, in his youth.

"There's no reason not to be cautious," he said. "Time is on our side, not the rebels. That so-called konfederacja of theirs is more ramshackle than usual, according to all accounts. At least half of them seem to be made up of foreign units—Czechs as well as Germans, mixed in with Poles and Cossacks. They'll lose whatever support they have each day the siege goes on. Whereas we . . ."

Prince Wiśniowiecki finished the thought for him. The

young man didn't have much military experience but he was an acute politician.

"Whereas for us," he said, "every day the siege goes on will garner us more support in the Sejm. Of course, we can't let anyone think we're deliberately stalling."

"We're *not* going to be deliberately stalling," said Łohojski. Again, he fought to keep a snarl out of his voice. He sometimes found Wiśniowiecki as annoying as Lubomirski. "I am not exposing our troops to possible danger when there's no need for it."

He pointed to the rise in the distance. "We will start there, and then expand our siege works as needed."

Kraków, official capital of Poland
Actual capital of Lesser Poland

Standing by the door inside the kitchen in the Cloth Hall that Denise Beasley had turned into a bomb-making facility, Christin George had her arms crossed over her chest and was contemplating her daughter at work. Denise was leaning over a cauldron, stirring the diesel fuel and soap with a ladle. As she worked, she began chanting a tune of sorts.

> *"Double, double toil and trouble;*
> *Fire burn and caldron bubble."*

"Sometimes, my kid's a little scary," Christin said to Laura Goss. The pilot was standing next to her, a little further away from the door.

Laura chuckled. "C'mon, Christin. Kids always like to play with chemicals. Hell, me and my brother Kevin once blew up our bathroom. Well, the sink, anyway."

> *"Fillet of a fenny snake,*
> *In the caldron boil and bake;"*

"Doing what?" asked Christin.

"Kevin said we were making rocket fuel. I didn't know if he was right or not—still don't—on account of I was nine years old at the time. The only thing I remember about it except *boom!* was racing out of the bathroom and that sugar was one of the ingredients."

> *"Eye of newt and toe of frog,*
> *Wool of bat and tongue of dog,"*

Christin and Laura had been friends for some time now, despite a ten-year spread in age and having nothing in common except both being lapsed Catholics. The friendship had developed because Hal Smith had employed Buster Beasley once, when he needed some welding done at his aircraft facility. Having nothing else to do that day, Christin had accompanied him. Getting bored after a while, she wandered into the front office where she found Laura pecking away at a typewriter. Hal had hired her not long after the Ring of Fire as his office manager and gofer. Mostly as a gofer, since her secretarial skills were minimal.

"You type even worse than I do," Christin had commented, after watching Laura for a minute or so.

Without looking up, Laura had grinned and replied: "So far as I know, I type worse than anybody. I'm thinking of taking a shot at a Guinness world record."

So had their friendship begun. Since marrying Buster, Christin had stopped her former partying habits, but she appreciated Laura's skill at the pastime and Laura enjoyed having a connoisseur to listen to her bragging.

> *"Adder's fork and blind-worm's sting,*
> *Lizard's leg and howlet's wing,"*

"Hey, Eddie!" Denise called out, without looking up from the cauldron. "I need more soap."

> *"For a charm of powerful trouble,*
> *Like a hell-broth boil and bubble."*

Half a minute later, Eddie came into the kitchen and handed Denise a little sack full of what Christin assumed was soap of some kind. Her daughter started pouring it slowly into the mix.

> *"Double, double toil and trouble;*
> *Fire burn and caldron bubble."*

His chore done, Eddie came over to Christin and Laura.

"How soon, do you figure?" asked Christin.

"More like what Mike figures, even if he keeps insisting he's not calling the shots."

Laura snorted. "Mike Stearns will stop calling shots when pigs fly."

"Which is what we were just speaking about," said Christin. "Flying, I mean, not pigs. How soon?" she repeated.

"Mike says the battle will start the day after tomorrow." Eddie nodded toward Denise. "She'll have enough bombs ready by then. Crack of dawn, Mike says. As soon as I can see well enough to get the plane off the ground and you can see the ground well enough to tell Little Miss Hellfire when to pull the levers and drop the bombs."

All three of them now turned back to contemplate Little Miss Hellfire at her work.

"You know what the scariest thing is?" Christin mused. "Denise had that whole chant memorized—every line of it—by the time she was eight years old. She got so interested she even read the rest of the play."

Laura's eyes widened. "She read Shakespeare's *Macbeth* when she was *eight*?"

Christin nodded.

> *"Cool it with a baboon's blood,*
> *Then the charm is firm and good."*

"Jesus!" exclaimed Laura. "That's downright terrifying."

The confluence of the Danube and the Traun
A few miles southeast of Linz

Hoping he might be willing to share some news, Julie Sims took her daughter out to visit Gustav Adolf at his forward headquarters on the triangle of land formed by the confluence of the Traun and Danube rivers. That was a gross violation of political and military protocol, looked at from most people's perspective. But Julie had her own view of the matter, at least when it involved the king of Sweden.

By now, she had the emperor's aides and adjutants reconciled to reality—or just browbeaten—so they made no objection when she came up onto the observation platform that Gustav Adolf had had built next to the two ten-inch naval rifles that guarded the confluence.

It probably helped that she had Alexi in tow. The girl had recently celebrated her fourth birthday and was of an age when children were irresistibly appealing to almost everybody. Some of the adjutants even smiled.

As did Gustav Adolf, when he saw Julie coming. The smile widened when his gaze moved down to look at Alexi.

"It's such a joy to watch them grow," he commented, when mother and daughter reached his side.

Julie just nodded. The only verbal response she could think to make would have been . . . undiplomatic. *How would you know, o mighty king? You probably spent as much time with Kristina when she was this age as Royal Custom requires. Maybe one day a month. Tops.*

"Any news from Kraków?" she asked.

The emperor shook his head. "Nothing beyond a veiled hint that the battle will begin the day after tomorrow."

Julie had to pull Alexi back a bit. The child had been reaching to play with the sword Gustav Adolf had scabbarded at his hip. "My husband's grousing that you should have assigned him to serve the Hangman Regiment as its cavalry force. He says those Slovenians they've got won't know one end of a horse from the other."

Gustav Adolf grinned. "Spoken like a true Scotsman. He's just bored with siege duty. Which, I will grant you, is as boring as watching paint dry, for a cavalryman."

He looked down at her. "And you?"

She knew what he meant. "I wish I were there, too." She lifted Alexi's little hand a few inches. "But I've got her to think about."

"You had her to think about when you flew up to meet the Turks in aerial combat. You still went."

Julie shook her head. "That was different. I wasn't exactly indispensable, but I was the best person for the job. At Kraków, I'd just be a civilian in the way."

They fell silent for a moment. Then, Gustav Adolf smiled again. "What was that so-very-appropriate remark by that up-time general of yours? The one with the peculiar middle name."

"William Tecumseh Sherman. 'War is hell,' he said. Boy, did he have that right."

Kraków, official capital of Poland
Actual capital of Lesser Poland

"You don't have to go, Jakub," said Judy Wendell. "You're not a soldier. Nobody thinks you are and nobody expects you to be."

His response was as predictable as the sunrise.

"No, I do. I cannot help lead a revolution if I am not prepared to share the risks."

"You said yourself you're the worst shot in the world."

Jakub lifted himself to a sitting position in the bed. "However, I am told by knowledgeable people that I would be bested by Secretary Abrabanel. I, at least, can hit the side of a barn."

Judy couldn't help but smile a little. "Better'n Becky can do, by all accounts."

She looked up at him for a few seconds. "Please come back to me," she said, knowing just how pointless it was to put that wish into words.

"We still have a full day before it becomes an issue," said Jakub.

Judy's smile this time was a wide one. "So let's not waste it, then."

Chapter 46

Airstrip south of the Vistula
Kraków, official capital of Poland
Actual capital of Lesser Poland

"And here we go," said Eddie, as the Dauntless lifted from the ground, heading east.

From the rear seat, Denise said: "This has got to be either the weirdest or the coolest family outing *ever*." She paused a moment, and added: "I'm using the term 'family' with what you call poetic license, you understand."

In the front passenger seat, Christin smiled but didn't say anything. The stronger Denise's attachment became to Eddie, the more resistant and prickly she got to any suggestion that marriage might be in the offing. Her mother found it quite amusing, because she recognized the pattern. That was exactly how Christin herself had reacted when her relationship with Buster started getting really serious.

Thankfully, Eddie was handling the situation exactly

the way Buster had—calmly, and with no effort to pressure or cajole the young woman involved.

Eddie reached the cruising altitude he'd decided upon—which was quite low; not more than five hundred feet off the ground—and leveled off. Meanwhile, Christin pondered the way she was now reacting to Jozef. Was she following the same pattern again?

She didn't think so. Jozef was the one who seemed nervous and twitchy. She was just . . .

Undecided.

She looked out the window at the ground passing below. Jozef would be approaching the battlefield himself now. Somewhere a few miles to the west a man born in the first decade of the seventeenth century was driving an armored coal truck built more than three and a half centuries later toward a battle that might decide—begin the decision, anyway—whether Poland would resume its forward progress or keep sliding back into medieval serfdom.

On his way into Kraków the day before, Eddie had flown over the Rudawa River. He'd reported to Jozef that the road that ran parallel to it was wide enough for the APC but that there would be some obstructions that needed to be cleared away—a couple of fallen trees and a small rockslide.

Jozef hadn't been concerned about that. He had two hundred hussars accompanying him, after all. They'd complain bitterly at the indignity of being reduced to manual laborers, but they'd still do the work since they could console themselves with the thought that it was really just part of the battle. Sort of like hauling fascines up to a moat, except further away.

"Coolest family outing ever," she pronounced.

Left bank of the Rudawa River
A few miles west of Kraków

"Mark warned me about this," Jozef complained, "but it's worse than I thought it would be."

He didn't so much as glance at the man sitting in the passenger seat of the truck's cab. He was leaning forward, almost hunched over the steering wheel, peering intently through the narrow slit in the armor plate that now covered the entire front windshield. Similar armor protected the two side windows.

Walenty Tarnowski was looking through the same sort of slit on his side of the windshield. "It's a real nuisance, I agree. All you can see is a small piece of the territory ahead of us. But we don't really have any choice, Jozef."

The mechanical engineer reached out and rapped the windshield with a knuckle. "This is called 'safety glass,' but it's not magical. A bullet that hits it squarely will pass through, even if it doesn't shatter the whole windshield. Besides, we're not driving very fast." He leaned in Jozef's direction to look at the instrument panel. "Twelve miles an hour, it says—and most of the time you're driving slower than that."

"Don't remind me," said Jozef, still sounding grumpy. "I'm starting to worry we won't get to the battlefield in time."

That was a little silly, and he knew it. Their arrival at

the battlefield would be the signal for the cavalry to charge out of the city, not the other way around. Half an hour either way wouldn't make any difference; even an hour or two wouldn't be disastrous. But Jozef was one of those people who disliked being late for anything. One of the things he'd found refreshing about Americans during his time in Grantville was that they were almost always punctual. That came from growing up in a society that had plentiful and accurate clocks; granted, it wasn't the product of superior character. He still found it preferable to the lackadaisical attitude of most of his fellow Poles— and Germans and Czechs and Italians, for that matter. The Americans marked off time in hours, minutes and seconds. Down-timers marked it off in matins, lauds, sexts and nones.

Another dip in the so-called road that Jozef hadn't spotted in time caused the APC to lurch. Again.

The effect was even worse for the four hussars in the gun turrets above, especially since they could only hold on with one hand, the other being needed to grip their weapons. But they were in a much better mood about it than Jozef was. First, because they didn't have to concern themselves with the actual driving. Second, because the feel of those same firearms was a source of great satisfaction, bordering on outright joy.

The four men in the turrets were the best marksmen of all the hussars who had fled Poznań. They cherished good guns as much as they did good lances and sabers— and these were far and away the finest guns they'd ever seen. "Hocklotts," the woman Tata had called them. She'd stockpiled a few in Breslau when the Silesian army marched out to aid the Galicians in taking Kraków.

The hussars hadn't been at all happy to hear about the role being played by the Silesians, true. On the other hand, the Silesian forces included Poles as well as Germans and they were being led by Gretchen Richter, who was regarded even by Polish hussars as not being one of the damn Swedish king's people. Not exactly, anyway.

Besides, there were those magnificent rifles! Accurate to several hundred yards—they'd fired a few shots to test the claims—and, best of all, they had an incredible rate of fire.

An APC armed with four such riflemen in the gun turrets would be fearsome on a battlefield. So they put up with being bounced around cheerily.

Cheerily enough, anyway.

Rynek Główny
Kraków, official capital of Poland
Actual capital of Lesser Poland

The Galician cavalry, which included the Cossacks, was gathered in the huge market square in the center of which stood the town hall and the Cloth Hall. It had been agreed by all parties that it would be better to let the Galicians use the Rynek Główny as a place to assemble while von Mercy's cavalry and the Slovenians gathered in the northern end of the city. The Bohemians and Slovenians were professional soldiers almost to a man.

The Galicians . . . not so much.

Most of them could claim to be veterans, true. But they were veterans of the sort of wars fought in the Ruthenian lands—what Jakub Zaborowsky somewhat sarcastically described as "freestyle" tactics and formations. If they tried to assemble in the small squares and narrow streets near the Brama Floriańska, Kraków's big northern gate, they'd almost certainly get themselves completely tangled up before they could charge out of the city.

As it was, the only thing that kept the Galicians in some sort of order were the Opaliński brothers, especially Lukasz. The Galicians weren't as familiar with him as they were with his older brother Krzysztof, but Lukasz exuded the sort of commanding presence that all hussars could recognize—and at some point or other, at least half of the Galician cavalry had claimed hussar status.

"He does look quite magnificent," commented Cecilia Renata, looking down into the square from her chamber in the Cloth Hall. Judy Wendell was standing next to her in the window.

"He seems like a pretty nice man, too," Judy said. "We spent weeks in close proximity to him in the carriage on the way back from Vienna, and he was cordial and courteous the whole time."

Cecilia Renata smiled. "You can leave off the—what do you call it?—sales pitch, if I remember correctly. Yes, Lukasz seems like a decent fellow and he's certainly not boring."

The young archduchess' expression tightened for a

moment. "I've done some discreet investigating, since you raised the idea. There doesn't seem to be the sort of womanizing in his history that made my husband in your universe such a difficult spouse."

She was referring to the current king of Poland, Władisław IV. In the up-timers' history, Cecilia Renata had married Władisław in this very year—1637.

"At least this time around you won't have to worry much about dying in childbirth—or losing any kids," said Judy.

In Judy's universe, Cecilia Renata had had three children by Władisław. The first, a boy, had died at the age of seven. The second, a girl, had lived less than a month. The third had been stillborn—and Cecilia Renata herself had died the next day. The exact cause of her death hadn't been in any of Grantville's historical records, but it was almost sure to have been the sort of infection that made childbirth such a risky business for women of this era.

But it was getting less and less risky by the day. Even the Americans' most hostile opponents were starting to adopt the up-timer practices when it came to sanitation and medical methods.

"I said, you can leave off the sales pitch."

Judy would have made a quip in response, but she'd spotted Jakub in the milling crowd of horsemen below.

This wasn't the first time she'd seen him riding a horse, but it was the first time she'd seen him do so while armed and armored. She was glad to see that he seemed at ease in the saddle. At least he wasn't likely to fall off in the coming battle and get trampled. But she wasn't at all happy with the so-called "armor" he was wearing, which was nothing more than a buff coat. She had a winter coat not much lighter than that hanging up in a closet in her parents' home in Grantville. It was great at warding off winter's chills, sure. But bullets? Or even a saber?

Jakub looked up, his eyes scanning the row of windows in the upper floors of the Cloth Hall. Spotting Judy, he waved his hand in greeting.

She waved back. Then, when she recognized the man sitting on a horse next to Jakub, she gave him a wave also.

Red Sybolt. *What the hell is he doing here? Are all men crazy?*

Judy wasn't sure of Red's exact age, but he had to be pushing fifty. On the other hand, he seemed to be at ease in the saddle himself despite—so far as Judy knew, anyway—never having spent a minute on horseback before the Ring of Fire. Of course, he'd spent a lot of time in a saddle since then, roaming around in Cossack territory with Jakub and Krzysztof.

"In any event," Cecilia Renata said, "it may all be a moot point by this evening." She nodded down at Lukasz, who was currently in discussion with one of the Galician hussars. "He may not survive the battle. Or, even if he does, may have been defeated. Possibly captured. My brother will be skeptical of the idea even if all goes well. He has a normal and rational Habsburg attitude toward rebels and revolutionaries. There is no way he would approve of my marrying into a lost cause."

Not for the first time, Judy was reminded of the vast

gulf between her and Cecilia Renata, despite their friendship. She couldn't imagine herself being that detached and cold-blooded about a possible husband.

There seemed to be a stir now, among the Galician soldiers near the northwestern side of the huge square. That was the direction of the gate they were planning to use when they made their sortie.

Looking back at Lukasz, she saw that he and his brother were pushing their horses forward, heading in the same direction.

She took a deep, slow breath. "It's starting," she said.

Linz, provisional capital of Austria-Hungary

The emperor of Austria-Hungary wasn't exactly glaring at Janos Drugeth, but his gaze was not full of favor and good will, either.

"Explain to me again," he said, "why your wife didn't get herself airlifted out of Kraków while she had the chance—along with my brother and sister. Who, must I remind you, are still the archduke and archduchess of Austria."

Janos had been wondering the same thing himself. From the few hints he'd gotten from Noelle in her—also few—radio messages, he was pretty sure his wife had decided to stay in Kraków because she saw some... interesting possibilities. And the same was evidently true of the two royal siblings.

None of which he wanted to discuss right now with Ferdinand III.

"Ah..." he said.

Cloth Hall
Kraków, official capital of Poland
Actual capital of Lesser Poland

"It's starting," Mike pronounced. He turned his head to look at Jeff Higgins. "You've got the Hangmen ready, right?"

Since the two of them were alone for the moment—that wasn't going to last long, judging from the sounds coming from the staircase—Jeff decided he could skip the formalities. "Stop fussing at me, Mike. You're just antsy because you're a so-called 'observer' and have to stay in hiding up here instead of joining in on the fun down there."

"'Fun!'" Mike snorted.

"Fine. The action. Of course I've got them ready. But I've got some time, still. We can't get out of the city until the Galicians have left." He glanced down at the activity in the huge square. *Activity,* in this instance, being hard to distinguish from *chaos and confusion.* "And that's going to take a bit, even with Lukasz cracking the whip."

He looked back at Mike. "Eric's riding herd on the regiment while I'm gone. And I am damn well going to exercise the privileges of rank and say goodbye to my wife. Speaking of which—"

Gretchen was the first one through the door, followed by Rebecca and Noelle. She went straight to her husband and gave him a long and passionate kiss.

Then, leaned away and took his head in both hands.

"Go," she said. "And come back."

Two hundred feet above the Polish countryside
A mile northeast of Kraków.

"And there they are," said Eddie. "Like ducks in a row."

Looking ahead, Christin saw that he was right. The siege guns the magnates had brought with them were now being manhandled into position just below the crest of a low ridge about half a mile from the city's walls.

Completely unsheltered and unprotected.

Glancing out the window to her side, Christin had to fight down a hiss of alarm. Eddie was flying so low she was amazed they weren't clipping off the tops of the trees they were passing over.

That was an optical illusion, she knew. They had to be at least one hundred feet above the ground and the trees below were almost all yews, which weren't usually more than half that high. Still, it was scary.

And exhilarating. *God, I'm an adrenalin junkie.*

"Are you ready, daughter of mine? It'll be the left lever first."

"Yeah, yeah, I got it," came Denise's voice from the back seat. "Don't worry about me and the bombing levers, Mom. Just make sure your rheumy old eyes gauge the target right."

Christin grinned. Like mother, like daughter. Adrenalin junkiedom *had* to be hereditary. Although her own mother had never shown any signs of the trait.

"Here we go," said Eddie, bringing the plane down still lower.

Christin would *swear* he clipped the top of one of the yews. She kept herself from squealing with glee, though. Denise might mistake that for a signal to drop the first bomb.

Chapter 47

Half a mile northwest of Kraków

Janusz Łohojski stared at the airplane coming toward him. He wasn't dumbfounded, but he was certainly puzzled. By now, after spending quite a bit of time a year earlier in Poznań, he was familiar with the up-time flying machines. One or another of them was almost always in the sky above that city.

But he'd never seen one flying this close to the ground. The oncoming aircraft was practically skimming the trees it was passing over, just east of the siege lines the magnates' soldiers were beginning to build. It was no more than a mile away now—and approaching very swiftly. He estimated it would pass over the rise where he and Prince Zasławski were overseeing the placement of the big siege guns in less than a minute.

What were they doing? There was something very menacing about the oncoming vessel, but it had been well established by Koniecpolski and his army that the enemy contraptions were insufferably good at reconnaissance but posed no real threat otherwise. Occasionally, they dropped bombs on the forces defending Poznań, but they did little damage. The airplanes were not powerful enough to carry more than one or two hundred pounds of explosives. Koniecpolski himself had once told Łohojski that he thought the USE Air Force simply did the intermittent bombing runs as a training exercise for their pilots.

The approaching aircraft couldn't possibly inflict any serious damage on the siege guns. Even if, by fortune, it dropped a bomb on one of the gunpowder stores, the most it could do would be to overturn the gun next to it—which wouldn't take more than a few hours to set back erect. No competent artillery officer—Zasławski had several of them, and was heeding their advice—would be foolish enough to keep a large supply of gunpowder near the guns themselves. There was no need to, except aboard ships. The big cannons took so long to reload that there was plenty of time to bring forward more gunpowder from stores in the rear.

Those stores would actually be better targets for bombs dropped from aircraft. But they wouldn't be easy to spot, as fast as the machines flew—and this one was coming directly at the guns in any event.

What were they doing?

Prince Władysław Zasławski was wondering the same thing himself—and was quite a bit more worried than the army's top commander. Łohojski was sitting on his horse on the crest of the rise, some distance away from the nine siege guns being muscled into position just behind the rise. Zasławski, on the other hand, was right in the middle of the battery, overseeing the work.

All the cannons belonged to him; bought and paid for out of his coffers. True, those were probably the biggest coffers in the Polish–Lithuanian Commonwealth except the king's, but guns this size were fiendishly expensive. So, the prince had insisted on keeping them with his own forces, which were also busily setting up siege works on either side of the rise.

He stood up in the stirrups to get a better look at the approaching enemy aircraft.

Noticing something out of the corner of his eye, Łohojski turned his head away from the approaching airplane to look at Kraków. To his astonishment, rebel cavalry were pouring out of the closest gate. A moment later, other cavalry started emerging from the big northern gate, the Brama Floriańska.

What were they doing? Now, Łohojski *was* dumbfounded. It was much too early in the siege for the defenders to attempt a sortie.

He heard another noise, similar to that being produced by the airplane. Turning his head still further to the right, Łohojski saw a bizarre, huge vehicle emerging from a copse of trees and heading toward the rise.

It took him a moment to recognize the thing, because when he'd seen it in Poznań it had not been festooned with banners. Nor had it had what looked like small turrets perched on the top.

The "APC," they called it. Koniecpolski had told him that his engineer thought the vehicle might someday prove quite useful.

Łohojski's mind finally processed what he was seeing.

The banners along the side of the vehicle as well as those flown from the turrets were similar to the royal banners but not identical. The coat of arms at the center of the white-and-red stripes was now a simple star.

That was an *enemy* APC—and the coordinated attack being launched against him had to have some underlying logic. It wasn't simply madness or stupidity on the part of an addlepated rebel commander.

Three seconds later, the logic began to unfold.

"*Now!*" shouted Christin. Sitting behind her, Denise immediately yanked the lever in her left hand.

A moment later, Christin repeated the call. "*Now!*"

Denise yanked the other lever. Then, rose up as far as she could in her seat to look out the window.

"Dammit!" she cried. "I can't see anything! Next time I run into Bob Kelly, I swear I'm gonna tear him a new asshole. What was he thinking?"

The girl's frustration was produced by the airplane's peculiar design. Kelly had originally built the Dauntless—which hadn't had that name yet—to serve a combined purpose. It would provide the Air Force with the same observational capabilities as Hal Smith's Belles and Gustavs, but would be able to haul more and bigger cargo because of the long and rather narrow construction of the rear fuselage.

Happily or sadly, depending on how you looked at it, the plane—now given the fierce name *Dauntless*—had been pressed into service as a bomber as well. To that end, a seat had been placed in the rear and a crude but effective system of wires and levers had been installed that enabled the person riding in that seat to eject the two bombs slung under the fuselage.

The downside to the new design was that the windows provided for the person in the rear seat were not only small, but perched high up in the fuselage.

A six-foot-tall man could have managed to look out of them easily enough.

Denise was five foot four.

"Mom! What the hell is happening?"

Christin didn't actually have any idea herself. Eddie had flown the plane so low that, racing at its top speed of perhaps one hundred and twenty miles an hour, they had passed beyond the siege guns before Christin could get a good look at the results of the strike. All she knew was that the bombs had worked. One of them had, anyway. Looking back as far as she could out of her own window, she could see the big flames now engulfing one of the siege guns.

Those same flames took down Władysław Zasławski.

He wasn't struck by any of the burning napalm himself, but a glob of it landed on the haunch of his horse. Frightened as well as badly burned, the horse reared up and threw him out of the saddle.

He landed on his back right next to one of the culverins. The impact stunned him, but he was not otherwise injured.

Until the powder stored next to the culverin exploded, and toppled it onto him.

He survived, because the gun didn't land on his head or torso. But it crushed his left leg and broke the tibia of his right.

He passed out from shock immediately, too soon to even cry out in pain.

Janusz Łohojski wasn't hurt at all, but it took him several seconds to bring his terrified horse under control. When he could finally pay attention to anything other than keeping himself in the saddle, he looked first to the oncoming enemy cavalry.

He understood now what the rebels were planning. That unexpected incendiary strike would panic the artillerymen, and in the confusion the oncoming enemy cavalry would try to seize the entire battery. With one bold strike, they would cripple the besiegers.

Zasławski would have to rally his own troops. If the youngster moved fast, he could establish a strong enough defense by the time the rebels arrived to drive off their cavalry.

Where was he? Looking around, Łohojski couldn't see him.

But he had no time to lose trying to find him. Łohojski was the top commander of the entire army. He had to get his own forces along with those of the other three magnates to come to Zasławski's support.

"Rally your men, Prince!" he shouted, and then galloped off.

Kraków, official capital of Poland
Actual capital of Lesser Poland

Looking through his binoculars from a window in the highest floor of the town hall's tower, Mike Stearns was almost as frustrated as Denise. He couldn't see much more than she could; partly because of the distance and partly because the rise blocked most of what he could see of the siege guns.

The one thing that was obvious, though, was that both bombs had gone off. Two fifty-pound bombs loaded with primitive napalm couldn't possibly engulf the whole battery in flames—but they didn't want to do that anyway. The plan was to duplicate Gustav Adolf's feat at Breitenfeld. They'd seize the enemy's artillery and turn it against them.

One of the gun's powder stores had been ignited, he thought. Beyond that . . .

He brought down the binoculars to look at the Galician cavalry. To his great satisfaction, he saw that the two Opalinski brothers were leading the charge.

Well . . . maybe not. Maybe it was two other hussars in full armor who looked like they might be the Opalinskis.

Good enough.

He lowered his binoculars and turned toward the photographer, who was leaning out of an adjoining window with a camera.

An *up-time* camera. One of the very excellent sports cameras that Mike had made sure his Third Division was supplied with—and one of which he'd brought to Kraków with him.

"You are getting this, yes?" he said.

The photographer was too intent on the work at hand to respond. Mike went back to looking through his binoculars.

The Galician charge had almost reached the rise, he

saw—and some of the Cossacks were starting to curl around its western slope. Make whatever jokes or snide remarks you wanted to about the indiscipline of the Galician cavalry. Those men could *ride*.

Mike was surprised to see that there was no sign of an organized defense on the part of the artillerymen or the infantrymen who should have been supporting them. Perhaps their officers had been injured—or simply weren't very capable.

At that point, having nothing further to do, the photographer climbed back down from the window.

"Do not teach your wife how to suck eggs," Rebecca told him frostily.

Half a mile northwest of Kraków

Under most conditions, the top officers in Prince Zasławski's army were quite capable. But they weren't very far removed from medieval retainers, either. So two of the three of them were wasting their valuable time yelling orders at the men trying to lift the culverin's barrel off of the prince.

The third one, *Regimentarz* Benedictus Wieczorek, was doing his best to get the prince's infantry to assemble on top of the rise. There were only two thousand of them, because Zasławski had concentrated on building his artillery and even the richest magnate could only afford to spend so much on his private army. But that was about the same number as those of the approaching cavalry, and if he could get the infantry steadied and in good field position on top of the rise, they'd be able to hold them off. At least two-thirds of them were pikemen, after all.

Napoleon Bonaparte had once said to a subordinate officer on a battlefield, "You can ask me for anything you like, except time."

The regimentarz was doing fairly well, actually. But he ran out of time. The Galicians came onto the rise and poured over it, killing everyone in their way, including Benedictus Wieczorek. It would be claimed by many of the Galicians afterward that he was cut down by Lukasz Opalinski himself.

Lukasz himself never made the claim—but he never denied it, either. It was too useful politically; and, besides, he *might* have. He cut down several enemies that day. He had no idea who they were, though.

The Brama Floriańska

"Pardon my language, Prince," said Jeff Higgins, "but this is fucking insane. You're the heir apparent to the imperial throne, damnation."

"No, Kristina is," replied Ulrik. "And please leave off the recriminations, Colonel. My mind is made up, I'm not going to change it—and I *am* the top commander of all Silesian forces. The only person who could overrule me is the Lady Protector of Silesia."

Ulrik swiveled in his saddle and pointed back to the town hall's tower. "And she's back there. And you seem to have misplaced your regimental radio."

Jeff scowled but didn't say anything. He had dark

suspicions about that mysteriously absent radio whose operator was normally at his immediate beck and call. He doubted if he'd ever be able to prove it, but he was pretty sure the radioman had gotten a big bribe from the prince.

Ulrik was normally as levelheaded as any man Jeff had ever met. But now and then, he'd dig in his heels over what he considered a point of honor—and when he did, he was immovable.

The Danish prince's longtime companion Baldur Norddahl could have warned him. The Norwegian had also once tried to persuade the prince to forego a dangerous mission. But Ulrik had still led his little flotilla of torpedo boats out to face Admiral Simpson's ironclads, the most fearsome warships on the planet.

You could even make a case that for him to lead the Hangman Regiment and half of the Silesian army out to face the armies of five Polish–Lithuanian magnates was a comparatively safe endeavor. But it wouldn't be wise to try to make it in front of Colonel Jeff Higgins.

"Fucking crazy," he repeated.

"They're all fucking crazy," said one of the Silesians guarding the Brama Floriańska, as he and his fellow soldier watched the Hangman Regiment marching out below them.

His companion grunted. "At least they're not sending us out. Just the damn Jews and the Polish dimwits—and these Hangmen fanatics."

The first soldier raised his eyes. The tail end of General

von Mercy's cavalry was still in sight. They were heading toward the space separating two of the enemy armies.

He was a mercenary, and a veteran, so he understood what von Mercy was trying to do: open a gap between two armies so he and the infantry coming behind him could crush one of them. He also understood how many men were likely to get killed in the doing of it.

Not him, though, he thought with satisfaction. Von Mercy had chosen to leave his Bohemian infantry veterans back in Kraków, along with the Vogtland irregulars, to defend the city against any possible enemy attempt to seize it during the battle.

Airstrip south of the Vistula
Kraków, official capital of Poland
Actual capital of Lesser Poland

As soon as the *Steady Girl* landed and taxied to a stop, Christin climbed out of the cockpit and rushed toward the hangar, where men were already pushing a cart toward the plane. Denise clambered out right after her and rolled herself under the fuselage. Those were *her* bombs being carted up to the plane, and she was damned if she'd let anyone else attach them to the hard points. They'd be sure to screw it up.

She could hear her mother shouting. "Move it! Move it!"

"What is it about moms," she muttered, "that makes them so bossy?"

Chapter 48

A mile north of Kraków

Jeff was wrong, actually. Prince Ulrik hadn't decided to march out with the Hangman Regiment and the other Silesian forces out of a stubborn and misplaced sense of honor. He'd done it with an utterly cold-blooded purpose, and a conspiratorial one to boot.

His co-conspirator had been Mike Stearns.

The commander of the Third Division had come to his chamber the night before the battle. After Ulrik had his servant let him in and then sent the servant out of the room—the Danish prince was far too canny to make the common mistake of seventeenth-century royalty and nobility of forgetting that servants have ears and mouths—he'd invited Stearns to sit.

"What can I do for you, General?"

"Since this expedition began you've complained several times that you felt useless."

Ulrik snorted softly. "Yes. I even borrowed one of your up-time phrases—'useless as tits on a bull.'"

Stearns smiled. "Well, as it happens, there's something you could do tomorrow that only you can do—only you, in the entire world."

"And that is?"

After Stearns explained, Ulrik rose and went to a side table. There, he poured himself a glass of wine. And then another, for the general. He returned to his seat, handed one of the glasses to Stearns—at no point did he ask him whether he wanted any wine; they were beyond that now—and drank about a third of his own after he sat down.

"Does your wife know what you're proposing?"

"No, I haven't told her—and I don't plan to. She'd have a fit."

Ulrik nodded. "That's wise, I think. She's a diplomat, not a soldier."

"It goes beyond that. I'm a revolutionary—like Gretchen, although my methods are different—and Rebecca isn't."

Ulrik's eyes widened. "I believe the whole world would disagree with you—including your wife herself. I have read her book, General."

Stearns smiled again. "So have I. Rebecca *supports* our revolution, there's no doubt about that. She's a brilliant woman—smarter than I am, for sure—so she also provides the revolution with theoretical guidance and justification. Not even Spartacus is in the same league, that way. But, in the end, she remains a student and a scholar. She's not—not quite, at least—the same sort of person as myself or Gretchen or Jakub Zaborowsky or Red Sybolt."

"Not willing to get her hands dirty, you're saying."

Stearns shook his head. "No, she'd be willing, if she thought it were necessary. She just wouldn't understand how to go about doing it in the first place. I don't think that woman has a ruthless bone in her body—and never mind that she devoted a whole chapter in her book to the need for ruthlessness when the revolution is threatened by hardened and vicious reactionaries."

Ulrik took another drink from his glass and set it down. "You, on the other hand, I believe to have several ruthless bones in your body."

"I have a whole bunch of them. From my prizefighter's knuckles on down."

Ulrik said nothing for a few seconds. Then, abruptly: "Did you get your hands dirty in Operation Kristallnacht, General?"

Stearns stared at him. Then, replied just as abruptly: "Yes. I did."

"I thought so." The Danish prince pursed his lips thoughtfully. "The official explanation has never struck me as very plausible. Anti-Semites are certainly vicious enough to commit such murders, but why would they do it? And in that manner? Mayor Dreeson and his companion were not killed as bystanders haplessly caught up in a melee. They were deliberately targeted at long range by an excellent rifleman. Why would anti-Semites start a riot in Grantville for the purpose of assassinating an elderly mayor and a Christian pastor? It was as if they deliberately attempted to infuriate people against them."

He picked up his glass and drained it. "So who did do it?"

"Ducos and his Huguenot fanatics. Not himself, but he would have given the order. We think the actual shooter was probably one of the men involved in the later assassination attempt against you and Princess Kristina."

"And the successful assassination of the Swedish queen. Both would have had the same purpose—to trigger another war against Richelieu."

"Yes."

"But you—I'm sure your man Nasi was involved also—chose to suppress the truth in order to unleash the CoCs on the USE's organized anti-Semites."

"Yes."

Ulrik rose, went back to the side table, and poured himself another glass of wine. He didn't offer to provide Stearns with any since the American general hadn't so much as touched his own wine.

Then, still standing at the side table, he drank half of it in one swallow before saying: "Dear God, that was *brilliant*. You've never told your wife about that either, I assume?"

"No."

"Don't. She wouldn't really understand."

"I don't *want* her to understand. Just because I have dirty hands doesn't mean I want to spread the dirt on anyone else, especially the person I love most in the world."

Ulrik nodded. "May I call you 'Mike'?"

So, here he was, riding a horse into a battle where he might very well get killed. From a normal diplomatic point of view, this was madness. The USE had taken great pains, after all, to keep its involvement with the Polish rebels as covert as possible. And now the crown prince of the

USE—which was what Ulrik was and everyone knew it, formalities be damned—was going to participate directly in a battle alongside those very same rebels?

Madness.

Unless . . .

The rebels *won*.

Won not just this battle but the revolution as a whole. At that point, a lasting and durable peace would have to be made between the USE and the Polish–Lithuanian Commonwealth. Two great nations which, given that one of them had the Swedish king for its emperor, had been engaged in savage hostilities for a generation.

Such a peace would be difficult. But not impossible. Not after the word spread—which it inevitably would, over time—that the crown prince of the USE had fought at Kraków right alongside his Galician allies.

From one viewpoint, it would be even better if he *did* get killed.

But there was no need to go to that extreme.

Even Mike Stearns had urged him to be careful.

They were nearing the front now. Ahead of them, von Mercy's cavalry was clashing with Polish hussars and the infantry was within three hundred yards.

"At least do me one favor, Prince," said Colonel Higgins.

"And that is?"

Higgins pointed to the rear, where the mounted infantrymen and their pack horses were bringing up the mortars.

"Stay back just a bit and take charge of the artillery."

Ulrik hesitated.

"Damnation, Ulrik!"—that was the first time the colonel had ever used his first name without preceding it with his title—"you'll be close enough to the action to satisfy anybody except Evel Knievel!"

The airplane passed overhead, flying very low. Ulrik looked up and followed its flight for a couple of seconds.

Who is Evel Knievel? he wondered.

Two miles north of Kraków

"*Now!*" shouted Christin.

"*Now!*" she shouted again, two seconds later.

The instant the second bomb was dropped, Eddie brought the plane up and sharply to the left. Ever since the battle began, he'd been careful never to give the magnates' troops a good target. The only time he flew low and straight was in the very last seconds of a bombing run.

Several musket men did fire at the plane. A pikeman got the tip of his blade within twenty feet of the fuselage, which was closer than any of the bullets came.

Half a mile northwest of Kraków

Within twenty minutes, Janusz Łohojski managed to get his own forces marshaled for a counterattack on the rebels who'd seized the battery on the rise. He even managed to persuade Potocki to commit his own army, although that would take longer.

Potocki was a solid fellow. Łohojski was confident that he'd bring his men up in time for the final surge against the rebels—sooner than they could get the big guns repositioned to fire on Łohojski himself, which was what mattered. From all he could see, the rebel force which had seized the battery was made up entirely of cavalry.

Cavalry were good—could be good—on the offense, if they caught their opponent off guard and sent them into a retreat. But for defense, which was what the rebels needed now, they were not nearly as good as infantry. They had no pikemen to fend off attackers, and the only guns they'd have would be pistols.

Łohojski himself had enough cavalry to ravage the rebels' flanks, but most of his force was made up of infantry. It would take them a bit, but they'd keep the enemy pinned on that rise. And then, once Potocki's army came up, they'd drive them back into Kraków and retake the guns.

They were less than a quarter of a mile away from the rise, now. Łohojski rode forward to get a better view of the rebels' dispositions.

The APC had reached the rise and taken position atop the crest. It wasn't much of a rise—not more than fifteen feet higher than the surrounding terrain—but it did give the riflemen in the forward turrets a superb view of the oncoming enemy.

The rifleman in the left front turret was a hussar by the name of Ambrozy Krampitz. When he spotted the horseman coming forward from the front ranks of the approaching pike-and-musket formations, he brought his rifle to bear on him.

It would be a long shot, but he thought it was within the capability of his marvelous new rifle. The weapon was far more accurate than anything he'd ever fired before.

He took careful aim . . . and squeezed the trigger. That had taken some practice to do it properly, since he was accustomed to firing matchlocks, which were so inaccurate that you just yanked up on the lever which served as a trigger.

Damnation, missed! Like most Polish szlachta, Ambrozy had a relaxed attitude toward blasphemy. It was disgraceful when a bad person did it. He was not a bad person.

He didn't *exactly* miss. The bullet didn't hit Łohojski but it did strike the flange on top of his helmet. It was a shallow glancing blow, with not enough force to either remove the helmet or twist it badly askew. But it certainly startled the commander.

He reached up a hand and felt the helmet. *What—?*

The next bullet struck the back of his wrist and shattered it. Shouting in pain and yanking on the reins, Łohojski brought his horse rearing up.

The rifleman in the other turret, Tomek Wrzesiński, had by then also brought his weapon to bear. His first shot struck Łohojski's horse in the throat. The animal screamed and toppled over, blood gushing from its neck.

Łohojski was a very experienced horseman. Despite the agony produced by his mutilated wrist, he managed to get his feet out of the stirrups and throw himself off the horse without letting it fall on top of him. The impact on the ground was hard, but didn't break any bones. Bruised and somewhat battered, he staggered to his feet; then, turned away from the enemy and began running—as best as he could, anyway—toward his own lines.

Wrzesiński's next shot missed him entirely.

Krampitz had taken more time to aim. His next shot struck Łohojski in the back of his right leg, a few inches below the knee.

It was only a flesh wound, since the bullet passed through the leg without striking a bone. But it was enough to cause Łohojski to stumble and fall on his knees.

The next shots fired by the riflemen in the turrets struck Łohojski almost simultaneously. Wrzesiński's bullet struck the back of his helmet and knocked it right off. It also broke his skull. Krampitz's shot struck him in the lower back, just below the edge of the cuirass. It missed any vital organs but caused a lot of internal damage and bleeding.

Łohojski collapsed. By then, a dozen of his cavalrymen had raced up and were now surrounding his body. Some of them dismounted to provide him with assistance. Others, still on horseback, fired their wheel-lock pistols at the far-distant APC—which was pointless, at that range, but angry men do pointless things.

"Do you think we got him?" asked Wrzesiński.

"Don't know," said Krampitz.

"Who was he, d'you think?"

"Don't know," said Krampitz.

Within a few minutes, the cavalrymen had brought Łohojski back to their own lines. He was still alive, but no longer conscious.

The officer who now took command of Łohojski's army was named Jerzy Dziedzic. He was an experienced and competent soldier, but Łohojski had selected him for the post because of his reliability, not his imagination and intelligence. Faced with a situation that confused him, Dziedzic chose the safest course, He ordered his men to take defensive positions while they waited for Potocki to bring up his army.

By then, the Galicians had the first culverin turned around and were starting to load it.

Airstrip south of the Vistula
Kraków, official capital of Poland
Actual capital of Lesser Poland

As soon as the *Steady Girl* landed and taxied to a stop, Christin climbed out of the cockpit and rushed toward the hangar, where men were already pushing a cart toward the plane. Denise clambered out right after her and rolled herself under the fuselage.

"Move it! Move it!" Christin shouted.

"Well, *I* won't be like that when *I'm* a mom," Denise muttered. "If I'm ever a mom at all."

Chapter 49

Half a mile north of Kraków

Lukasz Opalinski lowered the binoculars he'd been given by Jozef Wojtowicz and handed them back to him. The two men were standing atop the rise looking north.

"They're coming too quickly," he said. "We won't have more than two—maybe three—of the culverins ready to fire in time."

"You know more about these things than I do," said Jozef, "so I think you're right. That's how it looks to me, too." He put the binoculars back into the small holster he'd had made for them while he was still in Grantville. They were up-time made but neither fancy nor powerful—what the Americans called "opera glasses."

Having done that, Jozef turned his head to look at the APC. "On the other hand . . ."

Lukasz finished the thought. "Everyone who's ever been in a battle knows that cavalry can't break a solid and well-organized formation of pikemen—and unless I miss my guess, that's Potocki's army coming at us, which means they'll be both. For that, you need artillery, which we don't have. On the other hand, I believe that marvelous giant machine of yours will do better than even a battery of forty-two-pounders."

"It's worth a try." Jozef cocked an eye at his longtime friend. "I trust I can count on you to follow up with a proper charge."

"In the finest hussar tradition," Lukasz assured him. He glanced at the mob of cavalrymen who had gathered on the south side of the rise, most of whom were now out of sight of the oncoming enemy. "Well . . . enthusiastic tradition, anyway. But that'll be enough, Jozef, if you can shatter that formation of pikemen."

Before getting back into the cab, Jozef climbed into the interior of the former coal truck. He'd have much preferred to leave Pawel and Tekla in the care of a couple of hussars, who could be spared from the battle to bring the children to safety inside the city. But he knew they'd put up a fierce fight against the idea, and he simply didn't have time to deal with it.

When he reached the padded box in the middle of the interior, he leaned over the side. Pawel and Tekla were looking up at him. The two children seemed a bit worried, but not afraid.

"We're going into a battle," he told them. "I think you'll be safe but I want you to promise me you won't leave this box under any conditions."

"We promise, Papa," Tekla said. Pawel just nodded a few times, very quickly.

Jozef hesitated. Then: "I love you. So does your Mama." And he left.

By then, Jakub had reached the rise also. Behind him came the Silesian militia made up almost entirely of Polish farmers and German townsmen, along with those members of the former garrison of Kraków who had volunteered to join them. Thankfully, those volunteers included the two veteran sergeants named Michal Kozłowski and Nicolai Korczak. Jakub had found himself leaning heavily on their advice, since the Opalinski brothers had chosen to make him what the Polish military called a *pułkownik*—roughly the equivalent of a colonel in other armies.

From civilian to colonel in three days. Jakub was still trying to adjust to the idea. He understood the logic of it, which was political, not military. No one expected the Silesian militia to play much of a role in this battle. But for political reasons it was essential that they be actively involved, especially the Poles. That would simultaneously help blur the extent to which the Galicians were relying on the support of USE and Bohemian forces, as well as blurring the national character of Lower Silesia itself.

Gretchen had been particularly insistent on that point. She had come to the conclusion that she'd be spending most of her time and effort in the future in Silesia, not Saxony. In fact, she might very well have to resign her position as Chancellor of Saxony in order to be able to concentrate entirely on her position as the Lady Protector of Silesia. That was all the more true because she was bound and determined to turn Lower Silesia into a republican state. The only practical way to do that was to make Lower Silesia a province of the USE—and that couldn't be done unless the ethnic and religious identities of Silesia's inhabitants were subordinated to their political identity.

Most people of the time thought of the USE as "the nation of the Germans," but Gretchen didn't. Neither did any of the top leaders of the CoCs—nor did Mike Stearns. They wanted the USE to become the same sort of nation that the USA had been in another universe. A nation founded on citizenship and political principles, not blood and soil.

Jakub agreed with that himself, although in his case the nation he was dedicated to transform was his own Polish–Lithuanian Commonwealth. He still thought the idea of him being a pułkownik of a mostly Silesian unit was fairly ridiculous. But he could live with ridiculousness in a good cause.

Jakub was on horseback, unlike most of the members of his unit, who were all infantry. So he got to the rise a few minutes before the rest of them did. Once there, he went immediately to the Opalinski brothers to get their instructions.

The older of the brothers, Krzysztof, was officially the head of the Galician army. But it was Lukasz who had by now become the effective commander, at least on a battlefield.

"Just be ready to follow us when we launch the attack," Lukasz told him. "You won't be able to keep up, but it doesn't matter. One of two things will happen. Either we will smash Potocki's army and send them running, in which case all you will have to do is hold a lot of prisoners and tend to a lot of wounded men—theirs as well as ours. We're not Huns. Or we will be defeated and you will need to cover our retreat. In which case, a lot of you will die."

That was what Jakub had expected to hear. His two sergeants, Kozłowski and Korczak, had already explained the battlefield facts of life to him.

"Okay," he said. The Americanism was becoming as ubiquitous in the Commonwealth as it was in western parts of the continent. Poles were even more prone than most to adopt the word, being ever insistent on making the distinction between themselves—Europeans, through and through—and those half-Mongol Russian barbarians.

He then remembered to add, "Sir. And sir."

Lukasz and Krzysztof both grinned. "Relax," said the older brother. "We're Poles. We will damn well get rid of that idiotic *liberum veto*, but that doesn't mean we're becoming Germans."

A mile and a half north of Kraków

Jeff ordered the Hangman Regiment to take up a defensive position once they got within a quarter of a mile of the enemy. He would have preferred to do so earlier, to give his men more time to get ready, but there simply hadn't been any suitable terrain. Here, a dirt road ran parallel to a very low rise—not more than two feet, but that could make a huge difference on a battlefield, because the soldiers could fire behind shelter. That wouldn't have made much difference if they were still using muzzle-loading muskets, but the rate of fire the Hocklott breech-loading rifles gave them changed the whole equation.

Von Mercy had withdrawn his cavalrymen, partly to give them a rest and partly to see what the Hangmen could do. So, for the moment, the Hangmen were pretty much on their own. The Polish army they were facing—it was either Lubomirski's or Wiśniowiecki's; the intelligence they'd gotten wasn't clear—outnumbered them at least two-to-one, even if you included the Bohemian Jewish battalion which was serving the Hangman Regiment as a reserve force.

But Jeff didn't think the magnates really understood what they were facing. Their private armies had never encountered the accuracy and rate of fire that breech-loading rifles could produce. Nor had they encountered the sort of mortars that were even now being set up a hundred yards behind the riflemen now positioned along on the road.

Deciding he had time, Jeff trotted his horse back to the mortars.

He went first to Prince Ulrik, who had a somewhat glum expression on his face.

"I'm feeling useless again," he said. Nodding behind him, he added: "Major Krenz is doing all the real commanding."

"Eric's got the experience and you don't, Prince," said Jeff. "Just relax. If it'll make you feel better, contemplate the possibility you might still be struck down at any time by enemy fire, whether you're bossing around anybody or just looking good."

He examined Ulrik for a moment. "Which you do, by the way. I don't even want to think how much that armor cost you."

Ulrik's sour expression was replaced by a smile. "Cost my father, actually. I'm far too frugal to have bought something like this myself."

That was true enough. As many people had before him, Jeff was coming to the conclusion that, when the time came, Prince Ulrik was going to make one hell of a good emperor.

I can't believe I just said that to myself, Jeff thought. *"One hell of a good emperor." I can remember when my friends and I used to argue Democrats versus Republicans. Welcome to the year 1637.*

But that was immediately followed by a very different thought. *And welcome to the same year that has my wife in it. Ms. I-will-boil-you-in-oil revolutionary with the title of Lady Protector.*

He wondered what she was doing, right then.

Cloth Hall
Kraków, official capital of Poland
Actual capital of Lesser Poland

Gretchen was doing what millions of women had done throughout history, when their husbands were on the verge of combat. Trying not to think about it by keeping themselves busy.

Of course, that number dropped to hundreds—no, dozens; at most—if you only included women who were distracting themselves by plotting revolution.

In this instance, with two co-conspirators, Judy Wendell and Noelle Stull.

It was a peculiar trio, contradictory in more ways than Gretchen could count without getting dizzy.

She herself was a revolutionary dedicated to the overthrow of the European royal and aristocratic establishments. Who also happened to be the Chancellor of Saxony, the Lady Protector of Lower Silesia, and the wife of the colonel who commanded her nation's most famous—and fearsome—regiment. A nation which was ruled—to a degree, at least—by an emperor. The continent's most powerful emperor, in fact.

Noelle Stull was a former agent for the Americans who had played a central role in igniting Europe's revolution—but was a noblewoman herself now, the Countess of Homonna, as well as being the wife of the closest confidant of the emperor of Austria-Hungary.

Judy Wendell could claim to be the most homogenous of the three, since at least she bore no titles beyond the rather dubious Austrian one of "Serene Highness." More to the point, she was now the paramour of one of the Polish–Lithuanian Commonwealth's most prominent revolutionary leaders.

She also happened to be the best friend of an Austrian archduchess and was wealthier than most noblewomen. A fortune she'd begun to amass by selling dolls.

Go figure, as Gretchen's husband would say.

"All right," Gretchen said. "I agree"—she raised a stiff, cautionary forefinger—"*provisionally*, that Jakub's strategy is probably the best one. The most quickly effective one, at least. But I will have to refrain from open support of the idea and if Red Sybolt responds as we all think he will, I will support him. And that will not be a pretense, either. I *will* support him."

"Not a problem," said Judy. "In fact, Jakub himself would agree that that's the best tactic you could follow."

Gretchen snorted. The sound was half sarcastic; half... not. "He's clearly a student of Mike Stearns. He will use Red Sybolt the same way Mike has always used me." She pointed to the side, her finger now stiff with warning. "You can either negotiate with me or negotiate with the wicked witch from down below."

But there was no anger in her voice. Whatever suspicions she'd once had of Mike Stearns had been buried in the snow that fell on Dresden the same day that Stearns crushed the army of the counterrevolutionary brute Johann Banér just a few miles beyond the city's walls.

"And I'll do what I can to persuade Janos to give us his backing," said Noelle. She made a face. "Mind you, talking the emperor of Austria-Hungary into letting his kid sister marry a Polish revolutionary is . . . going to be tricky."

They all smiled at each other. Then Judy asked: "So, speaking of witches, when shall we three meet again?"

Airstrip south of the Vistula
Kraków, official capital of Poland
Actual capital of Lesser Poland

As soon as the *Steady Girl* lifted off the ground, Denise issued a loud "*Wheeeeeeeeeeeee*!" from the back seat, followed by: "Best family outing *ever*. Even if I haven't been able to see any of it."

"Stop grousing, dear," said her mother.

Chapter 50

Half a mile northwest of Kraków

Jozef saw no point in being subtle, so once he brought the APC off the rise and onto level ground, he just steered it straight toward the pike-and-musket formation which was now about two hundred yards away.

He didn't drive very fast—never more than ten miles an hour and usually less. Even going at that speed, he'd cross the distance separating the enemy from the APC in a minute or so. He was worried about getting the vehicle stuck in a ditch or hole or some other obstruction. Having to peer through a slit in the armor covering the windshield made for truly miserable visual conditions.

He began humming a tune, mostly to settle his nerves. He'd learned it in Grantville during his stay there. The tune wasn't quite appropriate to the occasion, but he thought it would do well enough.

Not more than five seconds later, Walenty complained. "I hate humming. If you insist on doing this, at least sing the blasted song."

Jozef smiled thinly. "As you wish."

He cleared his throat. Then:

"Oh, the shark, babe, has such teeth, dear,
"And it shows them pearly white—"

As he watched the monstrous vehicle coming toward his army, Mikołaj Potocki finally understood the rebels' full intent. He and his fellow magnates had been fools. They'd assembled their forces and marched down here with the serene confidence that their professional soldiers would have little trouble crushing a motley band of rebels. That would be even more true because a large fraction of the so-called konfederacja weren't "rebels" at all. They were foreign invaders.

But they'd miscalculated everything.

The magnates hadn't taken seriously enough the warnings they'd gotten not to underestimate the impact the new up-time technology could have on the battlefield. They hadn't grasped the shrewd manner in which the enemy had disguised their foreign troops by always maintaining an outward shell of Polish forces. The discord and disunity they'd been sure they would find simply wasn't there—at least, Potocki had seen no sign of it yet. In fact, the rebels seemed to be coordinating their units extremely well. Quite a bit better, being honest about it, than the magnates were managing.

And, finally, they'd never expected to encounter this level of military skill. Potocki had no idea who the rebels had for their top commander. The only possible candidates anyone knew about were the two Opalinskis.

But Potocki didn't believe that the brothers had the experience to plan and carry out such a shrewd strategy, applied with such deft tactics. They were both still in their mid-twenties.

He knew what was going to happen within a few seconds. It was a given, a certainty. The most stalwart pikemen in the world weren't going to stand their ground against such an inexorable behemoth.

All he could do now was save his army.

"Pull back! Pull back!" he shouted, waving his sword to the rear. "Maintain formations!"

That last was probably hopeless, but he had to try. If his men started withdrawing out of control, the retreat would quickly become a rout—and whatever might be the failings of the Galician cavalry, they'd already shown they were fierce. They would pursue his men and butcher them. Infantry on the run from cavalry were an easy target.

Jozef saw the first breaks in the enemy formations when he was less than fifty yards away from their front ranks. The mass of pikemen was parting before them— and not smoothly. Within seconds they were nothing more than a panicked mob, with pikemen in the path of the APC desperately trying to get out of its way and having no means of doing so except to clamber over their fellows.

Pikes were discarded—and as they came down, the blades inflicted wounds, a few of them fatal.

Jozef reached up and yanked on the cord controlling the air horn. Three times, quickly. That was the signal he'd established for the riflemen in the turrets.

✧ ✧ ✧

Tomek Wrzesiński had been on the verge of coming out of the turret anyway. Crouching in that narrow space with a heavy wooden lid covering the top of his turret was stifling and uncomfortable. Jozef had insisted on the lids in order to protect the riflemen from grenades that might be thrown at the turrets. Tomek appreciated the concern, but enough was enough. He'd never liked being in confined spaces.

He rose and shoved the lid aside. He heard it clatter on the top of the APC's armored roof, but didn't pay that any attention. He was scanning the area around him, bringing up his rifle and looking for targets.

Oh . . . and there were so *many* of them.

Tomek was a veteran and knew what he was seeing. The APC's charge had terrified the enemy pikemen and musketeers, and they were now starting to run. A few officers on horseback were trying to bring order to the retreat, but Tomek didn't think they'd have much success.

The APC came to a stop, providing Tomek with a stable shooting platform.

The enemy officers would have no success at all, actually. Tomek and his fellow marksmen would see to that. He brought up the rifle, took aim at the nearest officer, and shot him right out of the saddle. Not more than half a second later, he heard Ambrozy Krampitz's gun fire.

He didn't take the time to see the results. He had another target in his sights. At this range—fifty to a hundred yards—it was like shooting sheep in a pen.

Peering through the slit in the armor, Jozef decided he

would give the marksmen in the turret another minute or so before he set the APC back into motion. Tomek and the others could do a better job of shattering the enemy's leadership than he could. The APC was too clumsy for such work.

So, he went back to singing "Mack the Knife."

Jozef wound up just staying where he was. Before the minute was up, Lukasz and Krzysztof Opalinski pounded past the APC, with close to two thousand Galician hussars and Cossacks in their wake. Given the terrain, Jozef probably couldn't have kept up with them and it would be sheer folly to have his marksmen trying to shoot anyone while the APC was moving.

For him—and best of all, for his children—this battle was over.

"—Scarlet billows start to spread"

"That's a rather disturbing song," said Walenty Tarnowski.

Three hundred feet above the ground

"There's no target here, Eddie," said Christin, looking out of her window. Below, the Galician cavalry was wreaking havoc on their routed foes. They were too mixed up for Christin to want to take the risk of dropping bombs.

"Yes, I agree," he said, banking the plane to the east. "Let's go see how the Hangmen are doing."

From the rear, Denise piped up, mimicking Eddie's

voice. "'How the Hangmen are doing.' That's kinda sicko, Eddie."

A mile and a half north of Kraków

"And here they come," Jeff said softly. He was speaking to himself, since he was perched on a saddle about fifteen yards behind the front line of his riflemen. He'd found a rise of sorts—if you could call it that at all. The rise was no more than two or three feet higher than the surrounding terrain, but it still gave him a better view of the approaching enemy than he'd have had on the dirt road where most of the regiment had taken position,

It would take the enemy a bit of time before they arrived. Polish infantry formations weren't quite as rigid as Spanish tercios, but they would still never be considered "foot cavalry." More like "snail cavalry."

Well... "Tortoise cavalry," at any rate.

Jeff decided he still had time to check in with Prince Ulrik and Eric Krenz. He turned his horse and trotted back to the battery of mortars which was now positioned about fifty or sixty yards to the south.

"Are you all set?" he asked Krenz.

"All you have to do is give us the word. I think we're ranged in pretty well."

"Just make sure you don't come in short, Eric. I'm more concerned about friendly fire than enemy fire."

Krenz clucked his tongue. "You know, it's terrible for morale to have a commanding officer casting aspersions on his own troops."

"Not as bad as having your own mortars shelling you."

But he wasn't really worried about it. For all his flippancy, Eric Krenz was a very capable officer, as he'd proven a number of times by now.

Jeff trotted over to Ulrik, who'd taken position behind the left flank of the battery.

"All set?" Jeff asked.

Ulrik nodded. "As well as possible. To be honest, I wish the fighting would start. This is a bit nerve-wracking, just waiting."

"Yes, I—" Hearing a familiar sound, Jeff looked up. The *Steady Girl* was nearing them—and it was not coming at a tortoise pace. Jeff thought Eddie must be pushing the plane's limit when it came to speed.

It was coming very low too. Now, not more than one hundred feet above the ground.

The aircraft swept overhead. Turning, Jeff and the prince watched it race toward the enemy.

One bomb was loosed. Before it hit the ground, the second was loosed as well. Two closely spaced balls of flame erupted right in the middle of the enemy infantry.

"And here we go," said Jeff, heading back toward the road. He was cantering his horse now.

Prince Jeremy Wiśniowiecki had heard reports of the effect of the rebels' incendiary bombs but this was the first time he'd witnessed them himself. The first bomb had exploded right in the midst of a formation of pikemen, killing at least a dozen almost immediately. The ones who survived included many who were very badly burned. A number of them would not survive.

The second bomb had caused less harm. Either by

good fortune or simply because the devices could not be placed accurately when the aircraft was traveling at such a speed—that was the prince's own guess—it had overshot the next formation of pikemen and landed between them and a line of musketeers. None of the pikemen in that formation had been harmed at all. A fair number of the musketeers had been burned—badly burned, some of them, judging from the screams.

The incendiary devices were deadly, yes. But the prince didn't think the bombs had killed and injured any more of his men than a good cannon volley would have done. And even compared to siege guns, the aircraft's rate of fire was abysmal. Two bombs dropped—no more than two—and it had to return to its base somewhere on the other side of the Vistula to rearm. Perhaps it needed to refuel as well.

The aircraft would not return for at least half an hour, and by then Wiśniowiecki's forces would be grappling with the enemy—and probably already have routed them. There would be no target for the airplane that wouldn't risk killing many of the rebels as well.

It was time to crush this grotesque rebellion. The prince trotted his horse forward, raised his sword, and led his army on.

After Wiśniowiecki had gone no more than fifteen yards, the rebels began to fire. The range was absurd. Clearly, they were unnerved—as you'd expect from such people. Runaway serfs; Cossacks; debauched and depraved former szlachta. It was a wonder they'd had the nerve to rebel at all.

After the prince had come forward another ten yards, he was struck in the shoulder by a bullet. It was a frightful wound, but had the beneficial side effect of rendering the prince near-senseless from shock. He slumped in the saddle and slid off—which was fortunate, because at least some of the bullets that struck the aides and adjutants riding behind him, killing two of them outright and injuring two more, would have surely struck Wiśniowiecki himself if he'd still been erect in the saddle.

Three of the prince's longtime retainers rushed forward, picked him up, and carried him back to safety.

Stanisław Lubomirski had positioned his own army on Wiśniowiecki's left flank. Such had been the agreement between the two magnates. What they hadn't agreed on—and would have infuriated Wiśniowiecki if he'd realized what Lubomirski was doing—was that the voivode of Ruthenia was making sure his forces were lagging at least an eighth of a mile behind Wiśniowiecki's.

There had already been some unpleasant surprises since this battle began—the first of which had been the seemingly rash sortie by Kraków's defenders. Lubomirski knew that Łohojski had been badly injured and that Prince Zasławski seemed to have disappeared. And—possibly worst of all—there was a rumor that Potocki's men had been routed.

If there were to be any more surprises, Lubomirski intended to make sure he wasn't the one who discovered them.

When the courier brought him the news, Lubomirski

wasn't surprised. He hadn't seen Prince Wiśniowiecki fall, because he'd been too far away. But he had seen the sudden cessation of his army's forward progress and drawn his own conclusions.

So, that was that. Battles were won; battles were lost—and this one had been lost. Happily, the voivode of Ruthenia's army had barely suffered a scratch and he intended to keep it that way.

They would retreat to Kielce, he decided.

"That stinking son of a bitch," snarled Klimunt Wójcik. The regimentarz who had taken command of Wiśniowiecki's army after the prince was struck down was glaring to the northeast, watching Lubomirski's forces as they retreated.

Seeing the looks of apprehension in the faces of the two adjutants he still had at his side—he'd sent most of them out to steady the troops—Wójcik almost snarled at them as well.

But there would be no point to that. Nor would it be fair to them. With Lubomirski in full retreat—the same seemed to have happened to Potocki—and given the unexpectedly deadly fire coming from the rebels, Wójcik had no choice but to order a retreat himself.

And quickly—while maintaining disciplined formations. The Bohemian cavalry was out there somewhere. They could still cause great harm to the prince's army.

In point of fact, General von Mercy was pondering that same possibility himself at that very moment. He and several of his aides had taken position in a small copse of trees and he was observing the army that the Hangman Regiment had brought to a standstill.

Von Mercy couldn't tell whose army it was, at that distance. Probably Prince Wiśniowiecki's, but it might be Lubomirski's.

"Do we pursue?" asked one of his aides.

Von Mercy lowered the spyglass. "No," he said. "It's tempting, but this is really not our fight. All we needed to do for our king's purposes was help the Galician rebels hold Kraków. That, we've done—and done as well as anyone could ask for. We have business to the south and east. Let the Opalinskis and their followers hold what they can. They're on their own, now."

Airstrip south of the Vistula
Kraków, official capital of Poland
Actual capital of Lesser Poland

After the *Steady Girl* came to a stop, Eddie turned off the engine and slumped in his seat. Flying in combat, he had discovered, was a lot more draining than you'd think it would be, given that a pilot didn't really do much beyond sit on his ass.

"We still got two bombs left," Denise said from the back seat.

"Who would we drop them on? We won, child," said Christin.

"I'm not a child. Okay, I'm *your* child. I'll agree to that. But I'm not *a* child. There's an important distinction there."

Christin decided to leave that alone, lest her daughter start in on her new mathematical theories that had her being nineteen years old.

Probably twenty-two, by now.

"We could drop them in the Vistula. It's a river, so it's gotta have some fish in it."

"Denise, we are not going to go fishing with napalm bombs."

"Makes sense to me. You cook them at the same time as you catch them."

"She's still peeved with you because you made her sit in the back seat the whole time."

"I know," said Christin.

"I never got to see *anything*!" Denise complained.

"Your daughter's a little scary sometimes," said Eddie.

Christin nodded. "She gets it from me. When *I* was eight years old I didn't screw around with Shakespeare. I went straight for the top shelf stuff."

She began a little chant.

> *"Lizzie Borden took an axe*
> *And gave her mother forty whacks"*

A village seven miles north of Kraków

The men who'd taken him from the battlefield found a bed for Janusz Łohojski in a village whose name they didn't know. There was no one to ask because the villagers had all fled two days before the battle.

It wasn't much of a bed, as you'd expect in a hut that

belonged to a poor peasant. Just a straw pallet raised no more than eight inches off the dirt floor.

It had bugs in it, needless to say. Some of them were drawn to the blood that had seeped through his bandages. The blood had dried by now, but the insects didn't care. Scavengers of any size are not fussy.

The voivode of Kiev never regained consciousness. He died just before midnight.

Epilogue
The Anaconda Prospect

April 1637

Prague, capital of Bohemia

"It was such a strange feeling," said Morris Roth, who was sitting next to his wife Judith on a divan. "I was standing by the bed with Pappenheim. Edith was on the other side of the bed with the queen, monitoring Wallenstein's vital signs. Both of them were crying. And then..."

He looked away for a moment, as if composing himself.

"Then Edith looked up and told us that Wallenstein had died. And I felt a great sadness wash over me." He barked a little laugh. "Sadness, Judith! For Wallenstein! The same monster who tried to murder all of the children at the high school. Hundreds of them."

She took his hand and squeezed it. "People are complicated, Morris. That man may also have saved tens of thousands of children in the ghettos and shtetls of Poland and Ruthenia. Made it possible, anyway."

He sighed. "Yes, I know. It's why we moved here, after all. I still never would have expected myself to have that strong a reaction to his passing."

He got up and went to one of the windows. They were on the upper floor of the mansion, and that window provided him with a good view of Prague's ghetto. It was probably the largest Jewish community in the world.

Most of the wall that separated it from the rest of the city was still there. Not because Wallenstein had insisted on it—to the contrary; the new Bohemian king had given permission to tear it down—but because most of the city's rabbis insisted on keeping it in place.

The sight of that wall usually angered Morris, but today he was in a more contemplative mood. The two rabbis that he and Judith were closest to, Mordecai Levi and Isaac Gans, had approached him right after his return from Poland. They asked him—for the first time—if he might have some reading material relevant to what Morris called "Reform Judaism."

He lent them the *Gates of Prayer* as well as Rabbi Abraham Geiger's two volumes, written in the middle of the nineteenth century, *Judaism and Its History* and *Judaism and Islam.*

Whether anything would come of that, he didn't know. But he was hopeful. Just as he was hopeful that Wallenstein's "Anaconda Project" might eventually achieve the goal Morris had set for it. That goal had grown more ambitious as time passed. He no longer sought simply to save the lives of eastern Europe's Jews, he thought there was a good chance those lives could be improved in the doing—maybe even greatly improved.

"Have you spoken to Pappenheim?" Judith asked.

He turned away from the window. "Yes. Briefly, after the king died. I don't foresee any problems. His sole concern is to protect Wallenstein's legacy—which, for him, means ensuring that the regency succeeds in its purpose."

"And the Anaconda Project?"

"He had little to say about that—but what he did say was significant. His exact words were: 'I don't care what you do in the east, Morris. That was Wallenstein's ambition, which I always thought was probably a fantasy, at least for the most part.' So I asked him if he wanted me to bring the Grand Army of the Sunrise back to Bohemia."

He sat back down next to Judith. "His answer was . . . interesting. Let's call it that. He'd prefer for Bohemia to have only one army in it, which was his—or rather, the troops he left behind when he took the Black Cuirassiers to Linz."

"And you're supposed to do what, with your own army?"

"He said that as far as he was concerned, that was my affair. So long as the regency was not disrupted, I could do whatever I wanted—except bring the Grand Army of the Sunrise any farther west than Brno."

Judith pursed her lips. "That . . . *is* interesting."

"Isn't it?"

Kraków, official capital of Poland
Actual capital of Lesser Poland

"I didn't really do anything in the battle," Jakub told Judy, "except have my men round up a lot of prisoners—which included Prince Zasławski—and tend to the wounded. All the fighting was done by the men in the APC and the Galician cavalry."

"Has anything been decided about Zasławski?"

"His ransom, you mean?" Jakub shook his head, without lifting it from the pillow. To do that, he would have had to dislodge Judy, which he was not in the least bit inclined to do.

"No. We have some time, though, since there's no point starting a big fight over the ransom if there isn't one. There's no better than a fifty-fifty chance that Zasławski will survive. His injuries are pretty terrible. If he doesn't, we squeeze what we can out of his heirs for his body. If he does survive . . ."

"Is he really the richest magnate in the Commonwealth?"

"Who knows? It's not as if the magnates provide any public information on the subject of their wealth. He's certainly one of the richest. If he survives, his ransom will be huge."

"Do you really think it will be a big fight?"

"Oh, yes. The half-dozen militiamen who actually seized the prince are having visions of being wealthy themselves— and they have tradition on their side. The moment I propose establishing a widows' and orphans' fund like the one the Hangmen have, they will be furious with me."

Judy raised her head from his shoulder, which she could do without dislodging him. "I predict a lot of that in your future. Near future. When are you going to tell Red and Krzysztof what you plan to do?"

"Soon," he said.

"You're stalling."

"Very soon," he insisted.

Linz airfield
Linz, provisional capital of Austria-Hungary

Mike Stearns got out of the State Department's Dragonfly after the other passengers had already done so. Julie Sims had been waiting for him.

Impatiently.

"You gotta do something, Mike! You're the top USE commander here."

"No, I'm not. That would be Gustav Adolf you're looking for."

"I already talked to him. He thinks it's a good idea himself, if you can believe it. So it's up to you to put a stop to it!"

By then, his wife was at his side. "Put a stop to what?" Rebecca asked.

"What I'm calling Mailey's Madness. Do you know what that crazy woman is doing now? For Chrissake, she already got me a stupid medal—"

She broke off, seeing that Laura Goss was joining them.

"You're getting one, too."

"Getting 'one' what?"

"They're calling it—brace yourself—the 'Military Order of Mariana.' You and I are the first and only members. Talk about stupid!"

"For what?" Laura asked, frowning.

"Exactly what I said! It's ridiculous. We didn't do anything tougher than shooting fish in a barrel. Well, not much tougher, anyway."

She turned back to Mike. "I can't stop that because it was already a done deal by the time I found out about it. But there's still time to torpedo Melissa's latest crazy idea."

"Which is . . . ?"

The next words were practically wailed. "The fucking maniac wants to have a statue put up! Of me and Laura— right in the middle of one of the city's squares! Can you believe it?"

Mike took off his hat and ran fingers through his hair, while he pondered the problem. Which took possibly two seconds.

"Damn, that's a great idea," he said.

"*Mike!*"

"Oh, wow," said Captain Goss. "Just think of the party we could throw, unveiling something like that . . ."

"*Laura!*"

Kraków, official capital of Poland
Actual capital of Lesser Poland

Lukasz Opalinski stared at Jakub Zaborowski for a few seconds.

Then, issued a mighty snort. "That's utterly insane!"

He looked at the third person in the room, who was standing by one of the Cloth Hall's many windows. "Can you believe this silliness, Jozef?"

Wojtowicz kept looking out of the window for a few

seconds. Then, turned to face the two men seated in the center of the room.

"Actually . . . I can see a lot of advantages."

Lukasz was practically ogling him, now. His jaw had sagged open as well.

Jozef looked at Jakub. "You'll want something in exchange, of course. What is it?"

"Nothing personal. Politically?" Jakub's grin, as was often true, had an edge to it. "Oh, yes. I'll want a lot. We can start with the right of the congress—let's call it that, instead of the Sejm—to overrule any decision by the king."

"No *liberum veto*!" Jozef said.

"No, of course not. Majority vote."

Lukasz was looking back and forth between them. Finally, he clapped his mouth shut.

"That's nonsense!" he exclaimed. "Some decisions— military ones, especially—have to be made immediately. D'you know how long it would take to get a bunch of politicians assembled? Call it a congress, call it a Sejm, call it a flock of geese—it doesn't matter. You might as well call it whatever the name is for a herd of tortoises."

Jakub and Jozef looked at each other.

"He's got a point," Jozef said.

Scowling a bit, Jakub scratched his jaw. "Yes, I know. But I think . . . Yes, this would do . . ."

Imperial Palace (provisional)
Linz, provisional capital of Austria-Hungary

Emperor Ferdinand III glared at his two younger siblings,

who were seated next to each other facing him. They were in a small chamber, not one of the big ones Ferdinand used for public occasions—which this was certainly *not*.

"I'm trying to decide which of you is the more insane," he said. "My sister, who wants to marry a rebel—"

"I'm just *raising* the idea," interrupted Cecilia Renata. "I have no idea if the man involved would be in the least bit interested. Yet."

Ferdinand ignored that in order to concentrate his ire on Leopold. "And you! Wanting me to have you confirmed as a bishop—even take holy vows—so you can keep that one-eyed woman of yours as your open mistress."

He didn't bother to point out that doing any such thing would be explicitly forbidden by those same holy vows he proposed to take. Everyone in the room was of royal blood. For such as them, "holy vows" was a very elastic term.

The emperor's scowl was . . . imperial. "I'm sure the slut herself put you up to this."

For the first time, his younger brother glared back. "Minnie is not a slut!" snapped Leopold.

"No, she's not," chimed in Cecilia Renata. "Actually, she thinks Leopold is being silly. Minnie's perfectly content to have Leopold take on whatever spouse he might need to, eventually, so long as she and the child are provided for—and she doesn't even ask for much in that regard."

Ferdinand looked back at Leopold, who was still glaring at him. Then, back at Cecilia Renata, who was looking rather serene.

"Let's have the woman brought here, then," said the emperor. "So the sane aren't outnumbered by the lunatics."

Kraków, official capital of Poland
Actual capital of Lesser Poland

"You treacherous son of a bitch," said Red Sybolt. If he'd been a snake, he would have hissed the words. His shoulders were hunched like a cobra's hood.

He turned his angry eyes toward Krzysztof Opalinski. "Are you in on this, too?"

Krzysztof shook his head. His expression was more one of distress than fury. "No, of course not. I remain a dedicated republican."

"All right, then!" Red turned back to Jakub. "I'm warning you. If you go ahead with this goddam monarchy scheme, me and Krzysztof will immediately forge an opposition party and fight you tooth and nail."

Zaborowsky leaned back in his chair, with his hands planted on his thighs. "Oh, yes," he said. "I'm counting on it."

Linz, provisional capital of Austria-Hungary

Minnie looked around the small room. Her friend Denise would have called it a "living room" and immediately derided its skimpy dimensions.

It *was* small, by American standards. But Minnie was

satisfied with it. The apartment was clean and well furbished and had a nice kitchen. Best of all, Linz was a city under siege, jammed with people, and Minnie would have the place to herself. And Leopold, of course, when he came to visit.

And the baby, when he or she arrived. But by the time the baby could start toddling around, many things could have changed.

The siege could have been won. The siege could have been lost. Her employer might have summoned her back to Prague.

That had been one of the two conditions Minnie had insisted upon. She really enjoyed working for Francisco Nasi. The other condition was that she and Denise got to visit each other whenever they chose.

Who could say what the future would bring? It was even possible that after he became an ordained priest—which was not a requirement for being a bishop—Leopold might decide he had to respect his vows.

That was a very remote possibility, of course. It was more likely that a horse would learn to sing.

May 1637

Dresden, capital of the Province of Saxony

Mike Stearns' eyes went around the table, taking a couple of seconds to look at each of the people gathered there.

That done, he said: "Any hesitations? Any last thoughts?"

No one spoke. He turned to the man sitting to his right. "Jeff?"

"Are you kidding? I get a promotion *and* I get to stay with my wife." He looked across the table at Gretchen and smiled.

She gave him a quick smile in return, but her brow remained creased. Not with worry, though, simply with thought.

She turned to the man sitting to her right. "Are you sure you're ready for this, Joachim? The campaign is likely to get brutal. Not because of Ernst Wettin himself, whom I've always gotten along with, but because every reactionary in Saxony will throw their support to him."

"It can't be all that bad. Not one of those reactionaries is as ugly as I am."

That occasioned a little laugh at the table, in which everyone participated except Gretchen. In truth, Joachim Kappel was an extraordinarily ugly man. "Troll" was a word often used to refer to him. Fortunately, Kappel was as genial as he was ill-favored and handled his appearance by being the first to make jokes about it.

He shrugged. "To be honest, Gretchen, I'm much more concerned about what will happen if I *win* the election. I'm used to having you—and Tata, after you went to Silesia—here to tell me what to do."

"Tata's been gone for a while herself. You seem to have done fine."

"Yes, I think so. Still, becoming the chancellor of the province will be a challenge."

Gretchen studied him for a moment longer. Then she brought her eyes back to Mike.

"You can tell that damned emperor of yours—"

"Yours, too."

"Don't remind me. You can tell Gustav Adolf that if, as the Lady Protector, I do what he wants and declare unilaterally that Lower Silesia is henceforth a province of the United States of Europe, I will *also* declare that it is to have a republican structure and there will be immediate elections. And that every one of my decrees on religious freedom will stay in place."

"You can't organize elections immediately, Gretchen, as you know perfectly well."

"As soon as possible, then. I'm not putting up with this ridiculous title any longer than I have to."

"I'll tell him, but it's a moot point. Who could Gustav Adolf possibly want to establish as a hereditary ruler of Lower Silesia? There's no obvious heir apparent and he's almost as fed up with pretentious noblemen as you are."

He grinned. "Look on the bright side. At least you won't have to create your own established church the way he insisted you do in Saxony. Lower Silesia has such a jumble of denominations that even the most devoted adherent of *cuius regio, eius religio* would throw up his hands in despair."

That elicited another laugh around the table—again, participated in by everyone except Gretchen.

After the meeting was over, Jeff took Mike aside.

"I've got to give you fair warning. Once I make the announcement, I don't think you're going to have much of a Hangman Regiment left."

"I'll be surprised if there's anything left at all. You're

probably the most popular regimental commander in the army, by now—and what's just as important is that the Hangman has a higher CoC component than any other. Those men are all volunteers and they volunteered for a *cause*. We'll see what happens, but I'm willing to bet at least ninety percent of them will decide they'd rather fight alongside Polish revolutionaries than Austrian mercenaries. Especially if you're smart enough to design a nifty uniform for your new provincial army."

Jeff smiled. "I was thinking of adopting some of the Polish hussar notions of a proper uniform. Not the leopard skins and the ostrich plumes, though. That's a little much."

"Have you chosen a name yet?"

"You'd think a D&D aficionado would be able to come up with something dramatic, but all I've managed so far is 'Silesian National Guard.'"

Mike shook his head. "Don't. The obvious nickname will be 'the snuggies,' which is just about the last thing soldiers want to be called."

"I hadn't thought of that. Good point."

"How about your table of organization?"

"Oh, I'll stick with the USE's. I don't see any reason to get fancy about that."

"No fancy title for yourself, even? 'Brigadier' is pretty humdrum for the top commander of an entire army."

Jeff snorted. "We're talking about a provincial army. Which at the moment has exactly one regiment and some units that need to be reorganized. Should I call myself 'Generallisimo Higgins'? That'd be even more grotesque than Gretchen getting saddled with 'Lady Protector.'"

There was silence for a moment. Then, Mike said, very

seriously: "It's been a privilege to serve with you, Brigadier Higgins."

"Likewise, General Stearns."

Mike slapped Jeff on the shoulder. "And now let's call it quits with the formalities. You're not in my chain of command any longer, Jeff."

"No. Not for now, anyway. But who knows what the future will bring? If anybody ever starts prattling to you about what's likely and what's not, Mike, just point out to them that we're here either because of a cosmic accident or the divine will of God so shut the fuck up."

Kraków, official capital of Poland
Actual capital of Lesser Poland

Since all of them except the two youngsters had their own opinions when it came to the divine will of God, they observed a moment of silence rather than reciting any sort of grace. That had seemed odd to Pawel and Tekla, at first, but they'd gotten used to it soon. They had the practicality that came easily to children before it was beaten out of them by obsessive and superstitious adults. A moment of silence was shorter than grace so they got to eat sooner.

Jozef stretched out his hand. "Pass me the butter, would you, Denise?"

"You're gonna get fat," she predicted, as she passed it to him.

"I certainly hope so."

Hearing a soft chuckle, Denise looked at Eddie. "You think that's funny, too?"

Eddie was cheerfully shoveling potatoes onto his plate. "What is it with up-timers that you find virtue in misery and suffering? Anyone with any sense at all wants to get fat. You never know when famine might strike."

Denise and Christin looked at each other.

"Mom," said the daughter, "tell these dumb men that pessimism is its own form of misery and suffering."

"That's way too deep for me, Denise." The mother was spreading butter on her bread—and not stinting on it. "That's why they didn't let me skip my eighteenth year and go straight to nineteen, like they did you."

"Not funny, Mom. I *am* nineteen."

"What you are, girl, is someone who got planted in the middle of the Thirty Years War and has so far still managed to come up roses. That's an accomplishment at any age, trust me."

She lifted her glass of wine and held it up. "A toast, everyone."

Eddie and Jozef brought up their glasses. After a moment, so did Denise. A moment later, Pawel and Tekla raised their glasses of water.

"To the Ring of Fire," Christin said. "That brought us all together."

Cast of Characters

Abrabanel, Rebecca	USE Secretary of State; wife of Mike Stearns
Austria, Cecelia Renata, Archduchess of	Sister of Austria-Hungarian Emperor Ferdinand III and Archduke Leopold
Austria, Leopold Wilhelm, Archduke of	Younger brother of Austria-Hungarian Emperor Ferdinand III
Austria, Ferdinand III of	Emperor of Austria-Hungary; older brother of Archduke Leopold Wilhelm and Archduchess Cecilia Renata; married to Mariana, infanta of Spain
Beasley, Denise	Teenage girl employed as an agent by Francisco Nasi; informally betrothed to Eddie Junker; daughter of Christin George
Donner, Agathe "Tata"	CoC organizer in Dresden; close associate of Gretchen Richter

Drugeth, Janos — Hungarian nobleman; friend and adviser of Austrian Emperor Ferdinand III; married to Noelle Stull

Fakhr-al-Din — Druze emir

George, Christin — Mother of Denise Beasley

Goss, Laura — Captain in USE Air Force; pilot assigned to Rebecca Abrabanel

Gustavus Adolphus — See "Vasa, Gustav II Adolf"

Higgins, Jeffrey "Jeff" — Colonel, USE Army; husband of Gretchen Richter

Hugelmair, Minnie — Teenage girl employed as an agent by Francisco Nasi; friend of Denise Beasley

Junker, Egidius "Eddie" — Employed as an agent and pilot by Francisco Nasi; informally betrothed to Denise Beasley

Koniecpolski, Stanisław — Grand Herman of the Polish–Lithuanian Commonwealth

Krenz, Eric — Major, USE Army

Łohojski, Janusz — Voivode of Kiev; one of the Polish–Lithuanian magnates

Lubomirski, Stanisław	Voivode of Ruthenia; one of the Polish–Lithuanian magnates
Mackay, Julie	Sharpshooter; wife of Alex Mackay; née Julie Sims
Mackay, Alexander "Alex"	Cavalry officer in the army of Gustavus Adolphus; husband of Julie Sims
Mailey, Melissa	Leader of the Fourth of July Party
Mercy, Franz von	Bohemian general
Mizrahi, Moshe	Airship commander in the Gureba-i hava, the Ottoman Empire's air force
Murad IV	Sultan of the Ottoman Empire
Nasi, Francisco	Former head of intelligence for Mike Stearns; now operating a private intelligence agency in Prague
Nichols, James	American doctor

Opalinski, Krzysztof — Polish nobleman; Galician revolutionary leader; older brother of Lukasz Opalinski

Opalinski, Lukasz — Polish hussar; friend of Jozef Wojtowicz

Pappenheim, Gottfried Heinrich, Graf zu — Top general of the Bohemian army

Potocki, Mikołaj — Governor of Bracław Voivodeship; one of the Polish–Lithuanian magnates

Richter, Maria Margaretha "Gretchen" — Leader of the Committees of Correspondence; Chancellor of Saxony; Lady Protector of Lower Silesia; wife of Jeff Higgins

Roth, Judith — Wife of Morris Roth

Roth, Morris — Commander of the Grand Army of the Sunrise; one of Wallenstein's top advisers; husband of Judith Roth

Simpson, Thomas "Tom" III — USE Army artillery officer; husband of Rita Stearns; son of John and Mary Simpson

Sims, Julie	See Mackay, Julie
Stearns, Michael "Mike"	Former prime Minister of the Unites States of Europe; now a major general in command of the 3rd Division, USE Army; husband of Rebecca Abrabanel
Stull, Noelle	Countess of Homonna, married to Janos Drugeth
Sybolt, Bobby Gene "Red"	Former coal miner and UMWA activist; now a revolutionary leader in the Polish–Lithuanian Commonwealth
Ulrik	Prince of Denmark; betrothed to Kristina Vasa
Vasa, Kristina	Daughter and heir-presumptive of Gustav II Adolf; betrothed to Prince Ulrik of Denmark
Vasa, Gustav II Adolf	King of Sweden; Emperor of the United States of Europe; High King of the Union of Kalmar; also known as Gustavus Adolphus

Vasa, Władysław IV   King of the Polish–Lithuanian Commonwealth

Venceslas V Adalbertus   See "Wallenstein"

Wallenstein, Albrecht von   King of Bohemia

Wendell, Judith Elaine "Judy the Younger"   Barbie Consortium member; friend and companion of Archduchess Cecilia Renata

Wiśniowiecki, Jeremi   Prince of Wiśniowiec, Łubnie and Chorol; one of the Polish–Lithuanian magnates

Wojtowicz, Jozef   Nephew of Grand Hetman Koniecpolski; head of Polish intelligence in the USE; friend of Lukasz Opalinski

Zaborowsky, Jakub   Polish revolutionary leader

Zarfati, Abraham   Airship commander in the Gureba-i hava, the Ottoman Empire's air force

Zasławski, Władysław   Prince of the Princely Houses of Poland; one of the Polish–Lithuanian magnates

Afterword

The 1632 series, also called the Ring of Fire series, is now up to twenty-four novels and fourteen anthologies of short fiction, published by Baen Books. I am the author or one of the co-authors of twenty-two of those novels. (The two I was not involved with as an author are Kerryn Offord and Rick Boatright's *The Chronicles of Dr. Gribbleflotz* and Anette Pedersen's *1635: The Wars for the Rhine*.)

In addition, a few years ago I launched a publishing house of my own with the name Eric Flint's Ring of Fire Press, which enabled me to publish works in the Ring of Fire setting that Baen Books didn't have room for. Most of them are novels, and some are collections of short fiction. As of today, there are seventeen such volumes.

That's what has been produced in paper editions. There is also a bimonthly electronic magazine devoted to the Ring of Fire series, the *Grantville Gazette*, which has been in operation since May 2007. As of the month this novel comes out, the magazine will have published eighty-two issues.

The point to all this is that if you've enjoyed this novel and want to explore the Ring of Fire setting further...

Boy, are you in luck.

All of these titles, both in paper and electronic editions, are readily available.

You can find Baen Books' titles at its own website: https://www.baen.com.

You can find Ring of Fire Press titles at our own

website, which is https://ericflintsringoffire.com. They can also be found at Baen Books.

You can read the *Grantville Gazette* magazine at its own website, https://grantvillegazette.com, or obtain them through Baen Books.

Or, if you prefer, you can order any of these titles through Amazon, Barnes & Noble, Kobo and Smashwords.

And, of course, there's no law that forbids you from just walking into a brick-and-mortar bookstore. (Yes, they still exist. Lots of them, in fact.)

If you feel daunted by the complexity of the Ring of Fire series and don't know where to go from here, fear not. You can find a recommended reading order on the website maintained by fans of the 1632 series: https://1632.org/reading_order.

I should mention one more thing. A couple of years after we launched Ring of Fire Press, it dawned on us that since we'd already set up a publishing house there was no reason we couldn't publish works by other authors that were *not* in the Ring of Fire setting. The first such novel we published was Stoney Compton's *Incident in Alaska Prefecture.* Since then, Ring of Fire Press has published another eight such volumes and there are more on the way.

The sentence above was supposed to have been the end of the afterword. But a couple of weeks ago, a very old friend of mine died and I dedicated this book to him. I met Harry Meserve at UCLA when I was twenty-one years old. We were both graduate students in the history department. We became close friends, which we remained for the next half a century. Harry was the best man at my wedding to my first wife, Linda May O'Brien. I will miss him greatly.

—Eric Flint
December 2018

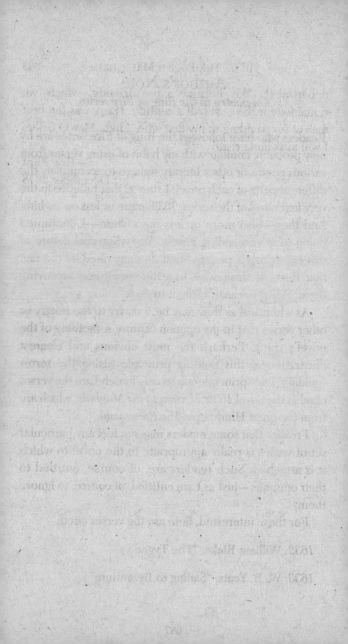

AUTHOR'S NOTE

For those interested here are the verses cited:

1632 William Blake 'The Tyger'

1633 W. B. Yeats 'Sailing to Byzantium'

Author's Note
On poetry in the Ring of Fire series

Readers who have followed the Ring of Fire series are by now probably familiar with my habit of using verses from various poems or other literary sources to accompany the different parts of each novel. I started that practice in the very first novel of the series, *1632*, more or less on a whim. And then—also more or less on a whim—I continued doing so in succeeding novels. The whimsical nature of this enterprise is perhaps best demonstrated by the fact that three of the novels have no verses accompanying them. Why? Because I forgot to do it.

As whimsical as they may be, I do try to use poetry or other verses that in my opinion capture something of the novel's spirit. Perhaps the most obvious and clearest illustration of this guiding principle (using the terms "guiding" and "principle" oh so very loosely) are the verses cited in the novel *1636: Mission to the Mughals*, which are from the great Hindu epic *The Ramayana*.

I realize that some readers may not feel any particular set of verses is really appropriate to the novel to which it is attached. Such readers are, of course, entitled to their opinions—just as I am entitled, of course, to ignore them.

For those interested, here are the verses cited:

1632: William Blake, "The Tyger"

1633: W. B. Yeats, "Sailing to Byzantium"

1634: The Galileo Affair: Robert Browning, "My Last Duchess"

1634: The Ram Rebellion: verses from the *Book of Ezekiel*, the Bible (King James)

1634: The Baltic War: W. B. Yeats, "Meditations in Time of Civil War"

1635: A Parcel of Rogues: Robert Burns, "Such a Parcel of Rogues in a Nation"

1634: The Bavarian Crisis: William Wordsworth, "Intimations of Immortality from Recollections of Early Childhood"

1635: The Cannon Law: nothing

1635: The Dreeson Incident: John Milton, "Paradise Lost"

1635: The Eastern Front: William Wordsworth, "Lines Composed a Few Miles above Tintern Abbey, on Revisiting the Banks of the Wye During a Tour, July 13, 1798"

1636: The Saxon Uprising: Alfred, Lord Tennyson, "Ulysses"

1635: The Papal Stakes: Edna St. Vincent Millay, "Renascence"

1636: The Atlantic Encounter: Wallace Stevens, "The Idea of Order at Key West"

1636: Commander Cantrell: William Shakespeare, *Troilus and Cressida*

1636: The Kremlin Games: nothing

1636: The Cardinal Virtues: not poetry but depictions of the four virtues

1636: The Ottoman Onslaught: Robert Browning, "Andrea Del Sarto"

1636: Mission to the Mughals: verses from the *Ramayana*

1636: The Vatican Sanction: Wallace Stevens, "Le Monocle de Mon Oncle"

1637: The Volga Rules: nothing

1637: The Polish Maelstrom: "Völuspá: The Prophecy of the Seeress" from *The Poetic Edda*

1636: The China Venture: Rudyard Kipling, "Mandalay"

1636: The Viennese Waltz (with Gorg Huff & Paula Goodlett)	978-1-4767-8101-3 • $7.99
1636: Mission to the Mughals (with Griffin Barber)	978-1-4814-8301-8 • $7.99
1636: The Ottoman Onslaught	HC: 978-1-4767-8184-6 • $26.00
1636: The Vatican Sanction (with Charles E. Gannon)	978-1-4814-8386-5 • $7.99
1636: The Cardinal Virtues (with Walter H. Hunt)	HC: 978-1-4767-8061-0 • $26.00
1636: The China Venture (with Iver P. Cooper)	HC: 978-1-4814-8423-7 • $25.00
1637: The Volga Rules (with Gorg Huff & Paula Goodlett)	HC: 978-1-4814-8303-2 • $25.00
1637: The Polish Maelstrom	978-1-9821-2472-4 • $8.99

THE RING OF FIRE ANTHOLOGIES
Edited by Eric Flint

Ring of Fire	978-1-4165-0908-0 • $7.99
Ring of Fire II	978-1-4165-9144-3 • $7.99
Ring of Fire III	978-1-4516-3827-1 • $7.99
Ring of Fire IV	978-1-4814-8238-7 • $7.99
Grantville Gazette	978-0-7434-8860-0 • $7.99
Grantville Gazette II	978-1-4165-5510-0 • $7.99
Grantville Gazette III	978-1-4165-5565-0 • $7.99
Grantville Gazette IV	978-1-4391-3311-8 • $7.99
Grantville Gazette V	978-1-4391-3422-1 • $7.99
Grantville Gazette VI	978-1-4516-3853-0 • $7.99
Grantville Gazette VII	HC: 978-1-4767-8029-0 • $25.00
Grantville Gazette VIII	978-1-9821-2425-0 • $8.99

Available in bookstores everywhere.
Order ebooks online at www.baen.com.

TIM POWERS

"Other writers tell tales of magic in the twentieth century, but no one does it like Powers."
—*The Orlando Sentinel*

ALTERNATE ROUTES

HC: 978-1-4814-8340-7 • $25.00 US / $34.00 CAN
PB: 978-1-4814-8427-5 • $7.99 US / $10.99 CAN

Ghosts travel the Los Angeles Freeways, and Sebastian Vickery must dodge spirits and secret agents as he seeks to stop an evil from the netherworld.

FORCED PERSPECTIVES

HC: 978-1-9821-2440-3 • $25.00 US / $34.00 CAN

Sebastian Vickery and Ingrid Castine are chased by ghosts and gurus as they rush to save Los Angeles from a god-birthing ritual.

DOWN AND OUT IN PURGATORY

PB: 978-1-4814-8374-2 • $7.99 US / $10.99 CAN

Tales of science fiction and metaphysics from master of the trade Tim Powers, with an introduction by David Drake.

EXPIRATION DATE

TPB: 978-1-4814-8330-8 • $16.00 US / $22.00 CAN
PB: 978-1-4814-8408-4 • $7.99 US / $10.99 CAN

When young Kootie comes to possess the ghost of Thomas Edison, every faction in Los Angeles' supernatural underbelly rushes to capture—or kill—boy and ghost.

EARTHQUAKE WEATHER

TPB: 978-1-4814-8351-3 • $16.00 US / $22.00 CAN
PB: 978-1-9821-2439-7 • $8.99 US / $11.99 CAN

Amongst ghosts and beside a man chased by a god, Janis Plumtree and the many personalities sharing her mind must resurrect the King of the West.